Silver Bells

FERN MICHAELS

Silver Bells

JoAnn Ross
Mary Burton
Judy Duarte

ZEBRA BOOKS
KENSINGTON PUBLISHING CORP.
http://www.kensingtonbooks.com

ZEBRA BOOKS are published by

Kensington Publishing Corp.
119 West 40th Street
New York, NY 10018

All Kensington titles, imprints, and distributed lines are available at
special quantity discounts for bulk purchases for sales promotion,
premiums, fund-raising, educational, or institutional use.

Special book excerpts or customized printings can also be created
to fit specific needs. For details, write or phone the office of the
Kensington Sales Manager: Attn.: Sales Department. Kensington
Publishing Corp., 119 West 40th Street, New York, NY 10018. Phone:
1-800-221-2647.

Zebra and the Z logo Reg. U.S. Pat. & TM Off.

First Printing: November 2008
ISBN-13: 978-1-4201-4410-9
ISBN-10: 1-4201-4410-3

eISBN-13: 978-1-4201-0758-6
eISBN-10: 1-4201-0758-5

10 9 8 7 6

Printed in the United States of America

Contents

Silver Bells
Fern Michaels
1

Dear Santa
JoAnn Ross
83

Christmas Past
Mary Burton
191

A Mulberry Park Christmas
Judy Duarte
293

Silver Bells

Fern Michaels

Chapter One

Amy Lee stood at the railing on the second floor of her palatial home in Malibu, staring down with quiet intensity at her guests, mostly employees and a few acquaintances. The occasion was her annual Christmas party. Why she even bothered she had no idea.

It had taken a crew of four three whole days to decorate the house from top to bottom. Another crew of three to decorate the outside. Christmas trees in every room, huge wreaths with red satin bows over all the mantels. Gossamer angels floated from ceiling wire, while a life-size stuffed Santa complete with a packed sleigh and a parade of elves circled the floor-to-ceiling fireplace that separated the great room from the dining room. The focal point of all the decorations.

The mansion was festive to the nth degree, and she hated every bit of it. She could hardly wait for midnight, when she handed out the gifts and bonus checks, at which point the guests would make a beeline for the door, having done their duty by attending the festivities.

Amy rubbed at her temples. She'd had a raging headache all day, and it looked like it was going to stay with her throughout the night. She knew she had to go back downstairs, paste a smile on her face, and somehow manage to get through the next hour. For the hundredth time she wished she was anywhere but here.

Here was California. While she lived in Malibu, she worked in Hollywood, where she and all the other movie stars worked. Phony and superficial Hollywood—just like most of the people she worked with. But she'd learned how to play the game, and it was a game. If you wanted the star status that she had, you learned quickly what the rules were. And then you stuck to them.

Amy always told herself she would know when it was time to get out. She wasn't sure, but she suspected the time was *now.* At thirty-three she was fast approaching has-been status. New, rowdy, outrageous, flamboyant starlets were giving the paparazzi a run for their money in their bid for stardom, and it was working. It seemed like the world couldn't live another day unless they read about one of the starlet's underwear or lack thereof, or getting busted for drunk driving while under-age or of age, then signing autographs for the arresting offi-cers or going to jail for ignoring the law. Autographs to the highest bidder as they were being fingerprinted. Transla-tion—big bucks at the box office.

She wasn't a prude, but she'd always prided herself on a certain decorum befitting her celebrity. She didn't flit from affair to affair, she didn't drink and drive, she didn't do drugs, and she absolutely refused to do nude sex scenes in her movies. One of the tabloids recently called her dull and said she wouldn't know what excitement was or an adrenaline rush if it hit her in the face. They were right.

Amy looked down at the dress she was wearing. It was a plain Armani scarlet sheath befitting the holidays, with a slit up the leg. It draped perfectly over her body. Just the right neckline, just the right amount of sleeve. She'd walked the red carpet enough to know she looked glamorous in her sparkling gown. Just like all her female guests looked glamorous. Once she'd heard a rumor that if you wanted to attend an Amy Lee party, you had better dress *down.* At the time she'd thought it funny. Now, it wasn't funny. Why was that?

Her head continued to throb each time she put her foot on one of the steps. Thank God she'd made it to the bottom without her head splitting open. She walked among her guests, chatted, patted arms, smiled, and even giggled at something one of her employees said. She risked a glance at her watch. Fifty minutes to go. Three thousand seconds. It felt like a lifetime.

It dawned on Amy that she'd been so busy with the party details that she hadn't eaten a thing all day. Maybe if she ate something, the headache would go away.

Amy made her way over to the buffet table. Earlier in the evening it had looked gorgeous, with a Christmas tree ice sculpture nestled in a circle of bright red poinsettias. The matching red candles had long ago burned down. Red candle wax pooled on the white tablecloth. The lobster and shrimp in their ice bowls, what was left of it, looked watery. The turkey and roast beef looked dry. The champagne fountain was as dry as the turkey and roast beef. She felt a surge of anger. Where were the people she'd hired to take care of the table? Outside smoking cigarettes, that's where. Did it even matter? When the last guest left, maybe she'd scramble herself some eggs.

Forty minutes to go. Two thousand four hundred seconds. What she should do was go to the sleigh, pretend her watch was fast, and start handing out the presents and the bonus checks. There were expensive token gifts for the other guests, so they wouldn't feel left out. Boy/girl gifts. Tomorrow it would be all over TMZ, Page Six, and anywhere else the gossips gathered. It was all part of playing the game.

Amy moved closer to the sleigh, touched her secretary's arm, and whispered. Word spread, and the guests started to mince their way toward the sleigh.

Twenty minutes later it was all over, and she was standing at the door wishing the last guest a Merry Christmas. Two weeks early, the last guest pointed out. "But then, my dear, you always were ahead of the curve." Amy forced a smile and stood in the open doorway until the last car pulled away from the driveway. The valet boys waved and walked down the driveway.

Amy turned to go inside when she looked at her oversize magnificent front door. She loved everything about the house, but the front door was special. She'd had it made of mahogany and gone to great lengths to find a lumber mill to round it out so that it looked like a cathedral door. Anytime she had been interviewed at home, the reporters had taken pictures of her front door. A memory. She was going to miss it. Her eyes burned when she looked at the huge silver bells attached to a glorious red satin bow. The bells were hammered silver, specially made. The tone was so pure, so melodious, it always brought tears to her eyes when they rang. Another memory. Maybe she'd take the bells with her.

Amy closed the huge door and locked it. Now she could relax. First, though, she walked about, turning off lights. The buffet table had been cleared and carried away. There was still noise in the kitchen, but she ignored it. She kicked off her heels and made her way to the sofa. She sat down, leaned back, and closed her eyes. It took a full minute to realize her headache was finally gone.

The multicolored lights on the artificial tree winked at her. How pretty it looked in the dim light of the great room. In broad daylight it looked like just what it was—a fake tree with a bunch of junk hanging off it.

As a child, back home in Pennsylvania, there had always been a floor-to-ceiling live tree that scented the entire house. Until that fateful Christmas when she was fourteen and allowed to go to the mall alone. Three days before Christmas, she'd gone to the mall with two of her friends. An hour into her shopping the police had come for her to tell her a gas explosion had rocked their house and killed her parents.

The days afterward were still a blur. She knew she'd gone to her parents' funeral, knew she stayed at her friend Katie's house until her aunt Flo, a writer of travelogues, could be found. A week later she'd been located in Madrid, Spain. She'd rushed home, swooped Amy into her arms, then swooped her out to California, where Amy had lived ever since.

There had been money, lots and lots of money that her aunt Flo invested for her. Huge insurance policies added to her robust nest egg. And the house was hers, too. The town had pitched in to repair the damage from the explosion, then closed up the house. Flo paid the taxes every year and said from time to time that they would go back, but they never did. Neighbors mowed the lawn in the summer and shoveled the snow in the winter. Kind people, caring people who had loved her parents. Flo said people in small towns looked out for one another. Amy believed it.

She'd cried a lot back then because she missed her parents. Not that Flo wasn't a wonderful substitute. She was, but it wasn't the same as having a *real* mom. Flo had enrolled her in everything there was to enroll in—gymnastics, soccer, choir, art classes, music classes, the drama club—everything to keep her hours full. But at night, when she was alone in her pretty bedroom, which Flo had decorated herself, she would cry.

Her world changed in her senior year when she had the lead in the school play. She'd given a rousing performance or so said the critics. A movie producer had shown up at the door five days later and asked her if she'd be interested in an audition with a photo op. Flo had raised her eyebrows and hovered like a mother hen in case it was some kind of scam. It wasn't. Flo continued to hover, saying college was a must. Amy had agreed, and the studio worked around her studies. Back then she did two movies a year, not little parts, not big parts, but big enough for her to get noticed. And then the plum of all plums, the lead in a Disney movie. Her career took off like a rocket. Flo still hovered until she convinced herself that Amy could take care of herself. The only thing Flo had objected to was the name change from Amanda Leigh to Amy Lee. But in the end, when her niece said she was okay with it, Flo stepped aside and continued on with her own career, which she had put on hold to take care of Amy.

Thanks to modern technology, aunt and niece stayed in

touch daily. Time and scheduling permitting, they always managed at least one vacation a year together.

Amy closed her eyes again as she ran the last phone call with Flo through her mind. Flo had called just as she was getting out of bed. She'd flopped back onto the pillows, and they talked for almost an hour. The last thing she'd said to her aunt before breaking the connection was, "I don't want to do this anymore, Flo. I want to go home. I *am* going home. Tomorrow as a matter of fact. I bought my ticket two weeks ago."

"Just like that, you're throwing it all away?" Flo had said.

"Well, not exactly. I have two more pictures on my contract, and I don't have to report to the studio till April of next year. I don't know if I'm burned out, or I just need to get out of the business. Come April, I might be more than ready to go back. I will honor the contract, so that's not a problem. Before you can ask, I am financially secure. You know I never touched my inheritance. I've got fifty times that amount from my earnings, and it's all invested wisely. I'm okay, so don't worry about me."

"Mandy, I just want you to be happy," Flo said. She'd never once called her by her Hollywood name. "I want you to find a nice man, get married, have kids, get a couple of dogs, and be happy. It's all I ever wanted for you. I'm just not sure you're going to find happiness back in Pennsylvania."

"We should have gone back, Flo."

"Woulda, coulda, shoulda. I did what I thought was best. For you. So, you're going to open up the house and . . . what . . . put down some roots?"

"I don't know, Flo. Maybe I'm looking for something that doesn't exist, and you're right, if I had wanted to go back earlier, I would have made your life miserable until you took me. The best I can come up with is, I wasn't ready to go back. I'm ready now, and I'm going. It would be nice if you could find a way to join me. Hint, hint."

"Darling girl, I met *a man*! He has the soul of an angel, and don't ask me how I know this. I just know it. He loves me, warts and all. He's a simple man, never been out of Madrid. He lives on a farm. Owns the farm, actually. Never been on an airplane. I'll ask him if he wants to spend Christmas with my movie star niece. He's seen all your movies, by the way. He thinks you're a nice-looking lass."

Amy laughed. "You getting married?"

"The minute he asks me, I am, but he has to ask first. I have to run, Mandy, I have an appointment I can't break. I'll call you tomorrow."

"Love you, Flo."

"And I love you, too."

Amy sighed. Flo had a boyfriend. At sixty-five, Flo had a boyfriend. Here she was, at thirty-three, without a prospect in sight. How weird was that?

Amy gathered up the sequined shoes that matched her gown. She walked out to the kitchen to see if the caterers had cleaned up thoroughly. The kitchen was spotless. She locked the back door and turned out the light. The great room had a master switch that turned off all the tree lights as well as the overhead lights. The outside lights were set on a timer that would turn everything off a little before dawn.

As she walked up the stairs to the second floor she found herself wondering if Hank Anders still lived back home. Her first boyfriend. The first boy who had ever given her a gift. Hank had been the first boy to kiss her. On the lips. She hadn't had a chance to tell him good-bye. Where was he right now? What was he doing? If he still lived in Apple Valley, would he remember her? Not likely, thanks to Flo and her transformation from small-town girl to glamorous Hollywood star. She'd had her nose done, gotten braces, wore contacts, and her hair was a different color. Flo had seen to it that her past stayed in the past. She'd never been able to figure that out. As far as her bio went, she was born and raised in California. Went to UCLA. End of story.

Or was it the beginning?

Chapter Two

Henry Anders, also known as Cranky Hank Anders, hefted his oversize suitcase off the carousel and looked around for his sister-in-law, who had said she'd meet him in the baggage area. When he didn't see her, he made his way to the closest EXIT sign. And then he saw her pushing a double stroller with the year-old twins, who were howling at the top of their lungs. He wondered if their high-pitched screams had anything to do with the way they were bundled up. Their mother looked just as frazzled as her offspring.

Alice Anders stopped in her tracks and threw out her arms. "Hank! I'm so glad to see you! I'm sorry I'm late. There was traffic, and my two bundles of joy here are overdue for a nap. I had to park a mile away. I'm sorry. I left hours ahead of time just so I wouldn't be late, and what happens, I'm late! Ohhh, I'm just so glad you're here. I was dreading going through the holidays without Ben. I had an e-mail from him this morning, and he warned me not to be late; that's why I left early. He said you hate to wait around for people."

Alice was a talker, he'd give her that. "No problem. Relax, Alice. I could just as easily have taken a cab or gotten a car service. I'm here, you're here, that's all that matters. The twins really grew since Easter. Ben said they're walking now."

An anxious note crept into his voice when he said, "He's okay, isn't he?"

Alice shoved a lock of dark hair under the bright red wool hat she was wearing. "As right as someone who's in Iraq can be. He said you're the only one he trusts to step in for him at Christmas. He was supposed to come back in September, but they extended his tour. This will be our first Christmas apart." Tears welled in her eyes as she gave the stroller a shove to get through the door Hank was holding open for her.

A blustery gust of wind whipped across the walkway. The twins howled louder. Alice dropped a light blanket over the top of the stroller to keep the wind at bay. One of the twins ripped it away, one pudgy fist shaking in frustration. The wind picked it up, and it was gone, just like that. Hank was about to chase it down when Alice stopped him. "It doesn't matter, it was an old one. Like I said, I parked a mile away, so let's get going. The sooner I get these two guys in the car, the sooner they'll calm down."

Hank didn't know what to say. He was certainly no authority on kids, babies in particular, so he just walked along, dragging his suitcase. He wondered if the twins slept through the night. Probably not from the look of the dark circles under Alice's eyes.

Out of the corner of his eye he watched his sister-in-law. Once she'd been slim and trim. Once she'd worn makeup and had a fashionable hairdo and she'd dressed in designer clothes. Today she was wearing a down coat of some sort that made her look forty pounds overweight. She was wearing jeans and sneakers, and her hair was up in a ponytail, the tail sticking out of the back of the bright red hat. Maybe marriage wasn't all that wonderful. Maybe he was lucky after all, even though at the time he thought his world was coming to an end when his fiancée had left him standing at the altar on their wedding day. He looked down at the twins, who were trying to poke each other's eyes out. Yeah, yeah, maybe he had dodged the bullet.

A twin himself, he wanted to tell Alice her nightmare was

just beginning when he remembered some of the things he and Ben had done growing up. Always in trouble, always fighting, always making their parents' lives anxious. Then again, maybe he wouldn't tell her.

Fifteen minutes later, Alice stopped in front of a dark SUV. He whirled around at the furious sound of a dog barking. Alice stopped, a horrible look on her face. "That's Churchill, the dog. Ben got him before he left for Iraq. He said we needed protection because we couldn't afford an alarm system." Hank thought she sounded like she would have gone into debt for the alarm versus the dog. "I think it might be a little crowded, but you'll be in the front seat. The dog sheds. And he poops everywhere. The twins step in it. He pees, too. I can never seem to catch him at the right time to let him out. He's a good dog, great with the boys. The lights are still up from last Christmas. Ben never got a chance to take them down before he had to return to Iraq. I have to get a Christmas tree. Ben wants me to send him a picture. Like I don't have enough to do without going out to get a Christmas tree. I wasn't going to get one. The boys are too little to know what a Christmas tree is."

"Uh-huh. Give me the keys, Alice, I'll drive and you can relax."

"Relax! That word is not in my vocabulary. The last time I relaxed was on my honeymoon, and even then I'm not sure I relaxed. It was *stressful*."

Hank decided he wouldn't touch that statement with a ten-foot pole. No sireee, not even with a twenty-foot pole. He offered to help strap the twins into the car seats, but Churchill had other ideas and growled at him. He slid into the driver's seat and turned on the engine. He hoped the heat would kick in. He was freezing.

The dog barked, and the twins howled and yowled as Alice walked around to the driver's side of the car and opened the door. She looked Hank square in the eye and said, "I can't do this anymore. I don't *want* to do this anymore. It's all yours!

The key to the house is the big key on the ring. You can get the damn Christmas tree, and you can decorate the house and you can clean up the poop and the pee and you can cook and clean and do the laundry and rake and take care of the yard. And you can tell your brother for me that I wish he had left me standing at the altar. There isn't much food in the house, so you'll have to go shopping, and let me tell you, that's an experience from hell. Good luck. The boys get a bath at seven. That's another experience that is right up there with hell. See ya!"

Churchill leaped over the seat to land in the front next to Hank. He threw his head back and howled, an ungodly sound that made the hair on the back of Hank's neck stand on end.

She was walking away! Actually walking away! "Hey!" he bellowed. "Where are you going? Come back here, Alice!" Obviously, she hadn't heard him because she kept right on walking. Must be the wool hat over her ears. He jammed the car in reverse and barreled down the aisle, coming to a stop next to her. He pushed a button and the passenger-side front window rolled down. "C'mon, Alice, you can't leave me with these kids and this dog. I know you didn't mean that; you're just venting, and I can understand how hard it's been. Get in the car. *Please*," he added as an afterthought. The twins had started to howl again the moment the SUV ground to a stop. Churchill leaped in the back and started to lick at the twins' faces. "Stop that," he shouted, to be heard over the din.

Alice was on the move again. He inched the SUV along to keep up with her. "Where are you going?"

"To get a manicure, a massage, and a pedicure. Then I'm going someplace where I can sleep for a week and get room service. Don't call me, I'll call you." She tossed her cell phone in the car window. Churchill leaped over the seat again and grabbed it before returning to the back. He started to chew on it. It chirped in protest. A moment later Alice ran between the rows of parked cars and was lost to him.

Hank sat for a full minute, the reality of his situation hitting him full on. Alice was gone. She'd meant what she said. He was stranded with year-old twins and a hundred-pound golden retriever that pooped and peed all over the place and chewed up cell phones, and there was no Christmas tree or food in the house. "Shit!" he said succinctly.

"Ben," he muttered under his breath, "when I see you again I'm going to kick your ass all the way to the Canadian border." He knew he'd do no such thing; he was just venting the way Alice had vented. He loved Ben even though he'd never understood why he'd wanted a military career. Major Benjamin Anders. It sounded so professional. When he got back from Iraq, he would be Colonel Benjamin Anders. Hank felt his chest puff out with pride at his little brother. Little brother because Ben was two whole minutes younger than his older brother.

As he tooled along Route 30, his mind raced. He knew squat about taking over a household. He lived in a town house, had a housekeeper, and never worried about grocery shopping. Hell, he didn't even know what to buy. And, he wasn't much in the kitchen department either, which meant he could boil an egg and that was it. And he could make coffee. He was a bachelor, for crying out loud. Now, in the blink of an eye he was suddenly a stand-in dad, a dog watcher, a chauffeur, a grocery shopper, and a cook. There was something definitely wrong with this picture.

Maybe he could get some help. The kind that lived in and did all those things. He could afford it. Or, he could send the bill to Ben. No, skip that idea. Not even majors make enough to pay for that.

Forty minutes later, Hank slowed for the red light on the corner. In five minutes he would be driving through the center of town. As always, he took a moment to savor the small-town warmth of Apple Valley. He cruised past the town square, noted the sleigh, the eight huge reindeer, and all the other Christmas decorations. Glorious wreaths with huge red bows were on all the sparkling white doors of the town's official buildings. The square was where the midnight candlelight Christmas was held. The whole town turned out. Kids in pajamas all bundled up, even dogs attended, with antlers on their heads and colorful green and white collars for the season. He loved Apple Valley and the people he'd grown up with. Right now, though, this very second, he hated it.

Churchill started to bark the moment Hank turned off Apple Valley Road, the main thoroughfare in town, onto Clemens Ferry Road, where his brother and he had been born and grew up. The old homestead. He blinked at the commotion going on at the house next to his old home. A fire engine, an ambulance, and the sheriff's car. Something must have happened to Albert Carpenter. Ben had just mentioned Albert in his last e-mail, saying he would be ninety-three the day after Christmas. He wanted Hank to invite him for Christmas dinner and make sure he got some presents. Albert Carpenter had been a substitute grandfather to both boys when they were growing up.

Hank felt a lump the size of a golf ball form in his throat. For years, Ben and the other neighbors had looked after Albert because there was no one else to do it. In fact, a few years ago, Ben had given him a puppy, a little white lapdog that Albert carried around. Ben said it added years to the old gentleman's life. He couldn't help but wonder if Alice had taken on caring for Albert along with her other duties. More than likely.

Hank pulled into the driveway, turned off the engine, and debated his next move. Churchill watched him with keen intensity. Would the dog bolt? How was he supposed to get two kids into the house at the same time? One under each arm. That had to mean the dog would bolt. Maybe. Out of the corner of his eye he saw the ambulance pull away. Out of the corner of his other eye he saw a white ball of fur streaking toward Alice's SUV. Churchill let out a high-pitched bark of pure happiness. Albert's dog. Who was going to take care of her? He knew it was a her because he remembered Ben saying Albert named the little dog after his wife, Sadie. Officially known as Miss Sadie.

Hank opened the door so he could get out without letting the big dog out of the car. He had to find a leash or something. Like that was going to happen. He looked around in a daze, the white fur ball yapping and yipping at his feet. Churchill continued to bark, growl, and howl at what was going on. The twins woke up and started to cry. "Oh, shit!" Maybe if he opened the door to the house, dragged the dog in, and shut the door he could do it that way. He'd have to come back for the kids. He was on his way to the door when he saw the fire engine and the sheriff's car leaving the neighborhood. That was when he saw the Range Rover in the Leigh driveway. The house must have been sold. He felt sad at the thought. Ben hung a Christmas wreath on the front door every Christmas even though the house was empty. First Albert, then the Leigh house. No, first Alice's fit. A trifecta of misery. Flo must have finally sold the house. He wondered why—it was in such perfect condition. He knew that for a fact because Ben told him that the sodality ladies did a spring cleaning once a year.

The front door slid open. Hank walked into the kitchen and grabbed a dish towel, which he carried outside and looped into Churchill's collar. With his homemade leash, he dragged the recalcitrant canine into the house. The fur ball followed and made herself comfortable on one of the family room chairs. Churchill took the other chair, but not before he lifted his leg on the bottom of it.

Hank lost it then. He marched over to the big dog, who looked at him defiantly. He stuck his finger to his nose and barked, "Do that one more time, and your ass is grass. You hear me? That means you sit out on the deck and look through the window. And I won't feed you either. Oh, Christ, the twins!" He raced to the door and back out to the car. It took him a good five minutes to figure out how to unbuckle the harness on the childproof seats or whatever they were called. A kid under each arm, he marched to the door and opened it. Alice said they could walk. He set them down and off they went. "I need a beer. Please, God, let there be beer in the refrigerator." There was no beer. He had to settle for a Diet Pepsi. Did all women in the world drink Diet Pepsi? He counted twenty-four cans. Alice must be addicted.

Hank looked around for a place to sit down. He was tempted to shoo Churchill off the chair, but one look at the retriever's face squelched that idea. Obviously, the chair was his. Miss Sadie looked at him with adoring eyes and yipped softly. "You just moved in, didn't you, you little shit?" Miss Sadie yipped again and put her head down between her paws. Yep, she had moved in.

Hank looked over at the twins, who were trying to crawl into the fireplace. He realized they still had on their winter gear and were sweating profusely. He removed it, closed the fire screen, then flopped down on the couch after he dumped a ton of toys on the floor. "I can't do this. I don't *want* to do this."

The sudden quiet alerted Hank that something was wrong. One of the twins, he didn't know which one, was trying to take off his pants. And then he smelled it. "Please, God, no. I've never changed a diaper in my life." Churchill jumped off his chair, trotted out of the room, and returned with a diaper clenched between his teeth. He let it drop at Hank's feet. Then he hopped back on his chair. Hank wanted to cry.

The TV suddenly exploded with sound. Churchill had the remote clutched between his paws. A cartoon show appeared. The twins squealed their pleasure.

"Alice Anders, you are a saint," Hank said as he prepared to change his first-ever diaper.

Chapter Three

Amy Lee, aka Amanda Leigh, walked through her old home. Everything was just as she remembered it. All these years later, nothing had changed. Thanks, she knew, to Flo, who stayed in touch with her parents' old friends.

Amy was glad now that she'd had the foresight to call ahead to a cleaning service, which had cleaned the house and turned on all the utilities as well as doing a week's grocery shopping. It was worth every penny in comfort alone. She was toasty warm, and there was even a load of wood on the back porch and a stack of logs and kindling perched on the end of the fireplace hearth. Maybe this evening she'd make a fire the way her parents had always done after dinner.

Her memory of that terrible time when her world had changed forever surfaced. This time she didn't push the memory away. Flo should have let her stay, at least for a while. She should have cried and been given the chance to grieve instead of being dragged across the country where every hour of her day was occupied so she wouldn't think about *that time*. Now, where had that thought come from? Had she secretly blamed Flo all these years for the person she'd become? Did she really want to look into that? Probably not. At least not right now.

It just boggled her mind that everything in the house

looked the same. The furniture was outdated, but that was okay. The oak staircase had the same old treads and gave off the scent of lemon polish. The furniture looked comfortable but worn. The house gleamed and sparkled, and it didn't smell like it had been closed up for years and years. Even the kitchen curtains had been washed and starched.

All the bedrooms and bathrooms were closed. She wondered why. One by one she opened them. The spare bedroom had a yellow spread on the big four-poster and crisp white curtains hanging at the windows. Flo had always slept in this room when she visited back then. A colorful braided rug was in the middle of the floor. Her mother had hooked rugs in the winter. Framed posterlike pictures hung on the walls—scenes from different cities that Flo had traveled to.

Amy backed out of the room and opened the door to her parents' room. Tears burned in her eyes. How many times she'd run to that bed and jumped in with her parents to be hugged in the middle of the night. She thought she could smell either the perfume or the talcum powder her mother had always used. How was that possible? She walked into the bathroom. All her mother's things were still on one side of the vanity, her father's things on the other side. She looked around as though time had stopped and never picked up again.

In one way, Amy was glad that Flo had left things the way they were. In another way, she wished she hadn't. She ran to the high four-poster and jumped up on it. She flapped her arms and legs this way and that like she was making snow angels.

Amy frowned when she heard a high-pitched siren. It sounded like it was right next door. She bolted from the room, which was at the back of the house, and ran to her old room, whose windows faced the Carpenter property on one side and the Anders property on the other. She watched as frantic EMS workers ran into the Carpenter house. She swiped at the tears forming in her eyes when, a while later, she saw the same EMS people wheel a gurney out to the ambulance. Not too long ago Flo had told her Albert Carpenter was in his nineties and in frail health. Such a nice man. His wife had been nice, too, to all the kids in the neighborhood. They'd always been partial to Hank and Ben. She was about to move from the window when she saw movement through the window facing the Anders house. She walked over to the other window, which afforded her a better view, and stared down at the man getting out of the SUV. Ben? Hank? It was hard to tell from where she was standing. Her heart kicked up a beat as she watched the scene being played out on the ground. Kids. Big dog. Little white dog. She burst out laughing as she watched the man run into the house to return and drag the dog into the house with a towel as a leash. She laughed even harder when she saw him straddle each child under his arms. A novice for a father. Ben? Hank? Her heart was beating extra fast. Not a good thing. So much for hoping that maybe . . .

Amy walked across the room to the rocking chair her mother had painted bright red because red was Amy's favorite color. She'd even made the cushions out of red velvet. Amy sat down and started to rock as she let her gaze sweep through the room. It was all just the same. Her boots were in the corner, her yellow muffler and matching wool hat, knitted by her mother, were on the coatrack by the closet door. Her navy peacoat with the gold buttons was still on the rack, too. Guess Flo thought I wouldn't need winter clothes in California, she thought.

From her position in the rocking chair, Amy could see the photos she'd taped to the mirror over her vanity. Most of them were of her, Hank, and Ben. Several of her friend Libby, who had moved away a few months before her parents' death.

Amy got up to check out her closet and dresser drawers. Everything was neat and tidy even after all these years. A lifetime ago. Time to let it all go. Time to lay all her old ghosts to rest.

Amy looked outside, surprised that it was already dark and it was only five o'clock. Time to think about a nice hot shower, some dinner, and a nice fire and a little television before she retired for the night. Tomorrow was another day. Tomorrow she'd go up to the attic and get down all her mother's Christmas decorations. Maybe she'd venture forth and get a real live Christmas tree. Not a glittery Hollywood tree but one that would smell up the whole house. Then she'd have that Christmas that never happened. The one she'd missed when Flo took her to California.

Maybe Christmas would be forever tainted. Maybe she couldn't get the old feelings back. Well, she'd never know if she didn't try.

Was it Hank or Ben in the house next door? She wished she knew. Maybe she should go over and knock on the door. People in Apple Valley did things like that. Most times they brought food to newcomers. She couldn't help but wonder if anyone would bring her something once they knew she was back home.

As she walked down the steps, Amy crossed her fingers. Let it be Ben next door. Let him be the married one. Maybe she could discreetly ask where Hank was. Find out if he, too, was married. She crossed her fingers tighter.

Back on the first floor, Amy opened the doors of the fireplace, laid some kindling, then stacked the logs the way she'd seen her father do. She had a fireplace in her California home, but it was gas. She'd used it once and was so disappointed with the effect it created, she'd never turned it on again. Within minutes she had a nice blaze going. In the kitchen she prepared a small salad to accompany the frozen TV dinner she popped into the oven. She uncorked a bottle of wine to let it breathe before she headed upstairs to shower.

Her first day home.

Home. Amy closed her eyes and almost swooned at the way the one word made her feel. She literally ran up the stairs, her heart bursting with happiness. She knew, just knew, coming back home to Apple Valley was the best decision of her life.

In the shower, she sang "Jingle Bells" at the top of her

lungs as she washed her hair and showered with her favorite bath gel, a Vera Wang scent she'd been using for years.

Thirty minutes later, Amy walked through the family room, where the fire was blazing cheerfully, and on out to the kitchen, where her dinner waited for her. She turned on the radio that was mounted under one of the kitchen cabinets. Holiday music invaded the old kitchen.

She was home. Eating in her old kitchen, using her mother's old place mats, using the same silverware with the green handles. It seemed the same, but it wasn't the same. The sugar bowl and creamer weren't in the middle of the table. Both her parents had always had coffee with their meals, even at lunchtime. Suddenly, Amy wasn't hungry anymore. She reached for the wine bottle and poured it into her glass. Flo had drummed into her head over the years that "you can't go home again," then went on to say some famous writer had said that. It wasn't until she was in college that Amy learned that the writer was Thomas Wolfe.

Amy sat down on what had once been her mother's chair and stared at the fire. She supposed you could go home again physically, but when you got there, you had to be realistic enough to know that time had passed, and it could never be recaptured. And recapture time was exactly what she had hoped to do by making this trip. How foolish she was to even think she could make that happen. The past was prologue.

Now what was she supposed to do until it was time to go back to California? Should she just eat, drink, sleep, watch television? Should she pretend it wasn't the Christmas season and ignore everything? Wouldn't that be a cop-out?

Maybe she should go next door and talk to Ben or Hank or whoever it was that lived in that house. There was nothing wrong with dropping in on old childhood friends. Was there? She tried to talk herself out of the idea by convincing herself that either Ben or Hank's wife wouldn't appreciate an unknown female dropping by—she looked down at her watch—at seven o'clock in the evening. Maybe she would do it tomorrow.

Before Amy could change her mind, she raced upstairs for her old peacoat. She was surprised that it still fit. She pulled the yellow hat down over her ears, wrapped the muffler around her neck, and was ready to go. A walk to the town square would be nice. She could take her time, look in the shop windows, and by the time she got home, she'd be wiped out and ready for a good night's sleep in her own bed. Her own bed. Five minutes later she was out the door, the key to the front door in the pocket of her sweatpants.

It was icy cold, the wind blustery and pushing her along as she walked down the street to the corner. Her feet already felt numb from the cold. No wonder, she thought, looking down at her feet. She wasn't wearing socks, and she was still wearing slippers, for God's sake. Stupid, stupid, stupid. Maybe she wasn't really stupid. Maybe she was just overwhelmed with being home and wasn't thinking clearly. She continued walking to the next corner, then she decided, yes, she was stupid, and turned around to go home.

How bleak and lonely Mr. Carpenter's house looked. Every other house on the street featured colored Christmas lights on their porches and shrubbery. Correction. Every house but Mr. Carpenter's and her house had colored lights. She made a mental note to get them down from the attic and hang them tomorrow. Maybe she'd hang some on Mr. Carpenter's house, too. She rather thought Mr. Carpenter would like that.

The Anders house was lit up from top to bottom. It looked like every room in the house was lit up. She looked around. The other houses on the street looked the same way. Families needed a lot of light, she decided.

Amy heard the sound when she walked across the lawn in front of the Anders house in a shortcut to her driveway. She stopped and pushed her hat above her ears to see if she could hear better. It sounded like a baby was crying. She listened hard, then heard a whimpering sound. She turned around and there by her front door was the beautiful dog she'd seen earlier. He looked even more golden under the porch light. She whistled softly, and the dog bounded over to where she was standing. "Hey, big guy, what are you doing out here all by yourself? Did you get loose? Like you're really going to answer me. I think you belong over there," she said, pointing to the door of the Anders house. "C'mon, I'll ring the bell, and before you know it, you'll be warm and cozy inside." The big dog walked alongside her as she made her way to the front door.

Amy rang the bell. Once. Twice. On the third ring she thought she heard a voice bellow, "Come in." She looked down at the dog and shrugged. She opened the door and stuck her head in. "Anybody here?" she shouted.

"I'm upstairs giving the twins a bath," came the reply.

"I brought your dog home. I think he might have jumped the fence. It's freezing outside. It's not right to leave an animal out in weather like this," she shouted again, anger ringing in her voice. As an afterthought she yelled again, "If you can't take care of an animal, you shouldn't have one. I'm leaving now," she said, backing toward the door, partially blocking it with her leg so the big dog wouldn't bolt.

The voice from the second floor thundered down the steps. "What are you, some know-it-all? If the dog jumped the fence, it doesn't mean I can't take care of him. Stop that! Right now! Now look what you did!" Two high-pitched wails of misery traveled down the steps.

The golden dog immediately raced up the steps, a white fur ball on his heels, yapping every step of the way.

"A thank you would have been nice. Doesn't sound like you're any great shakes as a parent either." Amy screamed out her parting shot as she closed the door behind her. "Stupid ass!" *And to think I couldn't wait to see you. Ha!*

Back inside her own house, Amy raced to her room for some heavy warm socks. She could barely feel her feet, that's how cold she was. Back downstairs, she tidied up the kitchen, poured more wine, then went back to the family room. She pulled at the cushions from the sofa and propped them up by the fire, her legs stretched forward. She added two more logs to the fire and sipped at her wine.

Two revelations in one day. 1. You can't have expectations when you go home again. 2. Ben or Hank Anders was not the boy of her youth. Screw it, she thought as she set the wine-glass aside and curled up on the old cushions. Moments later she was sound asleep.

She slept soundly only to be awakened hours later by the sound of her doorbell. Groggily, she looked down at her watch. It was after twelve. Who would be visiting at this hour? She ran to the door, turned on the porch light, and was dismayed to see the huge golden dog slapping at her doorbell. She opened the door, and he bounded in like a whirlwind. He ran over to the fire and lay down on the cushions.

Amy threw her hands in the air. "What's this mean? You moved out? What?"

The dog barked as he squirmed and wiggled to get more comfortable on the cushions. "Does this mean you're staying here for the night?" The dog barked again, laid his head on his paws, and closed his eyes. "Guess so. Can't say as how I blame you. He sounds like a . . . like a . . . big jerk."

Before she made her way to the second floor, Amy bent over to look at the collar on the big dog's neck. Churchill. "Okay, Churchill, see you in the morning."

Chapter Four

Hank Anders staggered down the stairs a little before midnight. He was beyond exhausted from the past few hours with the twins, and he now had a newfound respect for his sister-in-law. Where in the name of God was she? Probably sleeping peacefully in some five-star hotel after being pampered by a trained masseuse.

The two dogs looked at him warily. Churchill ran to the sliding glass doors off the kitchen that led to a little terrace in the back. Earlier he'd seen the area was fenced, so he let the dogs out. His nerves were twanging all over the place as he prepared a cup of hot chocolate the way his mother had always done when things got dicey. Well, as far as he was concerned, things didn't get any dicier than this.

Dinner had been a disaster. The twins didn't like hard-boiled eggs. They didn't like toast either. When they wouldn't eat, he'd belatedly checked to make sure they had teeth, and sure enough they each had six. Then he'd tried peanut butter and jelly, but they didn't like that either. All they'd done was smear it everywhere. The two dogs licked it up, to his chagrin. Milk from a cup was spilled on the floor and on the walls, leaving a sticky residue. The dogs licked that up, too. He finally found a can of ravioli and handed out spoons. Probably his tenth or eleventh mistake. At least he didn't have to worry about the dogs' dinner.

Bath time had been a total disaster. He wondered if Alice would notice, if she *ever* returned, that the wallpaper was soaking wet or that the linoleum on the floor was buckling where the splashed water had seeped under it. Probably not. Why should she? She had other things on her mind. God, where was she? Was she going to leave him here *forever* with her kids or until Ben got back? He shuddered at the thought. She'd be a fool not to. A five-star hotel, a pedicure, manicure, hairdo, facial, massage, certainly couldn't compare to this experience.

And who the hell was that person who brought Churchill back? And how had the dog gotten out in the first place? "Please come home, Alice. Please," Hank muttered over and over as he poured the hot chocolate into a cup.

Earlier, after the dinner the twins didn't eat, he had called the market and placed an order the clerk promised to deliver early in the morning. He'd lucked out when he called the only employment agency in town. The woman who operated it was running late and was still in the office. She'd promised a "day lady" or possibly a male nanny depending on availability and sir, we do not discriminate, who was capable of minding children and doing light cooking for $750 a week. He'd blinked at the amount but agreed. At that precise moment he would have paid triple the amount she quoted.

Hank was so hungry he thought he was going to pass out. He'd used the last of the bread, so he ate peanut butter and jelly right out of the jar. All of it. Though still hungry, he was too tired to rummage or try to cook something.

When Miss Sadie scratched at the door, he went over to open it. The little fur ball pranced in and looked up at the giant standing over her. She yipped and did a circle dance that probably meant something, but he didn't know what. He whistled for Churchill, and, when nothing happened, he turned on the outside light and whistled again. The small yard was lit up brightly, but there was no sign of the golden retriever. He ran out to the yard calling the dog's name, Miss

Sadie yapping and nipping at his pant leg as he raced around. Pure and simple—the dog was gone. "Aw, shit!"

Miss Sadie leaped up, snagged his pant leg, and held on. He tried to shake her loose, but she wasn't budging. Somehow he managed to get back into the house in time to hear one of the twins wailing upstairs. "I hate you, Alice Anders," he groaned as he made his way to the second floor. By the time he got to the boys' cribs, whichever one had been wailing, had stopped. Both toddlers were peacefully sleeping, thumbs in their mouths. Ben had been a thumb sucker.

Hank went back downstairs and opened the front door. He whistled and called the golden retriever's name. He felt like crying when the dog didn't appear. It was so cold and windy and he could see light flurries of snow in the lamplight at the end of the driveway. Miss Sadie was still protesting whatever it was she was protesting by yapping and whining. He told her to shut up in no uncertain terms. She growled, a funny little sound that made the hair on the back of Hank's neck stand on end. He'd read somewhere that little dogs could be killers.

Back in the kitchen, Hank looked at the hot chocolate in his cup. "Good for the nerves, my ass," he mumbled as he searched the cabinets for something a little more powerful. He finally found a bottle of scotch behind a giant-size bottle of ketchup. He removed the cap and swigged directly from the bottle. One gulp. Two gulps. Three gulps. "Where are you, Alice?" he singsonged as he made his way into the family room. "Please come home, Churchill." He immediately retraced his steps to the kitchen and made coffee. He stood in the middle of the kitchen as the coffee dripped into the pot. What kind of child-care provider was he? The worst kind, the kind that drank on the job, that's what kind. Well, that was never going to happen again.

Hank opened the door again and whistled for Churchill. He looked down at Miss Sadie, who just looked sad, like she knew Churchill wasn't coming back. He bent over to scoop the little dog into his arms. She cuddled against his heart, and he swore that she sighed with happiness. At least someone loves me, he thought. Either that or she's desperate for attention. More than likely she missed Albert.

The clock on the kitchen stove said it was one o'clock. What time did the twins get up in the morning? Not that he was going to be any more prepared for them when they did than he was when he arrived. He just knew Alice was sleeping soundly and peacefully on thousand-thread-count sheets while he was afraid to close his eyes.

Somehow he managed to pour his coffee and drink it without disturbing Miss Sadie, who appeared to be out for the count. Who was his earlier visitor, the one who brought Churchill back? Maybe the chick from next door, the one with the fancy set of wheels in the driveway.

As he walked around the well-lighted kitchen he felt sad that the Leigh house had finally, after all these years, been sold. And, without a doubt, the Carpenter house would go up for sale, too. This house, Ben's now, would be all that was left of the old childhood neighborhood. All the other houses on the street had recycled themselves, and, once again, small children played in the yards and even on the road because there was no traffic on the cul-de-sac. His memories seemed like they were a hundred years old.

Hank finally locked the door when he realized Churchill wasn't coming back. Obviously, the dog had jumped the fence. The best he could hope for was that the dog wasn't freezing somewhere. Miss Sadie squirmed, stretched, and licked at his chin before she went back to sleep. He just knew that Albert Carpenter had carried her around just the way he was doing.

Good Lord, how was he going to go to Albert's wake and funeral? He made a mental note to order flowers first thing in the morning. He'd have to find a babysitter. Suddenly, he wanted to cry all over again. How was he going to get the news to Alice? If she ran true to what she was doing, she wasn't going to be watching the news or reading papers. Ben needed to know, too. Tomorrow he would figure out what he was going to do about that.

The coffee had sobered him up, but he knew he couldn't sleep, so he switched on the television and watched a rerun of the daily news on Fox. Eventually he dozed, his arm around Miss Sadie.

Dawn was breaking when Hank finally stirred. Something had woken him. What? Miss Sadie was no longer sleeping in his arms. The house was silent except for a scratching noise on the sliding glass door. Miss Sadie wanted to go out. Then he remembered that Churchill was still missing. He ran to the door and opened it, but there was no sign of the golden retriever. What he saw made him blink. A good inch of snow covered the ground. Miss Sadie was no fool—she took one look at the white stuff, stepped over the threshold, squatted, and raced back inside.

Hank ran to the front door to see if the golden dog was waiting outside. He whistled and called. No dog prints could be seen in the snow. Shoulders slumped, he closed the door and went back to the kitchen to make coffee. While it dripped, and the twins were still sleeping, he used the first-floor bathroom to shower and shave. He wanted to be ready when the groceries and his new day lady arrived to take charge.

Fifteen minutes later, Hank was ready for whatever the day was going to throw at him. To pass the time until the twins woke, he checked out the little computer station Alice had set up in a small alcove off the kitchen. He was surprised when he clicked the computer on that it opened up to Alice's e-mail on AOL. At least he wouldn't have to worry about a password—it was all here, right in front of him. And there was an e-mail addressed to him.

Hank gawked at what he was seeing. Well, that certainly took a lot of nerve. He clicked on the e-mail and saw a to-do list. Not one word about where she was, what she was doing, or that she was sorry. A damn to-do list. He lashed out with his foot to kick the side of the little desk and was instantly sorry. He looked down at his bare feet and howled in pain, knowing damn well that he'd broken his big toe. What the hell else could go wrong? This was way beyond Murphy's law.

Hank read the list.

- Twins get up around 8. Diaper change. Dress.
- Breakfast. Oatmeal with milk and a little sugar. Applesauce.
- Lunch is soup, crackers, cheese cubes, and peaches.
- Milk as often as they want it.
- Dinner is whatever you want, cut up small or mash all food.
- Churchill gets fed at four. His food is in pantry in a bag. Do not let anything happen to that dog or Ben will kill you.
- Do the grocery shopping. List is on the fridge. Money is in the tea canister.
- Buy Christmas tree. Set it up. Decorate it. Buy wreath for front door. Hang wreath.
- Put gas in car, it's on empty.
- Give Churchill a bath today. His stuff is over the sink in the laundry room. Keep him warm. Build a fire and do NOT let him outside. Walk him. He can jump the fence.
- Twins get bath at 7. They like to play in the water. Do NOT flood the bathroom. They go to bed at 7:30. Give them a treat, ice cream will be fine if you buy it. They will scream for hours if they don't get it. Churchill gets a dog treat at the same time.
- Do laundry twice a day. Fold neatly and take upstairs. Do not leave in laundry room.
- Do not, I repeat, do not, drink while you are taking care of my sons.

Nursing his broken toe, Hank looked around wildly for something to hit, to smash. "In your dreams!"

Miss Sadie hopped up on his lap. She whimpered softly against his chest. "I can't do this, Miss Sadie. I wasn't cut out for this. How could she leave me here with this . . . this mess? Do you see how ill equipped I am to handle this? I don't even *want* to handle it. I bet ten dollars she's frolicking in some hot tub somewhere having a grand old time while I'm here . . . suffering. What's wrong with this picture, Miss Sadie?" The little dog licked his chin in sympathy.

Hank was on his second cup of coffee when the doorbell rang. Clutching Miss Sadie to his chest, he ran to the door just as the twins started to cry. He pulled it open to see the grocery delivery boy and directed him to the kitchen. He'd charged the food to his credit card when he ordered it, so all he had to do was tip the delivery boy. He took five dollars from the tea canister and handed it over. The boy looked at him in disgust, so he popped another five into his hand. "I used to get fifty cents for going to the store for my mother."

"Yeah, well, that was then, this is now. That's so like, some dark-age time. I have to buy gas, use my own car, and drive through snow and hope the person I'm delivering to isn't going to shoot me dead."

The kid had a point, Hank thought as he ushered him to the door just in time to see his new day lady/man walking toward the door. He groaned. Miss Sadie was yapping her head off, and the twins were bellowing at a high-decibel level. There was no sign of Churchill anywhere.

Hank sighed as he introduced himself to his day lady, who just happened to be an older man who said he was Mason Hatcher. He had quirky-looking hair that stood up in little spikes. Rosy cheeks, wire-rim glasses, and a mouth pursed into a pout. He wore a heavy black coat, sensible shoes with laces, and it looked like he had thick ankles. He was thick all over, Hank decided when Mason removed his coat, hat, muffler, and gloves and folded them neatly on the bench next to the door. Mason looked at him and said, "I don't much care for dogs."

"Yeah, well, the dog goes with the deal. And one is temporarily missing. I'm sure he'll be back soon. He's . . . a little bigger. I'll pay you extra for the dogs." Hank hated how desperate he sounded.

"We'll see," was Mason's response. "Now, where are my charges?"

"Huh?"

"The children. Where are they?"

"Upstairs, second door on the left."

Mason stomped his way up the steps as Hank made his way to the kitchen, where he started to unpack the groceries. There wasn't one thing fit for the twins. Obviously, broken toe or not, he was going to have to go to the market himself with Alice's list. Damn, his toe was killing him. And, to his horror, his whole foot looked swollen. He also had to go out to look for Churchill. *Don't let Churchill out. He can jump the fence. Ben will kill you if anything happens to him.* The words rang in Hank's ears until he thought he would go out of his mind.

It suddenly dawned on him that the house was very quiet except for childish laughter wafting down the stairs. Even Miss Sadie, her head tilted to the side, was aware of the sudden silence. A minute later Mason was walking down the steps, a twin in each arm. The little twits were gooing and laughing and tweaking the man's nose. How was that possible? He'd turned himself inside out to please them, and all they did was pinch, cry, and fight him every step of the way. Obviously, he didn't have the touch. The right touch.

"I have to go out," Hank said. He was stunned at his belligerent tone.

"I'd put on some shoes if I were you, Mr. Anders. It's freezing outside."

"I don't know how that's going to work, Mason. I broke my

big toe." If he hoped for sympathy, he wasn't getting any from this guy.

"Soak it in Epsom salts," Mason said without missing a beat. "When will you return, sir? By the way, is there a lady of the house?"

"When I'm done doing what I have to do is when I'll be back. I can't give you a specific time. There is a lady of the house but not right now. She's . . . well, what she is . . . she isn't here."

"I see. And you're in charge temporarily, is that it?"

"No, no, I'm not in charge. Well, I am, but I'm not. I know that doesn't make a whole lot of sense but . . . you, Mason, *are in charge.*"

"Very well, sir."

"Call me Hank."

"I can't do that, sir. You're my employer. The company frowns on familiarity. Will there be anything else before I feed these little angels?"

"Nope, that's it. See ya, Mason."

Shoes on, his toe throbbing, Hank dressed and left the house. His game plan was to ride around the neighborhood to look for Churchill before doing anything else. He'd start first by warming up the SUV and brushing the snow off the windshield. He turned around when he heard banging sounds coming from Albert Carpenter's house. Someone on a ladder was banging with a hammer and stringing lights, and who was it standing next to the ladder but Churchill!

"Hey!" he shouted.

A female voice responded, "Hey, yourself!"

"Do you need any help, other than my dog?"

"Your dog! This is your dog! I don't think so! He's mine now. Possession is nine-tenths of the law. I walked him. I fed him. And he slept at my house last night. That means he's mine. It was freezing out last night. He could have died out there. You just try and get him back and I'll . . . I'll . . ." The hammer drove a nail into the post with deadly precision.

"That's private property. What do you think you're doing anyway? Mr. Carpenter died yesterday."

"I know he died. God rest his soul. I'm hanging Christmas lights. What's it look like I'm doing? Furthermore, it's none of your damn business what I'm doing. Don't even think about stealing this dog from me. Just try calling him. I betcha five bucks he will ignore you."

Hank felt befuddled. That was a sucker bet if he ever heard one. Who was this person? She had yet to turn around, and she was bundled up like Nanook of the North.

His toe throbbing like a bongo drum, Hank whistled for the dog. Churchill ignored him. He called him by name. Churchill ignored him. He called out, "Good boy, come on now, I'll give you a treat." Churchill plopped down and put his head between his paws.

"I'll take that five dollars now."

It was like a lightbulb went off in Hank's head. "I know who you are. You're that know-it-all who brought Churchill back last night when I was giving the twins a bath."

Amy banged in another nail with the same deadly precision. "Wow! You figured it out. Guess you have a brain after all. He's mine, and he's staying with me."

"You're trespassing, you know. The old guy just passed, and you're hanging Christmas lights on his house. That makes you some kind of ghoul in my opinion. I wonder what the cops will do if I call them. I want my damn dog, and I want him now."

"Why don't you try taking him and see how far you get." The hammer swung again. The sound was so loud, Hank winced. "Go ahead, call the police. I'm just being a good neighbor. I know for a fact that Mr. Carpenter always had Christmas lights. In his later years he probably had someone do it for him. And just for the record, these are my lights. I didn't steal them, nor did I break into Mr. Carpenter's house in case that's the next thing you're going to say. Furthermore, you . . .you . . . buffoon, don't you think it's a little strange that a woman is doing this when someone of your . . . ilk should be doing it? Go bother somebody else. I'm busy."

Buffoon. Someone of my ilk. What the hell did that mean? His toe was throbbing so bad he wanted to bang it on the porch railing. Anger at his circumstances rippled through him. "Listen to me, you . . . you dog snatcher, I want my dog, and I want him *now.* He's a boy dog. Why'd you put that stupid red ribbon with a bell on him?"

The voice that retaliated was syrupy sweet. "It's like this, you clown. The bell lets me know where he is. This is the Christmas season, and red goes with the silver bell. For the last time, I did not snatch your dog. He came to me. He doesn't even like you. I can tell. Look at him, he's petrified of you. That's pretty bad when a dog doesn't like his owner. Did you abuse this poor animal?"

Outrage rivered through Hank at the accusation. Hank bent over to peer at the golden dog, who growled. "I would never harm an animal. I might have been a little sharp with him when he deliberately lifted his leg on a chair. He pees a flood. It took two towels to clean it up. He jumps the fence. I didn't know he could do that until this morning."

The voice was still syrupy sweet. "And I suppose you think I'm going to believe that . . . that ridiculous story. Let's get real here."

Hank was at his wit's end. His toe was killing him. "Are you always this nasty so early in the morning, or were you born this way?"

Four things happened at that precise moment before Amy could respond. Mason opened the front door to get the newspaper, Miss Sadie beelined out the door and ran at the speed of light to the Carpenter front porch, at which point Churchill leaped up to greet his new best friend and toppled the ladder. The know-it-all slipped and fell.

"Oh, shit!"

"Oh, shit, is right," Nanook of the North said as she rolled over in her down coat to survey the damage. Somehow or other the two dogs were now tangled in the string of Christmas lights that were twinkling off and on.

Churchill growled, his ears going flat against his head, a sure sign that he was perturbed at something.

Hank took that moment to stare at the woman on the floor, who was laughing hysterically. So this is what she looks like. Something teased at his memory then, something he couldn't put his finger on. She was so pretty it took his breath away. And she had the nicest laugh he'd ever heard in his life. He knew that laugh. Or he remembered it from somewhere. The question was where? "Do I know you?"

Amy was on her feet when she looked up at her old child-hood friend. "I don't know, do you?" She bent down then to try to untangle the string of lights the dogs were bent on chewing.

Hank wondered if a buffoon-slash-clown would do what he was doing, which was holding out his hand. "Hank Anders. I'm visiting next door for the holidays."

Amy stopped what she was doing, stood up straight, and looked him dead in the eye, hoping she wasn't giving away the delicious feeling coursing through her. "Mandy Leigh. It's been a long time, Hank." She crushed his hand in hers and saw that he tried not to wince.

"Mandy! It is you! Well, damn! In my wildest dreams I never thought we'd meet up again. You broke my heart when you moved away. I wanted to write you a hundred times, but no one knew where your aunt took you. California, we all thought."

"That's right, California," Amy said. "I've lived there ever since."

"Mom said your aunt Flo was a world traveler. We just assumed . . . no one ever came back. I thought the house was sold. Hell, I don't know what I thought. Look, I'm sorry about . . . about calling you names. This . . . it's a long sad story. Can we go for coffee or something? God, you're beautiful! You look just like I remember."

Amy laughed. "Is this where I'm supposed to say you're handsome?"

"Wouldn't hurt. Mom always said I was good-looking. So, can we do the coffee? I'll help you with the lights when we get back."

"Why not?" Why not indeed. Oh, be still my heart, Amy said to herself as she tidied up the porch, then replied, "Let's go to my house. I can make coffee, and I have some sticky buns. The kind Mom used to make when we were little."

As they walked toward the Leigh house, a light snow started to fall to the dogs' delight.

"Then you aren't mad at me?"

"Nah. I was just venting. I've been upset about Mr. Carpenter's passing. He was so good to us kids growing up. It's always especially sad when a person dies during the Christmas season. That's why I wanted to string up the lights. He used to love Christmas. Remember how we always made him a present?"

"Yeah. Yeah, I remember," Hank said softly. "I remember everything about that time. You really did break my heart, you know. By the way, Miss Sadie, the little fur ball, belonged to Mr. Carpenter. Ben gave the dog to him after his wife died. Churchill is Ben's dog. You're probably right about him not liking me. I was more or less thrust on him out of the blue. I might remind him of Ben. By the way, Ben is in Iraq."

"Sounds like you and I have a lot of catching up to do," Amy said, opening the front door of her house. *And he has no clue that I'm a movie star.* How wonderful was that? Pretty damn wonderful, she decided.

Chapter Five

Amy felt like she was walking on legs of Jell-O as she shed her outerwear on the way to the kitchen. Hank wasn't married. He was right behind her. In her very own kitchen. And he looked every bit as good as she dreamed. He was here. She was going to make him coffee and sticky buns. How good could life get? But the absolute best was, he had no clue that she was a movie star. A mighty sigh escaped her. She whirled around, not realizing how close he was. They literally butted shoulders. She looked into dark brown eyes that she remembered so well. She could smell minty toothpaste. In a liquid flash she could see something in his eyes, the same thing she was feeling. He blinked. She blinked, then Churchill broke the moment by jumping between them. Flustered, Amy backed away, and Hank sat down on one of the old wooden kitchen chairs.

The exquisite moment was gone. Hopefully it would return at some point.

Amy reminded herself that she was an actress. She could carry this off until she saw which way the romantic wind was blowing. "You know, Hank, I can make you a full breakfast if you like, or we can go with the sticky buns and coffee. Your call."

Hank looked up at the stunning woman towering over him.

He wanted to reach out and grab her. The old Mandy would
have smacked him for taking such liberties. He'd almost
kissed her. And his heart and his eyes told him she would
have been receptive to the kiss. This was a new Mandy.
Maybe he should step back and not be so . . . pushy. *Pushy?*
He cleared his throat. His voice sounded like a nest of frogs
had settled in his throat. "Whatever is easiest. Let's just talk."

"Great! Then it's sticky buns, juice, and coffee." As Amy
prepared the coffee and turned on the oven, she threw questions at Hank. "So bring me up to date. Do you come home
here to Apple Valley every Christmas? This is my first time
back." Was her voice too breathless, too giddy-sounding?
Maybe she should be more cool, a little aloof, instead of this
flighty person she'd suddenly become.

As Hank talked, Amy set the table with her mother's old
dishes. Plain white crockery with huge red strawberries in the
middle. Her mother had had a passion for strawberries for
some reason. Everything in the kitchen had to do with strawberries: the cookie jar, the canister set, even the place mats
were in the shape of strawberries.

"I remember these dishes. Your mom always served us
cookies and sandwiches on them. You always said if you had
to eat something you didn't like it made it okay because the
dish was so pretty."

Amy stopped what she was doing. "You remember that!"

"Well, yeah. I guess I considered it an important thing in
my life at the time. I don't have one bad memory of growing
up here in Apple Valley. Ben doesn't either. You never said
good-bye," Hank blurted.

Amy turned around as she fiddled with the pot holder in her
hand. "Flo . . . Flo whisked me out of here so fast I didn't
know what happened. I guess she thought I might . . . I don't
know what she thought. I used to cry myself to sleep. I wanted
to come back so bad, but there was nothing to come back to."

"Do you like living in the land of perpetual sunshine?"

"Yes and no. I really miss the change of seasons. I love

autumn, and I even like winter. The holidays here in Apple Valley are my greatest memory. How about you?"

"I live and work in New York. I'm an engineer, have my own business. I have nine employees, and we're doing pretty well. New York isn't that far away from Apple Valley. I came home once a month up until my parents died. Then Ben and Alice took over the house, and I came less and less. But I always came back for the holidays. Ben's in Iraq. He's a major in the army. He was supposed to be home by now, but they extended his stay over there. He's getting out when his twenty years are up. He has another ten years to go. Alice is . . . upset. She was so sure Ben would be home for Christmas. The last time he saw the twins they had just been born. The Army allowed him to come home on compassionate leave just before Christmas, when they were born. They're toddling around now, and they *have teeth.*" This last was said with so much amazement, Amy burst out laughing.

Hank wanted to confide in Amy, to tell her about Alice's great escape, but he decided against it because he didn't want to be disloyal to his sister-in-law. He decided to change the subject. "Are you going to go to Mr. Carpenter's funeral? I imagine the wake will be this evening. I'm going. I can pick you up if you want." Assuming Mason would babysit. No need to tell Amy about that either, he thought.

"I'd like that very much. I was going to order some flowers after I finished stringing the lights. Then you showed up . . ."

"I guess I came on a little strong. I'm sorry. I've been . . ." He was going to say upset with the way things were going, but at the last second finished lamely with, "Upset with Albert's death. He was special."

Amy poured coffee and removed the sticky buns from the oven. She let them cool as she poured juice into her mother's old jelly glasses. She hated the tremor in her hands.

"So tell me about you. What do you do in California?" There was horror in his voice when he said, "You aren't married, are you?"

Amy grinned. "Not even close. How about you?"

"I got close, but she left me standing at the altar. Best thing that could have happened to me. 'Course I didn't think that at the time."

Amy blinked, then she said, coolly, "You told me you would wait for me forever. Guess you didn't mean it, huh?"

Hank immediately picked up on the chill in Amy's voice. "I know I meant it at the time. I think by the time I turned twenty-one, I realized you weren't coming back to Apple Valley. I did try Googling you a while back. Nothing came up. I figured you got married, had a new name, and were living happily amid the orange blossoms and sunshine." It sounded so stupid even to his own ears, he couldn't imagine what she was thinking. He gulped at the hot coffee to cover his discomfort.

Amy's voice was still cool when she shoved one of the strawberry plates across the table along with two sticky buns and a napkin. "Guess you're a bachelor then. I thought you would have a bunch of kids by now."

Hank frowned. "Why would you think that?" What the hell was going on here?

Amy shrugged as she sat down. "Well, Ben is married. You're twins. Twins usually do the same thing. I'm sorry, I guess I shouldn't have said that. So, how do you like these sticky buns?"

"Quite good." They tasted like sawdust.

"No kidding. I think they taste like cardboard."

They looked at each other across the table. They were kids again, sharing a joke. They burst out laughing at the same time. Hank spoke first. "I was going to say they tasted like sawdust, but I didn't want to hurt your feelings. I missed you, Mandy. When you left I thought about you every day. Ben used to tease me, said I was in love with you. You know, puppy love."

"I was so crazy about you I couldn't see straight. Back then I believed we would get married after we finished college. I think that's why I was so upset when Flo took me away. I felt so lost and angry, but I was just a kid. I couldn't do anything about it. Every day I used to run to the mailbox thinking you'd find out where I was and write me a letter. I wanted to write to you, but I guess I didn't have the nerve. That might be more than you need or want to know."

"No, no, not at all. I was a mess myself after you left. My mom was good about it. She tried her best to explain what she thought happened. Even Ben did his best not to nag me, but he was getting off on it. You know how kids are."

"Yeah, I know how kids are. If you're not busy after we string the lights, I can make you lunch, or, if you like, maybe we could go to Andolino's for pizza. When I first got here I drove through town. Tony made the best pizza. I'll buy."

"Well, that's an offer I can't turn down. Pizza it is, and let me tell you, Tony's pizza has not changed; it's every bit as good as it was back when we were kids. His sons run the parlor now. So, are you ready? I'll meet you at Mr. Carpenter's. I want to check on . . . on the twins."

"Okay, go ahead. I'll clean up here and meet you on the porch. If you don't mind, I want to stop and get a big wreath for Mr. Carpenter's front door. We can order flowers at the same time. You okay with that?"

Hank shrugged into his jacket. "Absolutely. I just need ten minutes. Damn, I'm glad you came home this year." He was almost to the door when he turned around and came back. "Hey, if I want to ask you out, you know, dinner or something, should I call you up or what? I don't have your phone number. I need a phone number. Those tin cans we used to string between the houses aren't going to work. You know, a date."

A date with Hank Anders. That was the stuff dreams were made of. "Sure. It's 310-200-9999. What's yours?"

She wanted his number. Suddenly he felt light-headed. Hank pulled his wallet out of his pocket and handed her one of his business cards. He felt a jolt of electricity racing up his arm when his fingers touched hers.

Amy smiled.

Hank smiled.

And then he was gone. Amy sucked in her breath as she danced around the kitchen as the dogs pawed and yapped at her. "You don't understand, guys. I think I've been waiting all my life for what just happened. I am just so happy. So very happy."

The dogs yipped and yapped as Amy moved between the table and the dishwasher. When she started to sing "Jingle Bells," they howled. She laughed as she slipped into her heavy down jacket. "Hey, guys, it's snowing again!"

Amy, the dogs behind her, walked across the lawn to the Carpenter property. Hank was nowhere in sight. What was he doing? She looked at her watch. He'd said ten minutes. Now it was more like twenty. She shrugged. If he was blowing her off, then he was blowing her off.

Hank Anders watched Amy from the front window. His heart was beating so fast, he thought it was going to leap right out of his chest. The minute he'd gotten inside, he collapsed against the door. How was it possible that now, right at this moment, his childhood dream was coming true? He'd been *that* close. Close enough to kiss her. And not the kind of kiss he'd planted on her lips when they were thirteen years old either.

Mason, the new nanny, took that moment to enter the foyer. Alarmed, he raced to his employer. "Are you all right, sir?"

"Mason, my man, I'm about as right as a guy can get. How's everything going? I'm in love. Are the twins more than you can handle? Did I tell you I'm in love? Did they eat? They're kind of sloppy. This is such a great feeling. By the way, I found the dog."

Mason stared at his new employer. He met all kinds of people in his line of work. "I'm certain Mrs. Anders will be happy to hear that. Perhaps she's the one you should be telling. I'm happy for you. The boys are fine. They ate ravenously. They're playing in the family room. They've been changed, and I'm considering what to make them for lunch. About dinner . . . is there anything in particular you fancy?"

Hank gaped at the nanny. What the hell was he saying? "No, no, not Mrs. Anders." He motioned Mason to join him at the window. "Her. I'm in love with her."

Mason pursed his lips and glared at Hank, disapproval in every line in his face. "I see! Then my advice is *not* to tell Mrs. Anders."

"Dammit, no. That's not . . . I guess I didn't explain. I'm not the husband or the father of the twins. I'm their uncle. I live in New York. My brother is Mr. Anders. He's the husband, but he's in Iraq. I'm just visiting. Don't worry about dinner. Fix something for yourself. I have to go to a wake this evening. Can you stay past bath time? I'll pay you extra of course. Did anyone . . . you know . . . call?" Please, oh, please say Alice called.

Mason looked befuddled. All he could think of to say was, "I see."

"You already said that. What is it you see, Mason?"

"That things in this household are topsy-turvy. Or as my old mum used to say, at sixes and sevens. There were no phone calls. But, your e-mail has been pinging ever since you left. I assume that means you have messages."

Alice. Alice must have e-mailed again. "So can you babysit this evening?"

"Of course, sir. I charge twenty-five dollars an hour."

"Fine, fine!" Hank said as he leaped over the gates that held the twins prisoner in the family room. Just one big playpen. The minute the boys saw him, they started to cry. Mason was on the job immediately. A second later the boys were laughing and playing peekaboo with their nanny.

Hank clicked on the e-mail and was chagrined to see it was from his brother Ben and directed to Alice. He told himself he had to read the e-mail. Told himself he wasn't being sneaky. He had to find Alice for the boys' sake. It was such a sweet e-mail, Hank felt his eyes burn. Ben apologized again and again for not being home for the holidays. He thanked his wife for the recent pictures of the boys she'd sent him. He asked about the tree and who she was going to get to put it up. He said how much he loved her and couldn't wait to get back to her waiting arms. Then came the clunker that made Hank's back stiffen. *I know you said I shouldn't do it, but Hank will understand. He won't hassle us to repay the loan sooner than we're able. Hank's my brother. I'd do the same for him. I can see the stress and strain on your face. Photos don't lie, Alice. I know you're killing yourself with all you have to do. Start looking for someone to come in to help. With Hank coming for Christmas, he'll give you the money. This is no time for either one of us to be too proud to ask if we need help. I didn't get an e-mail from you yesterday or today. I hope nothing is wrong. Write me, honey. I love you. All my love, Ben.*

Hank clicked off the e-mail but saved it. "Mason!" he bellowed at the top of his lungs.

"Yes, sir."

"Can I hire you for six months?"

"I would think so, sir. Contact the agency and arrange it. I need to warn you, I'm in demand. I say that with all due modesty."

"Even with the dogs?"

"I suppose I can get a book on dog training."

"Good, good. Okay, I don't have time right now to call the agency. Will you do it and reserve yourself for the next six months. I'll . . . what I'll do is . . . throw in a bonus. Name it and it's yours," Hank babbled as he backed out of the door.

"Very well, sir."

A blustery gust of snow flurries slammed Hank in the face the moment he stepped outside. He laughed when he saw Churchill and Miss Sadie trying to catch the elusive flurries.

"Damn, I'm sorry, Mandy. The twins . . . and then there was an e-mail from Ben I had to read. You hung all the lights! You didn't need me at all."

"Sure I do. I waited for you to plug in the lights. Cross your fingers that they work."

Hank inserted the plug. Amy clapped her hands in delight. "I have a package of extra lights. It's amazing that they still work after all these years. Well, our work here is done. You can carry the ladder back to my house and put it on the back porch. Should I keep the dogs, or do you want to take them to your house?"

"Yours. The nanny doesn't have a dog book yet. Yeah, yeah, your house. My car or yours?" Then he remembered Alice said the SUV needed gas. "Yours. Alice said hers is low on gas. I'll fill it up later, but since I don't know how much driving we're going to be doing, let's use yours."

"Okay," Amy said agreeably.

Ten minutes later, the snow still swirling and twirling, Hank and Amy settled themselves in the big truck. "Pretty fancy set of wheels," Hank said. "Is it yours, or is it a rental?"

"I bought it when I got here. Mom and Dad's old cars are still in the garage. I didn't want to take a chance on either one of them. I knew I was going to need a vehicle. I might decide to stay on longer than I originally planned. I might even decide to drive cross-country when it's time to leave."

Leave. She was talking about leaving. Hank felt his loss. Well, he couldn't let that happen, now could he? "It's really snowing. Looks like it's going to keep up. If it does, maybe we could go sledding like we used to. We could pull the twins on the sled. I think our old sleds are still in the attic. You could use Ben's if you don't have one."

"Sounds like fun. I'm game. But not until I get the house set up for Christmas. You any good at setting up a tree?" She twinkled.

"The best tree-setter-upper there is. Takes two people, though. Ben and I always did it. It's the lights that are a killer. The tinsel can drive you nuts. Ben always insisted on hanging one strand at a time. It took all night."

"Really? Mom and Dad always did it after I went to bed.

When I woke up, there was this magnificent tree all lit up, with all the junk I made through my school years. We didn't have any fancy heirloom ornaments. How wonderful for you," she said sadly.

"I didn't know that, Mandy. What did you do for a tree in California?" Hank asked.

Amy bit down on her lip. "Flo wasn't big on cleaning up pine needles in July. She said that's how long it took to get them out of the house. We always had an artificial tree, and it glittered with shiny ornaments and white lights. The wreath on the door was artificial, too. It got a new red bow every year. We used to go swimming on Christmas Day and have a turkey. I did my best to sleep through the whole season."

"I upset you, didn't I? I'm sorry, Mandy. That wasn't my intention." Hank stretched out a hand to pat her arm.

Amy blinked away tears. "Well, we've arrived. Does Karen Powell still own OK Florist?"

"Yep. She expanded a few years back, added a nursery, and sells outdoor plants as well. Even trees. The parking lot is always full in the spring and summer."

A bell tinkled over the door when Amy opened it. She looked around. It was just the way she remembered. New merchandise, but the old beams were still there, with greenery and decorations dangling downward. "It looks like a Wonderland with all the trees. It's so festive, with all the greenery and red and white Santas. My gosh, I don't know what to buy. I want a little of everything."

"Then let's get a little of everything," Hank said happily. Damn, he was getting a large dose of Christmas spirit all of a sudden.

"Okay, but first I want to order the flowers for Mr. Carpenter so they can deliver them today. How about if I order a large arrangement and put your, Ben's, and my name on the card?"

"Sure. Sounds great. Oh, and will you include Ben's wife, Alice? Just tell me how much our share is."

"No problem."

Amy walked over to the counter and spoke to the girl behind the computer. She explained what she wanted, signed a card, and handed her a credit card. "I'm going to want a dozen or so of your poinsettias. All red. Shall I pick them out and put them by the door?" The frazzled clerk nodded as she punched in the order.

Amy and Hank spent the next hour picking out just-right poinsettias, knickknacks, and whatever pleased Amy. The clerk rang everything up while a young boy loaded the cargo hold of the Range Rover. She ripped off a tape and slapped it down on the counter in front of Hank along with Amy's credit card. "Sign on the X."

"No, that's not my card," Hank said, picking up the credit card. "Hold on, I'll get my friend to come in and sign the slip."

Hank walked over to the door and tapped on it. Amy turned around and smiled. He held up her credit card and motioned her to come inside. Without meaning to, he looked down at the platinum card in his hand and saw the name Amy Lee. He frowned. Who the hell was Amy Lee? What was Mandy Leigh doing with someone else's credit card?

Hank's stomach crunched into a knot as he stared at his old childhood friend as she walked toward him, a smile on her face. He realized at that moment he didn't know a thing about Mandy Leigh. All he knew was she was home for the holidays and lived in California. Otherwise, all their conversations were on the generic side. He'd been loose as a goose and opened up and confessed to loving her.

The name Amy Lee sounded so familiar. Did he know her when they were kids? Was she a client or a client's wife? Nothing was ringing a bell for him.

Who the hell was Amy Lee?

Chapter Six

It wasn't until Amy finished her third slice of pizza and drained the last of her root beer float that she realized she'd been doing all the talking. Hank had only eaten one slice of the delicious pizza, and his root beer float was basically untouched. He also had a strange look on his face. Like he wanted to say something or possibly ask her something and didn't quite know how to go about it. The words "moody" and "sullen" came to mind. She shook her head to clear her thoughts. She didn't need this, no way, no how.

Maybe he thought she'd spent too much money at OK Florist. He'd commented on her Range Rover, calling it a pricey set of wheels. Maybe he had a thing about women spending money. He'd been fine before they got to the florist, so whatever was wrong had nothing to do with Mr. Carpenter or the dogs. It had to be her. Something about her was suddenly bothering him. She racked her brain to try to recall what she might have said or done that would make him so quiet all of a sudden.

Well, she certainly wasn't going to worry about Hank and his moods. She had things to do and places to go. She fished some money out of her pocket and laid it on the table. After all, she'd invited him to lunch, so it was up to her to pay for it.

Amy got up and slipped into her jacket. The waiter approached and asked if she wanted change. She shook her head. "Are you ready, Hank?" she asked coolly.

"What?"

"I asked you if you were ready to leave. We came, we ate, I paid the bill, and now it's time to leave. Are you ready?"

"Yeah. Sure. My mind is somewhere else. I'm sorry, Mandy."

"I am, too," Amy said as she headed for the door. She slammed through the door, not caring that Hank walked right into it as it was closing. She ignored his yelp of surprise and headed straight for the car. Midway to the Rover, a young woman in a Girl Scout uniform rushed up to her. "Would you care to donate to Mr. Carpenter's funeral expenses?"

"What did you say?" The young girl repeated her question.

"I didn't know . . . of course." Amy emptied out her wallet.

"How about you, sir?"

"I didn't bring my wallet with me. Tell me where I can drop off my contribution. I'll do it as soon as I get home."

"Mrs. Masterson. She lives at 82 Cypress Street. She's in charge of the fund-raiser."

"Okay, thanks." Hank climbed into the Rover and buckled up. Amy peeled away the moment the door was closed securely. She clenched her teeth. If he thought she was going to start babbling, he needed to think again about his rude behavior. Some things were just not meant to be. So much for dreams and long-lost loves.

"The snow is really coming down," Hank said, in an attempt to make conversation.

The snow wasn't a question. So she didn't have to respond.

Hank eyed Amy out of the corner of his eye. He tried again. "That's pretty sad about Albert Carpenter. I knew he didn't have any family left, but I would have thought he had some savings, enough to bury him."

That wasn't a question either. So she didn't have to respond to it either. Instead, Amy concentrated on the falling snow and driving on the slick roads.

The rest of the ride home was made in silence on Amy's

part. She swerved into her driveway, turned off the engine, and hopped out of the Rover. "Don't bother yourself. I can unload the truck later. I have other things I need to do now. Do you want to take the dogs now, or should I keep them?"

Her voice was as cold as the snow falling all about him. Hank did a double take. He knew a brush-off when he got one. He'd had more than enough in his lifetime to know the signals. He took a moment to wonder if Mandy was bipolar. One minute she was on top of the world, and the next she was doom and gloom. She hadn't said a word on the drive home. "I'll take them," he said curtly.

"Fine," Amy snapped. She opened the door, and both dogs ran to her to be petted. Hank did everything in his power to get Churchill to go with him. He finally had to give up when the big dog bared his teeth. "Guess that's your answer, Mr. Anders."

Mr. Anders? "Yeah, guess so."

Amy moved to the door to close it. Then she added insult to injury, Hank thought, when he heard the deadbolt snick into place. He felt lower than a skunk's belly when he high-tailed it back to his brother's house.

What the hell is going on?

The house was exceptionally quiet. Instead of calling out, Hank walked out to the kitchen to see Mason puttering around at the stove. "Is there any coffee, Mason? Did anyone call?"

"I just made fresh coffee. No one called, but your e-mail is pinging again. I just put the boys down for their naps. My agency has booked me for the next six months. All you need to do is call to confirm and give them your credit card information. Is something wrong, Mr. Anders? You look . . . dejected."

Was something wrong? This guy was really astute. Hank wondered what kind of confidant he would make. He poured coffee. "What are you making?"

"Stew. I always make stew when it snows. The weatherman is predicting six inches of snow by morning. Did you go to the market, Mr. Anders? We need milk for the boys."

"Stew is good. I'm going to go to the market when I finish this coffee. I have to get gas, too. What I said earlier . . . you know . . . about me being in love. That wasn't true. Well, it was at the time, but it isn't now. I overreacted. Women are so . . . what they are is . . . hell, what are they, Mason?"

"Complex. Fickle. Manipulative. Selfish. Mind you, I don't know this for a fact, but I do read a lot. So, I guess what you're saying is the lady next door spurned your advances. Would that be a correct assessment, Mr. Anders?"

"It will do. I didn't do a damn thing. She froze on me. She goddamn well kicked me to the curb is what she did. What do you think about *that*, Mason?"

Mason opted to take the high road. "I think, sir, before I can comment, I would need to hear the young lady's side. As you know, there are two sides to everything."

"There must be something wrong with me. I was left standing at the altar a while back. The twins don't like me. The dogs don't want to come home. I don't get it. I'm a stand-up guy. I'm nice to old people. I've always liked kids. I'm generous, never ask anyone to do anything I won't do myself. My employees gave me a plaque that said I was the best boss in the world. I don't have dandruff. I use a top-notch deodorant. What the hell is wrong with me?"

"I don't think I'm qualified to comment on anything other than the boys. I think they sensed your uneasiness. In other words, you have little experience with toddlers. They sense your fear. I can't be certain, but I imagine it's probably the same thing with the animals."

"What should I do?"

"Try to repair the damage. Relax. Flowers might be an option. You need to be comfortable with yourself. I really think you should go to the market now before the roads become hazardous, Mr. Anders. The boys drink a lot of milk."

Hank looked over at the computer. He had the rest of the day and evening to check e-mails. Mason was right, he needed to get to the market and gas up the SUV. "Do you know how to bake a pie, Mason?"

"Of course. Doesn't everyone? What kind would you like?"

"Berry. Anything berry. I don't know how to bake a pie. I don't know how to cook. Period."

"Let me check the larder to see if the lady of the house has all the ingredients. I'll make a list for you, Mr. Anders."

Antsy with his inactivity, Hank walked into the living room so he could look out the window. He gasped when he saw Mandy and the dogs on Albert Carpenter's front porch. Mandy was stringing wire on the back of the giant wreath she'd purchased at the florist shop. Even from here he could see how huge the big red bow was. He'd wanted to hang the wreath with her. Was she making a statement of some kind?

Hank felt guilty and knew it showed on his face when Mason came up behind him with his list. He held out Hank's wallet. "I'm thinking you might need this."

"Thanks. I wasn't spying, Mason."

"If you say so, Mr. Anders."

"All right, I'm spying."

Mason cleared his throat. "Have you given any thought to speaking with the young lady and telling her whatever it is that's bothering you? It's entirely possible that she's reacting to something you did or said. For every action there is a reaction, Mr. Anders."

Hank snorted. "Try this on for size, Mason. Why would the lady in question be using a credit card, a platinum one no less, with someone else's name on it?"

"I'm sure there are many reasons why and how that could happen, Mr. Anders."

"Oh, yeah, name me one," Hank said belligerently.

Mason squared his shoulders. "Very well. Perhaps the card is in her maiden name. Perhaps it's a corporate card. Perhaps the young lady uses a pseudonym. And, Mr. Anders, is it any of your business to begin with?"

"I'm outta here," Hank barked as he opened the door. Slipping and sliding, he made his way to the SUV and turned on the engine and the heater while he cleaned the snow off the truck. He kept looking over at the Carpenter house, hoping Mandy would acknowledge him. She didn't. The dogs were so intent on romping in the snow, they weren't even aware of him.

"Screw it," Hank muttered as he backed out of the driveway. His first stop was the Masterson house on Cypress Street.

Ten minutes later he was ringing the doorbell. A pleasant woman opened the door and smiled at him. He reached for his wallet and explained that he was there to give a donation for Albert Carpenter's funeral.

"That's very nice of you but some very kind, generous person is paying for the funeral. Mr. Dial just called a little while ago. This same person, who I'm told wishes to remain anonymous, also paid for the church ladies to prepare a dinner after . . . after the burial. Everything has been taken care of, but thank you for stopping by."

Hank nodded and shrugged as he jammed his wallet back in his pocket.

Two hours later, Hank was back at the house, with the SUV gassed up and enough groceries to feed an army for a month.

He looked across the yard and saw that the colored Christmas lights had been turned on. Wise move. This way Mandy wouldn't have to get dressed and slog through the snow when it got dark out. The huge evergreen wreath on the door looked festive. He craned his neck trying to see into the cargo hold of the Range Rover to see if the contents had been removed. He couldn't see a thing with the falling snow and the tinted windows.

Disgusted with himself and his circumstances, Hank carried in the groceries. He smiled at the childish laughter coming from the family room.

While Mason unpacked the groceries, Hank made a fire, then settled himself on the floor, not close to the twins but just far enough away so they wouldn't pitch a fit. He watched them interact with each other as they played with their toys. From time to time they looked over at him to see what he was doing. He wiggled his fingers and made funny faces. Then he rolled across the floor and hid his face. It was all the boys needed. Suddenly they were all over him, yanking at his hair, sitting on his back, then rolling over themselves.

Hank sat up. The boys looked at him as much as to say, is the fun over? "You guys look just like your daddy. He's one lucky man. You're pretty lucky, too, to have a dad like Ben. I'm sorry your mom isn't here. She . . . I know she misses you, but she has some . . . issues right now. I think she'll be home for Christmas. God, I hope she comes home for Christmas."

The boys trundled off when they realized the giant on the floor was done playing. Hank rolled over and stared at the fire blazing up the chimney.

Where are you, Alice? He just knew in his gut that Alice would be able to explain Mandy's attitude. Women knew everything about other women. He sat up and moved over to the gate to step over it. Time to check the e-mails. He sniffed; the kitchen smelled just the way a kitchen was supposed to smell, fragrant and homey. He said so. Mason beamed with pleasure at the compliment.

Hank clicked on the e-mail and saw a note from Alice. Another list! Not a word about her return.

- The boys get a chewable Flintstone vitamin every morning. The bottle is on the kitchen windowsill.
- Trash pickup is tomorrow morning. Both cans are full. Separate the glass bottles from plastic. Containers in the garage. Bundle all paper products and put in separate bin. All bins are labeled in the garage.
- Buy gas for the snowblower. Container is empty. Otherwise, shovel the driveway.
- Wash Churchill's pee pads in Clorox.
- Lightbulbs on front porch are burned out. Replace them.

And that was the end of the list. Hank printed it out.

"I have to take the trash out, Mason. And I need to check

the snowblower. I think I'll walk to the gas station for gas. You have things under control here, right?"

"Yes, sir, I do. The pie is coming along nicely. The stew is simmering. I'm going to do some laundry. Do whatever you have to do."

"The boys need their vitamins. They're on the windowsill."

"I took care of that, sir."

"The pee pads need to be washed in Clorox."

"I've taken care of that, sir. The boys' laundry is washing now."

"You're right, Mason, you do have it under control."

Hank grabbed his jacket and entered the garage through the kitchen. He checked the snowblower. He had an identical one at home in New York, so he knew how to work it. Alice was right, though, it was bone dry, as was the gas container. He made fast work of bundling the paper products and separating the glass and plastic bottles. Then he dragged the heavy trash cans through the snow and out to the curb. How the hell did Alice do all this? He was huffing and puffing when he made his seventh trip down the driveway.

Should he start to shovel the driveway, or should he slog his way to the gas station for gas? He looked around for the shovel but didn't see one. He snorted as he grabbed the gas can and started down the driveway. He stopped in his tracks when he heard Churchill bark. He strained to see through the snow. Is that Mandy on the front porch of the Carpenter house? What the hell is she doing now?

"Hey, what are you doing?" he yelled.

"Decorating. Why do you care what I'm doing?" Amy shouted back.

Hank sucked in his breath and got a mouthful of snow. He didn't mean to say the words, they just popped out of his mouth. "Do you need any help?"

Amy strained to see through the swirling snow. She could use some help. "Yeah," she said before she could change her mind. Maybe she could get to the bottom of whatever it was that was bothering Hank.

He was on the porch a minute later, the orange gas can in his hand. "I was going for gas for the snowblower. I can do your driveway if you like. What are you doing?"

"I'm decorating Mr. Carpenter's front porch. I found all of our old decorations in the garage. Mom bought all of these reindeer one year and the sleigh. Don't you remember?"

"Yeah, yeah, I do remember. Your family won the prize that year for the best-decorated house. Why aren't you putting them up on your own front porch?"

Good question. "I'm not sure why. I just wanted to do something for Mr. Carpenter. He was always so big on Christmas even though he and his wife never had children. Remember how he used to say because he was a teacher all us kids were his children? Maybe it's a send-off of sorts.

"I came back home because I was trying . . . I wanted . . . I guess I was trying to recapture that last Christmas that I never had. You can't go home again, Hank," she said sadly. "I wish so much that I had come back sooner. I wish I had told Mr. Carpenter how much he meant to me growing up. I wish so many things. I guess I'm trying to make up for that. Is it right? Is it wrong? I don't know, and I don't care. I just need to do this. For me and for Mr. Carpenter."

Hank stared at the young woman standing across from him, tears in her eyes. "It makes sense to me," he said. "You're the one who paid for the funeral, aren't you?"

"How did you know?"

"I went to the Mastersons' to leave my donation. She told me an anonymous donor called Mr. Dial and paid for it. Tell me right now, who is Amy Lee? What were you doing with someone else's credit card? I didn't know how to deal with it."

Amy slid down on her haunches, her back against the front door. "Is that what your attitude was all about? Why didn't you just ask me?"

"Well, I didn't . . . All kinds of crazy thoughts were going through my mind. I was devastated when my thoughts . . . We were hitting it off so well. It was like a dream came true, then suddenly there was a glitch. I've been trying to deal with Alice and all that mess. So, who is Amy Lee? The name sounds familiar to me."

"Me. I'm Amy Lee. Flo and the studio wanted me to change my name. Flo wanted to wipe this place, my early years away. And yet she stayed in touch with the people here. She made sure the house was taken care of, cleaned and aired several times a year. It just never made any sense to me."

"Studio? What's that mean?"

"I'm a movie star. I work in Hollywood. I make pictures. Even got nominated for an Academy Award twice, but I didn't win."

"You're a movie star! Well, damn! I guess that's why the name sounded familiar. I haven't been to the movies in years and years. Are you good?"

Amy laughed. "I get by. I came back here thinking I wasn't going to go back to Hollywood. I had thoughts of retiring after I finish out my contract. I might be able to buy it out, at least that's what my agent said. I never understood how I could be good at something I didn't like doing. I still don't understand it. I've had enough. I'm not sure I want to stay in Apple Valley, though. I was hoping to find some answers here. I know now the answers are inside me. This place is just a memory, but I'm smart enough to know I have to lay it to rest before I can go on. My big regret is it's taken me so long."

Hank inched closer to Amy. "I don't know what to say. I feel stupid for jumping to conclusions. I'm sorry, Mandy. Or should I call you Amy?"

"My name is Mandy. I hated it that they took away my name. First my parents, Apple Valley, then my name. I was just a kid back then, and while I tried to deal with it, I guess I didn't do such a good job of it. What were you saying about your sister-in-law?"

Hank explained the situation. Amy burst out laughing and

couldn't stop. "I'm on her side. Boy, did that take guts. She must really trust you, though, to leave her kids with you."

"Well, I didn't do so good. Those kids hated me on sight. Churchill hated me and ran to you. I had to hire a nanny. A guy!" Hank said, his eyes almost bugging out of his head. "He had things under control in ten minutes. He cooks, does laundry. Hey, the guy is *IT*." Then he told her about Ben's e-mail. "So for my Christmas present to the family, I hired Mason for six months to help Alice. Ben will be back home by that time to pick up the slack."

"That's so wonderful, Hank! When are you going to tell Alice?"

"I can't tell her anything because I don't know where she is. She said she was going to a hotel to pamper herself."

"No, no, that's not what she's doing if their financial situation is so precarious. She's probably staying with a friend and talking it all to death. She was overwhelmed, that's the bottom line. I give her another day, and she'll be back. She's a mother, she won't abandon her kids. Trust me."

"You think?"

"I do, Hank. It's not easy being a single mom, and that's what she is with Ben away. It all falls on her. She's just one person, and there are just twenty-four hours in a day. She's frazzled. What you're planning on doing is a wonderful thing. I just wish there was a way to tell her to ease her misery."

Hank nodded. "So we're friends again, right?"

"Of course. If you help me get the sleigh over here, I can finish up while you go for the gas. Are we still going to the wake this evening?"

"Absolutely, but we might have to walk."

"I have boots, so it won't be a problem. Okay, let's go get that sleigh."

Hank reached for her arm and linked his with hers as they trudged across the lawns to Amy's garage. Minutes later, the sleigh was on Albert Carpenter's front porch, and Hank was on his way to the gas station that was only a block and a half away. He started to sing "Jingle Bells" as he trudged along. He looked down when he felt something hit his knee. "Churchill!"

"Woof."

"Hey, big guy, how're you doing? Where's Miss Sadie? Yeah, yeah, she's no fool, I bet she's sitting in that sleigh. It's just me and you, Churchill. You know what, I'm not even mad at you because Mandy's one in a million. You got good taste, I'll say that for you."

"Woof."

"Jingle bells . . ."

Chapter Seven

The caravan of cars leaving the snow-filled cemetery was several miles long. Albert Carpenter had been laid to rest, and the whole town had turned out to show their regard and to honor the man who had done so much for the education system.

It hadn't been a sad affair at all. More like a celebration of Albert's life. The wake that started at six the previous evening had gone on well past midnight to allow all the citizens of Apple Valley to pay their respects. They came in trucks, on sleds, on skis, and the sanitation workers had shown up on the town's snowplow.

During his teaching years, Albert had always conducted the Christmas Pageant, and when the actors took their final bow, the audience and cast alike had stayed to sing Christmas carols. And that's what they did this year before the funeral director closed the doors for the night. Until her passing, Mrs. Carpenter had been in charge of the refreshments. This night, Apple Valley's school principal did the honors.

So many memories had been shared, but the most poignant of all had been the story of Albert's financial problems that so few knew about. All his savings had gone to cover his wife's long illness. He'd been forced to take out a reverse mortgage that allowed him to continue to live in the house until his death. Albert Carpenter had died with just a few dollars in the bank, but he didn't owe anyone a dime. In fact, Charles Leroy from the bank said he'd made his final payment to the hospital just two months ago. Then he said something that brought tears to everyone's eyes. "Albert didn't want to join his wife until all his earthly debts were paid. It wouldn't look right or feel right knowing he was leaving others to pick up his slack."

Hank drove carefully in the long procession, no more than five miles an hour. "I thought the Apple Valley Band did a good job," he said. "You know what else, I'm glad you decided to decorate Albert's porch. I bet the town awards the prize to him this year. Posthumously."

"I liked that we all sang carols, just as we used to in school. It was sad, and yet it wasn't sad. He was so loved. Apple Valley and the people here are so special, Hank. There's so much kindness and goodness here. People actually care about one another. They help out and don't expect anything in return. It's not that way in California. Well, maybe it is, but I've never witnessed it. It's not just the season, is it, Hank?"

"No, Mandy, it's not just the season. This little place is just one of a kind. I used to think I should come back here and live, but then I told myself no, I needed to leave, to move on so someone else could move here and experience this life. For me to stay would have been selfish. Ben now. Ben was different. He said his roots were here, and he wasn't digging them up. This was home to him, and while he and Alice have lived all over, this was the place he always came back to.

"When we were growing up, the population was just a little under four thousand. Today it's almost six thousand. That's not a great increase, but it's something to pay attention to. I do know one thing for certain: I'll come back here to retire."

"Me, too," Amy said happily. "So, are we going to go sledding this afternoon or not?"

"I'm up for it, but first we have to go to the dinner at the church. I offered our services, but Father Mac said if he got any more volunteers, he'd have to move out. In other words, all we have to do is show up and eat. It's all under control. That was a good thing you did, Mandy."

Amy's face turned pink. She just nodded.

Hank pretended he didn't notice her discomfort. "I'm not sure, but I think I saw Alice at the cemetery. She was so bundled up, and the crowd was so dense, I can't swear to it, but I think it was her. She really liked Albert. Ben told me when she cooked she would always take something over. He was partial to peach pie, and she'd make it special for him in the summer when peaches were in season. When in the hell is she going to come home? It's almost Christmas."

Amy shrugged. "My guess would be when she can't stand being away from her sons one minute longer. Which is probably any minute now. Did you finish everything on her lists?"

"Almost. I have to get the tree and put it up. I guess I'm supposed to shop for the boys. I'm clueless in that department. Alice always decorates the house, so I guess I should do that, too, since she'll want to take pictures to send to Ben."

"I have an idea, Hank. Instead of going sledding, let's go get all our trees and set them up. I remember Mom saying you have to put it up in the stand, then let it sit for a day so the branches fall into place. I'd like to put one on Mr. Carpenter's porch, too. I think for sure that will make him a shoo-in for the Christmas prize. After we take care of that, we can go shopping for the boys. What say you?"

Hank reached over to take Amy's hand in his own. "I think that's a great idea."

Amy thought her hand was going to go up in flames. "Something's happening to us, isn't it?" Her voice was little more than a whisper.

Hank's response was husky, almost tortured. "Yeah. Yeah, something is happening. It's a good thing, isn't it?"

Amy laughed. "From where I'm sitting, a very good thing."

Hank squeezed her hand. She squeezed back.

The church parking lot was so full, Hank had to park two blocks away. Once they managed to get inside, they had to get in a line that wrapped all the way around the room and out the side door.

Amy found herself standing next to Karen Powell from OK Florist. They chatted a few moments while Hank met up with a friend of Ben's. "Do you have any extra poinsettias, Karen?"

"A shipment was due this morning. It might have been delayed with the snow, but sometime today for certain. Why?"

"Will you send two dozen plants to the Anders house? Hank and I are going to decorate it today. As a matter of fact, we're going to get the trees this afternoon."

"You might not know this, but I'm selling trees myself. We have them staked up in the nursery. You might not have seen them. And, we deliver!" she added, laughing.

Amy laughed. "Put us down for three trees. We'll stop by when we leave here and tag them."

"Will do."

It was after one o'clock when Amy and Hank climbed back into Alice's SUV to do some Christmas shopping. The crowds in the small village carried gaily colored shopping bags as they walked from store to store. Children bundled in snowsuits and mufflers pulled sleds filled with packages. Gaily dressed Santas stood in doorways handing out candy canes and hot chocolate. Holiday music wafted from loudspeakers mounted on the telephone poles that surrounded the square.

Apple Valley was small-town America at its finest.

"This is nothing like New York." Hank laughed as he accepted a cup of hot chocolate from an elf standing in the doorway of Jones's Pharmacy. Amy opted for a candy cane. They moved on, finally coming to stop at a small toy store. Inside, they turned into little kids, their selections outrageous until they stopped in their tracks, looked at one another, and reminded themselves the twins were just a year old. Sheepishly, they replaced the Barbie and Ken dolls and the catchers' mitts.

When they finally left the store, the stock boy tagged along behind them, their purchases piled high on a dolly. When they were loaded into the cargo hold and the door shut and locked, Hank turned to Amy, and said, "Do you think we'll have this much fun when we buy toys for our own kids?"

Whoa. She turned around hoping she could be cool. *Cool?* Amy's heart was beating so fast she thought it was going to leap right out of her chest. She struggled for a flip answer of some sort. Nothing came to her. Besides, Hank was looking at her so intently, she needed to respond. "Don't you have to ask me to marry you before the kids come? You haven't even kissed me yet."

"Not true," Hank said lightly. "I kissed you once, and I never forgot the feeling. That kiss lasted twenty-one seconds."

"You counted the seconds?" Amy asked in awe.

"Yeah. I thought I was going to black out. I was in love with you. I realized I was still in love with you the minute I set eyes on you."

Amy was so light-headed with Hank's declaration she reached for the side mirror to hold on to it. Hank had just said he loved her. That's what he said. The words were still ringing in her ears. All her dreams were finally coming true. She was supposed to say something. What?

Hank shuffled his feet in the snow. His voice sounded so anxious when he said, "Your turn."

The words were stuck in her throat. She wanted to say them. Instead, she leaned forward, grabbed his jacket in her mittened hands, and yanked him forward. She planted a lip-lock on him that made her head spin.

"Twenty-*seven* seconds!" she shouted gleefully when she came up for air.

The sound of handclapping brought both of them to their senses as a small laughing crowd moved off.

"Wow!" was all Hank could think of to say.

"That's it, wow!" Amy said. "You up for an encore?"

Hank groaned. He was no fool. He moved closer. All the

years of pent-up longing melted away when he brought his lips down on hers. This moment he knew seared his future. When he finally released her he looked into her eyes and saw what he knew was mirrored in his own. In a low, husky voice, he asked, "How many seconds?"

In a voice as shaky as Hank's, Amy said, "Are you kidding, I wasn't counting."

"Oh, who cares? You going to marry me?"

"If that's a proposal, the answer is yes."

Hank backed up a step. He looked to Amy like he was in a daze. She smiled.

He smiled.

"We should go to pick out the Christmas trees, Hank."

"Yep. That's what we should do," Hank said.

"But are we going to do that?"

Hank groaned as he opened the passenger-side door for her. "Yes, that's what we're going to do, but later, we are going to do other things."

"Promises, promises." Amy giggled. *My God, when was the last time I giggled? Never, that's when.* She leaned back and closed her eyes. She realized she had never been as happy as she was at this moment.

Hank laughed, a joyous sound. "There's something you need to know about me. I never make a promise I don't intend to keep. I don't know when I've been this happy," he blurted.

Amy laughed again. "Me, too. It's such a wonderful feeling. More so because it's the holiday season. Everything seems to be special during this time." Her voice turned serious a moment later. "But there's Mr. Carpenter and Alice. Are we being . . . ?"

"No. It was Albert's time. Alice . . . well, Alice made her own decisions. While we both understand that, we're doing what we think is right. We're doing what we can for Alice. Albert . . . is beyond our control. Somehow I think he would be very happy for the both of us. No, that's wrong, Mandy. I *know* Albert would be very happy for us. Okay, enough of all this. Are you ready to pick out the biggest, the best, the most-wonderful-smelling tree in the lot?"

"I'm ready, Mr. Anders," Amy said, hopping out of the truck.

An hour later they were covered in pine resin, but they had three trees that Hank said were the best of the best. The young guy working the tree lot shoved the trees through a barrel. They came out the other end covered in white netting. They watched as he loaded them into a pickup truck and hopped into the cab, where he waited for instructions.

While Hank paid for the trees, Amy explained where the trees were to be delivered. The young man nodded and peeled out of the parking lot, snow spiraling backward in his wake.

"Bet you five bucks those trees are home before we get there," Amy said, walking hand in hand with Hank back to the SUV. "Wait! Wait! We have to buy tree stands."

Together they walked back to the tree lot, where Hank picked out three stands capable of holding the big trees. He whipped out his credit card, paid for the stands, then they were on the way home. A light snow started to fall again as they hit the main road.

"Pay up," Amy said when Hank swerved into the driveway. All three trees were exactly where Amy had told the youngster to put them. Hank kissed her instead.

"That'll work." Amy giggled again. She felt like a teenager as she helped Hank cut away the netting to set up the tree in the stand on the Carpenter front porch. When they were finished, Hank stood back and said, "It's a beauty, perfect in every way. Tomorrow we can decorate it."

"Oh, it smells so good. Growing up, you could smell the tree all over the house. I loved it then as much as I love it now. I guess it's the kid in me. That won't change, will it, Hank?"

Hank for some reason knew this was a very important question, and he had to give just the right answer. "Memories are a wonderful thing, Mandy. Sometimes they fade in time, but if you work at remembering, then I think they'll be with you forever. The special memories. Like this one. Christmas was always the best time of year when we were kids. All the wild anticipation, the frenzy of the shopping, the tree, the snow, the way the house smelled. Ben and I used to talk about it. For the most part I think he and Alice pretty much duplicated everything. For them it was easier because they're in the house we grew up in. I know it was different for you after . . . but see, you still have those wonderful earlier memories." He looked at her expectantly to see if she was in agreement. She smiled, and his world was right side up.

"Okay, let's set up the tree for the boys. Then we can go back to your house and set yours up and do . . . other things. What say you?"

Amy giggled again. "Won't work, Hank. We have to decorate the house for Alice. I don't know why I say this because it's just a feeling. I think Alice is waiting until that's done before she returns home. Having said that, let's get to it. But before we get started, I think I'd like a cup of coffee. Your house or mine?"

"Well, since we have so much work ahead of us, I guess it should be the Anders house. I imagine the twins will be awake from their nap by now. I can't wait for you to meet them, and Mason as well."

"I have to let the dogs out first. I'll be over in a few minutes." Amy kissed him lightly on the lips before she tripped her way to her own front door.

Inside, she ran to the back door to let the dogs out, then leaned against it. She was shaking from head to toe. She was in love. Hank loved her. She loved him. How wonderful is that? Is this one of those Christmas miracles?

Was this love going to come with a price on it? Amy closed her eyes and thought about her home in Hollywood, thought about her contract, the few friends she had, and what her agent was going to say when she told him to buy out her contract. What would all those people on her payroll do if she turned her back on Hollywood? She could bonus them out and wish them luck in finding a new job. Was she getting ahead of herself? Probably, but she didn't care.

Hank had asked her to marry him, so that had to mean they would live where his business was. Maybe they could buy the Carpenter house from the mortgage company and have a home here in Apple Valley. She knew in her heart that Mr. Carpenter would approve. She rather thought Hank would approve, too. They could watch the twins grow up, and if they had kids of their own, they could play together. Win-win all around. She could hardly wait to tell Hank her idea.

The dogs scratched at the door to come in. She opened the back door to let the dogs in, and they all left together by the front door.

The twins squealed their pleasure when the dogs romped through the family room, Churchill leaping over the gate, Miss Sadie waiting patiently for Hank to lift her over it. Mason stood at the kitchen gate, his jaw dropping at the commotion. He put his fingers to his lips and whistled sharply. The twins stopped in midsqueal. Both dogs turned to look expectantly at the strange new person emitting the high-pitched whistle. "That will be enough of *that*. SIT!" Since both dogs were already sitting, they continued to stare at the person towering over them. "Very good. I am the Alpha. You need to understand that. Having said that, here is your treat for the afternoon." Mason handed out two dog treats, and hard crackers to the boys. Mason turned and was back a second later with a basket of dog toys that had been in the laundry room.

Hank nudged Amy. He hissed in her ear. "I don't know how he does it. He's unreal. Alice is going to be soooo happy. If she ever comes home."

"Mandy, this is Mason. Mason, this is Mandy, she's from California, and she's visiting. Next door."

Mason bowed low, then reached for her hand. "It is a pleasure to meet any friend of Mr. Anders."

"Mandy is a movie star. Her other name is Amy Lee."

"Ah. Am I to assume, sir, that things have progressed, and we are no longer in jeopardy?"

Hank blinked. The guy could talk in code, but he got it. "Yes, it's safe to assume that, Mason. By any chance, do you have any coffee made?"

"No, but I will be more than happy to prepare some. I just baked some brownies."

"I love brownies," Amy said. Mason beamed. The man does love compliments, Hank thought.

"We're going to set the tree up in the living room. Unless you have a better idea, Mason?"

"No, the living room will be fine. I think it best so the boys won't be tempted to play with the ornaments. And, of course, the animals have to be taken into consideration. I understand via the Internet that male dogs and trees are not compatible. I'll be in the kitchen if you need me for anything."

"That means we're dismissed," Hank whispered in Amy's ear.

The twins toddled over to the gate. Hank bent down and picked them both up. They giggled and laughed as they yanked at his hair and pulled at his nose. "I can't tell them apart," he confessed. "Come on now, give me a big kiss. Ohhh, that was sooo good. Give me another one." The boys obliged, and then they were done with the bonding and wanted down on the floor.

"I can see how they would be a handful," Amy said. "They're sweet as honey, and they both look just like Ben."

They watched for another minute or so as the boys rough-and-tumbled with the dogs, who were happy to play.

"Let's get to it, Mandy. We have a Christmas tree to put up." The doorbell rang and Amy opened it. "Oh, look, our poinsettias are here. I'll set them out while you bring in the tree. By the way, do you know where Alice keeps the decorations? You said she was big on decorating the house. We need to do that, too."

"Probably in the attic. I'll get them down as soon as we set up the tree. Just let me know when the coffee is ready."

* * *

It was four o'clock when Mason and the twins oohed and aahed over the couple's Christmas decorations. The tree was up, and it bathed the house in what Amy called a delicious balsam scent. She said she could smell it on the second floor. Poinsettias lined the stairway and were nestled in all the corners. The foyer held a small artificial tree, decorated with colored lights and tiny gossamer angels dangling from the branches. Amy surmised it had a special memory for Alice because of the care that had been taken when it was packed away. Fat ceramic Santas sat at each side of the door. Thick red candles were placed on each end of the mantel along with branches of live greenery that Hank cut off the bottom of the tree. Amy stuck bright red bows in and among the branches and dangled a few strands of tinsel. "Very festive," Hank said, taking Amy's arm in his. "Just think, next year we can do this in our own house." Amy just smiled. And smiled.

The twins gibbered and giggled as they pointed to the giant-size Santa standing next to the fireplace, his backpack loaded with colored boxes with bright red ribbons. Churchill sniffed it out. His intentions seemed obvious to all of them until Mason cleared his throat in warning. The golden dog lowered his leg and backed away, his tail between his legs.

"Good dog," Mason said as he handed out treats again, then opened the back door. Both dogs ran outside as the twins went back to pushing and shoving each other.

"No, no, no! We do not push, and we do not shove," Mason said as he wagged his finger at the boys. One of the boys, Hank wasn't sure which one, stomped his foot and started to cry.

"Sit down and fold your hands, young man. We do not slap and pinch our brother." The toddler sat down and folded his hands. He sniffed, but he stopped crying. Mason handed out raisins in small cups, and the boys were happy again.

"That guy needs to be cloned," Hank said.

Amy looked around. "I don't think there's anything left to

do here. I think I'm going to go home and take a shower. You want to come over for dinner?"

Hank grimaced. "That depends on Mason. I think he might want to go home early. Why don't you come over here? I'm sure we can find something to eat here. In fact, I know we can. He's cooking something that smells pretty darn good, and there are those brownies we bypassed when we had our coffee."

"Okay, if that's an invitation, I accept. We can put my tree up tomorrow. I'll cut the netting off and lean it up against the house. See you later."

Hank kissed her good-bye. He watched from the doorway until she was safely in her own house. *God, I am so happy.*

"It would appear you are in love again. Is that a clear assessment, Mr. Anders?"

"On the money, Mason. I asked her to marry me, and she said yes."

"You do . . . work fast. She's quite lovely. It would appear she returns your feelings. Is there any news on Mrs. Anders?"

"No, I'm afraid not. I'm sure she'll be back soon. God, I hope she comes back soon. The boys seem so happy. It bothers me. Don't they miss her?"

"Of course they miss her. They keep looking around for her. They whimper and suck their thumbs, but they can't talk, so you just have to figure it out for yourself. No one can take a mother's place. No one." This last was said with such vehemence that Hank winced.

What Mason said was true, Hank thought. It also explained Mandy's return and her search for yesterday.

Hank let loose with a long sigh. Thank God he had decided to come back to Apple Valley for the holidays. In doing so he was going to be able to help Alice in both the short and long term, and just by being here, he'd fallen in love all over again. If anyone could help Mandy lay her old ghosts to rest, it was him. He crossed his fingers hoping he was right.

Chapter Eight

Alice Anders paced the narrow confines of her friend's tiny apartment. Tears rolled down her cheeks. *Am I out of my mind?* No sane person would do what I've done. No sane person would abandon her home, her children, and her husband's dog. Even if Ben was a perfect dad, she'd fallen down on her job and screwed up big-time. That was the bottom line.

She looked down at the tabby cat circling her feet. Chloe was her name. She picked her up and cuddled her against her neck. This little animal didn't mess in the house, she had her own private sanitation boxes in the tiny laundry room and in the bathroom. She didn't make mistakes. And she cleaned herself religiously, unlike Churchill, who messed all over and rolled in mud whenever he felt like it. Giving him a bath always clogged the bathtub drain and then it was eighty-five dollars to get it unclogged. Her budget, stringent as it was, had ceased to exist months and months ago. Her credit cards were maxed out. She lived day to day.

She'd wigged out. How cool was that? More tears flowed. Ben was going to pitch a fit when Hank told him what she'd done. Chloe licked at her tears. God, how she ached to hold her sons.

Coming here to her friend's small apartment had seemed like the answer to all her problems. She'd gotten the idea when her best friend in Apple Valley, a first-grade teacher named Marie, had said she was going home to Seattle for the holidays. She'd given her the key and asked her to check on Chloe from time to time.

Her intention was to veg out, to fall back and regroup. To take bubble baths, to eat when and if she felt like it, to drink wine while she was soaking in a tub, and to sleep peacefully through the night with no interruptions. It hadn't happened that way at all. She was lucky if she slept two hours a night, and what sleep she got was fitful. There was no bathtub to luxuriate in, only a stall shower. She didn't have money for wine, and Marie didn't have cable television. She, too, lived on a budget.

The only thing she proved to herself was that she was an unfit mother. A slacker as a wife. She wasn't Supermom, and she never would be. That title would have to go to someone else, someone a lot more worthy than she.

Did the twins miss her? Probably not. Churchill hated her, so there was no point in even asking herself if the big golden retriever missed her. He probably hoped she never came back. The tears flowed again. She looked like a witch with the dark circles under her eyes. Her hair needed to be cut and styled.

Alice's wild pacing led her to the bathroom and the huge mirror on the back of the door. Well, if nothing else, she'd shed a few pounds.

What did Hank think about what she'd done? How was he coping? She wished she knew what he'd told Ben. Ben was going to be so disappointed in her.

Alice splashed cold water on her face, combed her hair, smoothed down the sweat suit she'd arrived in, and tidied the apartment. She made sure Chloe had bowls of food and water not only in the bathroom but the kitchenette, too. She cleaned the two litter boxes and put in fresh litter. She set the thermostat to seventy and sat down to drink her fifth cup of coffee. She didn't need this fifth cup of coffee. She was killing time, and she knew it. She'd made a mess of things, and now it was time to stand up and take the blame for what she'd done. She started to cry again. Like tears were really going to help her out.

It was totally dark now. Christmas Eve. It had always been the happiest time of the year, at least for her. Ben, too. How often they talked about how perfect life was here in Apple Valley. Especially at Christmastime. And she'd ruined it all. Her. No one else. She'd single-handedly ruined everything for everyone with her stupid actions. How in the name of God was she ever going to make this right?

By going home, a voice inside her head whispered, *You go back, you stand tall, you apologize and get your life back.* After . . . after she hugged and kissed her two little boys. She had to apologize to them, too, not that they would understand, but she'd do it anyway.

Still, she didn't move. Because . . . because she was a coward.

Alice stood up, drained her coffee, then washed out the cup and cleaned the coffeepot. She took one last look around the tiny apartment, checked on Chloe one last time by giving her a hug before she settled her in her little bed next to the sofa. She turned out all the lights, put on her heavy down jacket, and left the apartment.

Outside, Alice hunkered into her jacket as she made the long trek back to her house. There was little traffic, the citizenry of Apple Valley were secure in their houses, building fires, having dinner, and getting ready for the big man in the red suit.

It was bitter cold, and the tears escaping her eyes were freezing on her eyelashes. She barely noticed as she trudged along. She had to walk along the roadside because of the piled-up snow. Her sneakers were cold and wet. She'd never been more miserable in her entire life.

When she reached her neighborhood, Alice climbed over the banks of piled-up snow onto the shoveled sidewalk. How pretty it all looked, with the snow on the evergreens and the colored lights on the houses and in the trees.

Christmas in Apple Valley.

Soon the church choir would be out caroling. She and Ben always went caroling since they belonged to the choir. She'd had to give it up when the boys came along. She'd had to give up *everything* when the boys came along. Even Ben. She knew the thought was unfair. She'd known what it meant to marry a military man when she agreed to marry Ben. She had no one to blame for her circumstances except herself.

Alice rounded the corner to her street and stopped short when she noticed the crowds of people at Albert Carpenter's house. Then she smiled when she saw the front porch that was decorated to the nines. For sure the Apple Valley prize would go to this piece of property. How sad that Albert would never know how loved he was.

It looked to Alice like everyone had brought something to add to the decorations someone had been kind enough to set up. The tree was magnificent, with its twinkling lights. The boys would love the reindeer and the sleigh packed with gaily colored packages. Small statues lined the steps. Santas, elves, ceramic Christmas trees. Gossamer angels trailing red ribbons dangled on wires from the beams on the porch.

At first glance it all looked cluttered until you saw the homemade drawings, the cards tacked to the pillars that held up the porch. And then your second glance said it was the most beautiful sight in the world.

Alice tried to swallow past the lump in her throat. She just knew she was the only person in town who had not left something on that wide, wonderful front porch. Well, she would have to remedy that as soon as she could. Not because Ben would never forgive her if she didn't, but because she wanted to. No, that was wrong, she *needed* to do it.

Alice wondered if there was anyone in the whole world who understood what she had been going through with the exception of Albert Carpenter. She'd poured out her heart to him so many times these past months. For his comfort she'd knocked herself out trying to take care of him—she cooked for him, cleaned his house, shopped for him, and did his laundry. Not that there weren't others who would have helped, but she hadn't asked. She'd wanted to do it because he was like a wise old grandfather, and he dearly loved Ben and Hank and a little girl named Mandy Leigh. No, she was not Supermom or super anything. She was just plain old Alice Avery Anders. Triple A Alice, as Ben called her from time to time.

Alice moved on, and soon enough she was standing at her own front door. She turned the knob, but the door was locked from the inside. How stupid. She'd given Hank her keys. She rang the bell. The door opened. All she could do was stand there with tears in her eyes. Hank stretched out his arms, and she stepped into them. "Oh, Hank, I'm so . . ."

"Shhh. You don't need to apologize for anything. I'm just so damn glad that you're home. God, I can't tell you how glad I am. Come in, come in, it's freezing out there."

Alice stepped back and stared up at her brother-in-law. "I . . . need . . ."

Hank placed his index finger against Alice's lips. "No, you don't need to do anything but love those kids of yours. They're in the family room waiting for you."

Alice shrugged out of her jacket and ran to the family room. Like Hank, she vaulted over the gate and gathered up her twin boys, holding them close. Churchill and Miss Sadie vied for her attention. "Oh, God, I forgot about Miss Sadie. C'mere, you little bundle of love."

Hank backed away and bumped into Mason, who was wiping the corners of his eyes. "It would appear the lady of the house has returned. What would you suggest I do, Mr. Anders?"

"Well, after I introduce you to your new employer, you might want to go home to your own family and enjoy Christmas."

"Unfortunately, Mr. Anders, I don't have a family."

"In that case, Mason, how would you like to spend the holidays with us? As our guest."

"I think I would like that very much, sir. I would imagine Mrs. Anders will . . . ah, want to bathe her sons herself this evening, so I'll tidy up the kitchen. Is there anything else you need me to do?"

"Nope." Hank walked back to the family room and called out to Alice. "There's someone here you need to meet, Alice."

Hank drew Mason forward. "Meet your new nanny. Alice, this is Mason. Mason, this is Mrs. Anders. Mason is my Christmas present to you, Ben, and the boys. He's going to be here every day until Ben gets back home. The boys love him, and, if you can believe this, Churchill actually listens and does his business outside. He doesn't jump the fence anymore either."

Tears rolled down Alice's cheeks as she reached out to shake Mason's hand. The boys toddled over to him, begging to be picked up. "It's almost bath time, madam, do you wish to do the honors, or shall I?"

Alice looked like she was in shock. "I . . . really, Hank, I have a nanny until Ben gets home? Oh, God, you dear sweet man. How did you know that was what I wished for? Oh, it doesn't matter." She looked from Hank to Mason and said something Hank found strange. "If you don't mind, Mason, tonight I need you to bathe the boys. I have to go up in the attic to find something. From here on in, I'll do the bathing. I don't want to overwork you."

"Very well, madam."

"Do you need any help, Alice?"

Supermom Alice would have said no, she had it under control. This new Alice said, "Yes, as a matter of fact, I do." She bent over to kiss the boys again before she stepped over the gate. She literally ran up the stairs to the second floor, then up a third set of stairs to the attic. She whirled around at the top, and said, "The house looks so beautiful. Thank you, Hank. Perhaps someday I can make it up to you."

Hank nodded. "What are we looking for, Alice?"

"It's among the Christmas decorations. It's a string of silver bells that Mr. Carpenter gave Ben a lifetime ago. You have no idea what that string of bells meant to him. Each time we moved—and there were so many moves—he always made sure that string of bells went with us. He said you and Mandy got one, too. The sound was so true, so pure. I have to find it, Hank. I didn't leave anything on Albert's porch. There are so many people out there, so many mementos: the cards, the letters, the keepsakes. It just blew me away."

"There are several e-mails from Ben waiting for you," Hank said quietly as he rummaged through neatly labeled boxes.

"Did you read them?" Alice asked.

"Absolutely not!" Hank lied with a straight face. "Now that I know what we're looking for, I can search. Why don't you go and check Ben's e-mails."

Alice whirled around. The expression on her face was so fierce, Hank stepped back. "You know what, Hank, Ben's e-mails can wait. *This is important.*"

Hank didn't know what to say to that, so he didn't say anything. He kept rummaging in the ornament boxes, wondering what he'd done with his own set of bells. He vaguely remembered Albert giving them to him, but from there on it was a blur. Maybe he needed to say something light, or something meaningful. "I'm getting married, Alice. Mandy Leigh came back home for the holidays and we . . . we hooked up again. She helped me decorate the house for you."

"Hmmm. That's nice. Ben always said nice things about her." Alice whirled around and said, "I didn't mean it when I said I wished Ben had left me standing at the altar. Well, I meant it at the time I said it, but . . . you know what I'm saying, right?"

"Absolutely. You were just venting, and I understand that. Look, Alice, I could never do what you do every day, day in day out. I tried and couldn't do it. Ben is a fool for thinking you're some kind of wonder woman. And, I don't blame you a bit. That's why I had to hire Mason. He's the wonder in wonderful, and the boys really like him. So do the dogs."

"Hank."

"Yeah."

"Shut up. I have to take responsibility for my actions. I'm okay with that, and I appreciate all you did and for . . . for Mason. Please don't think I'm ungrateful, but right now I have to find those bells. Oh, God! Here they are. Look! Look! Listen!" Alice shook the bells, and suddenly Hank shivered at the pure melodious sound. The silver bells themselves were tarnished, the red ribbon holding them together was tattered and faded.

"Do you mind telling me what it is with the bells, Alice?" he asked gently.

Alice sat down on an old trunk. "Three or four months ago Albert talked me out of filing for a divorce. I was packed and ready to leave. I had taken him for his chemo treatment that day, and he was so sick, Hank. I mean really sick, but he sat me down and read me the riot act. He told me stories about his own up-and-down marriage. He said you have to work at it to make it worthwhile. He told me other stories about you guys when you were kids. He told me how Mandy was suddenly gone from your lives. He never judged me, never told me not to leave. Somehow or other he convinced me to stay without saying the words. He kept me sane, Hank."

"I see." And he did indeed see what she was talking about.

"I'm going over to that porch at midnight and ringing these bells."

"I wish I knew where I put mine."

"They're over there under the window in the box marked 'Hank.' Ben packed up your stuff after your parents . . . He said it was stuff you didn't want anymore."

Hank thought his heart was going to explode right out of his chest. He ran over to the box, popped the lid. He saw all kinds of junk he couldn't ever remember owning. The string of silver bells was wrapped in bubble wrap and tissue. They were just as tarnished, the ribbon just as tattered as the one Alice was holding in her hand. He shook them gently. Tears blurred his vision at the pure tone.

If Mandy had her set, all would be right with his world now that he understood what Alice was talking about. If she didn't, two out of three would be okay, too.

Down on the second floor, Mason was carrying the twins into their bedroom. They smelled like warm sunshine as Hank bent down to kiss each one of them. They reached out to Alice, who took them both into their room. She settled them in their beds, covered them, then sat down to read a story they didn't even hear; they were sound asleep. He watched her as she kept reading till the end of the story. She looked so motherly, so suddenly at peace he suddenly felt the same way.

Later on, downstairs, the bells in her hand, Alice sat down in the kitchen. She looked at the slice of homemade blueberry pie and the glass of milk waiting for her. She looked over at Mason and smiled.

"While you're eating, Mason and I will set up the gifts under the tree. This way you can enjoy the quiet evening. I'm going next door to see Mandy. If you need me, just call my cell phone."

Alice nodded. "Thanks, Hank, for everything."

Hank pointed to the laptop on the little desk. She nodded sweetly. "Just so you know, Hank, I love Ben with all my heart and soul."

"I know that, Alice. I'll see you later."

When Amy opened the door, she was holding a string of bells in her hand. "Oh, Hank, you aren't going to believe what I found. Look!" She held up a set of silver bells and shook them. Hank laughed and pulled his set of bells out of his pocket.

"Alice came home. She wants us to go over to Albert's porch and ring the bells at midnight. You up for it?"

"Oh, yes. I never decorated my tree, and I didn't set out any decorations," Amy said, pointing to the huge evergreen sitting in her living room in the middle of the floor. "I'm not sure what I was trying to . . . to find, to recapture. That time in my life is gone. This is a new beginning for me. I think for all of us. That in itself is a miracle as far as I'm concerned."

"I love you, Mandy Leigh. Always have and always will."

"And I love you, Hank Anders. I always have and always will."

When the clock struck midnight, three people stood on the Carpenter front porch. Silver bells rang, the sound clear, pure, and rich. High above, a kindly old gentleman ruffled his wings.

"Merry Christmas," he whispered above the sound of the bells that seemed to be ringing all about him.

Dear Santa

JoAnn Ross

Chapter One

The deer came flying out of nowhere, a flash of dark brown in a swirling white-on-white world.

At least it seemed that way.

One minute Holly Berry was driving on the winding, two-lane road that snaked through Washington's Cascade Mountains at a crawl, straining her eyes to see through the wall of white snow piling up too fast for even her furiously working windshield wipers to handle. The next minute she was fishtailing into a series of dizzying spins that a gold-medalist Olympic skater would've envied, sliding helplessly toward the edge of the cliff.

That's when she realized that it was true—your life really did flash before your eyes just before you died.

"You're *not* going to die," she insisted, as if saying it outloud could make it true.

After what seemed a lifetime, but in real time was only a few seconds, her SUV slammed into an ice-encrusted snowbank.

Then pow!

While her heart was pounding like an angry fist against her ribs, the airbag exploded from the center of her steering wheel in her face.

Which wasn't exactly like getting hit by a marshmallow.

Actually, it hurt. A lot.

It also filled the car with acrid smoke and a fine powder she'd managed to suck into her lungs as she'd shouted out a string of curses that turned the smoky air even bluer and would've made a sailor on shore leave proud.

Unfortunately, as soon as she'd opened her mouth, she'd sucked the stuff in, which triggered a coughing fit as she fought against the bag that was—thank you God!—quickly deflating.

That, and the fact she was alive, was the good news.

Once the huge white bag was out of her face, she could see that not only had it cracked the windshield, her dashboard looked as if a maniac had attacked it with a sledgehammer. And steam was rising from beneath the snowbank, hinting at a burst radiator.

Which was, she feared, just the beginning of even more bad news.

"And wow, isn't this just what you need?"

The rain that had been falling when she'd left her downtown Seattle apartment had turned to sleet as she'd crossed the bridge into east King County. She'd thought things were looking up as she began driving into the mountains and the sleet was replaced by a scattering of downy white flakes.

Unfortunately, by the time that deer had leaped in front of her, the damn snow had escalated into something close to a blizzard.

Dammit, she never should've swerved. Then again, if she'd continued to drive straight ahead, she would've risked hitting the deer, which could've resulted in it flying through her windshield onto her lap.

And wouldn't have that just been fun?

Since her electrical system seemed to have been killed, the windows wouldn't go down, so, shoving the deflated nylon bag out of her way, she cracked open the driver's door to let out some of the smoke. Which, in turn, let wind-driven snow come swirling in.

Retrieving her purse from where it had fallen onto the floor, she took out her cell phone and flipped it open. Unsurprisingly, given her remote location in these mountains, her screen showed no signal bars.

"And isn't this a fine mess you've gotten yourself into," she muttered as she wiped the air bag talc off her face with one of the wet wipes she always carried with her and tried to decide what to do next.

Holly had always prided herself on her practicality. Oh, she was aware that creative people were considered by many to be flighty. Unpredictable. Impulsive. Even undependable.

But just because she told stories for a living didn't mean that she didn't plan every single detail of her books. She'd plot the stories for weeks, even months beforehand, each and every scene carefully detailed on Post-its, color coded by character, and stuck onto the huge board that took up a major portion of her office wall. She never wrote so much as a first line without first knowing her characters' goals, motivation, and conflict. And each and every scene in each and every chapter was totally completed to her satisfaction before she moved on to the next.

Real life, to her mind, was no different. Which meant that her goal was to get herself out of this mess and her motivation was to do so before she froze to death—which was, needless to say, the ultimate conflict of man (or in her case, woman) against nature.

She knew the conventional wisdom was to stay with the vehicle so search teams could find her. The problem was that it could take several days for anyone to even realize she was missing. Oh, sure, the hotel in Leavenworth was expecting her this evening, but if she didn't show up, the desk clerk would undoubtedly just shrug it off as yet another undependable guest, and, since she'd given them her AMEX number to guarantee the room, they'd just run her card and not give her another thought.

Since the crash and subsequent air bag explosion had also disabled her dashboard GPS, Holly had no idea of exactly where she was. Actually, she'd begun to suspect that the calm female voice directing her over the mountains may have made a mistake, because although she'd never driven this way before, it seemed the highway should be four lanes, not the two that had, because of snowplows, narrowed down to about one and a half.

Unfortunately, the Washington state road map she'd bought as a backup was still sitting on her kitchen counter. The totally uncharacteristic oversight had her grinding her teeth even as she assured herself that just as she'd gotten her last heroine away from that serial killer, she could plot her way out of this predicament.

Holly's idea of exercise might be walking to Starbucks down the street from her apartment, but surely she could hike to wherever the next town was. And wouldn't movement keep her warmer than if she stayed here, shivering inside her disabled vehicle, like a damsel in distress waiting for a white knight in a shiny suit of armor to show up?

Of course, the flip side of that was that trudging through the snow could expend energy. Which wouldn't be good. Also, the sun was sinking lower and lower behind the mountains and no way did she want to risk becoming dinner for a mountain lion or bear.

Since this was, after all, supposedly a major road, surely the state would have the snow plows out working to stay ahead of the storm. A storm that hadn't even shown up on the weather channel. She'd checked the forecast before leaving her apartment.

Forty-five minutes later, as the snow kept falling and the sky darkened to a deep purplish blue, and her fingertips, even inside her leather gloves, had begun turning to ice, and Holly was beginning to get seriously concerned, she thought she heard the low drone of a car engine.

Of course, that could just be a hallucination.

Or a dream.

Didn't people fall asleep as they were freezing to death? She was sure she'd read that somewhere.

Using her gloved hand to wipe the steam off the window, she saw a fire engine red Ford Expedition, which dwarfed her stuck Highlander, come chugging out of the storm and pull to a stop.

Even as she could have sworn she heard a chorus of angels singing the "Hallelujah Chorus" from Handel's *Messiah,* the Expedition's door opened and a pair of long legs, clad in jeans and a pair of heavy PAK boots, swiveled out.

The rest of him, wearing a dark blue parka, followed. Despite those angel voices of joyous relief ringing in her mind, all the research over the years she'd done for her mystery novels had left Holly more distrustful than the average woman.

Still, while it was difficult to tell through the swirling snow, he didn't look like a serial killer.

Of course, neither had Ted Bundy. Who, now that she thought about it, just happened to have been from Washington state. As had the Green River Killer, along with several others, including the never apprehended Snohomish County dismemberment killer she'd used as a model for the villain in her first novel.

He was getting closer, his stride long and purposeful as he crunched through the snow.

Feeling as if she was in some woman-in-jeopardy movie, Holly retrieved her Zeus Lightning Bolt stun pen from her bag and slipped it into her jacket pocket.

Chapter Two

It was amazing how much a guy's life could change in twelve months, Gabriel O'Halloran considered as he cautiously made his way around the twisting switchbacks of the icy mountain road. This time last year, he'd been in Iraq, patrolling streets, dodging insurgent gunfire, praying like hell that he and his fellow Marines wouldn't get blown to pieces by an IED.

On a sixty-five-degree Christmas morning, while on patrol, his team had nearly walked into an ambush. Fortunately, one of the bad guys had gotten trigger-happy and begun to shoot as the first Marine entered the alley. Even better was that his "pray and spray" gunfire hadn't managed to hit anyone.

The battle, which was a long way from the peace the season was supposed to celebrate, lasted less than five minutes. The insurgents, knowing when they were outgunned, faded away, undoubtedly to fight another day.

As leader of the patrol, Gabe could have ordered the team to go after them. Deciding he didn't want to be responsible for any deaths on Christmas Day, they'd returned to camp in time for a traditional feast of prime rib, turkey with cornbread stuffing, mashed potatoes, and pumpkin pie, served up by a two-hundred-and-fifty-pound master sergeant wearing a red, white, and blue Santa Claus hat.

Now, here Gabe was, plowing his way through a frigging blizzard, tires crunching beneath the snow, the radio reporting road closures and accidents throughout the mountains, his eyes burning from trying to focus on the road as he doggedly made his way in near whiteout conditions home to a town that had boasted the teeming population of six hundred and twenty-five.

Six hundred and twenty-seven now that he and Emma had settled in.

Having spent his teenage years trying to escape his hometown, then intending to be career military, becoming a Christmas tree farmer and running an inn and bar wasn't the future he'd planned. Not by a long shot. But having seen a great deal of the world, despite the twists and turns his personal road had taken over the last few months, he had begun to enjoy himself.

Hell, he even had a dog, who was currently curled up in the backseat, snoring away like a souped-up chainsaw.

Couldn't get much more damn domesticated than that.

He'd just cautiously maneuvered around a particularly nasty S-curve, his studded tires crunching on the icy pavement, when he viewed an SUV partly buried in a snowbank. Pulling as far as he could off the road, he set the emergency brake.

The dog, having been born into a war zone, immediately sensed trouble. Choosing flight over fight, he scrambled off the seat onto the floor, where he somehow managed to curl up into a remarkably small ball, considering that the last time he'd been weighed at the vet, he'd come in at one hundred and thirty pounds.

"Stay," he told the dog as he retrieved the first aid kit—just in case—from the floor.

The dog looked conflicted. On one hand, or, more accurately, paw, he obviously wanted to stay hunkered down out of danger. On the other, he'd spent nine months of Gabe's thirteen-month second tour on patrol loyally sticking close to the squad of Marines who'd adopted him.

"Stay," Gabe repeated, holding up a hand. "Everything'll be okay."

Gabe hoped.

He'd no sooner jumped out of the Expedition when a woman stumbled out of the disabled Highlander. She was tall, leggy, and wearing a scarlet ski jacket, snug black jeans, and sheepskin-lined boots that rose nearly to her knees.

"Looks like you've gotten yourself in a little trouble," he said. "Are you all right?"

"I'm fine. Well, mostly," she allowed as his gaze swept over her, looking for injuries. "I swerved to miss hitting a deer." Before he could respond to that, she held up a hand. The red leather glove was thin, fitting her hand, well, like a glove, and while a nice look with the coat, wasn't all that practical for this kind of weather. "I know you're not supposed to do that, but it was all so sudden, and . . ."

She paused, as if picturing the moment he figured had been indelibly scorched into her mind. Emotions—especially fear—could do that to you. God knows he had memories that still, even after a year stateside, occasionally, when he least expected it, played in his mind.

Her hair—which fell in a trendy, expensive-looking cut that just skimmed her shoulders beneath a red knitted cap—was a strawberry blond, more gold than red. Her slightly slanted catlike eyes were moss green, her complexion, the part of it that wasn't already turning red and splotchy, which he suspected was the beginning of what could be some serious bruising, was as smooth and pale as top cream.

A sprinkling of freckles across the bridge of a cold-reddened nose, and a mouth that was a bit too wide, but eminently kissable, along with the way her diamond face came to a point in a slightly stubborn chin kept her from being perfect.

"And?" he prompted.

"This is going to sound crazy, but although I'm admittedly no expert, it didn't look like an ordinary deer. More like a—"

"Reindeer?"

"Exactly."

Which was, of course, ridiculous, Holly told herself.

Adrenaline, caused by the stress of the moment, must have caused her brain to fritz out, overlaying the actual event with other pictures in her memory. Pictures from the storybooks her father had read her so long ago.

He nodded. "That'd be Blitzen."

Leaving her staring after him, he strolled around to the front of the car and studied the hood buried deep in the snowdrift. The steam had quit rising from the radiator several minutes ago, but it didn't take a mechanic to know the poor Highlander wasn't going to be driving anywhere soon.

"Good thing the guard rail was there under the piled-up snow," he said. "Or you could've gone right over the edge and might not have been found until spring."

"Well, isn't that a lovely thought?"

She slipped a hand into her pocket and curled her fingers around the stun pen. Although he certainly looked normal enough (actually he was obscenely handsome, with slate gray eyes beneath black brows, a face that was all masculine planes and angles, and a jaw shadowed by a day's worth of dark beard wide enough to park his Expedition on), from that casually issued comment about the reindeer, she feared he might be a 5150, which a cop she'd once interviewed for research had told her wasn't merely an old Van Halen album but police code for a crazy person on the loose.

"And what do you mean, Blitzen?"

"He's a reindeer."

"So I've heard."

"Well, this one happens to belong to a friend of mine. He escaped from his pen yesterday." He opened the driver's door, looked into the car, and frowned. "Wow. Who'd have guessed an airbag could do that much damage?"

He looked down at her, eyes narrowed as he scrutinized her face. Then frowned. "You're going to have some bruising. And maybe a black eye." He skimmed a gloved finger beneath the eye in question. "But you're damn lucky you weren't burned."

That was, admittedly, one positive. "I guess I am."

Some people were touchers. Holly was not. Backing up a few steps, she flicked the cap off the marker-size stun pen, just in case. The salesman at the spy store had assured her that the electric arc that pulsated across the top of the pen would create a sharp, crackling sound, intimidating most would-be attackers.

And if that wasn't enough, the 800,000 volt output would drop a guy to his knees. Although it was supposedly able to zap those volts through clothing, Holly wondered how effective it'd be through all those layers of down parka.

"You seriously have a friend who owns a reindeer?" Her tone radiated her skepticism.

"Not just one. Eight."

"Next you'll be telling me he uses them to pull his sleigh."

"Actually he does." He gave her a slow, easy smile that was too charming for comfort and sent something turning inside her. Steeling herself against its charm, she told herself that Ted Bundy had probably used much the same smile to lure unsuspecting victims into his Volkswagen. "But Blitzen is the one who always seems to get antsy this time of year."

He had to be putting her on. Wasn't he? Feeling like Alice after she'd fallen down the rabbit hole, Holly wondered if she was hallucinating. Maybe she'd knocked herself out in the accident and was dreaming this entire conversation.

Because if she was awake, he could be seriously unbalanced. She took another step backward and, considering her escape options after she'd tasered him, hoped he'd left the keys in the Expedition.

"You know," he said, his midnight deep voice breaking into her tumultuous thoughts, "it's obvious that your rig isn't going anywhere anytime soon. And, as you've undoubtedly discovered, cell service here is pretty much non-available, so why don't you let me give you a ride into town, then we can arrange to have your SUV towed to a garage in the morning?"

That was obviously the logical thing to do. The *only* thing to do. But accepting that didn't stop every FBI serial killer profiling book she'd ever read for research to go flashing through her mind.

"Look." He folded his broad arms and seemed to be holding in a sigh when she didn't immediately jump at his offer. "If it makes you feel any better, I'm a former Marine."

The proud. The few.

And wouldn't he just look dandy on a recruiting poster?

While his service record was moderately encouraging, if it were true, it also could mean he was armed. Not that he'd need a gun to kill. From the size of those big, black-gloved hands, Holly suspected he'd be able to snap her neck before she knew what was happening. Before she could even turn off the safety switch on the stun pen and find a down-free place to jolt him.

She'd taken a self-defense course taught at the police station just last year. One of the basics she'd learned was GET—to go for the groin, eyes, and throat if attacked. Holly was considering the logistics of that when she realized he'd caught her checking out the G part of that acronym. Which was covered up by the heavy parka he was wearing, but given his size . . .

Heat flooded into cheeks that only moments earlier had been turning to ice.

"Sorry," Holly muttered, wondering about the chances of an avalanche coming down the side of the mountain to bury her and save her from further humiliation. "Suspicion comes with the job."

The humor in his gaze faded as he took a longer, more judicial look at her. "You a cop?"

"No. A writer. Mysteries." And just because she wrote about serial killers and psychos didn't mean she couldn't tell fiction from reality. At least most of the time.

She waited for him to ask if she'd written anything he'd read. Instead, his cheeks creased as he flashed another of those devastating smiles—who knew Marines had dimples?—and said, "Cool."

He held out his hand. "Gabriel O'Halloran. But most people, except my mother, call me Gabe."

"Holly Berry."

She waited for the inevitable joke about her name. It was especially difficult to escape this time of year.

Instead, he tilted his head. "The Holly Berry who wrote *Blood Brothers*? *Deadly Deception*? *Power Play*?"

"My publisher's fond of alliteration."

She was currently plotting her sixth book. The previous had garnered good reviews, even landing on some prestigious bestseller lists, and while she was no John Grisham, she was making a nice enough living.

"I thought you looked familiar. I've seen your photo on the back of your book covers. You're a lot better looking in person, by the way. Not that it's a bad photo. In fact, it's pretty cool, with you in that kick-ass long black leather coat, glaring at something in the distance, looking like you eat bad guys for breakfast, lunch, and dinner, then either shoot them or send them up the river for life plus ten.

"But . . . Shit." He shoved back the hood of the parka and dragged a hand through his wavy black hair. "Why don't you do me a favor and just shoot me and put me out of my misery before I dig this hole I'm sinking into any deeper?"

"I'm not armed." Holly figured the taser pen didn't really count and wasn't prepared to tell him about that yet. Just in case. "Besides, you're right. That's exactly the look the photographer was going for."

"Well, it worked. My mom's a huge fan."

"That's nice to hear."

A breath she'd been unaware of holding came out on a puff of ghostly white. He'd actually been kind of cute when he'd gotten all embarrassed. And that he had a mother—who made him smile when he talked about her—was a positive sign.

Until Ma Barker came to mind.

"Some moms read romance." The smile in his gray eyes

echoed the one on his sinfully chiseled lips. "Mine is into murder and mayhem."

"Well, thank her for me."

"I'll do that. So, now that we've introduced ourselves, and hopefully you've decided I'm not going to slit your throat once I get you alone with me in my vehicle, are you ready to get going?"

"I didn't think that," she lied as she recapped the pen and reached into the backseat of the disabled Highlander to retrieve her suitcase and computer bag.

"It's good that you're not a cop," he said conversationally, as he took the suitcase from her hand and began walking toward the Expedition.

"You don't like cops?"

"My dad's a cop and I like him just fine. He's sheriff of Cascade County. Which is where you are," he tacked on, in case she didn't know. Which, admittedly, she didn't. "He was an L.A. cop. I was in eighth grade when he turned in his shield and moved up here."

"That must've been a big change for all of you."

"My sisters—I have three—bitched for a long time about missing all their girlfriends."

"Totally understandable."

"I suppose." He shrugged. "But there was sure a lot of door slamming going on around the house for the first year or so. I missed the surfing. And the Cineplex, and, given that my hormones had just begun to kick in, all the girls in their itsy bitsy teeny weeny bikinis."

"I can see how that would be a loss," she said dryly.

Doing the math, since he seemed in his early to mid thirties, she guessed she hadn't quite made it into bikinis by the time his family had left California.

"But the change seemed to suit my mother and him, which was the idea. She transferred to teaching English at Cascade County High until she retired last year."

He opened the back of the Expedition, tossed in her case, and held out his hand for her computer, which she handed over.

"Dad says he never minded working the hard streets—burglary, murder, that sort of thing. It was the domestic disturbances that really got to him. Up here he mainly deals with tourists who don't realize that tossing back tequila shooters at a mile-high elevation has a helluva more effect on your bloodstream than it does at sea level."

He retrieved a black box, opened it, and took out some red plastic highway flashers. "There's also the usual barking dogs, mailbox bashing, and the occasional tree snatching. Pop's always said it's sorta like retirement, but he doesn't have to spend all his time fishing or playing golf."

Holly had climbed up into the Expedition and was just beginning to relax when a head that could've belonged to a small horse suddenly popped up over the top of her seat. She couldn't stop the slight sound—not quite a shriek, but close enough—from escaping her lips.

"Damn. Sorry about that." Gabe unzipped the parka, reached into an inner pocket, and pulled out a Milk-Bone the size of a dinosaur thigh, which he tossed at the animal, who snapped it out of the air. "I should've warned you about Dog."

Huge yellow canine teeth made short work of the cookie.

Holly, whose writer's imagination had kicked back into gear, immediately thought of Cujo. She also wished she'd left the cap off the taser pen.

"He's certainly large."

"Yeah. But you don't have to worry, because he's about as vicious as a newborn kitten." He climbed into the driver's seat and rubbed a hand over the dog's huge head. "Say hello to the lady, Dog."

The dog sat on his haunches and lifted a gigantic brown paw between the seats.

"Hello, Dog." The beast's furry tail began pounding the floor like a jackhammer when Holly shook his extended paw. She glanced up at Gabe. "That's his name?"

He shrugged. "I didn't want to get too attached to him. It seemed naming him would make it harder to leave him behind."

"Behind where?"

Wiping the dog drool onto her jeans, she looked back at the animal, who'd crawled up on the backseat and was now sprawled over what appeared to be a camouflage-colored sleeping bag.

"Baghdad. He was a stray pup running the streets. At the time he was about a tenth the size he is now and it was obvious he was on his own, so my squad started giving him food. Which, of course, had him adopting us back."

"I imagine that's not uncommon in such a situation."

"Not at all," he agreed. "A lot of the troops had camp dogs. Not only did it lift morale, some served as additional force protectors."

"Still, I'll bet those other troops didn't jump through whatever hoops it took to bring them back to America."

"No. But Dog was special. Although you could tell gunfire—and just about everything else—scared the hell out of him, he still insisted on going on patrol with us. He sniffed out an IED one day, which saved I don't know how many lives. No way was I going to leave him behind after that."

"Well, that's quite a story." She couldn't imagine the paperwork that it would have taken to get a stray dog from Iraq into America. "Sounds like you were lucky to have met each other."

"Yeah. That's pretty much the way I look at it, too."

"What kind of dog is he, anyway?"

"Beats me, but my best guess is a cross between a Great Dane and a Hummer."

After flashing her another quick grin, he crunched his way back through the snow and set up the flashers in both directions from the disabled Highlander.

"They'll go for thirty hours before the batteries run out," he told her when he returned. "Give us plenty of time to get a tow truck out here in the morning."

"I appreciate that. Of course, that leads to the problem of where I'm going to spend the night. Is there a town nearby?"

"Yeah. About forty-five minutes away in this weather."

"I guess I won't have any choice but to get a motel room there."

"That might be a little tricky this time of year," he said. "Given that it's a really small place and high tourist season. But we'll work something out."

She had an idea of what that *something* might be. If he was thinking she was going to spend the night with him, he was going to be disappointed. But, weighing her options, Holly decided she'd wait until they got to town to face that discussion.

"Were you serious about the tree snatching?" she asked, deciding to change the subject.

"Yeah. The timber industry's taken a hit these past years, but there's still some good money to be made in stolen trees."

"Really?" She looked up at the towering fir trees packed together beside the road. "How much money?"

His laugh was deep and rich and took a bit of chill from her blood, making her feel as if warm brandy had begun flowing in her veins. "Enough."

Sensing that he was laughing at her, she folded her arms. "Something funny?"

"Not about timber theft. A full grown old growth cedar can bring in five thousand bucks at a sawmill, and a larcenous guy could make a hundred thousand with a few days' hard work, so it's not as benign a crime like it sounds. But, like I said, it's a good thing you're not a cop, because your face gives away your thoughts."

He twisted the key in the ignition. The engine roared to life and began blowing blessed heat through the dashboard vents. "I could practically see the wheels of a possible murder-for-tree plot turning in your head."

"It has its possibilities," she allowed on a voice as chilly as the outside temperature. An intensely private person, Holly wasn't wild about anyone reading her so well. Especially since

Gabriel O'Halloran was the first person to ever have accused her of being that easily read. "Though at the moment I'm working on another idea. A black widow murder."

"Ah." He nodded as he pulled the Expedition back onto the narrow road. "The chirpy, white-haired owner of Black Forest Cookies who's accused of having poisoned six husbands."

"You've heard of the case?"

"Sure. Leavenworth's just on the other side of the mountains," he reminded her. "Maybe you could call it *The Cookie Caper.*"

She was about to inform him that his suggested title was more suited to a cozy mystery when she realized he was joking, playing with her alliterative title idea. Again, not exactly serial killer behavior.

"I'll take that under advisement."

Chapter Three

Having already had one accident that day, Holly was relieved when he kept the Expedition at a safe crawl, the yellow beam of the headlights bouncing off the wall of white stuff that continued to fall.

"We'll be in the town in another twenty minutes or so," he told her after they'd been driving approximately twenty-five minutes.

He'd turned the radio down, but she'd listened to a steady stream of road closures throughout the state. His voice sounded deeper and richer in the intimacy of the snow-shrouded silence.

"Okay, here's where I admit I have no idea what town that might be."

"Santa's Village."

"You can't be serious." Maybe he wasn't a stone-cold killer, or even 5150 insane, but once again Holly began to worry about him being delusional.

"It's the town's name, all right. Population six hundred twenty-seven." He glanced over at her. "It's also not on the way to Leavenworth."

She definitely would've noticed that town on the map while planning her trip. "Damn GPS."

Not encouraging was that she'd bought the faulty navigation system from the same guy who'd sold her the purse-size

Zeus Lightning Bolt taser pen. What if it turned out he was pushing fake Chinese stuff on an unsuspecting public? How many lives could that put at risk?

"Ah." He nodded as she filed the idea of a faulty taser away. She couldn't see it working in her black widow cookie killer story, but perhaps, like all the other bits and pieces of criminal behavior she had tucked away in her mind, it could prove useful down the road. "It told you to turn right at that crossroad outside Skykomish," he guessed.

"Exactly." Which was where she'd obviously gone wrong. "How did you know?"

He shrugged. "It seems to be a glitch in some programs. We've gotten lost drivers before."

"Who suddenly find themselves in Santa's Village."

"Yep."

Damn. "That's certainly a colorful name. Is it one of those cutesy theme towns?"

Leavenworth, where she'd been headed, had re-created itself from a dying timber and railroad town into a faux Alpine Bavarian Village, which reputedly drew two-and-a-half million tourists a year.

"It pretty much is." He glanced over at her. "Sounds like you're not a fan of cute."

"Cute has its place. Like puppies and kittens. Johnny Depp. I just don't celebrate Christmas."

"So, is that a religious thing? Or were you at some time traumatized by a department store Santa?" Easy humor laced his voice.

"Let's just say the rampant commercialism gets to me." Her tone, chillier than the snow falling outside, strongly suggested they drop the entire subject.

Holly hated Christmas. The whole Christmas season.

She hated the tinsel, the trappings, the decorated trees, the wrappings, and most of all, she hated Santa Claus, whom she'd quit believing in when she was seven years old.

"And here I would've guessed the season would be a big deal for you. Given your name and all."

"My father named me. *He* liked Christmas." Which was putting it mildly.

She couldn't remember all that much about her father, but she could recall him taking her to see them light the tree at Rockefeller Center every year.

They'd been living in New York City, and, although she couldn't remember it, she'd been told that she was a year old the first time she'd attended Macy's parade, dressed in an elf green snowsuit, perched atop her father's shoulders. The next year he'd put her on double runner skates and taken her ice skating for the first time.

Christmas, especially Christmas in Manhattan, had been nothing short of magical.

Then, the night Holly turned seven, while she was at home frosting sugar cookies for Santa with her mama, while out doing his annual Christmas Eve shopping, George Berry had been shot dead by a mugger who'd gotten away with three credit cards, forty-five dollars in cash, a Timex watch, and a Josephine Irish Cabbage Patch Kid with a pink dress and cranberry-colored pigtails.

Her mother had gone into what Holly now recognized as a deep clinical depression. So dark that she packed up what was left of their little family and moved them to L.A.

But despite the bright sun that was always shining above the palm trees, a dark cloud had settled over the house. And the next year, when Christmas rolled around again, there was no tinsel-draped tree. No presents. No trips to Macy's to sit on Santa's lap.

That was when Holly, in an attempt to bring some small ray of happiness back into their lives, had written to Santa.

She could still remember the letter. *Dear Santa,* she'd written in her very best second grade printing with a red pencil in the hopes the bright color would help it stand out from all those other millions of letters he probably received at the

North Pole. *My mama cries all the time since Daddy died. She says you can't bring him back to life. But this year, the only thing I want is a happy family. Like I used to have. Thank you and Merry Christmas to you and Mrs. Claus and all the elves and reindeers. Especially Blitzen.* For some reason, whenever her daddy had read her *The Night Before Christmas,* Blitzen had been her favorite. *Love, Your friend, Holly Berry.*

P.S. In case you didn't notice, being so busy with your toy factory and all, I'm living in California now.

Whatever she was thinking wasn't good, Gabe thought. Her lips were pulled into a tight line and she'd encased herself in enough ice to cover Mount Rainier. The lady was a touchy one. He also suspected there was a story there. One he intended to discover for himself.

Meanwhile, with her Highlander stuck in a snowdrift and the roads closed all throughout the mountains, it wasn't like she'd be going anywhere soon.

And neither was he.

Chapter Four

She stayed silent for a long time, seeming lost in thought as she watched the woods out the passenger window.

The only sound was the crunch of the snow beneath the tires, the slight scraping noise of the wipers as they struggled with the snow that was rapidly turning to ice, and the low drone of the voice on the radio announcing yet more road closures.

Her scent—reminding him of a vacation his family had taken to Vashon Island, where they'd gleaned fruit from a peach orchard—bloomed in the heat blasting from the dashboard vents.

He wondered if she smelled like that all over. Wondered if she tasted as good. Which had him imagining her lying on hot, tangled sheets while he ran his tongue down her smooth white throat. Across her collarbone. Then lower, over her pink-tipped breasts that he'd make wet with his kisses . . .

Fire shot, along with his blood, from his obviously fevered brain to his groin.

"I don't understand," she said as he shifted to adjust his suddenly too-tight jeans. "This storm wasn't even on the radar. I checked. The forecast was sunny, with temperatures in the high forties."

"Things change fast in the mountains."

"So I've heard."

"So, you're not from around here?"

He was hard and ached and short of pulling over to the side of the road and somehow getting her out of those tight jeans and boots so she could ride him hard and fast—which, unfortunately, wasn't an option, especially since he didn't exactly run around with a condom in his pocket these days—there wasn't a helluva lot he could do about it.

At least not for now.

Although it might not make a lot of sense, Gabe suddenly wanted to know everything about her—her favorite food, her favorite color (though he'd guess, from the coat, hat, and gloves, that would be red), whether she was a morning person or night owl, whether she liked her sex hot and fast, or slow and dreamy.

He wanted her both ways. First fast, then, once they got that out of the way, he'd take his time, touching her all over. Tasting her everywhere. Drawing out every sensation, warming every bit of her fragrant peach-scented flesh until she was begging for him to finish her off.

Then, what was really scary, was the absolute certainty that he'd want her again. And again.

"I've been in Seattle the past six months," she said, her voice breaking into a fantasy of being deep inside of her, feeling her contracting around him. "Before that I lived in L.A."

"Now there's a coincidence. Us both coming from the same town."

It didn't suit her, he decided. With that white as cream skin, she was the least likely California girl he'd ever seen.

"So, is your family back there?"

Significant other? Fiancé? Lover?

Or, oh hell, how about a husband?

"My father died when I was a kid."

"That must've been tough. I'm sorry."

"So was I." She exhaled a slight breath that told him she still hadn't quite gotten over it. "My mother's spent the past few years traveling."

"Lucky her." Having joined the Marines to see the great big wide world, Gabe wouldn't mind if he never left these mountains again. "But where's her actual home?"

"She doesn't have one. I mean she *really* travels. She works as a croupier on a cruise ship. So mostly she sails around the Caribbean. And occasionally along the Mexican Coast, what's called the Mexican Riviera."

"Sounds like an interesting gig."

And lonely, Gabe thought. Even though you'd be surrounded by people, wouldn't they mostly always be strangers? That was one of the things he'd liked about being a Marine. Semper Fi wasn't just some snazzy military slogan. It was a way of life. Once you got that service emblem pin at graduation, you became part of a family for life.

Not that he didn't love his own family. But after having grown up with three older sisters, it had been cool to have brothers.

She moved her shoulders in a small shrug. "Mom seems to like it."

Her tone didn't exactly ring with enthusiasm.

"Although you might not celebrate Christmas, to a lot of people it's a pretty big deal," he said. "So, can I take the fact that you're traveling to a murder trial over the holidays to mean that you don't have some guy waiting for you back in Seattle?"

She glanced over at him. "No. Why?"

The NO TRESPASSING sign was up and flashing in bright Day-Glo neon letters. A sensible man would back away. But, dammit, Gabe had been unrelentingly sensible for the past year. And more amazingly, celibate for two.

Maybe it was high time—hell, past time—to take a few risks.

Having never been one to play games, he decided to just lay his cards on the table.

"Because you're a good-looking, obviously intelligent woman and you pretty much had me from the moment you stepped out of that SUV. So, I just wanted to know if there's some guy out there I'm going to have to fight for your favors."

Her eyes widened. The smudge around the right one was growing darker. Yep, the lady was definitely going to have one helluva shiner.

"Well, that's certainly direct and to the point."

"I've never been one to beat around the bush. Or waste time playing games."

"I'm not one to play games either. But has anyone ever told you that you're a very unusual man?"

"Because I admire a woman with brains and looks?"

"No. Because, along with supposedly having a friend with eight reindeer and a sleigh, and living in a town called Santa's Village, you don't know anything about me."

"That can always be changed. And, for the record, about the town? It gets worse. Santa's Village bills itself as 'The Most Christmassy Town in America,' and you happen to be looking at the guy who not only owns an honest-to-God Christmas tree farm, but the Ho Ho Ho Inn."

"You have got to be kidding."

She was, unsurprisingly, less than impressed. He figured the usual guys she went for in the city were lawyers and stockbrokers who wore Armani suits and lived in penthouses overlooking Puget Sound.

"Hey," he said, "it's not like I named it."

Of course, admittedly, he hadn't changed the name either. He'd told himself that was because it was, in a way, a historical landmark. But it was mostly because Emma loved it.

After having been absent for so much of his young daughter's life, Gabe was willing to give her whatever she wanted. Within reason. And hey, his ego was strong enough not to feel the need to change the name to something his former Marine buddies wouldn't have ragged him to death about.

"I returned home last year and bought it from this couple who'd run it for the past thirty years and decided it was time to go lie in the sun and catch marlin and sun fish in St. Petersburg, Florida."

He could tell she thought he was crazy. And, hell, maybe he was. But he'd been starting to get crazy more and more back in the sandbox. And to Gabe's mind, the admitted wackiness of his hometown was a helluva lot better than the insanity of a war zone.

Chapter Five

"When do you think he's going to get here?" the five-year-old girl asked for the umpteenth time in the last hour.

"It's been snowing to beat the band," Beth O'Halloran reminded her granddaughter yet again as she took the basket of sliced potatoes out of the deep fryer and dumped them onto a plate next to a half-pound of Angus beef burger. "It takes time to get back up here from the city."

"I know." Emma O'Halloran's frustrated sigh ruffled her bright bangs. "But it's just taking forever!" She began pacing again, the heels of her pink cowboy boots clicking an impatient tattoo on the heart-of-pine plank floor of the Ho Ho Ho Inn.

"I know," Beth said sympathetically, stepping around the little girl to get the coleslaw out of the commercial refrigerator.

With three of her four children being daughters, Beth was accustomed to the amount of passion that could simmer inside even the youngest feminine body.

Emma stopped in front of the kitchen window again, pressing her nose against the double-paned glass, peering into the gathering purple darkness. "Do you think he's bringing my present?"

"He probably did some shopping," Beth hedged as she added the slaw to the plate.

"No. My real present!"

Beth sighed. They'd been through this before. Too many times to count. Although Gabriel had been, in some ways, easier than her girls, Emma was definitely her father's child when it came to tenacity. Once either one of them got something into their heads, it was nearly impossible to shake loose.

"Even if your father does decide to give in and get you that pony, I doubt he'd risk pulling a trailer up the mountain today."

"Not *that* present." The pink ribbon Beth had tied the unruly red-gold curls back with this morning loosened a bit as Emma emphatically shook her head. "I changed my mind. To something more special. Something I'm going to ask Santa for."

Beth sighed again as she thought about the palomino Welsh pony currently residing at Lucas Nelson's stable waiting to be delivered on Christmas Eve night. Although she'd personally thought the gift had been a little extravagant, she understood why Gabriel had bought it for his daughter. And it was a sweet little animal, she allowed. And docile enough for a child to handle.

Now, if Emma had changed her mind this close to Christmas, with the roads being closed, even if they could order a new present on the Internet, the delivery trucks wouldn't be able to reach town.

Well, no point in borrowing trouble, Beth decided. Whatever else her granddaughter had her heart set on now, Beth knew Emma would be over the moon when she got up on Christmas morning and saw the pony grazing in the small pasture behind the inn.

She held out the plate. "Here. Take this over to Ben Daughtry. He's sitting in the back booth."

"That's where he always sits."

"It's called tradition. Some people believe it's a good thing."

Heaven knows, until this past year, Emma's life had been unsettled enough. There were times Beth blamed herself for that. She and Will had visited their granddaughter three times a year and had never witnessed any signs of domestic trouble, but if they'd left the mountains and moved back to California, perhaps they might have been able to provide the stability they hadn't realized the little girl had been missing.

Then again, had she known about her daughter-in-law's illicit romance with her wealthy property developer boss while Gabriel had been overseas, Beth wasn't sure what she would or could have done. Surely e-mailing her son about his wife's adultery would've just given him one more thing to worry about during a time when he'd needed to keep focused on staying alive.

Unfortunately, life was a great deal more complicated than it appeared in those mystery books she liked to read, where problems were presented, then, in four hundred pages, neatly solved, with the bad guys behind bars and the good guys living happily ever after.

She watched the little girl carry the plate across the wood floor with the care that suggested she was walking on eggshells. Her teeth were worrying her bottom lip. Better fretting about a dropped cheeseburger than her daddy having an accident, Beth decided.

There may be state laws against child labor, but the way Beth saw it, this was a family business, Emma was most definitely family, and besides, having the child help out now and again made her feel useful, kept her out of trouble, and most important, tonight would hopefully keep her mind off her father's trip up the mountain.

Emma had reached Ben Daughtry's booth without incident. The sixty-something artist had moved here after being priced out of Seattle's Capitol Hill neighborhood, which, he'd complained, was having its bohemian roots overtaken by Starbucks and sushi joints. He'd never married, apparently choosing to direct all his energies toward his art, which, when he'd arrived had been—to her mind—disturbingly dark.

These days, rather than painting landscapes of a school of sharks attacking kayakers in Puget Sound, or King Kong atop the Space Needle fighting off attacking fighter jets, Daughtry earned a comfortable living creating seasonal watercolor greeting cards that all tended to make Santa's Village look like, well, a Hallmark card.

Beth suspected his former artist friends in the city would be amazed at the transformation of the man who'd arrived depressed and argumentative, but she wasn't surprised. She'd seen it happen many times, and although there were those few detractors who suggested that the town council was putting something in the water, she liked living in the kind of small town epitomized in old black and white movies and the Sinclair Lewis stories she'd enjoyed teaching to high school English classes.

Ben was good with children, she'd give the man that. After chatting easily with Emma for a moment, he took a pencil from the pocket of his red and green plaid shirt and quickly sketched something on a white paper napkin.

Emma studied it with a seriousness way beyond her age, then bobbed her head and beamed.

As the little girl returned back toward the kitchen, the napkin in hand, Daughtry dug into his dinner. Which was also the same thing he had every night, except on Wednesday, when, for some reason Beth couldn't fathom, he'd switch out the coleslaw for baked beans.

Her gaze drifted out the window. Although she would never admit it out loud, she was a bit concerned by the delay as well. Gabriel had blessedly escaped injury during all his years in the military, including two tours in Iraq and another in Afghanistan, but that didn't mean that a mother ever stopped worrying about her child.

Chapter Six

From high atop the town, bathed in the rising moonlight that cast a bluish glow over the snow, the small town of Santa's Village looked like the set of a model railroad. There appeared to be one main street—strung with, natch, bright red and green flashing lights—then a handful of others going off at ninety-degree angles. It was admittedly charming, if you liked the *It's a Wonderful Life* approach to the season. Taking the moonlit scene in, she decided the entire village couldn't be more than nine blocks square.

Winter-bare trees in front yards were strung with fairy lights and electric candles flickered in windows.

"Cute," she murmured dryly as they passed by a giant statue of Santa welcoming visitors to "Santa's Village, The Most Christmassy Town in America."

The part of her accustomed to editing her manuscripts wondered if *Christmassy* was even a word. The right arm, which had to be at least six feet from fingertip to shoulder, was automated to wave a manic greeting. It was, hands down, at the same time both the ugliest and scariest thing she'd ever laid eyes on.

"Granted, he takes some getting used to," Gabe said as he turned onto—what else?—Rudolph Road. "After about three months I just quit seeing him."

Holly figured it would take longer than that for her to stop seeing the oversize jolly old elf. As it was, she feared the scarily grinning Santa was going to appear in her nightmares. Looking a lot like Freddy Kruger wearing a pillow beneath a tacky red velvet suit.

The sidewalks were lined with lighted pine trees, and more lights, which flashed merrily, had been strung across the streets. Every storefront seemed to be trying to outdo its neighbor.

"Is the town decorated like this year round?" she asked.

"Pretty much," he allowed. "Though people do tend to crank things up a bit come Thanksgiving. Tourism has become a major industry here, especially since the timber business dropped off. Along with the Christmas junkies, we do get a lot of sportsmen and cross-country skiers."

"That's nice."

Holly had never understood the appeal of strapping sticks to your boots and trudging through miles of snow, but she figured it took all kinds to make a world. After all, not everyone enjoyed murder mysteries either.

They passed what she supposed must be the town square, boasting a white Victorian bandstand decorated in yet more white fairy lights. A towering Douglas fir blinked in multicolors, a crèche topped by a star and lit by a floodlight shared space with a menorah that had to be eight feet tall, with flickering red bulbs atop the candles.

"Nice to know Santa's ecumenical," she murmured.

"We try." When he made a left turn on Dasher Drive, Dog sat up and began paying attention. "Fortunately, the pagans signed on to the tree as their symbol and I've got a committee working on what to put up for Kwanzaa for next year."

"*You* have a committee?" Holly absently petted the huge head looming up through the space between the seats.

He shrugged. "I'm mayor. Which isn't any big deal," he told her before she might suggest it was. "The previous owner of the inn had the job, so I sort of inherited it along with the mortgage."

"Well, that's one way to avoid paying for a new election."

"There's not that much to do," he said. "Between the council, the school board, and the tourism bureau, the town pretty much runs itself. The main business has always been Kris Kringle's Workshop."

"Okay. Now you've got to be pulling my leg."

"Although it's a very fine leg—which seems to go all the way up to Canada, by the way—and there are a lot of things I'd like to do to it . . . beginning with starting at the ankle and nibbling my way up it . . . actually, I'm not."

"You're going to be disappointed regarding the nibbling," she said firmly. Just because he'd saved her from possibly freezing to death didn't mean she was going to show her gratitude by getting horizontal with him. "As for the workshop, if you are telling the truth, I'm starting to wonder what Kool-Aid you all are drinking here in this charming little hamlet."

His chuckle was deep and rich and stirred places in Holly she'd forgotten could be stirred. "Sam Fraiser's the seventh-generation owner, and although he's never actually laid claim to the title, a lot of people, and kids, in town believe he's the 'real' Santa Claus.

"Anyway, the workshop had been facing some lean years, make that decades, but all the problems with imports have made the shop's more traditional toys—like wooden planes, trains, and cars—more in demand. In fact, he got written up in the *Wall Street Journal* and *Business Week* last month."

"Okay." She gave the so-called Santa reluctant points. "That's admittedly impressive."

"A lot of people think so. Though the Fraisers have never been in the business for fame. In fact, my sister Rachel, who works as his accountant and business manager, says producers from *Ellen, GMA,* and *CBS News Sunday Morning* have called in the past few weeks, wanting him to appear on their shows, but he's turned them all down."

Holly had met writers who would run over their dear old grannies for such an opportunity.

"So, what is he? Some sort of hermit? Or another Una-bomber in hiding?"

"Gotta love a woman with a twisted mind." Again Holly found his deep chuckle way too appealing for comfort. "Actually, he told them it was his busy season."

"Of course it is," Holly said, not bothering to keep the sarcasm from sharpening her tone. "After all, he's got a big trip coming up."

"That's what he reminded them."

Forget about falling down the rabbit hole. Holly had just decided that somehow she'd gone into another dimension and landed in the Twilight Zone when he turned one more corner and the Ho Ho Ho Inn came into view.

You couldn't miss it. With those flashing red ten-foot-tall letters. But she'd been expecting some sort of tacky little motel-looking place. The type where you'd expect to find animal heads hanging on cheap paneled walls. Granted, the inside could still meet expectations, but the exterior was a surprise.

It was actually a compound of log and stone buildings nestled in a grove of fir trees. The lodge itself had a roof that soared two and a half stories high. The front was all glass and jutted forward like the prow of an ancient sailing ship. Perhaps a dozen smaller cabins were scattered around in the woods. Close enough to give a sense of a community, but far enough apart to allow privacy, if that's what a guest had come here seeking.

"Okay, I'm impressed."

"You were expecting, perhaps, the Bates Motel?" Rather than seeming to take offense, his voice held that humor she was beginning to find all too appealing.

"Something like that," she admitted.

"According to old-timers, the original main inn was more along those lines. But it burned down two years ago after it was hit by lightning. The owners had plans drawn up and had begun construction when they decided they didn't want to make that much of a commitment at that point in their lives.

So, they put it up for sale just when I got out of the service and was looking to make a lifestyle change. The top two floors are living area. I had soundproofing put in between the floors that allows me to live above the store without getting any of the downstairs noise."

"Lucky you." A warm, welcoming yellow light gleamed forth from the windows. "And it's stunning. But you've got to admit the signage is a little tacky."

"More than a little," he agreed. "The thing is, it fits the town's building code. I could've left the flashing lights off, but decided to put them back up because my daughter loves them."

"Your daughter?"

"Yeah." He pulled up in front of the lodge, parking between an ancient VW bus that had been painted in geometric squares reminiscent of the Partridge Family tour bus and a trendy Lexus crossover. "Emma's five. Needless to say, she finds all the kitsch in the town to her liking."

"I can imagine." Memories of her own childhood Christmases in New York, which she'd buried deep inside her long ago, stirred. From habit, Holly rigidly tamped them down. It figured that the first guy she'd found appealing in months was not only married, but a player. "How does your wife feel about it?"

"Wife?"

He cut the engine and turned toward her, a quick spark firing in eyes that had turned to flint. The easy humor was gone and the mouth that had been so quick to smile was drawn into a hard, tough line. For the first time she could see the warrior dwelling inside the friendly Good Samaritan inn owner.

"What the hell would I be doing hitting on another woman if I had a wife waiting for me at home?"

She shrugged. "People cheat all the time. You wouldn't be the first married person to fool around."

In fact, although she wasn't prepared to share the fact, she'd lost her virginity her freshman year of college to her English Lit professor, who'd neglected to mention a wife who'd just happened to be away on sabbatical studying the Brontë sisters at University College, Oxford.

The ironic thing about that whole sad affair was that at the time the Brontës had been her favorite authors, and the dark, broody, and overly temperamental professor had reminded her of Heathcliff.

"Other people may cheat." Something else came and went in Gabe's eyes. Something Holly couldn't quite read. "But not me. No way. No how."

He was suddenly looking at her as if she were a stray dog. No, worse than a stray, given the story of him having adopted that oversize mutt who was currently whining impatiently to get out of the SUV—he actually *liked* strays.

"Okay." She held up a hand. Obviously she'd misread the situation. "Since I just met you, I'll have to take your word for it. But may I point out that you're the one who hit on me. Talking about nibbling on ankles and such." Just the thought of all the other body parts representing the "such" was enough to make her blood run a little hotter. "Then, out of the blue, you brought up your daughter."

"You've never heard of a single dad?"

"Of course. I've just never actually met one."

The line of his jaw hardened. "Well, you have now."

Apparently he'd had enough of the conversation because after muttering a rude curse, he opened the door and climbed out. Not quite understanding how the mood had taken such a drastic turn, just because she'd made an understandable mistake, Holly didn't wait for him to come around the front of the Expedition, but jumped out and placed a hand on his arm.

"Look," she said. "I'm sorry if I offended you. That wasn't my intention." She offered a smile of contrition. "Especially after you rescued me from turning into a popsicle."

He looked down at her hand. Then cursed again. It might've been mild for a Marine, but it still wasn't a word Holly had said more than once, okay, maybe twice in her life.

"Hell. While we're sharing apologies here, let me offer you

one for overreacting. My only excuse, not that I have much of one, is that you hit a hot button I didn't realize I had."

As they stood there in the snow-covered parking lot, Gabe looking down at Holly, her looking up at him, something stirred in her. More complicated than lust, it felt uncomfortably like need.

"Okay," she said through lips that had gotten suddenly dry. "So, we're even. No harm. No foul."

As quickly as the winter storm had swooped down over the mountains, his grin was back, quick and, dammit, sexy as sin. "Gotta love a woman who can use a sports metaphor. I don't suppose you eat meat?"

"I've been known to eat a bloody steak from time to time."

"How about carbs?"

"A steak without a baked potato or fries is like a day without chocolate." She shrugged. "What's the point?"

The air was biting, the snow continued to fall, but Holly was feeling warmer and warmer inside as his eyes swept over her face.

"I don't suppose you've watched ESPN on occasion?"

She tossed her head. Flashed him a flirty smile she didn't even know she had inside her. "I'll see your ESPN and raise you. I happen to subscribe to the NFL network."

"Be still my heart." He patted the front of the parka with that wide gloved hand that she was no longer worrying about breaking her neck. No, it was the other things she was imagining it doing that could prove really dangerous. "I'm not absolutely positive, but I think I may have just fallen in love."

"Don't get overly worked up," she said as he opened the back of the Expedition and got out her things. "I only signed up because I was thinking about writing a book about a crazed fan who killed off players from rival teams.

"Although that concept didn't quite work out, I kept the network, because, while I couldn't tell you an option play from a quarterback sneak, what's not to love about hunky guys in shoulder pads with tight butts running around in spandex?"

"I'd never thought of it that way."

"Now there's a surprise." Although the single former Marine Corps dad was certainly no Rambo, the testosterone he oozed was definitely of the heterosexual variety.

Toughening herself against it—and him—she turned and began walking down the narrow path someone had shoveled from the parking lot to the front door.

Chapter Seven

The sweep of headlights flashed in the window.

Over the sound of the wind in the tops of the trees, Beth heard a truck door open and shut. Then, surprisingly, another.

The door to the combination inn/restaurant/bar opened a moment later and Gabriel entered with a woman who looked vaguely familiar.

"It's her!" Emma hissed.

"Who?" Beth looked closer.

"My present!"

"What present?"

"The one I decided I wanted more than a pony," Emma insisted on an impatient huff. "My new mom!"

"What?"

"See." The little girl shoved the napkin at her grandmother. "I had Mr. Daughtry draw her for me, so Santa would know exactly what she looked like."

Beth studied the pencil sketch, then looked back at the woman stamping the snow off a pair of calf-high chocolate-hued Uggs.

Daughtry's sketch wasn't as detailed as a photograph. But there was no mistaking the resemblance. The artist had captured the pointed, stubborn chin, the wide mouth, which was smiling in the sketch, unlike the real woman whose intelligent green gaze was sweeping over the room.

It was only a coincidence, Beth assured herself, as her granddaughter ran across the wooden floor to greet them. Just random luck. Just as it was only the chill of the night air that had caused the goosebumps to rise on her skin.

Revealing a speed that belied his size, Dog streaked past Gabe into the inn just as Emma came barreling toward him.

Then she skidded to a stop in front of Holly Berry, staring up at her with the awe that the adolescent boy Gabe had felt upon his first sight of a *Playboy* Playmate of the Month foldout.

"Hi." Her little voice was breathless, her face beatific.

"Hi, yourself."

The woman won huge points with Gabe when she returned his daughter's smile. Meanwhile, Dog came screeching to a halt with the scratching sound of claws on the wooden floor, rolled over, and waited for Emma to start scratching his stomach, as she always did.

"I'm Emma."

"I'm Holly."

The little girl's eyes lit up as Dog began wiggling on the floor, trying to get the attention he'd grown used to receiving. "Like Christmas Holly?"

"Exactly like that. I was born on Christmas Eve, so although my mother was pushing for Caroline, my father, who was a huge fan of Christmas, won the argument."

"That's cool." Emma's beaming smile could have lit up the town of Santa's Village for a month. "Maybe your daddy would like to live here. This is the most Christmassy town in America."

"So I read on the sign." When Dog, tired of being uncharacteristically ignored by his small owner, let out a deep rumbling bark, Holly absently began scratching his belly. "Unfortunately, my father died when I was young."

"That's too bad." Rosebud lips pulled into a pout Gabe recognized all too well. Even a five-year-old female, he'd discovered, could be every bit as capricious as the older variety, and Emma's emotions could swing in a wide arc. "My daddy almost died in Afghanistan. But he saved a bunch of people in a big battle and got a medal."

"Well." Holly glanced up at him. "That's very heroic."

Gabe cringed inwardly. He hated talk of heroism. "I was just doing my job," he insisted as he always did when either his mother or daughter brought it up. His father—having been a grunt in Nam—was wise enough to let sleeping dogs lie. So to speak. He took off the parka and hung it on the rack on the wall. "Same as any other Marine would've done."

"Hmm."

He could tell Holly wasn't exactly buying that, but was grateful when she didn't push for details. Instead, she stood up again and swept an appraising glance over his daughter. "I like your outfit."

Emma preened like a Junior Miss Cascade Rodeo Days finalist as she skimmed a small hand down the front of the pink fringed faux suede skirt. "It's my cowgirl outfit." She stuck out a small foot. "See, I have boots to match."

"I've never seen pink cowgirl boots before." Holly gave them an admiring appraisal.

"They're special. My aunt Julie sent them to me from Calgary. That's in Canada."

"I know."

"She went up there to compete in the barrel race in the Calgary Stampede, which is this really big, famous rodeo. But she fell off her horse and broke her arm."

"That's too bad."

"Not really. Because she fell in love with the doctor who put her cast on."

Holly won additional points with Gabe by smiling. Not just a phony patronizing one for show, but a real one that crinkled the corners of her green eyes. "Sounds like a lucky break."

"That's what Aunt Julie says. Especially since she'd never, ever"—red curls danced as Emma shook her head—"fallen off her horse before. My uncle Jeremy—he's the doctor she married—says it was kismet. That's kinda like magic. Like Ariel saving Prince Eric from drowning, and falling in love with him."

"Sounds like it to me," Holly agreed, exchanging a glance with Gabe, who rolled his eyes. She suspected the family had very few secrets with this pint-size Paul Revere living among them.

Not that she'd pump a little girl for information about her father. Even if she was interested in the man. Which she wasn't.

Liar.

"Did Daddy bring you back from Seattle with him?" Emma asked.

"Part of the way." He'd shoved his fingers into the front pockets of his jeans, his thumbs arrowing downward, drawing her attention to his 5-button fly. "I had an accident, and he came along just in time."

"That's what heroes do," the little girl said, as if she were an authority on such matters. "Like Aladdin did when he rescued Princess Jasmine when she was about to get her hand cut off for giving an apple to a poor beggar."

"The world according to Disney," Gabe murmured, once again sounding more than a little uncomfortable at being stuck atop that pedestal his daughter had created for him.

"Nothing wrong with fairy tales," Holly murmured back, even though her own mother had never allowed her to read them. Or go to Disney movies.

Better, she'd said, for little girls to grow up believing in reality. Of taking charge of your own life. Because waiting around for knights in shining armor and expecting happily ever after endings could only lead to heartbreak.

Still, Holly hadn't needed to spend a bundle talking about her childhood with some Freudian shrink to make the connection between her father's murder and her having grown up to be a mystery novelist.

Perhaps NYPD had never managed to catch George Berry's killer, but in Holly's stories, the bad guys were *always* captured by the final chapter, justice prevailed in the end, and the good guys—and women—went on to live happily ever after.

It was, in its own way, every bit a fantasy as the one those romance novels her best friend, Jeanine, who ran the Body Beautiful Day Spa next to the Starbucks down the street from her apartment, gobbled up like chocolate-covered coffee beans.

"Which is why they call it fiction," Holly had been quoted as saying just last week during an interview on Seattle's KOMO's *Northwest Afternoon* program.

Since selling her first book the same week she graduated from college, for the past seven years crime had been Holly's business. And fortunately, since people seemed to be endlessly fascinated by murder and mayhem, business was good.

Still, she was intrigued by the idea of this hottie Marine sitting in a theater, or even on a couch in his living room, watching *The Little Mermaid*.

"Ms. Berry has had a long day," he said on a mild tone that nevertheless brooked no argument. Holly figured the quiet authority must have served him well in the military. "We need to see about getting her a room for the night."

"She could stay with us," Emma volunteered quickly. A bit too quickly, Holly thought. "We've got lots of room."

"I think Ms. Berry might feel more comfortable with other arrangements."

His fingers curved around Holly's elbow as he led her across the room, which she was surprised to find tastefully decorated for the season. The fragrant green fir had been draped in white fairy lights, its branches adorned with what appeared to be hand-carved ornaments. Fresh wreaths hung on the windows, and the staircase was wrapped with pine garlands.

There were no animal heads on the walls, no inflatable snowmen or waving Santas.

Unfortunately, there was a juke box from which Lonestar was promising to be home for Christmas.

Yeah, right, Holly thought.

Great group. Stupid song. In fact, it was, thanks to her own personal history, her least favorite song ever recorded. Unfortunately, this particular one seemed to have been covered by anyone who'd ever picked up a microphone and it was impossible to get through the holiday season without being bombarded by various versions.

At least the country edge to this rendition kept it from being as saccharine as the one by The Carpenters, which had come onto the Highlander's radio as she'd left Seattle.

The kitchen had been built with a large window, allowing diners to watch their meals being made. It also, Holly thought, enabled the kitchen staff to keep an eye on their customers, thus allowing better service. The smells emanating from the room outfitted with what appeared to be state-of-the-art equipment made her mouth water. Then again, all she'd had to eat since that bagel this morning had been a thermos of coffee and a package of M&M's.

The fire he'd told her about probably made it impossible for the long check-in counter to be original, but it certainly looked antique. Perhaps an old bar from an 1880s saloon. She ran a finger over the crease in its polished surface and imagined a bullet skimming by during some long-ago gunfight.

A woman, with fashionably silver hair cut in a short bob, wearing a white chef's apron over jeans and a blue Seattle Seahawks sweatshirt came out of the kitchen.

"It's about time you got home." She wrapped her arms around Gabe's wide shoulders, went up on her toes, and kissed his beard-roughened cheek. "I've been a little worried."

"I was delayed." He ran the back of his hand down the side of her face, the gesture easy and natural, demonstrating yet again that he was a man comfortable with physical displays of affection. "Holly, this is my mother, Beth O'Halloran. Mom, this is—"

"Holly Berry." Twin dimples that echoed her son's creased in her cheeks as she smiled. "I'm a huge fan."

A slender gold ring flashed in the twinkling white lights of the Christmas tree as she held out her hand. "Welcome to the Ho Ho Ho Inn."

"Holly had an accident on the road," Gabe revealed. "She swerved for Blitzen."

"Sam said he'd gotten out again," Beth agreed. "But, thank heavens, he's back home now." Hazel eyes swept over Holly's face. "Let's get some ice on that eye while I fix you some dinner."

"I was thinking perhaps, since we're booked solid, she could stay with you and Pop until her SUV's fixed and the roads open again," Gabe suggested.

"Well, now, of course you'd be welcome," Beth agreed. "But as it turns out, we've a lovely one-bedroom cabin that just opened up today. The Davidsons' daughter went into labor early," she informed Gabe. "Even if they could get over the mountains, which they probably can't, since your father's been out putting up road closure barricades all day, they understandably decided to stay in Portland."

She smiled at Holly. "They've been regulars since their daughter, Madison, was about Emma's age. We'll miss them, of course, but it's a lucky timing for you."

"It seems to be." Holly decided her luck had definitely been mixed the last few hours.

"Is Madison okay?" Gabe asked.

"Better than okay. The Davidsons are now proud grandparents of twins."

"That's good news."

The genuine warmth in his tone suggested he knew the new mother. Which only made sense. Of course, there could also be a history there, Holly considered. She couldn't imagine many teenage girls not noticing Gabriel O'Halloran. Especially in a town this small. As the idea of a Christmas vacation fling with a hunkier younger version of the Marine single dad came to mind, Holly felt a little twinge of something that felt uncomfortably, ridiculously, like jealousy.

"Fabulous news," Beth agreed. "Anna sounded over the

moon about being a new grandmother when she called to cancel. Why don't you take Holly's things over to the cabin, Gabriel," she suggested, "while I fix her something to eat."

"I'll help," Emma chirped up. "Do you like gingerbread?" she asked Holly.

"Doesn't everyone?" Holly responded, suspecting that was the answer the little girl wanted to hear.

"Good. Because Gramma makes the best gingerbread in the whole world. I helped her make it this morning."

"Emma's quite the little helper," Beth agreed, her smile once again reminding Holly of her son's. "I don't know what I'd do without her."

Five minutes later, Holly was sitting at a small table in the kitchen, a bag of frozen peas wrapped in a dish towel against her eye, while Beth whipped up a serving of the daily special—gravy-smothered chicken fried steak and mashed potatoes.

Even as she could practically see the dinner attaching itself to her hips, Holly, who was more accustomed to nuking a Lean Cuisine or takeout Chinese, couldn't deny it smelled heavenly.

If she was going to get stranded somewhere, a town called Santa's Village definitely would've been her very last choice. Well, at least right above hell.

Still, as Emma chattered on like a little red-haired magpie about her various aunts and uncles' adventures, and Beth bustled around the kitchen with an ease a finalist on *Top Chef* would've envied, Holly decided it was actually rather pleasant.

When Gabe's mother put the white plate in front of her and she discovered the calorie-laden dinner tasted even better than it had smelled, she decided she could have done a whole lot worse.

Chapter Eight

The cabin, which was stone and wood on the outside, was warm and cozy, with overstuffed furniture covered in sturdy fabric designed to take a lot of abuse. The furniture was an eclectic mixture of pine and other woods, the plank coffee table wide enough to encourage visitors to put their feet up.

Someone—it had to have been Gabe—had lit a fire in the stone fireplace while she'd been eating dinner. There was a powder room and large but cozy combination living room and kitchen separated by a granite-topped counter downstairs. Upstairs, in the loft, was a bath with separate shower and oversize whirlpool tub that looked out onto the dark expanse of forest, and a bedroom boasting a king-size four-poster bed created from logs.

Yellow plank pine walls glowed like warm butter beneath the wrought iron chandelier. A second fireplace, this one gas, flickered in the corner and a Native American print quilt and pillows covered the bed.

A smaller blanket, bordered in deep brown and blue woven petroglyphs, hung on the wall opposite the bed. A fanciful figure in colors ranging from red to bright yellow stood in the center of the blanket.

"It depicts a spirit quest," Gabe told her as she paused in front of it, "symbolizing a young brave seeking his destiny.

The petroglyphs were designed after those found near the Columbia River. They've been dated back to over ten thousand years. The ones on the stones," he said. "Not the blanket."

"It's lovely," she murmured. The woven wool was incredibly soft to the touch. "It must've been nice. To believe in such a thing."

"Nice?" He tilted his head and looked down at her.

"That's not exactly the word I mean. More life affirming. The idea of a quest to follow your fate."

"And you don't believe in that idea?"

"I believe we all make our own fate. . . . What?" she asked, after a long, humming moment when he didn't respond.

"I was just thinking how I used to believe that, too. When I left town on, I guess you'd have to say, my own spirit quest."

"Which led you into the Marines."

"Yeah. Where I learned that despite all the training, despite being a member of the strongest military in the world, fate has a helluva lot more to do with life than most of us want to admit."

Suspecting that he'd seen a lot during his years in the service, Holly didn't want to argue. Besides, if she was going to get technical, she suspected fate had played more than a little part in that Manhattan murderous mugger being on the street corner that long-ago Christmas Eve.

"Well." She blew out a breath. "Thanks for rescuing me. And for the place to stay. And the dinner."

"The Ho Ho Ho Inn prides itself on its hospitality."

She couldn't help smiling.

"What?" His chiseled masculine lips quirked just a bit in response to her smile.

"I was just thinking how amazing it is that a big tough Marine can say the name of this place with a straight face."

His rich, warm laugh was every bit as intoxicating as the buttered rum Beth O'Halloran had insisted on sending with her in a foam to-go cup, along with a plate of ginger spice molasses cookies.

"Believe me, it took a while." His eyes warmed like gleaming pewter in the glow from the wrought iron chandelier's candelabra bulbs. "Nearly as long as it took me to get used to the idea of being an innkeeper."

"It seems a little—" She paused, taking time to find the right word. "*Staid* for someone who's obviously accustomed to more action."

"Which is precisely why I'm happy with staid for the time being. Plus, there's Emma to think of."

Holly wondered how he'd ended up in America's most Christmassy town the single dad to a little girl. Where was the former Mrs. O'Halloran? If there'd even been one.

"She's darling. And going to be a heartbreaker when she grows up."

"Oh, Lord. I don't even want to think about that." He'd unzipped the parka he'd put back on to walk her to the cabin, and now rubbed a hand against his chest. "I'm thinking about locking her in a closet at puberty and letting her back out at thirty. Or seeing if I can talk her into a convent."

"Well, those are two possible solutions." She wondered if her own father would've felt the same way. Felt a tinge of the sadness at the idea she'd never know.

"Probably not the most practical," Gabe allowed. His lips were still smiling, but his heavily lidded eyes, as they moved slowly, intimately over her face, were not.

"What?" she asked, her voice uncharacteristically soft after another long, drawn-out pause.

"I was just thinking about fate." Thoughtful little lines appeared at the corners of those unreasonably sexy eyes. Once again demonstrating he had no concept of personal space, he ran a hand down her hair. This time Holly did not—could not—move away.

"What about it?"

"How if all of the events of the past few years hadn't conspired to bring me back to this place I always swore I wanted to escape, I wouldn't have happened to have been on that road today." He combed the long, dark fingers of his left hand through her hair, which was still a bit damp from having walked out into the snow again from the inn to the cabin. "Just a few minutes after you'd run into that snowdrift."

"It was more like forty-five minutes," she managed through lips that had gone ridiculously dry.

"Then I guess I'm damn lucky that fate kept some other guy from getting there before me."

At this moment, Holly was almost hoping that some other man had. Someone like, perhaps, Sam Fraiser, the owner of Kris Kringle's Workshop, out searching for his runaway reindeer. If only she'd been rescued by the village's own personal Santa, she wouldn't be so tempted by those lips that were getting closer to her own.

And she definitely wouldn't be going up on her toes to help him close the gap.

"Gabriel." His name came out on a ragged breath.

"That's funny." His free hand slid beneath the back of her sweater, roughened fingertips warm against her flesh.

"What?"

"The only person who's called me that since sixth grade is my mother." He drew her closer. "But it sounds really, really different coming from your lips."

He lowered his mouth and brushed at those lips with a feather-soft touch that was more temptation than proper kiss. The hand on her back was both gentle and confident as it pressed her even closer against him.

"Say it again." His breath was warm against her lips. He tasted of coffee, and cinnamon gum, and desire. A desire that was ribboning through her own veins.

"Gabriel." The archangel's name came out on a shuddering breath. "Please."

"Please yes?" His lips continued to drift over hers in a slow, lazy seduction that was as enticing as it was enervating. "Or please no?"

Although her taser pen was back inside her bag, which was currently lying on the coffee table in the other room, Holly knew she could stop him. She had, after all, taken that protection course at the police station, and while she might not be able to break bricks with her bare hands, she knew moves that could have him writhing on the floor gripping his wounded balls.

But she knew that she wouldn't need those GET skills with this man. Knew that she could simply step away and he'd stop.

But, oh God, his mouth was so amazingly clever. The almost kisses so tempting, drawing her into complacence, even as they excited.

Telling herself that it was only because it'd been a very long time since she'd been with any man, that this hot, intoxicating pleasure had nothing to do with Gabriel O'Halloran himself, or the admittedly unusual circumstance that had landed her in first his SUV, then his arms, Holly twined her arms around his neck.

"Yes, dammit."

Chapter Nine

She closed her eyes, expecting the former Marine to ravish, to take what she was so willingly offering. But instead, she felt the curve of his lips against hers.

"Well"—his voice, husky with lust, but tinged with humor, had her toes curling in her Uggs—"since you put it that way."

Needs. Hunger. Lust. They surged through Gabe, battering away at his hard-won self-control, demanding satisfaction.

In response to her demand, he crushed her against him as his lips turned hard. Fueled by his own burning hunger, driven by her uninhibited response, he wanted to devour her—her warm, ripe mouth, her hot, peach-scented skin, which was practically melting beneath his now roving hands.

His tongue was in her mouth, his hands were beneath the sweater on her breasts, and as he pressed against that soft, womanly place between her thighs, he felt about to burst all five metal buttons beneath his fly.

Too fast, he told himself as her mouth clung to his and her silky soft hands dove beneath his sweatshirt. Too soon. Although his aching body was shouting at him to take her the hell to bed, now, when he did make love to her, and Gabe had every intention of doing exactly that, he wanted to be able to take his time. To give, as well as take.

DEAR SANTA
137

When her greedy touch went lower, her fingers slipping between denim and skin, he grasped hold of her wrists.

Not yet ready to quit, he pinned her hands to the wooden post of the bed and slowed the pace, lips plucking at hers again, rather than devouring, his tongue leaving the lush hot moistness of her mouth to skim a slow, tantalizing circle around her parted lips.

"Dammit." His breath was rough. Ragged. His body ached and his damn heart hadn't pounded against his ribcage this hard since the last time he'd been on a battlefield. "Do you have any idea how much I want you?"

And because he did want her, more than was either reasonable or safe, he let go of her and backed away.

"I think that was fairly evident." Her eyes were wide, and just a little unfocused, which was sexy as hell, as she rubbed her wrists.

"You didn't say no," he reminded her.

"Would it have mattered?" On a flare of heat, she tossed up that stubborn, pointed chin.

"Hell, yes." She might as well have slapped him. "I've never been into forcing women."

"Like you'd ever have to," she muttered.

The mood was disintegrating. Like morning mist that rose from the lake each summer, only to be burned away by the sun. But her tone, rather than sexy warm, or even annoyed hot, had turned as chilly as the icicles hanging from the cabin's eaves.

Women, Gabe thought. From five to twenty-eight—and he knew exactly how old she was because he'd taken the time to Google her while she'd been in the kitchen with his mother—they could all be as capricious as the damn weather.

"You met my mother."

Because it was impossible to be this close to her and not touch, he linked their fingers together and led her out of the room and down the stairs, away from the temptation of that king-size bed.

Not that the lack of a bed would stop him if he put aside principles and just went for what he wanted. Especially since he was really, really tempted to drag her down onto the rug in front of the stone fireplace.

But hadn't he learned the hard way that people could get hurt when you only thought about your own sexual needs?

"Do you think she'd have raised a guy who didn't respect women?" he asked.

"No." Holly blew out a breath as they reached the front door. "And it's not just her. I watched you with your daughter. You're a nice guy, Gabriel O'Halloran."

"Terrific." Because his body still wanted her, still ached with the need for her, and because she'd just reminded him that Emma was waiting in bed for him to read the Grinch story to her, Gabe laughed. A harsh, rough sound from deep in his throat. "Kittens are nice. Boy Scouts and TV weathermen are nice. Believe me, sweetheart, a lot of the things I want to do with you don't begin to fit into that category."

He skimmed a finger beneath the eye that, despite the ice pack his mother had given her, was still blossoming into one hell of a shiner.

"You've had a stressful day." His mother's response to stress came to mind. "Why don't you take a long, hot bubble bath and relax?"

Hell. The words had no sooner come out of his mouth than Gabe regretted them. Because they stirred up images of being naked with her straddling his legs in that oversize tub. And afterward, smoothing lotion the scent of ripe peaches over every inch of her porcelain-pale skin.

"Get some rest." He plowed forward before she might just go insane and invite him into that bathtub with her. "Since breakfast comes with the cabin, and you obviously haven't had time to go shopping, I'll see you in the morning."

He skimmed a finger down her nose. Then, before he could change his mind, he turned and walked out of the cabin into the dark and snowy night.

Chapter Ten

Holly stood at the door, watching him walk out of the yellow circle of light from her own porch back to the inn. White flakes continued to fall, shawling silently over the land, and once he'd been swallowed up by the snow-swirled darkness, she could have been the only person in the world. Which was all it took to kick Holly's imagination into high gear.

She hadn't been all that wild about the cookie murders, anyway, having already written a black widow killer. But six weeks ago, although she'd never allowed herself to believe in writer's block, she'd run smack into it.

She'd always read three newspapers a day looking for story ideas. Desperate, and with a deadline approaching, she'd added two more papers and more magazines than anyone could read in a lifetime.

She began taking tabloids home with her frozen dinners from the supermarket. Okay, her audience might not want to read about bat boy being found on a melting glacier at the North Pole, or the *Titanic* being discovered by a lunar rover in a previously uncharted sea on the moon, but there were a lot of crimes profiled between those newsprint pages. Unfortunately, none had gotten her balky muses—who seemed to have gone into permanent PMS—to cooperate.

Neither had Court TV. Nor any of the other true-life crime

shows that seemed to run 24/7 on cable. It had been desperation, and a need to be anywhere away from home on Christmas, that had had her driving over the Cascades to Leavenworth.

And that same desperation had landed her in the arms of a hottie ex-Marine who had her feeling things she'd forgotten she *could* feel. Tingling in places she'd never known she could tingle.

But now, as she closed the heavy wooden door, she thought about all the things that might be lurking out there in the dark winter night.

Mountain lions, perhaps? Although bears were supposed to hibernate, surely once in a while a rogue one might come out of its den to go searching for food. Or wolves, which, thinking about it, the wind in the top of the trees sort of sounded like. Did they have wolves in Washington?

But even as that idea caused the hair to rise on her arms, she didn't write about killer animals. Well, actually she did, but Holly had always thought human animals could be far more terrifying due to their propensity for evil.

What if a woman was alone here in this very cabin while a serial killer lurked outside, armed, with a huge hunting knife— with a serrated edge and ugly blood groove—hidden in his boot?

But what was the woman doing here, out in the middle of nowhere? Perhaps her car had broken down?

No.

Holly shook her head as she took the plastic lid off the take-out cup and sipped the buttered rum, which while no longer ex-actly hot, was still warm. That was too close to real life. It wasn't always easy keeping fact and fiction separate, and bringing her own experience into her story could very well blur the line.

So . . .

She began to pace the wooden plank floor, her mind spinning with possibilities. What if it just wasn't a lone woman at risk— which brought to mind all those Halloween slasher stories—but a young mother? With a small son.

No. A little girl. With hair the color of a newly minted penny, who was clever and funny and chattered like a magpie.

Although Holly hated putting children in jeopardy, even in books, there was admittedly something visceral about the idea. Something that her readers could connect emotionally with.

"But what would they be doing out here in the middle of nowhere?" she asked herself out loud.

Running from something. Or someone. Hiding out. Perhaps to keep the little girl safe?

Holly felt a stirring in the far reaches of her mind and realized that she'd just hit on something that had appealed to one of those bitchy muses who'd been refusing to cooperate.

"That's it. She's running from her husband." A dangerously possessive psychopath who'd do anything, stop at nothing, to get her back.

Of course, she considered as she took another sip of the cooling rum, even if her beleaguered heroine knew every martial art in the world, and was armed to the teeth, she'd still be in danger.

Unless . . .

"There's a hottie sheriff in town." That worked, she thought. So long as he was self-assured enough not to overpower the heroine's autonomy. "Maybe former military."

She nodded, liking that idea. "A former Navy SEAL." Which was a possibility, but she'd also written SEALs in her second and fourth books, which had been set in San Diego and Virginia Beach.

"Maybe a former Marine." Her mind immediately spun up an image of thick black hair and steely gray eyes. "Who's come back to his hometown and taken on his father's job as sheriff."

That worked, Holly decided.

She went over to the kitchen table, where Gabriel had left her laptop, took it out of the case, and sat down to work.

As the words started flowing, like water from a magical well, and her muses finally began to cooperate, Holly decided that she wasn't the only one who found the hunky inn owner an inspiration.

Chapter Eleven

It was the knock on the door that woke her. Sitting up, Holly looked around the unfamiliar surroundings.

It took her a moment to realize where she was. Aha! The inn out in the middle of the Cascade Mountains, where she'd landed after wrecking her Highlander. She squinted, trying to read her watch.

"Ten in the morning?"

She never, ever slept past seven. Except that time two years ago, when despite having a shot, she'd come down with the flu. Or, when she'd been writing madly until deadline. Which is exactly what she'd been doing last night.

She vaguely remembered saving her story. Then e-mailing it to herself, just in case some crazy electrical storm surge might come along to fry her laptop.

Then she'd dragged herself upstairs where, because even with the central heat there was a chill in the air, she'd put on her flannel pajamas, after which she'd fallen into bed.

Then crashed. That had been, what? Two hours ago?

She thought about ignoring the knock, rolling over, burying her head in the thick cloud of down pillow, and going back to sleep. But what if it was something concerning her Highlander? What if the tow truck driver had already arrived with it?

Rubbing the grit out of her eyes with her knuckles, she

padded in sock-clad feet downstairs, opened the front door, and found herself looking a long way up into Gabriel O'Halloran's apologetic gaze.

"Sorry. It looks as if we woke you up."

"I worked late." She ran a hand over her hair, which, if it was behaving in its usual bedhead fashion, was undoubtedly stuck up in all directions, looking as if she'd put her finger in a light socket.

A small bright head peeked around his jean-clad thighs. "Wow." Bright eyes swept over Holly's face. "Does your eye hurt as bad as it looks?"

Amazingly, she'd forgotten all about that. Lifting a finger to her face, Holly couldn't quite refrain from flinching as she touched the bruised skin beneath her eye. "I don't know how bad it looks," she said, even as she feared the worst. "But it's okay."

"That's good. I had a black eye in September, after I got in a fight with Jimmy Jones—he's one of the big kids, in second grade—on the playground because he said Santa wasn't real." Pink lips turned down in a moue. "He's not a very nice boy."

"Doesn't sound like it, hitting a girl," Holly agreed.

"Oh, I hit him first," Emma said casually. "Daddy said I was wrong, even though he told a fib about Santa." She glanced up at her father, who nodded resigned confirmation. "Gramma was worried you'd be hungry. So we brought you breakfast. So you can eat before we go out and get your tree."

The scent of fresh brewed coffee rose enticingly from the brown paper bag Gabe was holding. As uncomfortable as she was, letting the former Marine see her in her flannel jammies and spiky hair, not to mention whatever her eye must look like, there was no way she could resist a morning jolt of caffeine.

"That's very considerate of your grandmother." She moved aside, allowing them into the cabin, and folded her arms across her breasts. "What's this about a tree?"

"It's an inn tradition." Gabe put the bag on the butcherblock counter, took out a tall cardboard cup, and handed it to her.

"Thanks." She took a sip and nearly wept.

"My pleasure." He skimmed a look over her, and amazingly, instead of cringing, if the light in his eyes was any indication, actually appeared to like what he saw. "As for the tree, like I said, it's an inn tradition. Everyone who stays here gets to choose their own from the farm."

"Thanks," she repeated as she took another, longer drink. It was hot, dark, sweet, and caused a much-needed jolt to her system. "But as soon as my Highlander gets fixed, I'll be on my way."

But not on to Leavenworth. After the nearly twenty pages she'd written last night, Holly had committed to her runaway wife and psychotic, possessive husband story. The cookie-baking black widow would have to wait.

"Ken Olson, of Olson's Auto Repair, took his tow truck out to bring in your rig a bit ago," Gabe said. "You've probably got at least a couple hours until he's got it back to town and checked it out."

"Well." Holly supposed she couldn't expect things to move as quickly up here in the mountains as they might in the city. "I appreciate your help with that. But I'm really not into the whole tree thing."

"You don't like Christmas trees?" When Emma's eyes widened to saucers of disbelief, Holly felt like the Grinch who stole the little girl's Christmas.

"I like them just fine," she said. "It's just . . . well, I've never had one."

Emma gasped. "Never?"

"Well, not since I was seven."

Gray eyes, replicas of her father's, narrowed as they skimmed over her face. "Wow! That was a really, really long time ago."

"Sorry," Gabe said as Holly choked on her coffee. "We're still working on the concept of tact."

"It's okay." Holly wiped her lips with the back of her hand. When Gabe's gaze followed the gesture, she knew they were thinking the same thing. Of that hot kiss they'd shared last night.

She could also tell that she'd hugely disappointed his daughter.

"Daddy grows the very bestest trees," Emma said fervently. "We could find you the neatest one ever. To make up for all the Christmases when you went without one."

"I think maybe Ms. Berry would just as well forgo the tree hunting experience," Gabe told his daughter gently.

"But, Daddy, everyone else at the Ho Ho Ho Inn has a tree." The little girl's voice rose perilously close to a whine.

Something occurred to Holly. "Don't you have school today?" she asked. Surely she hadn't worked through an entire weekend?

"I'm in kindergarten," Emma confirmed. "Which is just half days until I get to first grade next year. But we had a snow day. Which is even more special because now I get to go with you to pick out the most perfect tree."

Although the child was only five years old, it was like trying to stand up to a velvet bulldozer. Holly exchanged a look with Gabe. He shrugged, letting her know that it was her call.

"Let me get dressed," she said. "And we'll go see what we can find."

"Awesome!" A small fist pumped into the air. "We brought you doughnuts, too. Since you missed breakfast."

She held out the brown paper bag. There was a bear claw, a filled doughnut, and a flaky croissant.

"If I lived here, I'd be the size of Mrs. Santa within a week," Holly said. Then, seeing the frown lines on the small forehead, she managed a reassuring smile. "They smell delicious."

Emma nodded, the worry lines smoothing. "The lemon-filled doughnut is my favorite. That's why I picked it for you."

Holly lifted her gaze to Gabe again, who was watching her carefully. As if she'd hurt a little girl's feelings? Holly didn't know what the father and daughter's backstory was, but she did know how it felt to be a child and have your life pulled out from under you. As Emma's must have been.

"Lemon-filled are my very favorite kind," she said, then

watched him blow out a breath she suspected he'd been unaware of holding. She didn't care what he'd said. Gabriel O'Halloran *was* a nice guy.

Holly took a knife from the drawer, cut the doughnut in half, and put one of the halves on a small plate from the open shelf over the sink. "But I don't think I can eat them all myself. So why don't we share?"

"Okay." The cheerful child was back as she shrugged out of her coat and mittens and happily carried the plate over to the table.

"I'll be right back down," Holly said. "As soon as I get dressed."

She'd just started up the stairs leading to the loft, when Gabe caught hold of her arm.

Holly glanced back over her shoulder.

"Thanks," he said, with a heartfelt appreciation that didn't surprise her as much as it might have only a day earlier.

That he loved his daughter was more than a little obvious. Although she wasn't about to envy Emma for having the father she herself had always dreamed of, Holly nevertheless found herself warming to him. And not in the sexual way she'd experienced last night. But something deeper. And, oddly, more unsettling.

"I've never gone tree hunting before," she said. "I'm looking forward to the experience."

The oddest thing was, the words that were meant to reassure both father and daughter were absolutely true.

Across the room, Emma was licking lemon filling from a small thumb, oblivious to the look Gabe was sweeping over her.

"You look good enough to eat," he said.

She refrained, just barely, from running her hand down the front of the cream pajamas covered with deep red cherries. "If you're hungry enough to eat flannel, there's a bear claw in that bag with your name on it."

His deep rumbling laugh followed Holly up the stairs and

into the shower, staying with her while she quickly blow-dried her hair and tried to cover up the purple and blue pouch of swollen skin around her eye.

And his laugh was still there, warming her blood in a not unpleasant way after she'd dressed.

There had to be some kind of mind-altering Kool-Aid in the water, Holly decided as she headed back down the stairs to willingly go on a Christmas tree hunt.

Chapter Twelve

Emma was bundled up like a snow princess in her Hello Kitty pink hooded jacket lined with white faux fur, matching pink snowpants and boots, and fuzzy pink mittens, when Holly came downstairs. The expectation on her face was so bright Holly felt she needed to put on her sunglasses.

"Emma," Gabe said, not taking his eyes from Holly, "why don't you go check on Dog. Ms. Berry and I will lock up and be out in a minute."

"Okay." She obediently went outside.

"Now that she got her way, she'll be sweet as a sugar plum for at least the next ten minutes," Gabe said. His wry grin creased his cheeks in a way that made Holly want to lick those dimples.

"She's darling." To keep her hands out of trouble, Holly turned her back and slipped her arms into the scarlet ski jacket she'd hung on the wall hook last night. "And you're good with her."

"It's taken some adjustment on both our parts," he surprised her by admitting. "But we're getting there."

His fingers brushed the back of her neck as he lifted her hair from beneath the collar. Like everything else about the man, the casual touch proved unnervingly seductive.

"I don't mean to pry, but did your wife die?"

Emma's mother would have been young, but having written a serial killer who targeted soccer moms in her fifth book, Holly knew that youth wasn't always enough to keep that old boogie man Death from claiming another victim.

"No." His tone was curt, but in the short span of time it took for her to turn back around, his face had set in a not unfriendly, but unreadable mask.

"Sorry," she said as she plucked her knitted hat from the rack. "As I said, I didn't mean to pry. Besides, it's none of my business—"

"I'm beginning to think it just might be." He seemed nearly as surprised to hear himself say that as she was to hear it. "But, the thing is, it's not a pretty story. Not all that unusual, either, unfortunately. But definitely not something I want to talk about when I'm headed out on a beautiful winter day with an even more beautiful woman."

"Oh, that's good." She drew in a short breath. "Do you practice those lines? Or do they come naturally?"

"I don't know, since, having grown up with three older sisters who never let me get a word in edgewise, I've never exactly been the talkative type." He tilted his head and studied her, the same way he had last night. Slowly. Silently. Intimately. "Come here."

Holly could no more have resisted that husky invitation than she could have sprouted gossamer wings and flown to the moon.

"I thought about doing this all night," he said as he enveloped her in his arms. She felt her body melting. Degree by enervating degree. "About holding you again." He brushed his lips against her temple. "Tasting you again." His mouth skimmed down her cheek. Nuzzled her neck. "You smell like sugar cookies this morning."

"It's the vanilla in my lotion." She tilted her head, giving his lips access to that little hollow in her throat where her pulse was beating so hard and fast she wouldn't have been surprised if he could hear it. "I have a friend who runs a day spa. She creates personalized scents."

"I'm sure she does a dynamite business. But I have the feeling you don't need any extra embellishment." His tongue slid silkily up her throat, from that wild bloodbeat to brush the line of her jaw before encircling her lips. "Though I have to admit, sugar cookies are one of my favorite things."

"I dreamed of this," she said, as her hands stroked his shoulders.

They were wide and strong and capable of carrying heavy burdens. Just like the small-town sheriff in the story she'd stayed up all night writing. There was no point in denying that Gabriel had been her inspiration for that gentle, but tough, defender of women and children.

"Of you. And me. Together."

It had been after she'd pictured the sheriff shooting the psycho husband dead. Oh, she hadn't gotten to that scene yet, but she could see it as clearly as if it was running on her HDTV. She'd had it in her head when she'd fallen into bed, thinking of the abusive bad guy's scarlet blood staining the pristine moonlight snow.

Once again, justice had prevailed. As it always did in a Holly Berry mystery.

But her muses, and her unconscious mind, had a different ending. As she'd discovered when she'd dreamed of the hero making slow, amazing love to the heroine, in front of a fire blazing in a stone hearth, while the little girl slept the safe, protected sleep of innocents in her pink canopied bed upstairs.

She could feel his lips quirk against hers. "Was it a good dream?"

Holly tilted her head back. "What do you think?"

"I think"—his lips plucked at hers, punctuating his words as he made her blood sing—"that there's no way you and I couldn't be spectacular together."

And then, as if to prove his point, his mouth swept down and took hers. Hard and fast, the sudden punch of heat literally rocking her back on her heels, warming all the cold, empty places inside her.

It was the strangest thing, she thought, as the amazing kiss went on and on and on. His mouth was still on hers, but somehow she could feel it in every cell of her body. Shooting out her fingertips, her toes, curling in her stomach, making her nipples tingle and that hot, needy place between her thighs ache.

"If we were alone," he groaned into her mouth, one large hand holding her intimately against his lower belly, where he was rock hard and swollen, "we'd finish this."

"Yes."

Somehow, as he'd dragged her into the heat, both arms and one leg had wrapped around him. Reality had receded as he'd made love to her with only his wickedly clever lips, teeth, and tongue. At this moment, Holly would have said *yes, yes, yes!* to anything, everything, Gabriel had in mind.

As he'd done last night, he backed away. His hands on her shoulders, his eyes on her face, which, she feared, was not only bruised, but flushed the crimson color of her jacket.

"Unfortunately, right now, we have a tree to hunt down." He bent down and kissed her nose. Then her lips again, the brief flare of heat ending too soon. "So, hopefully you'll be issuing me a snow check."

"I think you mean a rain check." Although she'd never been the type of woman to go to bed with a man she'd just met, Holly was definitely issuing one to this man.

"Maybe that's what you call them in Seattle." He grinned, took away the leather gloves she was about to put on, and replaced them with a pair of insulated blue gloves covered with white snowflakes.

"My sister Rachel is a serious skier," he explained. "She was on the Olympic team that went to Japan in '98 and her closets look like an REI warehouse. Since your own gloves didn't look that warm, I stopped by her house this morning before coming over here."

"That's very thoughtful." They might not go with her coat, but they definitely looked warmer.

"We do our best to keep our guests comfortable here at the Ho Ho Ho Inn. And, getting back to my plan of nibbling every fragrant inch of your sugar-cookie-sweet body, here in Santa's Village, it's a snow check." He picked up the conversational thread. "We're a little different from the rest of the planet."

As she walked out into the bite of an icy winter's morning and saw the huge sleigh pulled by—count them!—*eight* reindeer, there was no way Holly was about to argue that claim.

"Blitzen, I presume?" she asked with an arched brow.

"Back left, right in front of the sleigh," Gabe said without a touch of irony in his tone.

She narrowed her eyes at the brown, antlered reindeer who'd caused her accident. In turn, he returned a blank, brown-eyed stare.

"So, what happened to Rudolph?" Holly asked.

"He's make-believe," Emma volunteered from the backseat of the huge red, gold, and black sleigh. Dog sat beside her, long tongue gathering in snowflakes that continued to fall like feathers from a patchy blue and gray sky. "From the song. 'Rudolph the Red-Nosed Reindeer.'"

"Of course. I'd forgotten that."

"I can sing it for you." Without hesitation, she began to do exactly that.

"There's still time to change your mind," Gabe murmured.

"No." Between the coffee and the mind-blinding kiss, she was already too awake to go back to sleep anyway. "Besides, I'm looking forward to seeing an actual Christmas tree farm."

The weirdest thing was, it was true.

Five minutes later, Holly was snuggled beneath a pile of blankets next to Gabe, who was actually driving the sleigh.

"You're very good at this," she said. Even Blitzen seemed to be obeying the light flick of the reins.

"I've had a lot of practice. Sam Fraiser, that'd be—"

"The village's very own Santa Claus," Holly said.

Although she couldn't quite keep the wry tone from her voice, there was no way she was going to question the reality of the man the little girl singing in the backseat had gotten in a fistfight over.

"Yeah. That's him. Well, he's been loaning the rig out to the inn for a long time. It sorta adds to the appeal, and bringing the tree back on that rack at the back of the sleigh is more colorful than strapping it to the roof of the Expedition. Also, back when I was in high school, I picked up some extra Christmas bucks driving tourists around during the holidays."

Picturing the teenage boy he must have been, Holly had no problem at all imagining long lines of high school girls waiting for rides.

"How does this tree hunting thing you've got going work during really bad weather?" she asked.

"I don't know, since this is my first winter running the place and we haven't had any so far this season. This storm might have closed the roads because of the snowpack and ice, but it's still nowhere near the blizzards the place can get. I suppose, if the weather got really nasty, most guests would prefer to stay inside by the fire and let me bring their trees to them."

That was probably the case, Holly thought. But as the harness bells jingled merrily, the metal runners crunched against the snow, and Emma segued into "Frosty the Snowman," she decided they'd be missing something special.

"Oh, they really do look just like Christmas trees," she said on a little appreciative intake of breath as they approached the acres of fir and spruce trees lined up like little blue-green conical soldiers.

"That's the point," Gabe said. "And I don't want to burst any bubbles, especially since you're not a real fan of the holiday in the first place, but although they're trained to grow into a more pyramid shape than, say, pine trees, they still need to be trimmed and shaped at least once a year."

"They're still lovely." Again, she meant it. "The only thing missing are lights, glass balls, and angels for the tops."

He bent his head toward her, lowering his voice for her ears only. "The angel's sitting right here."

"Flatterer," she said. When she turned her head, their lips brushed.

"It's not flattery if it's true."

He pulled up on the reins, clucked lightly, and the reindeer came to a stop next to a big gray barn. A huge fresh wreath made up of spruce boughs hung above the closed double wooden doors of the barn, and trees, wearing red bows fashioned from outdoor velvet ribbon, flanked either side. A hand-painted sign offered sleigh rides, cocoa, hot apple cider, free disposal bags, and the loan of saws and axes for the do-it-yourselfers.

"We closed down this past weekend because the previous owner always gave his employees the last week of December and all of January off to spend with their families," Gabe said. "But if anyone in town wants a tree, they know they're free to come cut one."

"Doesn't that invite tree theft?"

"I suppose it could, though there's not as much profit in second- or third-growth trees," he said as Dog jumped down from the backseat and set off across the field, snow flying, chasing after a squirrel.

"Poor guy never catches them," Gabe said with another of what she was beginning to think of as his trademark grins, "but that never stops him from trying."

"Maybe the fun is in the chase," she suggested.

"There is that."

Taking Holly's word that she could certainly climb out of a simple sleigh herself, he lifted Emma down.

"How can anyone ever decide?" Holly asked.

She had a vague memory of going to a neighborhood lot with her father, and him carrying a tree back to their apartment, but there couldn't have been more than twenty or thirty to choose among. Here the forest of conifers seemed to stretch on for miles.

"You have to look and look and look," Emma informed her. "But all Daddy's trees are the best. You can't pick a bad one. Do you know Nordstrom?"

"Of course." Part of the appeal of Seattle, when she'd been looking for a new place to live, had been the fabulous downtown flagship store.

"Well, one of Daddy's trees is on the front of their catalog this year."

"I'm impressed."

Gabe shrugged broad shoulders. "We're local. It only made sense."

Holly knew men, both in L.A. and Seattle, who'd be broadcasting such a coup through a bullhorn.

"Good try," she said. "But I'm still impressed."

As perfect as every tree appeared to Holly, Emma seemed determined to find the "most bestest" tree. This one was too skinny. Another too tall. A third's branches were too close together. A fourth's were too far apart.

"How about this one?" Holly asked finally, after the search had stretched on for an hour.

Emma's lips drew together into a thoughtful line as she looked a long, long way upward.

Holly, who was holding her breath, realized that Gabe, standing next to her, was doing the same thing.

Emma let out a long, happy breath of her own.

"It's perfect," she pronounced. "Better even than the one that lady from Nordstrom picked."

Not bothering to hide his relief, Gabe took the hatchet and saw he'd retrieved from the barn, and, after making sure Emma and Holly were standing out of the way, lay down on the ground and began to saw.

Less than three minutes later, the tree toppled to the snow. While he was wrapping the snowy branches in netting, Emma gathered up a handful of snow and, giggling, stuffed it down the back of Gabe's jacket. Which had him, in turn, expertly packing a snowball that he then threw at his daughter.

"Holly!" the little girl shouted as she ran a zigzag retreat through the trees. "You have to help! It's girls against boys."

Holly had never, in her memory, taken part in a snowball fight. But as Gabe chased after his daughter, Holly chased after him, throwing herself at his legs, causing him to crash to the ground, with her sprawled on top of him.

"Damn, you're pretty good. For a city girl." Wrapping his arms around her, he rolled over, so she was lying beneath him. "But guess what, sweetheart, you and half-pint over there just happen to be outmanned."

Laughing, and a little out of breath, Holly shoved against him. "Let me up, you big bully."

"In a minute." His body was warm against hers, his eyes hot. Holly wouldn't have been surprised if all the snow on the mountain melted from the way he was looking at her. "Your nose is red."

"So's yours." Reaching out, she grabbed a handful of snow and washed his face with it.

"You realize, of course," he said, using his superior strength to press her deeper into the snowdrift, "that you're daring to take on a United States Marine."

"Yeah, yeah," she responded breathlessly, as she wrestled beneath him. "The few." She scissored her legs around his. "The proud." Using the instructions the Seattle cops had taught her during that class, she managed to flip their positions so she was now lying on top of him. "The oversexed."

"Got that right." When he cupped her butt with his gloved hands and pressed her against him, she realized that he'd allowed her to overpower him. "As I intend to prove to you tonight."

Before she could respond, Emma had returned and was standing over them. "The girls won," she decided.

"They always do," Gabe agreed. "At least in this family."

"Why don't you kiss Holly?" Emma suggested. "To show you surrendered."

"From the mouths of babes," he murmured. "I hereby surrender to the superior super power of females." Lifting his head, he brushed his lips against hers. While still cold, they managed to send a burst of heat through her veins.

"Okay." Before she got into more trouble, Holly stood up. "On behalf of the female forces, I accept your surrender."

"Consider this lone, lowly male your prisoner. Do with me as you please," Gabe said.

"Funny you should mention that," Holly shot back just as Dog, looking like the abominable snow beast, came loping up to him and swiped a huge tongue down Gabe's face.

"God, I knew I should've left you back in the sandbox." Laughingly pushing the ball of wet fur away, Gabe stood up and began brushing the snow off the front of Holly's jacket.

She did not immediately brush his hand away.

Unable to remember the last time she'd felt so carefree, Holly laughed as they walked back toward the sleigh.

Memories danced through her mind. Of hot roasted chestnuts and gaily decorated store front windows, and holding the hand of a man she suspected she'd gazed up at in exactly the same way Emma was looking up at Gabe.

And, although it didn't make any sense at all, Holly oddly felt as if having landed here in Santa's Village, she was catching a glimpse of what her life might have been.

Chapter Thirteen

The excitement of the day had obviously gotten to Emma, who fell asleep in the back of the sleigh on the ride back to the inn.

"Blessed silence," Gabe murmured.

"I think she's darling," Holly said.

"You're not going to get any argument there," he agreed. "Sometimes, like out of the blue, it'll dawn on me that she's actually my child, you know, the seed of my loins, all that sort of thing, and I'll just feel knocked flat."

"She's fortunate to have you."

He shrugged. "We're both lucky."

Gabe knew Holly was curious. Knew he was going to have to tell her what happened. But since his mother had already warned him about Emma thinking that this newcomer to Santa's Village had been sent to be her new mother, he feared his daughter might just be pretending to sleep. She had, after all, proven herself to be a fairly good little actress.

He was going to have to talk with Emma about Holly. Explain that while Santa had many great qualities, and while maybe he might be able to fit a pony in this sleigh, which turned magical when he drove it, he wasn't in the habit of delivering actual *people* to good little girls and boys. He wasn't looking forward to the conversation. It seemed kids grew up way too fast these days, and his daughter was already five going on twenty.

"After I take her back to the inn and we drop off your tree, I'll take you over to Olson's, so you can talk to Ken about your Highlander," he said to Holly.

"Thanks. I'd appreciate that. I also have some shopping to do."

"If you want to make a list, I can pick some things up for you," he offered. "Consider it part of the service."

"That's nice. But since I have a feeling I'm going to be here for a while, I might as well check out the town."

"Your call," he said agreeably.

Twenty minutes later, he'd carried his daughter—who actually did appear to be sound asleep—upstairs and tucked her into bed.

"An advantage of living above the store, so to speak," he said as they drove the short distance to the center of town in the Expedition, "is that there are always a lot of people around willing to watch out for her. It makes it like a large extended family."

"That's lucky. Especially with your mother working there."

"Not just my mother, but one of my sisters. Janice, who graduated from Washington State in Hospitality Business Management, is in charge of the rentals. From keeping housekeeping on their toes, to arranging for repairs, decorating, the whole nine yards. Even mostly the kitchen stuff, though Mom's beginning to take that on more and more now that she's retired. Which allows me to concentrate on the farm."

"I'd like to make it a year-round destination. Maybe have some classes on conservation, invite the school kids to have field trips during planting season, and since it's located on the other side of the lake, maybe even get into boat rentals, bait and tackle, that sort of thing."

"Sounds as if you're really settling in."

"Yeah." Gabe was surprised about that. He hadn't been sure the move from California to this small mountain town would work out. But at the time, not wanting to leave Emma with sitters while he worked some 9-to-5 job, or worse yet, become a cop like so many ex-military, and like his own dad had done, hadn't been an option, either.

"Her mother left us," he said, deciding the best way to handle those questions she'd been too polite to ask was the same way he'd done everything else in his life. Just straight out.

"I'm sorry."

"I guess I was, too. For a while. But it was mostly wounded pride. And it wasn't as if we'd had what anyone could consider a real marriage. I met Lila while I was stationed at Camp Pendleton. She was a civilian secretary working on base. I thought she was pretty, which she was. I also thought I was the hottest Marine ever to come down the pike."

"I don't know much about the military. But from all those commercials I see on TV and in the theaters, I'd suspect that's pretty much the Marine mindset," she said mildly.

He chuckled at that all too accurate appraisal. "Can't argue with that. Neither one of us was looking for anything serious. Then she got pregnant."

"I see."

Gabe wasn't certain anyone actually could understand his and Lila's relationship. Since he hadn't understood it himself at the time. Not even after it had crumbled down around them, leaving a vulnerable little girl amidst the rubble.

"She didn't really want to be a mother. Had never planned to be." He remembered the conversation as if it'd happened yesterday. "Said she liked kids okay. Other people's kids."

"Not every woman feels the need to define herself by motherhood," Holly said quietly. He could tell she was walking on eggshells.

"How about you?"

Although he knew he was getting way ahead of the game, he'd wondered about that long into the night. As much as he wanted to take Holly Berry to bed, once his mother had told him about his daughter's belief that this woman was destined to be her new mom, he hadn't wanted to risk hurting Emma.

As Lila had told him when she'd greeted him at their house with her suitcases already packed, he'd already spent too many years thinking only of himself. Of his own wishes and needs.

Well, that had certainly changed. And although he wasn't going to deny that he missed sex—a lot—and there were a lot of women in town who'd been more than open about their willingness to let him put his boots beneath their beds, if only for a night, he'd screwed around with too many of those sex candidates in the backseat of his Camaro IROC-Z back in high school. And although those days and nights parked out by the lake had been fun, he wasn't really in a mood to relive them.

And then, as always, there was Emma. From what he'd been able to glean from their conversations, there had been more than one man in his wife's life while he'd been away keeping the world free from terrorism. No way was Gabe going to put a revolving door in his bedroom.

Although celibacy definitely wasn't a natural state, he'd been doing just fine. Until he'd driven around that S-curve and come across Holly Berry, who was causing all his good paternal intentions to pretty much fly out the window.

"If you'd rather not talk about it . . ." Her voice broke into his thoughts.

"No." He shook his head to clear it. "You'll probably hear different versions of the story anyway, if you're going to stay here for any length of time. You might as well know the truth. I talked Lila into having the baby. I promised that it'd be good. That we'd be a family."

"Like the one your mother and dad made with you and your sisters."

"Good guess. Being a male and pretty clueless about the nuances of relationships, I didn't realize that my parents' relationship hadn't come easy for them. That they'd worked at it every day. And that part of the reason for them moving up here had been because Dad had gotten so stressed out at work it was impacting the rest of their lives."

"Admittedly, I don't have any experience with a close-up and personal view of marriage," Holly said quietly. "But I suspect no child really understands what's going on outside his or her own self-centered world."

"That's probably true." He sighed. "So, Lila had the baby. I was in Panama at the time. During Emma's very short lifetime, I've done two tours in Iraq, and another in Afghanistan."

"That doesn't allow much time for being a husband. Or father," Holly allowed.

He slanted her a look. "Good point. And one Lila made right before walking out the door. She's now married to her former boss. A property mogul who builds shopping centers. They live in some McMansion in a seaside development outside San Diego. He's a nice enough guy. But he doesn't want kids. Especially one who isn't biologically his."

"That's his loss."

God help him, he didn't just *want* Holly Berry. He liked her. A lot. Liked her intelligence, her tenderness, and her matter-of-fact way of cutting to the chase. She might prove a challenge, but a guy would always know where he stood with her.

"Yeah. I remember standing there, thinking that here I was, a tough battle-hardened Marine who'd been on the front lines against al-Qaeda and the Taliban, but I had no idea how to take care of a little girl. Hell, the only thing in the house turned out to be Chunky Monkey ice cream and Lucky Charms cereal and since either my mother or the Marines had fed me all my life, I didn't even know how to make out a grocery list."

"So you came home."

"Not at first." He remembered those early days. "I didn't want to run back home to my parents because I think it would've been too tempting just to hand Emma over to my mother and sisters, who were certainly more than willing to help out. I'd missed out on most of her life. I wanted, needed, to build a bond between us before I brought others into our life."

"Well." She blew out a long breath. Her eyes, including the one she'd put a little powder on while he'd been in the inn putting Emma to bed, were bright with a suspicious moisture. "That's very impressive."

"No." Gabe might not be an expert in parenting, but of this one thing he was very sure. "It's not. Because women do it every day. All over America. The world. Hell, look how well your mother raised you, and I'll bet there weren't any people handing out single mother medals."

"She did the best she could," Holly agreed. "Under difficult circumstances."

Haltingly at first, she told him about her father's murder. Although he'd seen death, killed bad guys himself, Gabe found the circumstances of George Berry's death even more terrible. Especially given the way it had obviously shattered his daughter's small family.

"So," she wrapped up, "my mother moved to L.A. and, well, with all the palm trees and sunshine, we sort of just let the Christmas season slip away."

There was a lot more there she wasn't telling. Having spent the first thirteen years of his own life in southern California, Gabe knew that while it definitely wasn't anything like here, most people still celebrated the holidays. Hell, each December his mother had put a tree in every room, created crafty, handmade ornaments, and directed the kids' pageant at church, while his father would fill up the front yard with the plywood reindeer, snowmen, angels, and wise men he and Gabe would spend the summer making on the table saw in the garage. Thinking back on it, Gabe suspected their electricity bill between Thanksgiving and New Year's probably doubled from all the lights.

Speaking of lights . . . Gabe was tempted to suddenly look up and see if a lightbulb had just lit up over his head.

"What?" Holly asked, sounding defensive. And no wonder. Here she'd just opened up and shared a story he suspected she didn't tell often, if at all, and he'd laughed.

"I just realized why, of all the towns in America, my parents moved to this one. They've always been Christmas junkies."

"I'm beginning to think that may not be such a bad thing," she admitted.

"Well, you're definitely going to be making up for lost time."

They shared a laugh, putting their individual difficulties behind them as they enjoyed the moment. And each other.

Chapter Fourteen

"A week?" Holly blew out a frustrated breath. Dragged a hand through her hair.

"At least," Ken Olson, of Olson's Auto Repair, repeated. "Sorry. But this isn't the city. It's hard to get parts over the holidays. Especially with all the roads closed."

"But surely you have radiators." She looked around the garage that was packed concrete floor to ceiling with car parts that Ken, a major packrat, had collected over more than fifty years in the business. "Maybe a refurbished one that'll get me back to the city?"

"Well, now, I might be able to find one that'd fit your vehicle," he allowed, the unlit cigarette Gabe had never seen him without bobbing between his lips. "But the thing is, you've got more trouble than a radiator. Your fuel level float's flat busted, and the flange on your alternator's cracked, plus, your power steering pump's leaking fluid, the front struts don't look good, and I sure wouldn't want to send you back down the mountain with those brake linings."

He took off his red and green plaid wool cap with the shearling earflaps and scratched his head. "No telling what might happen. And without you having an airbag anymore. Well, shoot, I'm sorry, ma'am, but my conscience would just

eat away at me like battery acid if anything happened to a
pretty young thing like you."

Holly dragged a gloved hand down her face.

Then turned to Gabe. "I don't suppose there's a car rental
place in town."

"There's a small Avis outlet," he allowed. "Out at the airfield.
But they ran out of cars two days ago. And right now . . ."

"I know," she huffed, "with the roads closed, they can't bring
any more in."

"That's pretty much it," he said sympathetically. "If you
need transportation, the family's got enough vehicles to lend
you one."

"That's very generous. And I might take you up on that,"
she said. "But that doesn't get me back to the city."

"What happened to Leavenworth?"

"I've changed the story. I don't need the cookie lady anymore." She drew in a deep breath. Let it out. Repeated. Remembering when his sister Janice was studying yoga, Gabe
figured she was trying to find her center.

"Why don't you let me take you shopping," he suggested.
"Whatever happens, you're going to want some coffee and
chocolate, at least."

Her eyes narrowed. "How did you know about the chocolate?"

He shrugged. "Hey, I have a mother and three sisters. Plus,
I may not write mystery novels, but the M&M wrappers
stuffed into your Highlander's ashtray were sorta a clue."

Despite her obvious frustration, more, he suspected because she'd lost control over the situation, than the actual
problems with her SUV, she laughed at that.

"You're right. It's the obvious solution. And I appreciate the
offer."

After she'd settled back into the Expedition, Gabe said, "I
just remembered. Mom asked me to give Ken a message to
take home to his wife about the inn's Christmas Eve party. I'll
be right back."

"I'm sure not going anywhere," she said.

He walked back into the garage where Ken was standing beneath the lift, changing the oil on an old Dodge Charger Gabe's brother-in-law Jack had spent two years restoring to its old muscle car–days glory.

"Thanks," he said. "Appreciate it."

"No problem," Ken said, the cigarette clenched between his nicotine-yellowed teeth. "Glad to be able to help out by keeping the little lady in town a bit longer. Writes books, the missus told me. About murders and such."

"Yeah. She's good, too." Gabe had stayed up most of the night reading *Blood Brothers,* a story about good and evil twins.

"Doesn't look like she'd write them kind of stories," Ken said. "Figure that's more along the lines of a guy job. She's a looker, that's for damn sure."

"You're not going to get any argument from mc about that."

Gabe was halfway to the Expedition when the older man called out, "Good luck."

As he headed off to the North Pole Mercantile, drinking in the scent of sugar cookies and very desirable woman, Gabe figured that thanks to Mother Nature, he'd already gotten pretty damn lucky.

The market was a surprise. Although there were fresh trees and wreaths, which Gabe confirmed were from his farm, for sale in front of the store, and the expected towering pyramid of poinsettias inside, it was as well stocked as the neighborhood grocery store around the corner from her apartment. In fact, Holly thought, as she put a bag of pebbly Clementine oranges into her cart, it seemed to have even more fresh fruits and vegetables.

Gabe, it seemed, was particularly popular. They couldn't get down an aisle without some female stopping to chat. Most often that chat included an invitation.

"Sorry," he said, after the third such interruption, this one by a brunette wearing ski pants so tight she must've had to lie down to zip them up, a sweater beneath her open coat that looked as if it'd been sprayed onto her double-D silicone-enhanced breasts, and a pair of high-heel boots that were admittedly good-looking, but ridiculously impractical. If she wasn't careful, she could slip on the ice and break her neck.

And wouldn't, Holly thought acidly, remembering the way she'd put her hand over Gabe's on the cart handle, that be a terrible shame.

"Must be tough, being the town's hottest bachelor," Holly said dryly as the brunette sashayed away.

"It's a dirty job," he said with a quick grin.

"And how fortunate for all the women of the town you're willing to do it." She turned and reached for a blue box of pasta.

"It's not that way." He leaned over her, his chest pressing against her back as he reached over her head and plucked the box from the top shelf. "Actually, until you came along, I was living a pretty much celibate life." He tossed the box into the cart. "Let me be more specific. *Entirely* celibate life."

Holly glanced around. She'd never, ever thought she'd be discussing such things in public, let alone in the pasta and tomato sauce aisle of the North Pole Mercantile, but she had to ask.

"For the entire time you've been here?"

He nodded. "And the year before that."

"Wow."

"Yeah."

"I don't want to get personal." She lowered her voice. Leaned toward him. "But since you brought it up—"

"No, I definitely don't have a problem in that regard."

She hadn't thought so. "Still, that's a long dry spell." Even longer than her own.

"I was out of the country the first year," he reminded her. "And, like I said, I don't cheat."

Having learned about his wife's affairs, Holly understood the flare of heat he'd displayed when she'd accused him of hitting on her when he had a wife at home.

"The last year has been complicated. And, like you said, it's been a long dry spell." His pewter eyes swept over her face with all the impact of a caress. "One I'm hoping to change."

"You never know." She tossed her head in a flirtatious way that was so not typical for her. "Play your cards right and I might invite you over to dinner tonight. If you think you can get a sitter."

"Sweetheart, all it would take is for the women in my family to know I had a date and they'd be standing in line to have Emma spend the night with her cousins."

"Well, then. How do you feel about lasagna?"

"My favorite thing," he said promptly. "So long as we're having sugar cookies or peaches for dessert."

Because it had been too long since he'd kissed her—at least since he'd parked the car in the lot twenty minutes earlier—he bent his head and brushed his lips against hers.

Mindless of the fact that she was in a public store, Holly allowed her own lips to cling. And cling. Until the unmistakable sound of a throat clearing behind them broke through the silvery mist clouding her mind.

"Sorry." If he was at all embarrassed, Gabe didn't reveal it. He moved aside. "Merry Christmas, Mrs. Whetherton," he said with a friendly smile.

Beady black eyes as sharp and dark as a crow's took in the two of them. "Merry Christmas, Gabriel," the woman, who looked to be at least in her eighties, said. "And it's about time to see you spooning with a woman. Your poor mother has been despairing about you ever giving her another grandchild."

Her gaze swept over Holly, as if checking out her breeding credentials. "You'll do," she decided before continuing down the aisle.

Rather than be embarrassed, or offended, Holly surprised herself by breaking into laughter.

* * *

Because she wanted some time to herself to explore the town, Holly asked Gabe to take the groceries back to the cabin for her.

"It's less than five blocks," she pointed out. "I walk a lot farther than that in the city. And it's stopped snowing."

His forehead frowned. "If you have any trouble—"

"Gabe." She touched a hand to his cheek. "You're not a Marine any longer. You don't have to save the entire world. Besides, I'll be fine. Really."

"I need to split cord wood for the inn. I guess I'll just work off some of my sexual frustration on some logs."

"Don't work it all off."

He laughed, a rough, harsh sound edged with need. "Sweetheart, where you're concerned, that's not possible."

Holly knew exactly how he felt.

Chapter Fifteen

The town was surprisingly charming. Oh, overdone, certainly, if you weren't a fan of Christmas, but still, once you looked beneath the tinsel and trappings shouting out from the storefront windows, there were really lovely locally hand-crafted items inside the shops. Many that would easily belong in the trendy galleries of Seattle's Fremont and Pioneer Square neighborhoods or even Kirkland, known as the Monterey of the West, across Lake Washington.

Telling herself she wasn't really becoming a Christmas shopper, that she was just paying back a kindness, she bought a lovely cashmere scarf, woven by a local artisan, in soft shades of cream, moss green, and gray, for Beth O'Halloran.

Once she'd done that, well, of course she needed to find something for Emma. Which was when she decided to check out Santa's Workshop.

The building was housed in what appeared to be an old brick warehouse at the end of North Pole Lane. The minute she walked into the gift shop, Holly decided the place definitely lived up to its name. The floor-to-ceiling shelves were filled with dolls (cloth and baby dolls, with not a Barbie or Bratz to be seen), stuffed animals, and what, although she was no expert, even she could see were beautifully crafted wooden cars, trains, airplanes, and boats.

"Welcome to Santa's Workshop." A woman, wearing a red wool blazer over a cream ribbed turtleneck and an ankle-length, slim green and red plaid wool skirt, greeted Holly with a remarkably familiar smile.

"You're Rachel O'Halloran."

"Got it in one." The dimples that had been a dead giveaway deepened. "And you'd be Holly Berry."

"News travels fast."

"Honey, around here, it's like lightning. By the time you got back from cutting that Christmas tree this morning, everyone in Santa's Village probably knew your height, weight, hair color, and what you did for a living. Speaking of which, I like your books, by the way."

"Thank you."

"No, thank you. Sometimes life is just so damn cheery here, I enjoy diving into a good, gory murder. Especially on those days I feel like murdering my own kids. I have three, all boys, which can be a challenge, just like their uncle."

"Gabe was a challenge?"

"Since everyone already knows about you, including, now that you've gone shopping, that you prefer the yellow packet artificial sweetener over the blue, and that you're cooking my brother lasagna tonight, and it's obvious that he's taken with you, it's only fair that we women stick together. God knows, he's never been all that talkative, so I doubt he's shared that much with you."

Holly was beginning to understand exactly why Gabe wasn't all that chatty. Especially if his other sisters were at all like this one. "He told me about his marriage breaking up." The minute she'd heard the words leaving her mouth, Holly wished she could have called them back. Although obviously his family knew at least some of the circumstances, she felt as if she'd betrayed a confidence.

"Did he now? Well, that shows Mother's right. As usual. The boy's definitely serious."

Holly was equally uncomfortable that she and Gabe had

been a subject of discussion. One of the things she liked about being a writer was it allowed her to live a very private life.

"He's not exactly a boy," she felt obliged to point out on his behalf.

"Well, that's certainly true enough," Rachel allowed. "Going into the Marines really changed him from that hell-bent for trouble kid who wrecked that car he'd borrowed from Kendall motors when he was fifteen—"

"Gabe stole a car?"

"Well, he was planning to take it back," Rachel assured Holly. "It wasn't exactly his fault Margaret Whetherton was such a horrible driver. She's always been a menace. You've no idea how relieved everyone in town was when her doctor grandson came down from Bellingham and took the keys to her Caddy away. Now we all take turns driving her around so she won't feel tempted to get back behind the wheel.

"Anyway," she continued, amazing Holly when she didn't so much as pause for a breath, "Gabe wasn't a bad kid. He just wasn't happy about leaving L.A.—not that any of us were, but at least we girls had each other—and having your dad be town sheriff, as bad as it was for us, because of all the boys who were afraid to try to so much as get to second base for fear of Daddy shooting them, had to have been worse for Gabe because there was so much expectation put on him. Like what they say about being a preacher's kid. If you know what I mean."

She stopped. And flashed another of those smiles. When the pause lasted longer than a second, Holly decided she'd just been invited to respond.

"I can see how that would be the case. I was an only child. So I always felt like I had to be perfect at everything."

"That's exactly how I felt." Rachel nodded her dark brunette head. "Although, of course, I wasn't an only. But birth order has onlys and eldest, which is where I fall in the family, pretty much fitting the same model. So, are you here to visit? Or to buy something?"

"I was hoping to find something for Emma."

"What a lovely idea." She flashed another of those Gabe replica smiles. "Especially since she believes you're going to be her new mama."

"What?"

"Uh-oh." Gabe's sister had the grace to flush. "I guess I let that cat out of the bag. So, Gabe didn't tell you about her Christmas wish?"

"No. It didn't come up."

Holly couldn't decide whether she was glad or not that he'd neglected to share that little bit of information. Then decided it could've only made this morning's tree hunting expedition uncomfortable. But it did explain why the little girl had been so eager for Gabe to kiss her. Obviously she'd been doing a little matchmaking.

Which wasn't all that surprising, Holly decided, remembering how many of the men she'd tried to set up her mother with over the years. Including her fifth grade teacher, her pediatrician, and the guy who came by their house every month to read their electric meter.

"Well." Rachel tilted her head. "I guess, staying at the inn as you are, you would've figured it out pretty soon. Let me show you some of the stuffed animals Emma was looking at when she visited last week."

Holly was trying to decide between a fluffy panda bear and a pink and purple polka dot elephant when the door at the back of the room, which she guessed led into the actual workshop, opened, and a tall, lanky, silver-haired man wearing cowboy boots, jeans, and a western snap-front shirt entered the gift shop.

"Well," he said on a western drawl that possessed just a bit of twang. "If it isn't Holly Berry, come to pay us a visit."

She'd begun, just a bit, to buy into the tourism aspect of the town, but if this was the guy they were putting forth as Santa Claus, someone obviously needed to call Central Casting.

"And you must be Sam Fraiser?"

"That's me." He held out a huge hand that was nicked and scarred from a lifetime of carving wood. "Welcome to Santa's Workshop." He glanced down at the two stuffed animals she was holding in her hand. "Go with the elephant."

"I guess you know that because, deep down, you're Santa Claus?"

"That and the fact that the colors match her bedroom," he said.

"And you'd know that how?"

"Because she's one of those little girls who wakes up at the crack of dawn and can't wait for her family to come over before checking out her Christmas presents. So, she and Gabe worked out a deal. Instead of hanging her stocking on the family room fireplace mantel, they put it in her room. That way, she's allowed to look through it on Christmas morning while she waits for the adults to get things ready."

He winked. "Last year I put in a coloring book and a set of crayons that kept her busy for a while. This year I'm thinking about a Game Boy. They come in pink now, you know. And there's a Powerpuff game I think would keep her occupied until Gabe gets up."

"Whatever happened to handmade wooden toys and baby dolls?" Holly waved a hand toward all the shelves.

He slipped his hands into the front of his jeans. Rocked back on the heels of his Tony Lamas. "Do you have any idea how many children there are in the world?"

"No." She folded her arms. "Why don't you tell me?"

"A bunch. So, sometimes the only choice is to outsource."

"Of course." She gave him a long look. "You know, you don't exactly look like a jolly old elf." In fact, now that she thought of it, he was a dead ringer for Paul Newman. The older, still sexy one, not Hud.

"Yeah, I know." He rubbed a shaven jaw that was nearly as broad as Gabe's. "My wife put me on a low carb diet a few months ago. Said that with obesity becoming such a serious problem among not just adults, but children, it's important for Santa to set a good example."

"Your wife sounds very wise."

"She's smart as a whip," he agreed. "Has kept me on my toes all the years we've been together. And while I occasionally miss potato chips, and still have cravings for Mrs. Fraiser's apple cobbler, I've gotten used to it. For the children's sake."

It was a good act. But that's all it was. An act. And for some reason she couldn't quite understand herself, although she felt a little ridiculous arguing the subject, especially in front of Gabe's sister, who was watching with undisguised interest, Holly couldn't just let his claim go unchallenged.

"You're not really Santa Claus."

Blue eyes narrowed even as the friendly smile stayed on his lips. "You're sure of that, are you?"

"Of course." Oddly, since it didn't make any difference in the grand scheme of things, she was beginning to get frustrated. "I'm an adult. I know Santa doesn't exist. That he's merely a lovely myth told to children. Partly to get them to behave."

Fraiser rubbed his chin. "That sounds vaguely familiar. Maybe you've watched *Miracle on 34th Street* recently?"

"I don't watch Christmas movies."

"Actually, I know that," he said. "Which is a shame. But I was merely pointing out a similarity."

"Look," Holly said in an exasperated breath. "I think it's lovely that your family has run this toy shop for so many generations and that the things you make here bring children pleasure. I also think it's great the way the town reinvented itself to bring in tourism."

"Is that what you think we did?"

"Winnie Jenson, the clerk at the checkout at the market told me that the post office does a huge business postmarking Christmas cards with the Santa's Village, America's Most Christmassy Town postmark."

"That's true," Rachel entered into the conversation. "But

it doesn't bring in revenue. It also causes more work, which is why—"

"So many people in town volunteer to help out," Holly interjected. "Mrs. Jenson already told me that. And, as I said, I think it's a great marketing idea. But I don't play games, Mr. Fraiser. I'm a realist."

"Yet, you tell tales for a living," Sam Fraiser pointed out.

Damn. He had her there.

He smiled. "Take the elephant," he suggested gently, effectively declaring the topic closed. "She'll love it. Meanwhile, it's been lovely finally meeting you in person, Holly Berry."

It wasn't until the elephant had been rung up and wrapped in paper with a smiling, red-cheeked bearded Santa printed on it, and Holly was a block away, that his words sunk in.

"What did he mean, *finally*?"

The question puzzled her until she'd turned onto Dasher Drive, headed back to the inn. From what Gabe's sister had said, the gossip line worked at lightning speed in Santa's Village. Obviously Fraiser had heard about her arrival in town.

That settled to her own satisfaction, Holly began thinking ahead toward the evening.

Chapter Sixteen

Anticipation, Holly thought, as she bathed in the oversize tub—after stealing a nap so she'd be rested for the evening ahead—then smoothed on the peach-scented lotion Gabe had first mentioned wanting to taste, could be a bitch. It wasn't as if she were some virgin bride getting ready for her wedding night. She'd had sex lots of times before.

Okay, probably not nearly as many as he'd undoubtedly had. But how hard could it be? She not only wanted his hot, rock-hard Marine body, she liked him. Which was, to her mind, even more important than chemistry. So why were her nerves so tightly tangled they felt on the verge of snapping?

Her cheeks were flushed, more from emotion than the warm bath, and her hands were shaking so hard she'd nearly poked her eyes out with her mascara tube.

Somehow they made it through the dinner, which hadn't been that much of a problem. Anyone could throw together some lasagna, after all. She'd learned to make the dish when she was only a few years older than Emma, during a time when her mother's depression had kept her in bed for days at a time.

"If you want," he said, as they sat in front of the fireplace, sipping on the brandy he'd brought over with him, "I can come over tomorrow and help you trim the tree." A tree that was currently sitting in his garage because he'd warned her that if she'd taken it inside with all that snow and ice on it, she'd end up with it snowing inside the cabin.

"I'd think Emma would want to help."

"She's the one who brought it up."

"Ah." Holly nodded. Took another sip and wondered if bringing up the topic of Emma's Christmas wish would ruin the sex part of the evening.

"Rachel told me she told you about Emma." He'd put his arm around her shoulders and now smoothed a hand down her hair. "I hope it isn't going to make things uncomfortable for you."

"No." She'd thought about it a lot while soaking in that bubble bath. "I'll be careful that she doesn't get her hopes up and make it clear that you and I are merely friends—"

He lifted a brow. "Is that all we are?"

"Well, friends with benefits, which she doesn't need to know about. Don't worry, Gabe. I understand how vulnerable she is. And how much she wants a complete family."

"Yeah." He brushed his lips against the top of her head. "I can see how you would understand that."

They sat there, listening to the music he'd brought over that was playing on the CD player. It was something classical, familiar, but Holly couldn't quite identify it. She'd been grateful, after having the carols blasted to her from the loudspeakers all over town, that he'd left the holiday music at the inn.

"I read one of your books last night," he revealed. "*Blood Brothers*. You kept me guessing until the end which brother was going to turn out to be the evil prostitute serial killer."

"My take on Jack the Ripper." She smiled a bit. "With a touch of Dr. Jekyll and Mr. Hyde thrown in."

"Well, like I said, you kept me turning pages. My mother's obviously got terrific taste in authors, because you're really, really good."

"Thank you." The compliment, which, if she were to be brutally honest with herself, was just one person's opinion, should not have given her so much pleasure. But it did.

Silence fell over them again.

"This isn't as easy as I thought it was going to be," she said finally as she stared into the flickering orange flames of the fire he'd built when he'd first arrived.

He put a hand beneath her chin. Gently turned her head toward his. "I'm not sure it should be that easy," he said.

Gabe had figured out that nothing about Holly Berry was going to be that simple. Which was fine with him, really, because he'd never trusted things that came too easily.

"Admittedly, some people might consider this rushing things," he said, his eyes echoing his encouraging smile. Wanting to soothe, as much as he wanted to arouse, Gabe kissed her, a satiny meeting of lips, a mingling of breath. "But it doesn't seem too fast to me. And it damn well isn't going to end up a one-night stand."

"Not for me either," she admitted throatily.

He smiled. Took both their brandy snifters, placed them on the coffee table, then stood up and held out his hand.

As if it was the most natural thing in the world, she put her hand in his and together they walked, side by side, up the stairs to the loft. The storm that had brought all the snow that had landed her in the village had moved on, leaving the sky a vast canvas of black satin studded with icy crystal stars.

Silver moonlight streamed across the sheets as she pulled back the comforter while Gabe turned on the gas fireplace, causing sparks to flare.

Then he took her in his arms and lowered his head until their lips were close, not quite touching. "I want you to know, absolutely, that this is important to me."

"I do." Her breath shuddered out as he stroked her throat with the pad of his thumb. "It's important to me, too."

Those gorgeous creases in his cheeks deepened. Just when she thought he was going to kiss her, really kiss her, Gabe tilted his head so that his lips grazed her cheek. Her mind spinning, she moaned softly as his firm, but snowflake-soft lips skimmed around the curve of her jaw to her other cheek.

She turned her head, trying to capture those tantalizing lips, but his mouth deftly evaded hers, gliding up her bruised face, where she feared the heat raging beneath her skin had burned off the mineral powder concealer she'd applied so carefully earlier this evening.

His breath warmed the hollows of her cheeks, her temples. When it whispered gently over her eyelids, they fluttered closed and she forgot all about worrying about how her black eye might look.

She couldn't think. Couldn't breathe. Every fiber of her being was so brilliantly, radiantly alive, concentrating on the drugging feel of his clever hands as he undressed her, piece by piece, then following the blazing trail those broad hands made with his mouth.

Finally, it was her turn. Holly took her time, as he had, pulling his sweater over his head, allowing her mouth to drink in the taste of his heated skin. Her blood pounded in her veins as she stripped away the rest of his clothes.

Then somehow—was it possible to float?—they were lying on the moon-spangled sheets, hands touching, lips exploring, soft sounds of desire filling the air as they became lost in each other.

When Holly would have hurried, Gabe slowed the pace, as if intent on savoring every moment. Her body felt as if it had been turned to liquid, flowing heatedly beneath his touch, which promised erotic delights. When his fingertips plucked at her sensitive nipples, she arched her back. But already his hands had moved on, leaving only a lingering sense of pleasure and a steadily rising need.

His hand spanned her stomach, causing a weakening warmth there before continuing downward. When his tantalizing touch skimmed up the inside of her legs, and his thumb flicked against that damp, ultrasensitive place between her thighs, her entire body began to tremble.

Just when she felt on the verge of shattering, wanting, needing to treat Gabe to the same sensual pleasure, she shifted, so she was lying next to him, exploring his body as he had hers, entranced by the contrast of his surprisingly soft skin pulled taut over steely muscle.

She skimmed her lips down his damp chest and drew a shaky groan. Dipped the tip of her tongue into his navel, and had his fists knotting the sheets. The sheer masculinity of him was both powerful and beautiful at the same time, and suddenly, Holly wanted nothing more than to feel him inside her.

As if reading her mind, he caught hold of her shoulders and flipped her over, taking a moment to sheathe himself in the condom he'd placed on the nightstand after lighting the fire.

Bracing himself over her, he looked deep into her eyes.

"Now," he said.

"Now," she whispered.

He surprised her. Dipping his head for a soft, tender kiss that for some reason seemed more intimate than everything else they'd shared.

Their hands linked. Watching each other, they joined. Bodies. Minds. Hearts. He began to move, driving her deeper into the mattress, plunging into her hot slick heat until she cried out his name. When he felt the rippling waves of her climax, Gabe surrendered the last of his control. With one last mighty thrust of his hips, he filled her completely, giving in to his own release.

He could still feel her inner tremors as they lay there together on the hot, tangled sheets, pulses of passion continuing to spark between them.

"I wanted this." He lifted his head and brushed the damp hair away from her face. She still had a few red scrapes from the airbag and her poor swollen and discolored eye looked as if she'd gone ten rounds with Evander Holyfield, but he'd never seen anyone so beautiful. "From the minute you stepped out of that Highlander."

"I know." She smiled beneath his thumb as it stroked her love-swollen lips. "At least I sensed something spark. I wanted you, too." She smoothed a hand down his damp back.

Over his butt. "That is, once I got over worrying about you being a serial killer. Or a 5150."

"A 5150?"

"A crazy person." She sighed as he kissed her again. "On the loose."

"I am crazy." He deepened the kiss. "About you."

Not wanting to go into the local drugstore and buy rubbers for tonight, which would've allowed every damn person in town to know that he'd been about to get naked with Holly Berry, Gabe had been grateful that his brother-in-law Jack, who'd been trying to get him laid since he'd first come back to town, had shown up two weeks ago with an invitation to dinner and a box of Trojans.

The double date his sister had ambushed him with hadn't worked out. The third grade teacher had been sweet and pretty and had, with a few little hair flips and a lip-licking thing that women did, let him know that if he wanted to get lucky when he took her home, she'd go along with the program.

But there hadn't been any chemistry. Not so much as a twinge on his part, and if she'd been totally honest, he suspected she hadn't really been all that hot to jump his bones either. Just lonely. Or more likely, tired of being alone.

Which he could goddamn understand. And identify with. Just not enough to do anything about it with someone he didn't want to have to talk to over a breakfast table the next morning.

Rachel had complained he was too picky. That it was time to move on. Jack had suggested he just drive into the city, pick up some hot chick in a bar, and go for it without overanalyzing it. That, Jack had decided, was the best way to get over whatever mental block against sex his cheating wife must've saddled him with.

As much as he'd appreciated them caring about him, Gabe had ignored both their advice. But as the moon rose higher in the star-studded sky, and he and Holly Berry made love all night long, Gabe was damn grateful for the condoms.

Chapter Seventeen

It was a time of mistletoe and magic. Of cocoa, and carols, and walking hand in hand down snowy lanes. Although she'd spent twenty-one years of her life avoiding Christmas, over the next five days, as if determined to make up for all she'd missed growing up, Holly allowed Gabe to coax and cajole her into experiencing the joy and fun to be had during the holidays in "The Most Christmassy Town in America."

Although it had been obvious that Emma's sacrifice to forgo helping decorate the tree had been a matchmaking attempt, Holly insisted the little girl help, and as the three of them hung the wooden ornaments they'd picked out together at Sam Fraiser's shop, when Gabe had lifted Emma high to put the red-haired angel on top of the fragrant blue spruce, Holly felt as if they were becoming a family.

A feeling that intensified as she attended the school's Christmas pageant, sitting in metal folding chairs with the entire O'Halloran clan. They watched Emma, clad in a long white nightgown Gabe's sister Janice had sewn for her and angel wings Holly, Beth, and Rachel had spent an entire evening gluing sequins and tinsel onto, sing "Hark the Herald Angels Sing" and "Away in a Manger."

"I didn't forget my lines," she said as she flung herself into Gabe's arms after the play.

"You were perfect," he said.

"Better than perfect," Holly seconded. "In fact, when you were singing, I felt as if I was listening to a real, live angel."

Emma beamed. "This is," she said on a long, happy sigh, "my bestest Christmas of my whole life."

Gabe met Holly's eyes over the top of his daughter's bright head. "Mine too," he said, his voice roughened with the desire that seemed to grow, rather than diminish, each time they'd made love.

The auditorium was filled with parents and children. The scent of cedar mingled with the happy buzz of holiday conversation and snatches of carols as students continued to sing, not as a performance, but for their own enjoyment.

But all that faded away, and once again, as always happened when he looked at her that way, Holly felt as if they were the only two people on the planet.

"I'll make that unanimous," she said.

The annual Ho Ho Ho Inn Christmas Eve party, unsurprisingly, given that Gabe's sister Janice appeared capable of being CEO of a Fortune 500 company, went off without a hitch and was a smashing success.

By the time the evening had come to an end, Holly figured she'd danced with just about every male between the ages of fifteen and ninety in town. Including Daniel O'Halloran, a tall, rugged, still handsome man who looked, Holly guessed, exactly as Gabe would look in his fifties. He was also even less talkative than his son, which wasn't surprising, given that he'd spent so many years living with a wife, three daughters, and now a granddaughter who was showing early signs of someday claiming Rachel's conversational crown.

No longer bothering to pretend that their relationship was casual, after the last guest had drifted out the door, Holly went upstairs with Gabe and Emma, who, after a day of ice skating on the lake, snowwoman building, topped off by the party, had fallen asleep the minute her head had hit her pink Powerpuff Girls pillow.

It was like a scene from Currier & Ives. Outside the soaring window, fat white snowflakes floated down from the moongilded sky, turning the forest, and the lake beyond, into a winter wonderland.

Inside, a red and orange fire crackled in the grate and two stockings—one for Gabe and another for Holly—hung from the mantel. Emma's own stocking was, as Sam Fraiser had claimed, hung in her bedroom.

Holly was sitting on the leather couch in front of the fire, her feet up on the coffee table, sipping brandy, as she had their first night together, gazing at the Christmas tree that was decorated with the same wooden ornaments that hung on her own tree and the one downstairs, along with blown-glass balls Gabe had told her had been handed down from his mother, and red and green construction paper chains. She'd never felt more content in her life.

"It was a good party," he said.

"The best," she agreed. "That was nice of you to eat Mrs. Fraiser's pork rinds. I think you and your mother were the only two people who actually tried them."

"I didn't want her feelings to be hurt. They're pretty gross, by the way. Gotta feel sorry for Sam, being on that low-carb diet."

"Speaking of Sam, I noticed he wasn't at the party."

"Never is," Gabe said.

"Because it's his busy night."

"Exactly."

Holly was in too good a mood to argue something that no longer mattered. If Sam wanted to pretend to believe he was Santa Claus, what harm was there in the entire town going along with the idea?

"It's perfect," she murmured.

He followed her glance to the tree. "The construction paper was definitely the final touch."

Holly smiled. She and Emma had made those chains together at a table downstairs in the restaurant two days ago. "Definitely. But I was talking about my life. Right now, at this frozen moment in time, it's positively perfect."

"You know," he said, with what she could feel was studied casualness, "if you were to hang around here a while longer, we might manage to work our way up to absolutely, positively perfect."

"Why should I leave?" she asked with a feigned casualness she, too, was a very long way from feeling. "I can work anywhere. Everyone's so friendly and welcoming." She ran her finger around the rim of the brandy snifter. "And, of course, there's Emma. And Dog." She smiled down at the huge dog who was currently snoring away in front of the fire. But as soon as the lights went out and the adults went to bed, Holly knew he'd sneak into Emma's room. "And, of course, you."

"I saw this interview you did on YouTube the other day," he confessed. "While you were over at the cabin writing."

"Ah." She nodded. "I know which one you're talking about." She'd been nervous, as she always was when the spotlight was turned on her, but she'd thought it had come out well enough. "About life imitating art after that strangler appeared to be using one of my books as a how-to guide."

"That's the one. Anyway, you were talking about how you plot everything out beforehand, with all the Post-its and index cards and notebooks."

"That's the way I always worked," she agreed.

Until coming here. Every afternoon she'd spend two or three hours writing, and without any forethought, the words had been flowing as if from some magic well. Not wanting to send her muses back into sulk mode, Holly hadn't questioned the change in process. Just welcomed it. Although she did occasionally wonder if again, it had something to do with the magic of this place. Or, perhaps, just how Gabe had her opening up to so many new experiences and ideas.

"This past week I've been more of a go with the flow kind of girl."

"Then you won't panic if I give you something you might not have planned for? Something personal?"

"Well, I was really hoping for a George Foreman grill," she said on an exaggerated sigh.

Surprisingly, he didn't smile. In fact, he seemed unreasonably nervous. "Next time."

He bent down, and from behind the stack of packages beneath the tree, took out a small, gilt-wrapped box.

Holding her breath, Holly slipped the ribbon off it. Carefully took the tape and paper off. Inside the black velvet box, an antique diamond ring, set in white-gold, glistened like a glacier.

"It's my grandmother's," he said. "If you'd prefer something more modern, that's cool, too, but I knew if I bought a ring here in town, you'd hear about it before I could get it home, so I figured that perhaps, this could stand in as a promise, and later, we can go to the city, and—"

"Why would I want to do that?" she asked. "When this is so perfect?" Not just because she honestly found the filigreed ring lovely. But because of its history. A history that connected Holly with Gabe's family.

She slipped it onto her finger. "It fits." Perfectly.

"I'm glad." His shoulders, which had looked as stiff as if he'd been standing at attention on a Marine parade field, loosened, revealing his relief. "I love you, Holly. More than I ever thought was possible."

"I know the feeling." She reached into her bag and took out an envelope. "I didn't buy you a gift either, for the same reason," she admitted. "But I wanted to give you something. So, I wrote you this."

She'd poured her heart out for nearly a dozen pages. Sharing the years of sadness, some she hadn't even realized she'd been suffering. And how, since meeting him, her entire life had changed. All because of the wonderous joy of loving this very special man. And his equally special child.

She watched him, her heart in her throat, as he read the deepest secrets of her heart. Her yearnings. And her conviction that despite everything she'd been brought up to believe about fate being merely an appealing myth, her entire life had been leading her here.

To this place.

To this man.

When he lifted his head, his eyes were bright with suspicious moisture. "Thank you."

Simple words, but she'd already come to accept that Gabe was a man of few words. It was the emotions behind those words that counted.

He drew her into his arms. Kissed her long and deep. Then drew back. "Every time I look at you, every time I kiss you, I fall in love all over again."

She smiled. Touched her hand to his cheek. "Then don't stop looking," she suggested. "Or kissing."

"Don't worry. I plan to keep on doing it for the next fifty years."

"And then?"

"And then we'll just continue kissing our way to our centennial anniversary."

"Oh, I do like how you think," she said on a breathless laugh.

She was about to suggest they move into his bedroom where they could move beyond the kissing part of the evening, when he drew back.

"That's funny."

"What?" She followed his gaze to beneath the tree.

"That box wasn't there when I arranged all the packages before the party."

He left the couch again and picked it up. It was wrapped in green paper with Santa's smiling face. The same paper Rachel had wrapped Emma's elephant in.

"The tag says 'To Holly. From Santa,'" he read.

"Good try." She smiled even as she shook her head.

"I swear." He lifted his right hand. "I've never seen this box before."

Holly didn't believe him. But, because she loved him, she played along with the game, opening the package.

Inside, lying on a bed of red satin, was a yellowed envelope, addressed in red pencil to Santa Claus, postmarked twenty-one years earlier, from Los Angeles, California.

"It can't be," she said. When her fingers began trembling too much to open the envelope, she held it out to Gabe, who pulled out a folded piece of lined filler paper.

"'Dear Santa.'" He read the all too familiar childish printing out loud. "'My mama cries all the time since Daddy died. She says you can't bring him back to life. But this year, the only thing I want is a happy family. Like I used to have. Thank you and Merry Christmas to you and Mrs. Claus and all the elves and reindeers. Especially Blitzen.'"

"He was always my favorite," Holly murmured.

"Helluva coincidence," Gabe said.

"That's one word for it."

Gabe continued reading. "'Love, Your friend, Holly Berry.' There's a P.S. 'In case you didn't notice, being so busy with your toy factory and all, I'm living in California now.'"

"How on earth?" Her mind was spinning with possibilities. Dazzling, gilt-edge possibilities that were as wonderful as they were impossible.

"There's more. I think you'd better read this for yourself." Gabe handed her the letter.

Below the careful printing Holly remembered laboring over was a note, written in a big, bold, masculine scrawl. *My Dearest Holly. Please forgive the delay in answering your letter. Some Christmas wishes just take a bit longer to fulfill. Merry Christmas back to you and, of course, your own special happy family, Gabriel and Emma. Love, Santa Claus.*

Christmas Past

Mary Burton

Chapter One

Nat King Cole crooned on a bargain CD player as Nicole Piper set down her half-eaten peanut butter sandwich and picked up a Baby's First Christmas snow angel. She moved to a small silver vintage Christmas tree perched on her dinette table. The tree's aluminum bristles caught the light streaming in the window.

She'd found the Christmas tree at a fall yard sale. The tree's twenty-dollar price tag had seemed high at the time, but the vendor had assured Nicole the tree was a steal. Still, she'd worried over the extravagance and had negotiated the price down to eighteen dollars. Two dollars was loose change to most, but not for her. Her budding photography business barely brought in enough to support Nicole and her infant daughter.

The tree might have been unnecessary, but she was glad now she'd bought it. Its sparkling branches were not only festive but its bold, quirky style suited her new life.

Nicole hung the angel front and center on the tree, taking a moment to adjust it so it was straight. It was the only ornament on the tree. "So what do you think, Beth?"

Her eleven-month-old daughter lay on a blanket in the small

living room just feet from the dining area. Beth's feet and hands curled around a half full bottle of baby formula. She tossed Nicole a sloppy grin and went back to her bottle.

The child was oblivious to everything but her chubby fingers, which methodically closed and opened around her bottle. Nicole smiled. This was how it should be. It was Nicole's job to worry, not Beth's.

Nicole finished off her sandwich and carried her plate to the kitchenette. The apartment was furnished with a blue hand-me-down sofa with a pullout bed, which Nicole used nightly, a few end tables, a TV that only picked up local stations, and a round café table with one chair and a high chair. Near the sofa was Beth's white crib. Unlike the rest of the room, the crib was not used or hand-me down. It was a stunning piece of furniture that looked as if it had been plucked from a magazine. A gift from Nicole's friends, the crib indulged the only child she'd ever be able to have because of birth complications.

The third floor walk-up apartment would have looked a bit sad if not for the large photographs on the walls. Nicole had taken the black and white portraits in the last year. The nontraditional images had odd, quirky perspectives that completely captured the likeness and character of her subjects. Nicole made her living taking commercial portraits, but these images were shot during the precious free moments she had. They were also going to be part of a modest January show at the 1864 Gallery.

Nicole picked up a lukewarm cup of tea and sipped it as she stared at the pictures. They represented a huge milestone because they symbolized her return to the art world after almost a three-year absence.

When she'd been married to her late husband she thought she'd never be an artist again. All her energy had gone to surviving her husband's abuse. Now, the past was behind her and she was creating again. She'd forgotten how exciting and joyous it felt to see her photographs materialize in the developing tray.

To think she'd almost lost her art. To think she'd almost lost her life.

As if sensing her unease, Beth pulled her bottle from her mouth, craned her neck in search of Nicole. Seeing her mother, the baby gurgled.

Nicole grinned back and winked at her child. Satisfied, Beth returned to her bottle.

Beth's father, Richard Braxton, had been a charming, clever, and violent man. He'd lured Nicole into his life almost five years ago. They'd met in San Francisco when he'd darted out of the rain and into her studio. He'd quickly won her heart and before she thought, she'd married him. Within a year, he'd turned her life into a living hell.

Finally, after three years of marriage, she'd summoned her courage and fled across the country to Virginia. Not realizing she was pregnant, she'd changed her name and gone into hiding, knowing that Richard would kill her for leaving.

Those weeks had been tense and terrifying but Nicole had been determined to rebuild her life, even after she'd discovered she was pregnant.

Braxton, furious when he'd discovered she'd left, had tracked her down to Richmond, ready to kill Nicole and Lindsay O'Neil, the woman who'd sheltered her.

Nicole and Lindsay had been saved, but just the memory of that hot July day had Nicole crossing the room and double-checking the three deadbolt locks on her door. She'd been checking locks a lot lately. For reasons she couldn't explain, she'd felt that Richard had somehow risen from the dead and was watching her.

That was ridiculous, of course. "The man is dead," she whispered. "Richard can't hurt you anymore. The nightmare is over." Logic did little to quell the sudden knot in her belly that always formed when she thought about Richard.

Turning from the door, she stared down at her daughter, who looked so much like her father. Her dark hair, brown eyes, and long lean hands ensured that there'd be no denying who'd sired the child. And yet despite the physical similarities, Beth was pure light. No darkness. She was the best part of Nicole.

The front doorbell rang, startling Nicole from her thoughts. The baby dropped her bottle and rolled on her stomach to watch her mother move toward the door.

Nicole smiled at Beth and kept her tone light when she said, "Who could it be?"

The baby gurgled.

Nicole peered through the peephole. She smiled when she saw Lindsay O'Neil's blond hair tied in a trademark ponytail, which accentuated her sharp profile. Lindsay wore a baby front pack, which held her three-month-old son, Jack. She wore a lightweight jacket, red sweater, and jeans. In her hand, she held a brown shopping bag.

Sighing out her tension, Nicole unfastened the lock and opened the door. "Merry Christmas." Nicole tossed in a big smile, determined to forget her worries about Richard.

Lindsay grinned, leaned forward, and kissed Nicole on the cheek. Jack grunted between them, unhappy about being gently squished, and the women laughed. Lindsay, patting her son on the bottom, came into the apartment.

Nicole closed the door behind her and clicked just one deadbolt into place.

"So what brings you downtown?" Nicole asked. "I thought you'd be helping your mother-in-law with the big party." Lindsay's in-laws owned a restaurant called Zola's and each Christmas they closed their doors to the public and had a huge party for friends and family. Nicole and Beth planned to attend.

"I stopped by Audrey's early this morning. She's cooking like there's no tomorrow. I tried to help but she shooed me out of the kitchen. However, she asked me to drop these few things off with you." Lindsay set her bag down on the kitchen table by the tree and pulled five to-go tins from the bag. "Nice tree."

"Thanks."

"It's vintage?"

"So I hear. I just liked the way it sparkled."

Lindsay carried the food into the kitchen and stacked the tins on the counter. "Audrey thinks you're too thin. There's enough ziti and bread here to sink a battle ship."

Nicole laughed. Lindsay's in-laws, the Kiers, had taken her under their wing when she'd moved into this apartment. They'd given her furniture, rugs, and lamps. "That's sweet of her."

"This is your first Christmas with the baby. They worry about you." Concern darkened her gaze a fraction. "I worry about you."

Lindsay ran the women's center and was passionate about stopping domestic abuse.

"We're doing great." And that was the truth. "We're settling in nicely."

Lindsay held her gaze an extra beat. "You're sure? You have dark circles under your eyes."

"That's actually a good thing. I was up cropping pictures and framing them for the exhibit." She held up her hands. "Have a look around at my latest."

Lindsay's gaze trailed to the images as she moved around the room studying each carefully. She stopped at a black and white portrait of Kendall Shaw, a local news anchorwoman. Kendall and Nicole—the diva and the artist as their friends liked to say—were an unlikely pair but had struck up a close friendship when Nicole was pregnant. "When did you take this?"

"A week ago."

Moody shadows accentuated Kendall's stunning cheekbones and powerful eyes and the use of sepia tones made Kendall's skin look like silk. "Very powerful. Does she like it?"

"I haven't shown her yet." Nicole nibbled on her bottom lip. Like many artists she constantly questioned herself. "Do you think she'll like it?"

"Most definitely. And I know her husband would love a print."

"Good. Because that's what I'm giving them for Christmas." She also had a picture of Lindsay and Jack ready to give on Christmas Day.

Lindsay faced Nicole. "So you're ready for the show?"

"Yes. And it's exciting and terrifying."

"You'll knock 'em dead."

"I'm no longer the sad, desperate woman I was when I showed up on your doorstep two years ago running from Richard. Really."

Lindsay unbuttoned her jacket and Jack gurgled in his front pack. Beth's fat hands and sock feet slapped the carpeted floor as she crawled toward Nicole and, gripping the fabric of her mother's jeans, pulled herself up.

Nicole picked up Beth, unsure of why she'd just referenced Richard. She'd not spoken his name in more than a year. "So I hear that the Kiers' party is a huge deal." She'd been invited last year but late-term morning sickness and fatigue had kept her away.

"Oh, it is. It's an extravaganza. You haven't lived until you've seen the food."

"Can't wait." Beth grabbed Nicole's nose. Nicole captured the little girl's hand in her own and kissed it.

"David Ayden is also going to be there." Lindsay watched Nicole closely for a reaction.

Nicole's stomach fluttered. Homicide Sergeant David Ayden was a widower with two teenage sons. He'd been a good friend to her after Beth was born. They'd had dinner several times with his boys and Beth. He and the boys had helped move furniture into her apartment. They'd laughed a lot and despite the dozen years between their ages, seemed to be on the same page about so many things.

At Beth's christening, he'd pulled her aside and out of the blue had kissed her on the lips. The kiss had been sensual and so full of promise. An unexpected heat skyrocketed through her body. She'd kissed him back, wrapping her arms around his neck.

After the kiss, he'd said he'd wanted *more* than friendship. She'd been stunned, excited, and scared all in the same instant. Ayden's lean body, rawboned features, and thick blond hair excited her and she liked him so much. It would have been so easy to love him.

Love. Just the idea of love terrified her. She'd loved Richard and had nearly lost herself. And the thought of loving and losing herself to anyone else had her pulling away.

"*I can't,*" she'd whispered.

The desire and longing in his expression melted first to confusion and then to embarrassed hurt. Sloppily, she'd tried to explain, but she sounded like a confused child. He nodded, stoically accepting her wishes. She'd left the christening feeling awful. A few times she considered calling him, but never did. What could she say?

Nicole felt her cheeks warm when she remembered some of the sexual fantasies she'd had involving him. "He's doing well, I hope."

Lindsay arched an eyebrow. "The holidays are never great for him. His boys are going to stay with his late wife's parents this Christmas so he's covering the office. But he will be at the party."

Nicole remembered how his scent had clung to her hours after the kiss. "I'm glad. I'd hate for him to be alone."

Lindsay's gaze didn't waver from Nicole's face. "I saw the kiss he planted on you at Beth's christening."

Color rose in Nicole's face. "I didn't think anyone saw."

"I was the only one. What happened?"

"I just wasn't ready."

Lindsay studied her a beat. "That's fair enough. You had a lot of healing to do this year." A grin lifted the edge of Lindsay's mouth. "Still, just the mention of his name makes you blush."

Her face grew warmer. "I won't lie. The idea of seeing him again excites and scares me."

Lindsay lifted a brow. "I get the *excites* part, but why are you afraid? Ayden is not Richard."

"I know. I know."

"But . . ."

"But caring or loving someone is just too dangerous. The cost is too high if things go wrong."

"You deserve to have a good man in your life, Nicole. Don't let Richard steal your future."

The thought that Richard could still be controlling her made her mad. "He's not. This is *my* choice."

"Okay." Lindsay always had a sense of when to back off.

Nicole inhaled deeply to calm her rapid heartbeat. "So what else is in the bag?" She peered into the shopping sack and saw an envelope addressed to her. "What's that?"

"Believe it or not, it's a letter that was addressed to you. It was mailed to my old town house. I guess the sender knew you were living with me at the time. Anyway, it was delivered to the town house next door and the bonehead that lived there never took the time to drop it by my place. He just moved out and the rental company found it. They called me and I picked it up."

Curious, Nicole picked up the padded envelope. Her name and address were typed neatly on the mailing address label of an Alexandria, Virginia, law firm, Wellington and James. The postmark was August 15, a year and a half ago. Richard had been dead nearly a month when the letter had been mailed.

"I was curious about Wellington and James so I looked the firm up on the Web. They have a site."

Nicole laughed. "Ever the detective's wife."

"I'm a natural snoop." There was no hint of apology in her voice.

"So what did you find out, Nancy Drew?"

"Not much. It's a small firm owned by two women. Charlotte Wellington and Sienna James. Everything written about them was positive. They did mostly corporate work but have branched into criminal law."

Beth gurgled and grabbed the edge of the envelope. She'd have put it in her mouth if Nicole hadn't set her back down on her blanket and handed Beth her bottle. Nicole pulled the tab on the edge of the envelope and tore it open. Flecks of padding cascaded to the floor as she dug her hand inside. Her fingers brushed the hard edges of a DVD case. "What's this? There's no letter."

"Pop it in the DVD player and let's see." Lindsay's tone had grown serious.

"It bothers me that there's no letter." Hard lessons had taught Nicole that surprises never boded well. She put the disc in the machine and hit PLAY. Immediately, Richard's face flashed on the screen. Dark slicked-back hair and olive skin accentuated sharp piercing eyes and even white teeth.

Nicole's stomach immediately clenched and tears filled her eyes. Seeing him nearly made her sick. She had forgotten how intense and frightening his gaze could be. With a trembling hand, she shut the TV off. "Oh, my God."

Lindsay pushed EXIT and pulled out the DVD. "God, I am so sorry. I had no idea. You don't need to see this. Just smash it into a million pieces."

Sweat beaded on the back of Nicole's neck. "How could he have sent this? He died a month before it was mailed."

Lindsay pursed her lips. "No doubt he set something up with the attorneys before he came to Richmond."

"Richard was always good at looking at all the different angles." Nicole's hands trembled and a chill cut through her body. "I don't understand."

"I do. He figured if he failed to get you back, he'd have this tape sent to you. It's just another way to terrorize you." Lindsay shut the TV off.

Nicole pulled in a ragged breath. Richard's plan was working. She'd gone from excited and happy to terrified in seconds. Beth gurgled on her blanket. Nicole glanced down at her daughter and reminded herself she had nothing to be afraid of. Richard was dead. She was free. "Turn the TV back on."

"Nicole, let it go. You don't have to watch this. Don't give him the chance to upset you."

She folded her arms over her chest. "No, Lindsay. I need to see his face, look him in the eye, and tell myself I am not afraid."

Lindsay looked unconvinced. "You don't need to prove anything."

"I need to know I can do this."

"It's not necessary. I know you're not afraid."

Nicole pulled the remote from Lindsay's long fingers. Her throat tight, she reloaded the DVD and pointed it at the TV. She hit PLAY.

Richard's face reappeared. Her stomach clenched, but her gaze didn't waver. He would not rule her life. She would have the last word.

Richard's flashing white teeth reminded her of a hungry wolf. "If you're watching this, Christina . . ."

Christina. That had been her given name—the name Richard knew her by. But when she'd fled Richard and moved east she'd changed her name. At first the name Nicole Piper had been a temporary name. But after Richard's death, she'd discovered she had no desire to take back her old name. It had too much sadness attached to it. So she'd changed it legally.

"If you're watching this, Christina, then it means things didn't end between us as I planned." His smooth, cultured voice was maddeningly calm. Clearly he still believed that he was going to win their cat and mouse game. "But I couldn't leave you without a parting gift as a token of my love. Because, Christina, I do love you so very much." He smiled and absently adjusted the gold signet ring on his right pinky. "You remember Vincent, don't you?"

Nicole hit PAUSE. "Vincent was his assistant. He was a very nasty man who often did Richard's dirty work."

Lindsay frowned as she dug her cell out of her pocket. "I should call Zack." Zack Kier was Lindsay's husband. He was a homicide detective with Henrico County Police. "This is a police matter."

Nicole nodded. "As soon as I've seen it." She hit PLAY.

Richard continued. "Vincent killed that friend of yours, Claire Carmichael, that woman that helped you escape San Francisco."

Nicole could barely breathe. Claire had lent Nicole money and even found a beat-up car for her to drive. Later, Nicole learned that Claire had been horribly tortured. Her shop had been burned and all the evidence that could be used against her attacker destroyed. Her killer had never been caught, though police had believed it was Richard. But if Vincent had killed her that meant he'd gotten away with murder.

Lindsay pulled in a shocked breath. "My God. Claire's family was devastated by her death. They never had closure and still pray the murder will be solved."

Losing a daughter would be a fate worse than death.

Richard had paused for effect on the tape. Smiling wider, he continued. "If you want the evidence that proves Vincent killed Claire, go see my attorney. Her name is Charlotte Wellington of Alexandria, Virginia. Ms. Wellington is authorized to give the information only to you. Go to her and get the evidence if you want to prove Vincent killed Claire."

Nicole's eyes narrowed. "Why would he do this?"

And then as if to answer the question Richard never heard he said, "My hope is to prove to you that I didn't hurt Claire. I love you. I just want you back in my life, Christina."

Lindsay shook her head. "The man doesn't know the meaning of the word."

Nicole felt sick as she shut off the TV.

"Do you think he's telling the truth?" Lindsay asked.

Nicole's head was spinning. "I don't know."

"He was a pro at playing games."

Nicole sighed. "I know. But I owe it to Claire to find out." Anger overrode her fear.

Lindsay set her jaw. "You can't do this alone. I'll come with you."

Nicole shook her head. "No. But I'd appreciate it if you could watch Beth."

"Of course, I'll watch her. But you can't go alone. Let me come."

"No, Lindsay." Her friend's concern touched her deeply. "Richard is my mess and I plan to clean it up once and for all."

"Dad, I feel kinda like a creep for leaving you here alone at Christmas." David Ayden smiled at his oldest son, Zane. The boy had his mother's eyes. Caleb was behind him, kneeling and zipping up a ski bag.

They were at the train station standing on the platform. The boys were taking the train to a ski resort in the West Virginia mountains. He was going to miss them like hell but knew they needed to get away and have a good time. And his in-laws had been lobbying for months for this trip. "I want you two to go and have a good time. Your grandparents can't wait to have you."

Caleb rose. "Why don't you ditch work and come?"

"It's my turn to work the holiday. I've had the last couple of Christmases off." The department had given him the time after his wife's death. He and Julie had been married for sixteen years. She'd died of cancer. "But my number has come up. And your grandparents are so excited about the ski trip and I want you to have a good time." He could make it through a few days alone.

"Hey, why don't you call Nicole," Caleb asked. "I bet she doesn't have plans."

Zane glared at his brother. "They broke up, doofus."

A subtle tension settled in Ayden's lower back. "We were never *together*. We were just friends."

Zane stared at his father an extra beat. The kid had spotted the attraction his father had had for Nicole. Wisely Zane now decided not to share his thoughts.

The train engine released a whoosh of steam.

Ayden was grateful for the distraction. "You boys better get on the train. I don't want you missing it."

"So are you working the whole time?" Zane asked.

"Most of it. I've got the Kier party on Christmas afternoon."

"Ah, man," Caleb said. "We're gonna miss that. I love that party."

"I'll eat your share of pasta," Ayden joked. He refused to let his boys see that he was going to miss them. He hugged Zane close and then Caleb. "Don't eat too much crap in the dining car. Your grandmother is going to feed you lunch."

Zane grimaced at his brother. "Tell that to the human garbage can."

Caleb shot his brother a murderous glare. "Who's got the mega bag of M&M's in his backpack?"

They would go round and round like this for hours if Ayden let it continue. *Just put them on the train.* That's what Julie would have said. *Let the kids eat some junk. It's Christmas.* "Go."

The boys hugged their dad one more time and then climbed the three steps to the train. Ayden waited on the cold platform until he saw the two settled into their seats. The boys waved, trying to shoo him away, but he remained until the train engine roared to life and the cars started down the tracks. When the caboose finally faded from sight, he turned and headed to his car.

He crossed the parking lot and slid behind the wheel of his Crown Vic. He started the engine and waited until the heater had defrosted the already chilled windshield.

The boys were going to have a great Christmas. This was a good thing for them all. He didn't mind the work, and how many times had he wished for a little quiet in his own house? Only now he suspected the quiet wouldn't be a peaceful one.

Why don't you call Nicole?

The words rattled in his head as he put the car in DRIVE. He'd not seen her since April. Since the day he'd kissed her. He'd thought they had something. Hell, he was even thinking marriage. But she'd pulled away from him. She'd had tears in her eyes when she'd told him she wasn't ready. She wanted to be friends.

Friends. He wanted to be her friend. And her lover and her husband. He'd wanted to help her raise her daughter. He'd wanted the whole damn package. But he'd not been able to say all that. Instead he'd nodded, shoved his hands in his pockets, and kept his tone cordial. She'd said she'd needed space. And he'd been willing to give it to her. Only he couldn't just be friends. It was all or nothing.

Through mutual friends, he'd kept up with Nicole over the last six months. He'd not asked about her but listened when friends talked. Nicole's two closest friends, Lindsay and Kendall, were married to homicide detectives in his department, so he caught bits and snatches of information from time to time. Business was doing well. An upcoming art show in January. Beth was crawling.

Ayden had managed a few dates over the summer and fall. They'd been nice diversions but nothing had made him want a second or third date. None of the women had compared to Nicole.

"Shit." All or nothing had gotten him a fat load of nothing.

His phone rang. "David Ayden."

"Ayden, it's Lindsay." Her voice sounded like a whisper.

"Everything all right?"

"Yeah. I just don't want Nicole to hear me. She's in the bathroom."

He gripped the phone. "What is it?"

"It's not good."

Ayden's mood darkened as he listened to the details. "Send her to my office. And tell her if she doesn't come I'm sending a squad car for her."

Chapter Two

Nicole gripped the DVD in her hand as she climbed the staircase to the second-floor offices of the county's homicide department. Today, there weren't many people on the floor, which usually buzzed with ringing phones and chatter. The silence gave the place an eerie quality that underscored the tension radiating from every muscle in her body.

As she moved down the carpeted hallway her mind slipped back to the day she'd met Claire Carmichael.

The breeze of the San Francisco Bay had left her skin chilled as she'd pushed through the front door of the new age shop. Bells above her head jingled and the delicate scent of lavender hung in the air. Her hands trembled.

Her body ached inside and out and bruises darkened her arms. Last night with Richard had been the worst ever. Unprovoked, he'd hit her. She'd tried to calm him, but he'd been inconsolable. He'd pinned her on the floor of his office and savagely raped her. He'd told her over and over that she was his until he decided he was finished with her. She knew then if she didn't leave he would kill her.

As the shop's scents enveloped her, her heart was hammering in her chest as she clutched her designer bag close to her. She glanced out the picture window half expecting to see Richard striding toward her. She wouldn't have long before he realized she was gone. And if he found her . . . God, she didn't want to think how he'd punish her for this rebellion.

"Hello?"

"Be right out." The woman's voice was strong and cheerful and Christina remembered when her own voice sounded like that.

Christina drew in a deep breath. Everything was going to be fine. She repeated the mantra several times before beaded curtains behind a display case full of crystals and unicorns fluttered open.

A smiling woman with kind eyes moved toward her. She wore a loose-fitting dress and had tied her hair up in a bun. She wasn't much older than Christina but possessed a grace and wisdom that stretched far beyond her years.

"Can I help you?"

Christina moistened her lips. "I saw you speak at the community center a few months ago."

The woman's eyes sharpened. "On domestic violence."

"Yes."

"I remember you. You stood in the back of the room."

"Yes." It was all she could do to speak without breaking down into tears.

"You're in trouble."

Tears welled in her eyes. "Yes."

The woman moved past her, flipped the OPEN sign to CLOSED and locked the front door. "My name is Claire."

"I remember. Claire Carmichael."

She smiled. "Good memory. Come in the back and we can talk."

"I've got to get out of town. I don't have much time."

"Does your husband know you've left?"

"It's just a matter of time."

"Then we've got a few minutes."

"I have to warn you, my husband is Richard Braxton. He's a violent, evil man. If he finds out you helped me, he'll be angry."

Claire didn't hesitate. Bracelets jangled on her wrist as she wrapped her arm around Christina's shoulders. "Don't you worry about me, honey. I can take care of myself. Now let's figure out how we're going to get you out of San Francisco."

Nicole paused and closed her eyes. *I can take care of myself.* Claire's words haunted her. Nicole brought evil into Claire's life and she'd died horribly because of it.

She moved toward Ayden's office, knowing she'd do whatever she could to avenge the woman who had been so kind to her.

Nicole stopped at the office in the corner. On the wall rested a placard that read SERGEANT DAVID AYDEN. The door was ajar. She couldn't see Ayden but she could hear his deep, rich voice. It sounded like he was on the phone. Nicole drew in a breath and knocked.

"Yeah, come in." He sounded gruff, annoyed.

Feeling like an interloper, she pushed open the door. Ayden stood with his back to her, the phone pressed to his ear. He wore a white button-down shirt and khakis. Clipped on the left side of his dark belt was a cell phone and on the other side his gun. A lean waist accentuated broad shoulders and military straight posture.

When the door hinges creaked he turned. His expression was dark until he saw Nicole. For a brief instant there was a softening in his blue eyes and then it was gone. "Let me call you back." He hung up the phone. "Nicole."

"Hi." Her voice sounded hoarse and full of emotion.

"Lindsay called me and told me about the DVD." He moved around the desk. There was an edge about him as he moved and he radiated an energy that suggested that he knew how to fight if need be. He was a good father who had been a good husband. But under the calm facade lurked a warrior.

Suddenly she felt awkward. She held out the DVD. "This is what I received."

Frowning, he nodded. He took the DVD from her, careful not to touch her. Behind his desk was a small television equipped with a DVD player. He popped it in. "Can you handle this?"

She hated the idea of seeing Richard's face again. "Yes."

Ayden nodded and hit PLAY. His expression grew savage as Richard spoke. After the recording ended he shut it off. "I've heard enough about Braxton but have never seen a video of him."

Nicole swallowed. "He had quite a presence in person. He could silence a room when he entered." She remembered all the parties they attended and the strained expressions of the people he did business with as he spoke to them.

Ayden's jaw tightened and released. "I've already placed calls to the lawyer's office in Alexandria. Charlotte Wellington is not being cooperative. She's pledged to protect her client and has told me she won't release information to anyone but you. If I want the information, I'll have to get a search warrant."

She frowned. "It's almost Christmas."

"And there's not a judge to be found to sign a search warrant under these circumstances. None will be back until Friday at the earliest."

Nicole felt boxed into a corner. "I can't let Claire's parents go another Christmas without closure." She shoved her hands into the pockets of her black leather jacket. "This is so like Richard."

Ayden's jaw tightened but he didn't say anything.

She didn't want to drive up I-95. The roads would be jammed with holiday travelers and the weather forecasters called for snow. And then there was Beth. She couldn't drag the child along with her. Lindsay would watch her, but her friend already had a hectic schedule. Despite all the reasons not to go Nicole heard herself saying, "I'll drive up there now.

If I hurry I can be back by this afternoon. Lindsay said she'd watch the baby."

Ayden's frown deepened. "You don't have to do this. We'll have a court order by the weekend."

"Claire went out on a limb for me and it cost her her life. This is the least I can do for her."

"The traffic and weather are going to be a nightmare."

She managed a shrug just to show him she could handle it all. "It won't be that bad." She checked her watch. "I'll call you when I get back to town."

No way in hell was Nicole going to the Washington, D.C., metro area by herself today. He wasn't going to let scum like Braxton jerk her chain like this. "I'm coming with you."

She shook her head. "No. I can do this alone."

Nicole had to be one of the strongest women he knew. And one of the most beautiful. Even now, standing this close to her made his heart tighten.

"I'm going." His statement had force behind it. "Let me make a couple of calls."

"Ayden, you don't have to do this."

He reached for his phone and dialed a number. "Yes, I do. Besides, I wouldn't trust that car of yours to get around the block let alone up and back to D.C. today."

She straightened. "It's a good car." Claire had given it to her.

He grinned. "We'll take my car."

She started to pace back and forth. He could see that this whole mess with her late husband was tying her into knots. If he had his way, he'd dig the guy up from his grave and knock the crap out of him.

Detective C. C. Ricker picked up her line. "Ricker."

Ayden filled Ricker in on the details. "You can cover the fort today?"

"No sweat. Do what you need to."

"Thanks."

He hung up and moved across the room to get his coat off

the back of his door. As he passed he caught Nicole's scent. Soft. Delicate. Like her. She wore faded jeans and a loose sweater but neither hid the curves of her figure. Her hips had rounded a little since her pregnancy but it suited her. He much preferred this look to the images he'd seen of her when she'd lived with her husband. The one picture that stuck in his mind had been taken at a charity ball. Her too-thin frame was clad in a red designer gown and her long, ebony hair and makeup had been professionally done. As stunning as she was, she'd reminded him of a plastic doll not a woman.

Now thick hair hung in a loose shag around her face and she wore only a hint of makeup. The combined effect made it hard for him not to stare. He'd hoped maybe these last few months would have tempered his response to her but they hadn't. If anything, it had magnified.

He shrugged on a gray overcoat. "Let's get going."

"Ayden, please stay. You don't have to do this."

"My boys are out of town and there is nothing happening here. And, like you said, we'll be back by dinner."

A crease knotted her forehead. "I don't like taking help."

"There is pride and then there is foolishness. Besides, we both know Braxton was a sneaky bastard. Who the hell knows what is waiting for you up there?"

She nibbled her lip. "I hadn't thought about that."

"Braxton was never honest or predictable and there is no reason why he should start being upfront now."

She considered his words. "You're right. I'm rushing in like a fool."

"You're no fool. You're trusting and kind. He knew that when he made the tape and he is taking advantage of it."

He pressed his hand into the small of her back and guided her out of the office. They moved past the cubicles, down the steps, and out to the parking lot where his dark Crown Vic was parked. A blast of cold air cut across the asphalt making her wince. Her leather coat wasn't heavy duty and he almost chided her for the choice. He stopped himself. She didn't need another man telling her how to live her life.

Ayden opened the door and she slid into the cold interior. He moved around the front of the car, got behind the wheel, and fired up the engine. He turned on the heater but cold air blasted them. "It'll take a moment to heat up."

"I'm fine."

"Your lips are blue."

She arched an eyebrow. "It's the newest shade this season."

He grinned, put the car in gear and headed toward the main road. "Pink looks better on you."

A silence settled over the car as he maneuvered through the traffic on Parham Road and got onto the interstate. Soon, they were northbound on I-95. "With luck it'll be less than two hours."

The heater finally was pushing out warm air and she held her hands to the vent. Her nails were short and her hands chafed.

"You've been working in the darkroom again." He kept his gaze on the road ahead but out of the corner of his eye he saw her turn to him.

"How'd you know that?"

"Your hands. Looks like you've been using developing chemicals. And I remember you saying the commercial stuff is mostly digital now."

She curled her fingers as if to hide their rough edges. "I heard you were a good detective."

He wanted to keep the conversation light and away from Braxton. "So I'm right."

"You are. I've got a show opening in January. Nothing huge, but it's a start."

"Congratulations. That's no small feat. You must be busy."

A half smile tugged at the edge of her lips. "Most days I barely have time to brush my hair. Between the baby and the business and the art there's barely time to breathe, but somehow it's all coming together."

No mention of a man. Good. "You're still doing mostly portraits?"

"You remembered?" She sounded shocked.

He remembered everything about her. "You said something once about not doing landscapes anymore. That people were more your style now."

She relaxed when she talked about her work. "That's right. Something in me changed, so it stands to reason the art would change as well."

He fumbled to find more things to talk to her about. "How's Beth doing?" He'd thought he was over the baby phase in his life and didn't want more children, but he'd fallen for that little girl as hard as he had for Nicole.

Nicole's eyes glistened with pride. "She's great. She's crawling now."

"Tearing the place up?"

"Every chance she gets." She shifted toward him. "How are the boys?"

"Great. Zane was accepted to Virginia Tech."

"Wonderful. And Caleb, he should be looking at college soon."

"He wants to go to Tech, but his grades are borderline. We'll see."

If his two teenage sons were in the backseat they'd be busting a gut laughing watching their old man struggle to make conversation. He never lacked for words when it came to them or to work. But with Nicole the sentences did not flow. He wanted to talk about the kiss they'd shared in April and if she was ready for more now. But he didn't want to push her. So he lapsed into silence and kept his mind on the thickening traffic. At the horizon a thick band of gray clouds promised snow. As awkward as all this was, he'd never have let her go alone.

As minutes passed, he noticed that Nicole folded and unfolded her fingers a few times. Something was on her mind.

Finally, she turned in the seat and faced him. "I owe you an apology."

That caught him short. "How so?"

She moistened her lips, hesitating, as she seemed to gather her thoughts. "Back in April. When you kissed me."

Her candor surprised him a little. He cleared his throat. "Nothing to apologize for."

"I gave you really mixed signals that day."

"You had a lot on your plate. It's okay to not always know what you want."

She sighed. "It's not that simple. I mean, I really liked it when you kissed me. It was a great kiss."

"But . . ."

"But it felt like everything between us was happening so fast."

"You're right. We were getting close quickly." He'd welcomed the fast pace.

She smoothed her hands over her jeans. "My courtship with Richard was very quick. I jumped in without thinking. I swore I'd never do that again."

He didn't like any comparison to Braxton. "I would never hurt you."

"I know." She pressed her fingers to her forehead. "I'm messing this up. I know *you* would never hurt me."

When Ayden's wife had been alive, they could read each other's thoughts. With Nicole it was all uncharted territory. Frightening and exciting. "So your point is?"

"When you kissed me, I hadn't felt like *that* in a really long time. It just about knocked me off my feet. And I guess that kind of intensity scared me."

"Fair enough." Gratefully, his voice remained steady.

She moistened her lips. "I'm not in a position to make any promises or commitments, but if you want to get together again, I'd like that."

He gripped the steering wheel, praying he kept the car on the road. "Define together."

She didn't answer right away. "Sex."

As much as he wanted her in his bed and his life, he hesitated, "Why are you bringing this up now?"

"I don't know. I guess that video kinda rattled my world. I mean, the feelings for you have always been there, but the video reminded me we only have today."

"Okay." He could barely process this. "Are you sure this isn't about getting back at Braxton?"

She thought for a moment. "No, it's not."

He believed her. "Okay."

"I'll warn you. It's been a while and I might not be any good at it anymore."

"I doubt that's true."

"How do you know?"

"The way you kissed me in April."

"Oh." A frown creased her forehead. "That was good?"

"Yeah."

She tugged at a loose thread on her cuff. "Just remember I can't make a commitment."

"What makes you think I want one?"

She blinked. "Because that's the kind of guy you are. Rock solid. The marrying kind. I don't know if I'll ever marry again."

She was right. He did want her long term. But if this was all she could give him, then so be it. "All right."

"All right, what?"

"I accept your terms. Sex with no commitment."

Surprise widened her eyes a fraction. "I don't believe you."

He glanced at her and held her gaze just for a moment. "I'm fine with that."

Nicole blushed. "Oh."

"Surprised?"

"Well, yeah." She shook her head.

"What's the term? Friends with benefits?"

She laughed. "Yeah."

"We're still friends, I hope?"

"Of course."

"Well, then we'll work the benefits out."

She shoved her fingers through her hair. "Okay."

He was glad to see he wasn't the only one who was nervous. Unsure of what else to say, he sunk into a silence and kept his attention on the I-95 traffic. Snow had started to fall and it was getting harder and harder to see. The traffic was beyond thick now and cars were bumper to bumper the last few miles.

Soon they took the eastern side of the beltway around the Washington, D.C., metro area and took the Old Towne Alexandria exit. They wound their way through snowy cobblestone streets until they reached the law offices of Wellington and James. Ayden parked the car in the firm's lot.

"This weather isn't looking so good," he said.

The clouds were gray and plump with moisture. "Do you think we'll be able to get back tonight?"

"I don't know. We'll know better when we get a look at the roads after this meeting."

"Maybe it'll go quickly?"

He wasn't optimistic. "Let's hope."

They got out of the car and he met her on her side. Nicole was very aware of him—his scent, the way he towered over her, and the firm pressure of his hand on the small of her back. A jolt of energy shot up her arm.

He guided her into the law offices of Wellington and James. The building was located on Union Street and was at least a hundred years old. It had a brick facade and steps and black wrought iron railing. The front door was painted a bright red and a brass knocker hung in the center. A full lush green wreath with a velvet crimson bow hung from the door.

Ayden pushed open the door and they entered the lobby. The reception area was small but nicely decorated. It wasn't to her tastes—very colonial and very old Virginia. But it was nice. A Chippendale couch and chair hugged the exterior walls and an Oriental rug warmed the floor. A mahogany desk with a state of the art phone sat across from them. It all looked antique and expensive.

"This would have been the kind of place Richard would

have chosen," she said. "It would have suited his ego to know he had an old firm that was well connected. He always insisted on the best."

"We'll see."

Despite the wreath on the outside door, no Christmas decorations adorned the interior. And no one sat at the receptionist desk to greet them. They stood there for a couple of minutes before Ayden cleared his throat. Seconds later they heard quick, purposeful footsteps in the back hallway.

A woman appeared. She was dressed in a sleek dark suit, white shirt, and tasteful pearls. Rich, full, auburn hair hung around her shoulders and framed an oval face. A high slash of cheekbones made her look like a model.

Nicole shifted her stance when she got a good look at the lawyer. This woman would have been Richard's type. He liked polish and sophistication. The bastard had tried to ingrain that same sleekness in her. On their first date he'd suggested that a change in her eye shadow would enhance her eyes. And like a fool she'd changed the shade for him.

Nicole glanced at her faded jeans, old sweater, and scuffed leather jacket. She took a perverse satisfaction in her disheveled appearance, knowing Richard would have been appalled.

"May I help you?" The woman's voice was as cultured as her appearance.

"I'm Nicole Piper," she said clearly. "I received a package from your office. You have something for me."

"I'm Sergeant David Ayden. I called earlier," Ayden added.

The woman lifted a brow as her gaze settled on Ayden. "You called about Christina Braxton."

"I no longer use that name," Nicole said.

The woman's gaze flickered to her, but she showed no reaction to the comment. She was clearly accustomed to hiding her thoughts. "My name is Charlotte Wellington." She extended a manicured hand. She possessed a surprisingly strong grip. "It's so nice to meet you."

Ms. Wellington released her hand and took Ayden's. She

held his hand an extra beat, a subtle appreciation glowing in her eyes.

Nicole felt a pang of jealousy but tamped it down. Ayden wasn't hers. She had no holds on him.

Amusement flickered in Ms. Wellington's eyes when she looked at Nicole. "If you two will follow me into the conference room, I will get your file."

The two followed Ms. Wellington down a short hall. Off to the side was a small conference room with a round table. The walls were painted cream and paintings of various English hunt scenes decorated the walls.

As Nicole shrugged off her dark jacket, Ayden moved behind her and reached for it. This close, his scent enveloped her and his fingertips brushed her bare skin at the nape of her neck as he pulled the jacket from her. The innocent touch set her nerves on fire.

Ayden seemed unmoved as he draped it over an empty chair. Her heart was racing. He shrugged off his own coat, laid it over hers and took the seat beside her. Broad shoulders brushed hers.

"This should be interesting," he said.

"Yes."

"Are you okay?"

She wasn't even close to okay. "I just want this over with."

"It will be soon."

Ms. Wellington returned and sat at the head of the table. "Please excuse the lack of staff today. I let everyone go early for the holidays."

"Thank you for staying to see us," Ayden said.

"Are the roads as bad as I think?" she said easily.

"Not too bad yet, but they'll be a mess soon enough," Ayden said.

Ms. Wellington nodded. "They're calling for five inches."

Nicole tempered her rising temper. She'd lost all patience for polite conversation since she'd left Richard. "Can you tell me what Richard left me?"

"Yes." She removed an unopened manila envelope from her folder. "Mr. Braxton retained my services about eighteen months ago."

"In July?" Ayden asked.

"Yes. He stopped by only briefly and appeared to be in a rush."

Nicole's insides tightened with anger. Her husband had been in a rush to get to Richmond, so that he could kill her. "May I see the envelope?"

Ms. Wellington pressed long fingers over the folder. "First I will need to see identification."

"That may be a problem," Nicole said. "As I said, I have changed my name."

The woman lifted a brow. "Do you have anything that identifies you as Christina Braxton?"

"No. I didn't bring anything with that name on it when I left California. My driver's license says Nicole Piper. And you addressed the envelope to Nicole Piper."

Ms. Wellington pursed her lips. "But I'm to give this information only to Christina Braxton. Unless you have identification, I cannot release the information to you. Mr. Braxton was very specific. He only wanted me to give the envelope to Christina Braxton."

Frustration ate at Nicole. Everywhere she turned Richard was screwing with her life. "I don't know what to tell you."

"Can you give me your social security number?" the attorney asked.

Nicole drew in a breath. She rattled off the number.

Ms. Wellington raised an eyebrow and nodded. "And your home address in California?"

Nicole held a tart remark. "Twenty-three Pacific Breeze."

"Correct again."

Nicole leaned forward. "And just to save you the trouble of asking, Richard's middle name was Alonzo. His mother's maiden name was Rodriguez and his birthday was May second."

Ms. Wellington met her gaze and held it a moment. "You've made your point."

"May I see the folder?" Her patience was ready to snap.

"Just sign here. It's simply a statement that shows you've accepted responsibility for the contents."

Nicole took the pen and paper. "Which name should I sign?"

"Christina Braxton."

Aware that Ayden was watching her she signed her old name, adding flourish to the C and B as she'd done in the old days. She pushed the paper back toward the attorney, grateful to have it away from her.

"I will leave you two alone," Ms. Wellington said. She tucked the paper in a file and rose. "Just let me know when you're finished."

"Thanks." Nicole didn't raise her gaze from the envelope. When the attorney had closed the door behind her Nicole looked at Ayden. Suddenly she was afraid. "I can't open it."

She knew Richard. He had brought her up here to terrorize her. That's what he liked to do best.

Seeming to understand her hesitation, Ayden nodded. Grim-faced, he ripped open the sealed edge with his thumb and glanced at the contents. "Damn it to hell."

Chapter Three

"What is it?" Nicole felt her throat tighten with dread.

Ayden laid the pages face down. "Pictures."

Her heart felt as if it would explode in her chest. "What kind of pictures?"

His jaw tightened and released. "Pictures of a murder scene. Claire Carmichael's murder scene."

She felt sick. "Taken by the police?"

"No. The killer." He laid his hands on the pictures, clearly unwilling to let her see them.

She blew out a breath. "How do you know that?"

Ayden tapped his thumb on the table. A small muscle pulsed in his tight jaw. "She's still alive."

Nicole raised a shaking hand to her lips. She didn't want to picture her friend at the mercy of a killer, but dark, frightening images flashed in her head. Nicole knew Claire's face had been cut dozens of times with a razor.

Smoothing unsteady hands over her thighs she tamped down the fear that clawed at her. She was so glad that Ayden was here now. "Is there anything that tells us who the killer is?"

"Not at first glance, but forensics and the San Francisco

police need to go over these." He glanced in the envelope. "There's also a key on the bottom."

"A key?"

He pulled the key out and handed it to her. She picked it up and studied it.

"A safety deposit box key?"

"That's my guess." He fished in the envelope again. "There's a card in here as well. It gives the name of a bank."

Bitter anger roiled inside her. "So he's sending us on a scavenger hunt?"

A hunter's intensity radiated from Ayden. "It appears so."

"This is so like Richard. So damn controlling." Tears threatened. "I'm so tired of him ruining my life."

Ayden laid his strong, calloused hand on hers and held her gaze. "Richard Braxton is dead. He has no more holds on you. You are in control of all this right now. You can stop now and we can turn this over to the local cops."

"No. No. I want to end this once and for all. Like I've said before, I owe Claire this much." She straightened her shoulders. "Let's go to that bank."

Something akin to pride glistened in his eyes. "All right. We'll go to the bank now." He checked his watch. "With luck, we'll be on the road back to Richmond in an hour."

She nodded but she didn't believe that they were going to be headed south in sixty minutes. Something deep inside her whispered that their journey was only just beginning.

They rose and Ayden helped her on with her coat. He called out to Ms. Wellington.

Ms. Wellington appeared from an office at the end of the hallway. She moved with confidence and efficiency yet didn't seem rushed. A neatly plucked eyebrow arched. "Have you gotten everything you needed?"

Ayden studied the woman. "We have for now. But I may return to ask you a few questions."

"I won't share information about my client. Attorney-client privilege." She was so full of righteous indignation.

Anger sparked in Ayden's eyes. He pulled out the pictures and held them up so that only Ms. Wellington could see them. "Have a good look at these, Ms. Wellington. Your client is responsible for this."

She glanced at the pictures. For a moment her well-cultured veneer cracked as the horror of the images penetrated her brain. But just as quickly, Ms. Wellington cloaked her emotions and she met Ayden's gaze. "I had nothing to do with that."

He hoped the pictures scared her. "But Mr. Braxton did. I believe he or his associate killed this woman."

"I don't know anything that can help you."

Nicole was the one who spoke up. "Her name was Claire Carmichael and she helped me escape my husband. If not for her I'd be dead now, I know that. What you see in that picture . . . that's what Richard—your client—did to punish her for helping me."

"As I said, I had nothing to do with that," she said evenly.

"We didn't say you did," Ayden replied. "But your client did, and I would hope you would help police put that monster behind bars."

Ms. Wellington swallowed. "I can't reveal discussions I had between my client and me, but if there is another way I can help, then I will, of course."

Ayden didn't seem all that mollified, but he accepted her statement. She likely didn't have anything to do with the murder but she was protecting the killer. "We'll be talking again soon. Can you tell me where this bank is?"

She glanced at the card. "Just around the corner, not one hundred yards from here." She gave them directions and followed them to the front door.

"There's a small inn two blocks from here on the Potomac. Layfette House," Ms. Wellington said. "In this mess the roads will be gridlocked by now. Most people don't know about the inn so it will be the last to fill up."

Ayden nodded as he turned up the collar of his jacket. "Thanks."

Nicole and Ayden left the lawyer's office. Outside the air had turned bitterly cold and the snow fell faster. The heavy downpour wouldn't let up for a while. Nearly an inch of snow had accumulated on the streets and a white blanket covered Ayden's car.

He captured Nicole's elbow and they headed out into the snow. They opted to walk the two blocks instead of taking the car and risking not finding another parking space.

In this historic section the snow, combined with the green wreaths on the town house doors, brick sidewalks, and candles burning in the windows, made the area all the more charming. If not for this dark errand she and Ayden had been given, she would have loved to have slipped her hand into his and walked these streets and savored the beauty.

But she would do neither.

Flecks of snow dusted Ayden's blond hair. Blue eyes bore into her. "It's going to be okay."

"I want to believe that."

Warm calloused fingers wrapped around her chilled hand. "Believe it."

With him this close, touching her, she knew that she could do anything. Somehow everything would be fine and she didn't need to be afraid. She felt hopeful. "Okay."

They walked on the hundred-year-old brick sidewalk down Union Street. In the distance, the Potomac River meandered past as the snow accumulated along its icy shores.

Within minutes they were at the bank doors. Ayden reached forward and pulled on the brass handle. The door was locked. Confused, he checked his watch. "They shouldn't be closed."

Nicole glanced to the left and spotted a sign. "Closed early for snow. Will reopen tomorrow. I can't believe this. The roads aren't that bad yet."

He removed his cell from his pocket and dialed a number. "Let me call the state police and see how the roads are doing. If they're okay we'll head home and come back tomorrow."

She hated the idea of having to leave and return, but resolved that it would have to be done. "Okay."

Ayden asked for a Captain Lou Fraser and waited only seconds before the other man's deep voice cut through the lines. Ayden's eyes softened when he smiled and spoke to the man who was clearly a friend. When he smiled, it took years off his appearance and made him, well, dashing. She found her heart beating faster as she stared at him.

He hung up the phone and looked at her. "The interstate is a nightmare and the alternate, U.S. Route One, is just as bad. If we leave now we'll be sitting in our car for eight hours."

Her heart sank. She'd never spent a night away from Beth. "I've got to get back to my baby."

"You can call Lindsay and let her know. Beth will be fine with her."

"I know. I just don't like being separated from her." Feelings of worry always plagued her when she thought about her child. That was par for the course with motherhood. But now in the face of Richard's evil all she wanted to do was hold her baby.

"She'll be fine," Ayden said. "And you will be fine."

"I know."

"The inn Ms. Wellington mentioned is a block from here."

She sensed any hotel in this tony section of town would be expensive and she was forced to admit, "I can't afford a room. My budget is tight."

"I've got it covered."

"That's kind of you, but I can't have you pay for me. You've done so much."

"I don't mind helping."

She sighed. "I appreciate this, I really do. But it seems since I left Richard someone has always had to help me. It's hard being grateful all the time."

He studied her a moment. "After Julie died, everyone jumped in to help me and the boys. It was great at first. I don't know how I'd have made it without the help. But it got old after a while. I just wanted to get back to some kind of normal."

"Exactly. I don't want to be anyone's charity case anymore."

He studied her. "The county's valor awards are coming up in the summer. What if you take the headshots for the program? We don't have a budget to pay you, but . . ."

She smiled, grateful. "I'd be happy to take those pictures."

"Then we're even."

"I doubt that will ever happen."

"Let's see if they have a couple of rooms at this inn." He rubbed his hands together, trying to get warmth in his fingertips.

"Right. Yes." His logic was doing little to soothe her frantic feelings but she had no choice.

They backtracked their steps and drove to the inn, which was at the river's edge. The three-story brick building, like the rest of this area, was at least a couple hundred years old. Green wreaths with red bows hung in all the windows and single candles flickered in each. They ducked under a blue awning that extended from the entrance over the sidewalk and hurried up the stairs.

Ayden pushed through the front door and instantly a rush of warm air greeted them. To their right a fire crackled in an ancient fireplace, an Oriental rug warmed an old plank floor, and hunter green walls gave the room an old-world feel.

Across the room stood a ten-foot Virginia Pine Christmas tree. Faux electric candles and strings of dried apples draped the tree and miniature glass teardrop ornaments hung from the branches. The place smelled like apples and cinnamon.

Ayden guided Nicole to the desk across from the tree. Behind the thick wooden desk stood an older man with thinning gray hair and dark-rimmed glasses. He wore a blue suit, white shirt, and a red tie. A red silk handkerchief peeked out from his breast pocket.

The man glanced at Ayden and immediately straightened. "Yes, sir?"

"We need a couple of rooms." Ayden slid his hand into his pocket.

A couple of rooms. Despite their conversation in the car, he was trying not to rush her. She was touched by his concern, which made Nicole want him more.

The clerk's gaze darted between the two as if he was trying to figure out what they were about. Nicole could just imagine the thoughts racing through the clerk's head. She looked like a bohemian artist with her dark hair, turquoise scarf, and leather jacket, while Ayden looked like the poster child for conservative with his dark knee-length coat, white button-down shirt, and khakis.

"We don't have a couple of rooms," the man said. "We've had an influx of calls in the last thirty minutes. The beltway is clogged and a lot of folks are trapped in town for the night." Ayden frowned. "But I do have one room. It's a small. Just one double bed."

Ayden glanced at Nicole. "What do you think?"

Nicole tripped over the pros and cons. Should they stay? Go elsewhere? Maybe the roads weren't that bad. They still might get home. And then there was the promise of sex that hung between them. She heard herself say, "We'll take it."

Ayden seemed to swallow a smile. "Any port in a storm?"

Nicole nodded. "Right."

"Any luggage?" the desk clerk said.

"No." Ayden spoke with a stern confidence that allowed no room for questions.

Nicole felt herself blush. This all felt so illicit though it was anything but. Perhaps it was because she had not been with a man in almost two years, but it wasn't like she was a silly virgin. There'd been Richard, of course, and before him a couple of boyfriends. But the idea of just lying in the same bed with David Ayden made her mouth go dry.

Nervous energy shot through her as she watched him accept the room key. She stared at his rough, calloused hands and her mind skipped to an image of those same hands touching her bare skin. She'd not been touched in so long.

"Hungry?" he asked.

"Uh, yes."

He smiled. And again he looked so different, so attractive. "Me, too. There's a restaurant over there."

"Sounds good."

They moved into a tiny café. The place was nearly full, but there was one table by the window. The hostess took their coats and promised to have the table ready in a few minutes.

"I need to call Lindsay and let her know where I am."

"Sure."

She reached inside her oversize purse crammed full of pacifiers in zip-top bags, spare diapers, toy keys, and a wallet held together with a rubberband. She glanced up at Ayden a bit apologetic. "My cell is in here. Somewhere."

"No rush."

Her hand skimmed the bottom and her fingers brushed the phone. She snapped it up. "Gone are the days when all I needed was a couple of bucks and my driver's license."

"That's traveling light."

"That's what I did after college. I'd pick up and go into the mountains and shoot sunrises and sunsets. Often I just slept in my car."

He frowned. "That's dangerous."

"I never thought twice in those days. Now I think twice, three times." She pushed her bangs off her face and dialed Lindsay's number.

On the fourth ring she heard Lindsay's breathless, "Hello."

"Lindsay, it's Nic. How's it going with the kids?"

Ayden turned away to give her privacy.

In the background, Nicole heard banging pots. On that end the noise had to be deafening. "Is that Beth?"

Lindsay chuckled. "And Zack and Jack."

"Your head must be ready to explode."

"I'm used to the noise at the women's center. So when are you going to be back?"

"Tomorrow. The roads are blocked by snow."

"We barely have a dusting down here. But I'm not surprised you guys are getting it up there. D.C. always gets more snow."

"So you're okay with Beth for the night?"

"Of course. She is a doll."

The genuine kindness in Lindsay's voice eased her nerves. This would have been impossible without Lindsay's help. "Thanks."

"So," she said, dropping her voice a notch. "You and Ayden having a good time?"

Heat rose in her cheeks. "He's very kind."

"That's not what I'm digging for."

Nicole glanced over at Ayden, who'd turned toward her as if he sensed he was now the topic of conversation. His gaze bore into her and then flickered away. "I've got to go."

"Which is code for he's standing right there and you can't talk."

"Exactly."

"Before you go, remember the man is nuts for you and a little fun might be just what the doctor ordered."

"Thanks for the advice." She hung up to the sound of Lindsay's laughter.

Outside snow coated the large deck that overlooked the Potomac River. They moved into the restaurant. When Ayden sat across from her, she leaned forward. "Thanks for all you've done."

"Stop saying thank you."

"Right."

The hostess seated them at the table by the window. They had a stunning view of the river and the snow falling outside.

A tall officious man wearing an apron over his white shirt, black vest, and pants appeared at the table. He greeted them in French.

Without thinking, Nicole responded in French. The waiter raised an eyebrow. In French he said, "Ah, you speak French, madame."

"*Oui.*" As she conversed with the waiter she was aware that Ayden watched her. When they'd placed their drink orders, the waiter left.

"I'm impressed," Ayden said. "Where'd you learn to speak like that?"

"My parents and I lived in Paris for three years. I was about fifteen. Dad worked for a magazine and he was the Paris editor for a while."

"I never knew that about you."

She folded her hands in front of her. "It was a great time."

"I've never been to Europe. My folks' idea of a vacation was Virginia Beach for a long weekend."

"I've heard it's fun."

"To a fifteen year old it was paradise. You miss Europe?"

"Yes. Someday I hope to take Beth there."

The waiter arrived and served Ayden his coffee and Nicole her glass of wine. Normally, she never drank, but today she needed to settle her nerves. The waiter took their orders and left.

Absently, Ayden lined up the fork and the knife until they were straight like soldiers. "So where else have you lived?"

"After Paris we were in London for a while and Rome before coming to L.A."

"You speak Italian?"

"Yes. And German. I have an ear for languages."

"Your parents have passed away?"

"Yes. They were older when I was born. They died shortly after college. I used my small inheritance to start my first business."

"I don't know as much about you as I thought."

"You know all the bad stuff. You know about Richard and all the darkness that went with him. You've seen the worst. Believe me, it wasn't always like that."

"So what other hidden talents do you have?"

She'd not had wine in so long the few sips had already melted through her. It was nice not to have such a bare-knuckle grip on everything. "I'm a decent baker. Mom insisted I learn to cook. She was Irish and old-world in some ways. A good woman knows how to cook. And I love to camp. Like I said, I didn't think twice about picking up and heading into the mountains alone for a few days."

He frowned. "You met Lindsay in L.A."

"We knew of each other. But we didn't hang out much. She was so driven and I was just a free spirit." A smile played on her lips. "Funny. Now I'm the one that's uptight all the time and she's the most relaxed I think she's ever been in her life."

"I can't guarantee you'll be the free spirit you once were. Kids have a way of changing things."

"How have the boys changed you?"

"I used to ride a Harley."

She laughed outright, trying to picture him sitting on a bike. "When was that?"

He hesitated as if he didn't want to admit how long ago it really was. "A few years back."

"Were you with the department then?"

"No, that was college. I did a couple of years at the community college and then joined the department. I finished up going to school part time at VCU."

"And the rest is history?"

"Right."

"How long have you worked homicide?"

"Fifteen years."

"Long time."

"Yeah."

She sipped her wine, wishing it would wash away all the worries and fears and leave her with this relaxed cozy feeling forever. "What's a favorite Christmas memory you have?"

He frowned and for a moment seemed pensive. "I think it was the year the boys were about four and five. Both were so excited about Santa. But I was working a lot in the weeks up to Christmas and I was hardly home. Julie and I barely saw each other. I had to work on Christmas Eve. I arrived home about six A.M. Julie was up making coffee. I kissed her when I heard the boys' feet hit the floor. They came downstairs like they were possessed. I remember feeling bad because I hadn't had time to put the tree up for Julie. Then I saw the light in her eyes. She was so excited. I followed her to the closed living room doors.

When she opened the doors it was like she'd opened it to a dream. The tree was up, lit, decorated, and surrounded by gifts. Like magic. Later I told her I was sorry I hadn't gotten her a gift and she told me my presence was present enough. The boys were jumping up and down begging to get inside. And I remember feeling so damn lucky."

She could see the memory brought him sadness. "Hey, let's make a promise right now not to talk about the past or the future tonight. Let's just keep things in the present."

Ayden smiled. "That would be good."

She traced the rim of her glass with her fingertip. "So what do we talk about?"

He sipped his coffee. "How about us? We didn't come to any conclusion." The glimmer in his eyes reflected growing desire.

Nicole sipped her wine. In the car she'd been tense and tight. Now she felt relaxed, open, brave even. She wanted Ayden. He not only made her feel safe and secure but sexy and confident.

If she didn't act on her feelings now, she'd lose her nerve. "How about we just stop talking and go up to the room?"

Ayden's shocked pleasure gave her the satisfaction of knowing she still had the power to make a man go weak at the knees. She'd forgotten just how exhilarating that felt.

His gaze on her, Ayden signaled the waiter. "Box up our lunch and send it up to our room . . . in a couple of hours."

Nicole didn't hear what the waiter said. She was only aware of Ayden rising. She stood and together they moved toward the elevators.

Charlotte Wellington sat in her office staring at her phone. Beside it was a half-full glass of scotch. In college she'd dreamed of being a lawyer and making a difference. She'd hung out her shingle and expected to take the world by storm. And for a time she'd tasted stunning success. She'd quickly made a name for herself, purchased this building, and hired three other associates.

And then two years ago, the bottom had fallen out. The interest rate of the subprime loan she'd taken out to buy this building had adjusted. Her monthly payments had gone up by almost two grand. Nothing that should have been too devastating, but through a series of flukes, she'd lost her top five clients. She'd been faced with no income and rising expenses.

Charlotte had let go two associates and sublet a few of the office spaces; however, the changes hadn't been enough. She'd been faced with bankruptcy.

The thought of poverty terrified her. She'd grown up poor, knew what it was like to skip a meal, and she'd worked hard to create Charlotte Wellington and she'd fight tooth and nail to keep what she'd had.

And then Richard Braxton had walked into her office eighteen months ago with a huge retainer check and made three simple requests: mail a letter to his wife, hold a sealed envelope until she arrives, and when she claims the envelope, make one phone call.

Simple, easy, quick money. Almost too good to be true.

But she'd been too desperate to look too closely or ask too many questions.

Charlotte had gratefully accepted the check and mailed the letter. She'd all but forgotten about it until today when Detective Ayden had called.

In the last year, the firm had begun to regain ground. She'd refinanced the building and had just been hired for a high profile criminal case. Things were looking up.

And then Detective Ayden had shown her the pictures that she'd held in the envelope for more than a year and a half.

Devastating images of blood and pain and tears burned her brain.

Charlotte swirled the amber liquid in the crystal glass and then took a hearty sip. She'd had nothing to do with that woman's murder but still she felt the slice of guilt.

Now, she had one last task to perform for Richard Braxton

and she could wash her hands of the man. Dial a number, let the phone ring three times, and hang up.

Charlotte picked up the phone. What was Braxton planning? She tapped her fingers on the phone's numbers. Her gut was telling her not to make this call. But she'd accepted the fee and agreed to fulfill her contract to her client who'd come into her life when she was most desperate. That had to be worth something.

She picked up the phone and dialed all but one of the numbers. Her heart hammered in her chest as she stared at the buttons. Just push the last number. Her nerves tightened.

Quickly she hung up.

Charlotte sat back in her chair. Images of the woman in the pictures flashed in her mind again.

The woman's eyes had been haunted with pain and fear. She'd known she was going to die. Her agony must have been incredible.

Charlotte gulped the rest of her scotch. She couldn't take her gaze off the phone, nor could she summon the courage to complete the call.

Chapter Four

Ayden and Nicole didn't speak as they rode the elevator in silence to the third floor. Amazed at the blend of nerves and desire in his gut, he guided her to the door and opened it with the key.

Nicole walked into the room. Her movements were careful, deliberate. He knew she wanted the sex; knew she was primed for it. But he wished he could read her mind or the subtle expressions on her face.

Ayden closed the door softly behind him. He wouldn't worry about tomorrow. It was all about now.

Nicole dropped her purse in a chair and faced him. She smiled and moistened her lips as she shrugged off her jacket.

He was so hard he could barely think. He'd long thought he was past the wild passions that drove his teenage sons to distraction. Now it was all he could do to string two thoughts together.

She moved toward him and stared up at him. Her deep brown eyes telegraphed her desire. She slid her arms around his neck and rose up on tiptoes. He banded his arms around her narrow waist and drew her against him. Her full breasts pressed against him.

Driven by a primal desperation, he leaned his head down

and kissed her. The first kiss was gentle. He didn't want to overwhelm her. But the taste set him on fire.

Ayden tipped his head forward and rested his forehead on hers. His heart raced in his chest. "I want you so much."

Nicole knew that he wanted her. She could feel his desire rolling through him and tensing his muscles. And still he held back because he seemed afraid she'd somehow break. She needed to show him that she was a flesh and blood woman.

"I am not a piece of glass." Her voice sounded husky. "I'm not fragile and I'm tired of people treating me like I am."

To add weight to her words, she kissed him on the mouth again, teasing the edges of his lips with her tongue. When it opened she explored his mouth.

Her kiss tore down whatever barriers stood between them. Groaning his desire, he kissed her back, taking control of what she'd started. He threaded his fingers through her hair and fisted it in his hands. He drew her head back so that her neck was exposed and he kissed the hollow.

Nicole arched back, pressing her breasts up for him. She was still nursing her child part time so her breasts were full and ripe with milk. Her nipples hardened.

Ayden drew his head back and stared down at her breasts. Desire burned in him as he leaned down and unfastened the snaps that trailed down the center of her blouse. With each snap, a bit more of her pale skin became exposed to his gaze. When the V of her blouse dipped below her breasts, he unfastened the bra's hook between them. The soft peaks tumbled free with a small bounce and he bent his head and kissed her nipples.

Nicole sucked in a breath and arched her back. "You are driving me nuts."

"Good."

Smiling, she stepped back from him. He watched with keen, sharp eyes as she unfastened the last of the snaps of her blouse and let the fabric fall from her shoulders. She wrestled free of her bra.

She stood before him half naked and nervous, aware that her body was not the sleek, narrow figure that she'd once had. She'd grown curves and a fullness that she'd not been able to lose after the baby.

"God, you are beautiful." His gaze drilled into her as he stripped off his jacket and laid it on a chair. Carefully he removed his gun and phone from his waistband and laid them on his coat. He stripped off his shirt and the protective vest under it. He moved toward her and cupped her breasts again. He teased the tip of her nipple with his tongue and she closed her eyes and let the sensation build again.

With fumbling hands, Nicole reached for his pants' button. She unfastened it and the zipper and slid her hand over him. He was hard and ready and she knew neither of them would last much longer.

He pulled her hand away. "It will be over before it starts."

"Come into me now."

"I want this to last." The words sounded as if they'd been ripped from him.

"We have all night."

That's all he needed to hear. He backed her up until the back of her knees pressed against the back of the bed. She fell back against the mattress and scooted to the center. Ayden was on top of her in an instant. He straddled her thighs and unfastened her pants. Carefully he unzipped the jeans and she lifted her hips so that he could tug the fabric off her. He tossed them on the floor.

She wanted him inside her now. Waiting was not an option for her.

Ayden pulled off his undershirt and threw it aside. Again he kissed her breasts and licked at the soft pink nipples. Soon he moved to the hollow between her breasts and then began to kiss the tender flesh of her belly.

As if reading her thoughts Ayden smoothed his hand over

her hips. "I love your body." He noted a small butterfly that she'd had tattooed on her hip a few months ago. "What's this?"

"A bit of rebellion, I suppose." She grinned. "I feel a little silly now when I think about it. Most people will never see it."

He kissed the butterfly. "Very sexy."

Nicole pushed his pants down his hips, exposing him. The invitation was too much for him to guard against. As she cupped her breasts, Ayden pulled in a breath and pushed into her.

Nicole was tight, wet, and so soft he thought he'd come in that instant. God, but he wanted to savor this moment. He'd learned not to count on tomorrow or the next time. He'd learned that all he had was now.

He moved inside of her slowly at first. She groaned her pleasure and, lifting her pelvis, took all of him to the hilt. She smoothed her hand over his buttocks and cupped his flesh. He pushed into her harder.

A primal fierceness grew stronger and stronger in him and soon there was only her and their desire. He moved in her faster. She matched him stroke for stroke, goading him and begging him for more.

She was a polite, civilized woman but her lovemaking was hot and frantic. Desires he'd held at bay for so long broke free and with a groan he shoved inside of her.

Nicole undulated and moved, driving them both toward insanity. She circled her lush breasts with her fingertips and he could stand it no longer. He moved faster and faster.

She moaned and arched her back, calling out his name as she gripped the sheets with her hands.

He came inside of her, draining every ounce of himself into her.

Ayden collapsed against her, resting his face in the hollow of her neck. Their heartbeats hammered against each other. Both their bodies were slick with sweat and they breathed hard as if they'd just finished a long race.

Nicole traced circles on his back and finally when he had the strength, he rolled on his side. He pulled her against him, spooning his naked body against her backside. Possessively, he draped a hand over her body and cupped her breasts.

"That was wonderful," she said. Already her voice sounded sleepy.

He nuzzled his face into the hollow of her neck. She smelled of roses and lingering desire. "Yeah."

Within seconds her breathing slowed and she drifted off into a peaceful sleep.

He'd not felt such a sense of rightness in a very long time. In this moment, there were no bad guys, no stresses, no worries. Just this soft, loving woman asleep in his arms.

I love you.

He wanted to whisper the words in her ear. But knew now was not the time. She might have given him her body, but her heart was another matter.

When the phone rang, Denny Smith was startled from a nap. He'd dozed off in front of the wide-screen TV, the fall football game highlights blaring around him.

He jumped to his feet. For a moment he didn't recognize the ring and was confused. And then it hit him that the ringing came from the phone that had been on the charger on his hip for eighteen months. He had never been without the damn thing that had remained stubbornly silent.

He moved to the phone and noted the incoming phone number. Braxton's attorney. As instructed he didn't answer the phone but waited for the ringing to stop.

Braxton had come into Denny's life eighteen months ago with a suitcase full of cash and a request. When the phone rang, it was time to kill Christina Braxton.

Braxton had made him swear to keep the phone for five years. If the phone didn't ring in those five years, he was off the hook and could keep the money.

But if the phone rang, Denny was to find Christina at an Alexandria bank. He was supposed to abduct her and kill her.

Braxton had paid extra, demanding that her death not be quick. Once Denny delivered her body to a guy named Vincent, he'd get a final bonus.

He'd figured the whole scenario was odd. Why not just off the bitch? Be done with her. Denny's number one rule was to keep it simple.

But Braxton had a gripping obsession with his wife. The woman had infected him. He still hoped that he would get her back and return to California with her. If anyone was going to kill his wife, Braxton had said, it was going to be him. He would be the one to drain the light from her body.

The hit was just insurance in case Braxton failed, which he'd not planned on doing.

But Braxton did die. He'd been killed in his attempt to steal his wife. Dumb bastard. He'd made the whole scenario too damn complicated.

"Simple is the way to do things. Not complicated."

Denny had expected Christina to take Braxton's bait soon after his death. But she hadn't. And he'd been forced to wait.

Some would have written the deal off when Braxton had died. After all, who kept a promise to a dead man?

But Denny prided himself on honor. A man in this business was only as good as his word.

Denny pushed out of his reclining chair and went to the armoire across the room. It was made of walnut and its lines were plain. It was easier for him to think when things were uncomplicated.

From the armoire he pulled out a gun safe, dialed in the combination and pulled out a .22 revolver. The gun was hardly fancy or high-powered. A TV crook would have picked a semi-automatic or something exotic. But those kind of guns jammed and they left shell casings.

His .22 could kill just as easily and he avoided complications. He slipped on his gun holster and stuck the gun inside. He shrugged on a brown leather jacket that made him look like a biker.

Denny stopped by a wall mirror and combed his hands through his thick black hair. His first stop would be the bank. That's where the attorney was to send the woman. Braxton had promised she'd be delayed at the bank at least two hours. Plenty of time for him to nab her.

Chapter Five

Nicole wasn't sure how long she'd dozed. She only knew that she couldn't remember the last time she'd felt more relaxed or content. The restless energy that had dogged her for so long was gone. In this room, with Ayden's body spooned against hers, all felt right with the world.

Ayden traced his hand along her naked thigh. His touch wasn't possessive, or seductive even. It was familiar, tender, as if he'd touched her a thousand times. For a moment, promises of a future with Ayden whispered in her head. They were sweet, alluring, and tempted Nicole to open her heart. She stopped. She and Ayden had right now. And now would have to be enough.

She rolled on her back and the sheet slipped away from her full breasts. Ayden had propped his head up on his hand. "How long have you been awake?"

He smiled. "Just a little while."

She suspected it had been more time than that.

Ayden moved his hand to her flat stomach and traced circles around her belly button.

Her heartbeat kicked from slow to high gear. She traced

her hand down his flat abs, stopping just below his waist. Already he was hard and ready for her.

"How about you roll on your back," Nicole said. She scrambled to her knees. Dark hair brushed her shoulders and caressed the tops of her breasts. She wasn't sure that he would. That he would let her be in control.

Amusement and a warming desire sparked in his eyes. "Yes, ma'am." He rolled on his back and tucked his hands behind his head. He didn't take his gaze off her and reached forward to brush her hair aside so that he could see her breasts.

Nicole moistened her lips and straddled him. His erection brushed her inner thigh. She laid her hands on his chest and smoothed them down his flat belly as she leaned forward and kissed him on the lips. The searing kiss brought his hands up to her hips and he cupped her buttocks.

Heat rose up in Nicole. She wanted to take her time, to savor their lovemaking, but already she burned to have him inside of her. He teased her nipples until they were hard.

Hoping to temper her desire, Nicole leaned back out of his reach. Her heart thumped wildly. She was so moist. She kissed him hard on the lips and he threaded his hands through her thick dark hair.

Her hand slid down his belly until it wrapped around his hardness. She could tease him and not lose herself to the pleasure.

A growl rumbled in Ayden's chest when she wrapped her fingers around him. "You're driving me insane," he said.

"That's the plan."

In a quick move he freed himself from her and rolled so that he now had her under him. He straddled her.

"I'm in charge," she said with breathless excitement.

"Maybe some other time when I'm not about to explode."

Some other time. This wasn't just one night for Ayden. He wanted more. Nicole wasn't sure that she could give him that, but for now she wanted him so badly that she refused to argue.

She smiled and opened her legs. He pushed inside of her and she gripped the sheets as he moved faster and faster in her.

When the explosion came, they collapsed against each other, their bodies slick with sweat.

Denny quickly discovered that the bank had closed early because of the snow. He'd been thrown for a second before he remembered the lawyer. She had seen Christina Braxton, otherwise she would not have called.

He smiled. He'd wanted to meet Charlotte face to face for more than eighteen months. He'd done some checking when Braxton had tossed out her name. She'd come up hard like him and had scraped her way to the top. She wasn't no country club miss. She was trailer park. Like him.

He'd kept his eye on her and checked on her from time to time. He'd never approached her. Just watched from afar when the mood struck. She was a looker. Long legs. Red hair. More than once he'd imagined that red hair splayed on a pillow as he buried himself between her creamy white legs and strangled the life from her.

Now that he was actually going to meet her, he felt a bit nervous. As tempted as he was to try her out this afternoon, he knew he wouldn't. The job came first.

Keep it simple.

He arrived at the law offices of Wellington and James just before five. He wasn't sure if anyone would be there. Most of the town had cleared out because of the snow and holiday. But when he tried the front door he was pleased to discover it was unlocked. Braxton had said that Charlotte Wellington was a hardworking woman. In fact, if she'd not been working late that summer night, Braxton wouldn't have hired her.

Denny pushed through the door, careful to be as quiet as possible, and then he locked the front door behind him. Better he had surprise on his side.

He paused at the doormat by the front entrance and wiped

his feet before crossing the carpeted floor to the hallway that led to the back.

The place looked very fancy, high-end. Classy. For Denny, he didn't care so much about the class. As long as he had his cars to work on and money for good beer, he was content. He worked just enough for people like Braxton so he didn't have to get a real job.

Denny reached to the holster in the hollow of his back and pulled out the .22. He screwed a silencer on the tip. He also carried a knife and brass knuckles but hoped neither would be necessary.

The offices down the narrow hallway were all dark except the last on the left. Good. He moved down the hallway, his soft-soled shoes soundless on the hardwood floors.

He tensed when he heard the rustle of papers and the squeak of a chair. Quick and easy was all he was asking for. He put his gun behind his back.

Denny paused inches before the threshold. From this angle he could see Charlotte, who sat behind her desk, her head bent forward. This close he could see that her skin was as pale as a china doll's and her reddish hair hung loose around her shoulders like spun silk. She wore a frown and her right hand clenched her pen.

He moved to the doorway and watched as her gaze flickered up to him. First, green eyes sparked with surprise, then confusion, and then fear. He liked the fear.

"May I help you?"

Even her voice sounded rich.

Suddenly, he wasn't in such a rush to get back to his car. Christina Braxton wasn't going anywhere until the weather broke.

Simple, you dumb bastard. Keep it simple.

The voices chanted in his head. The last time he'd ignored the voices he'd almost gotten arrested. That had been in New York five years ago. And since then he'd faithfully heeded the advice.

But today, he resented them. New York was a long time ago. And didn't he deserve a little fun?

A touch of complicated wouldn't hurt.

"Do you work for Wellington or James?" The question was meant to rattle her cage some more.

Charlotte lifted a neatly plucked brow like she was queen of the world. "I *am* Wellington."

He didn't mind the spark of anger. She had pride, a great rack, and she was smart. Not such a bad combination. "Sorry, Ms. Wellington."

She rose and he could see that her dark skirt hugged a narrow waist and hips that rounded out just right. "What can I do for you, Mr. . . . ?"

"Smith. Mr. Smith." Denny let his gaze flicker over her figure. So nice.

He moved into the office knowing that invading her space would set her on edge. Experience had taught him how easy it was to unnerve someone just by getting too close. Upsetting Charlotte gave him a perverse pleasure. "You the only one here today?"

"No, I'm not."

The faint flicker in her glance told him she was lying. "Come on, there's no one else here right now."

Charlotte Wellington reached for the phone on her desk. She wasn't one to play games. Too bad.

Smiling, he swung the gun out from behind his back and pointed it at her. She needed to understand that he was in charge. "No phone."

She dropped her hand, but to her credit, remained as calm and cool as if they were the best of friends. A rack. Brains. And now balls, so to speak. He liked breaking this one.

"What do you want? I don't keep much cash on hand." She kept her gaze direct as she nervously moistened her lips.

"Not looking for money." He moved closer until he was only a foot from her desk. This close he could smell her perfume.

Rich. Spicy. "You sure don't look like any of the lawyers I've ever worked with. Mind if I call you Charlotte?"

She raised her chin. "I'll take that as a compliment. And no, you may not call me Charlotte."

That bit of sass made him laugh. "You should be complimented, *Charlotte*. It's meant as one."

She arched an eyebrow. "You got a first name, Mr. Smith?"

"Denny. Denny Smith." Why not give his name? She'd not be telling anyone.

She was doing her best to look unruffled but he could see that she was scared. The rapid rise and fall of her chest. The way she fisted and unfisted those long, manicured fingers. "No reason to be scared, Charlotte. I'm not going to hurt you."

"What do you want, Mr. Smith?"

"It's the holidays, Charlotte. Why are you working here all alone?"

"I'm not alone."

"Charlotte, come on. I know when you're lying. I always know when people lie. I kinda have a gift for that."

"I'm working today because there's a mountain of paperwork that needs to be done. My boyfriend is going to be here soon. We have a party to go to."

In all the times he'd checked up on her, a boyfriend had never materialized. The gun still trained on her, he sat in the leather chair across from her. He crossed his legs. "Sit."

Charlotte hesitated just a fraction and then sat down. She tapped her index finger on her desk.

"I can almost hear your mind working."

"Really?"

"You're wondering what I'm going to do."

"I'm wondering when my boyfriend is going to get here."

"You don't have a guy. Your life is this office. I know. Because I've been watching you."

Her skin paled and her eyes darkened for a moment. "What do you want, Mr. Smith?"

He shrugged. "You called me, Charlotte."

"What do you mean, I called you? I've been working all day."

"Three rings, Charlotte, and then a hang up. If you're the only one working here today, you called me."

Tension tightened her spine and she sat so straight he thought he'd hear her spine crack. "I called a number."

He was really enjoying himself. "My number."

Fear did flicker in those green eyes now. "I hung up. We never spoke."

"I've been waiting for that call. You see, we had a mutual friend. Richard Braxton."

He straightened the cuff of his pant leg, which had gotten a little twisted when he'd walked here. "The bank was closed, so I decided to come to you. I need to know where Mrs. Braxton is, Charlotte."

Charlotte's heart hammered in her chest and it took all her resources not to show her fear. But when she thought about the pictures in the file that Detective Ayden had shown her, she nearly cracked. Since she'd made the phone call, she'd done a few Internet searches, trying to find out what had happened to Claire Carmichael. The *San Francisco Chronicle* told her what she'd needed.

Those images of Claire swirled in her head now as she faced the man. She was grateful she didn't know where Nicole Piper had gone. She prayed she'd fled this damn city. "She left here about two hours ago. I don't know where she went."

He relaxed back in his chair and tapped his index finger on the butt of his gun. "Getting the truth out of someone with the first question is sorta like hitting the lottery, Charlotte. A one in a million shot. And in my thirty-eight years, I've never hit the lottery."

She laid her long fingers on her desk. Keep him talking. Don't panic. "I promise you, Mr. Smith, that I don't know where Christina Braxton went. Her late husband instructed me to leave her alone when she opened her package. He then told me to call you. I've done only what he asked."

"Was she alone?"

Her lips flattened. She didn't want to tell him anything. But a sprinkle of truth always made the lies more believable. "There was a man with her."

Mr. Smith scratched his chin. "You think they left the city?"

Her voice remained steady. "Yes."

"Please. The roads are a mess."

"She was determined to get home. Chances are they're stuck on the beltway somewhere."

"I don't think so, Charlotte. My guess is that they're in a hotel or restaurant. What was the man's name?"

"Ayden. I think he was her boyfriend." She wasn't certain about that one. It was just a vibe she'd gotten from them. She debated whether or not to tell Denny that Ayden was a cop, and then decided not to. If she didn't get out of here alive, it would be better for Ayden if Denny wasn't expecting to meet an armed cop.

Mr. Smith seemed to consider what she'd told him. "My bet is they landed in one of the four hotels near here."

"I told you they left."

"You're lying." He leveled his gun at her heart. The amusement in his eyes vanished and they hardened with a look that chilled her.

Simmering panic exploded. She arched back in her chair trying to press herself through the leather. "Look, we both work for the same man. There's no reason to kill me. I'd be a fool to withhold information from you."

He leaned forward. "Christina Braxton is trapped in this town somewhere until morning. I'll find her within an hour."

"Then just leave me. I won't say a word. I swear."

"Like I'm gonna buy that one. Besides, I like you when you're afraid, Charlotte. It makes your pale skin blush and the sharpness in your gaze fade."

Silent, she stiffened.

"Stand up, Charlotte." He rose and gestured upward with his gun.

Charlotte's legs felt like rubber and she could barely draw

in a deep breath. Even as images of the Carmichael woman flashed in her head, she rose and met and held his gaze. "I don't want to die, Mr. Smith."

"Who does, Charlotte?"

"I'll beg if that's what you want." Maybe she could get him to lower his guard. "Denny, please."

The smile deepened in his eyes. "Take your blouse off, Charlotte."

A rush of cold trickled down her back. "What?"

"Take it off, slowly."

She lifted her chin. "No."

"I'll only ask one more time."

Tears welled in her eyes. "No."

Without fanfare, he fired. The bullet struck her in the side, tearing through her flesh like hot steel. For a moment she just stood there stunned, as adrenaline pumped through her system. And then the pain came in a hard punishing wave and she dropped forward on her desk.

His expression remained so damn calm. "I should just kill you. But I've thought about this moment for so long. And it is Christmas. Take your jacket off."

Blood seeped from her wound and stained her blouse. Pain robbed her of breath. He was going to rape her and then kill her. Terror nearly paralyzed her. But she dug deep and summoned the shreds of her courage.

Carefully, she rose and started to unfasten the buttons of her jacket.

His eyes glistened. "Don't rush it, baby. Don't rush it."

It took little effort to wince as she shrugged it off. She glanced down and saw a letter opener and made a point to drop her jacket over it.

"Take your blouse off."

She started to unfasten the pearl buttons of her blouse. His gaze settled on the swell of her breasts. She used that moment to place her hand on the jacket over the opener.

"Lace bra," he said. "I knew you wore lace."

Charlotte pretended to wince and double forward. Her hand over the hidden letter opener, she dropped to the floor and pulled both the jacket and opener with her. She curled up in a ball and dug the opener out.

Slow, purposeful footsteps creaked against the floor as he moved around the desk. "Get up, Charlotte."

She gripped the letter opener. She'd never be able to kill him or stop him, but if she could delay him long enough, she could escape through the bathroom door located next to her desk. This building was old and the walls and doors were thick.

The soft-soled shoes appeared by her face. "Get up, Charlotte. You're being dramatic. That bullet didn't hit any vital organs."

In one swift move she jerked the letter opener forward and rammed it into the top of his shoe. The man screamed and fired his gun. This bullet went wide and hit the floor by her head.

"Shit." He recoiled a second.

She scrambled to her feet and dashed to the bathroom. He grabbed a handful of her hair and yanked her back against him. Pain attacked every nerve ending in her body.

"Not smart, Charlotte," he hissed. He shoved her forward against the desk so her stomach dug painfully into the wood. He pressed the gun to her head as he fumbled with the hem of her skirt.

She screamed. Tears rolled down her face.

He jabbed the butt of the gun into her wound and she nearly blacked out from the pain. Somehow she remained conscious. Her fingers brushed a crystal paperweight on her desk.

Denny pushed his thigh between her legs.

Seizing the few seconds she had, she gripped the paperweight and swung back with it with all the force she could muster. The blunt edge caught his jaw and tossed him off balance. Hair ripped from the roots as she tore free and dashed to the bathroom. This time she was able to slam the door and lock it.

"Damn you," he muttered.

She pressed herself against the wall farthest from the door and dropped to her knees. Her entire side was wet with blood.

She waited for a pounding or the pop of bullets. Neither came. Outside there was a deadly calm. And then she heard the scrape of furniture over her floor.

"I got to hand it to you, Charlotte. You're a whole lot more than I expected." He sounded breathless. He was hurting. Good. "That fancy desk of yours is in front of the bathroom door, in case you're wondering. You aren't going anywhere, but don't worry, I'll be back when I take care of Christina. Then we'll finish what we started."

Charlotte glanced down at the plume of blood growing on her silk blouse. "Monster."

"Happy holidays, Charlotte." His voice sounded so pleasant, as if they were old friends. "And I'll be sure to lock up on my way out and leave a note saying you'll be closed until next Monday. Don't want anybody stopping by."

She listened as his uneven footsteps faded down the hallway. In the distance the front door closed.

Gripping her midsection, Charlotte pulled herself up and moved to the door. It was jammed shut.

She was trapped.

Chapter Six

Tuesday, December 23, 5:00 P.M.

Ayden sat in the darkened corner of their hotel room watching Nicole as she slept. Making love to her had rekindled everything he'd felt for her and more. He'd do whatever it took to protect her.

He glanced at the envelope they'd picked up at the law offices. He'd gone into the hallway and called San Francisco PD and spoken to a Detective Rio about the Carmichael murder. California authorities had theorized that Braxton had killed the woman but they had never been able to prove it. He told them about the photos and the twisted treasure hunt he and Nicole were on now. With luck they'd nail the killer and Carmichael's family would have closure. Rio had been excited about the development. The Carmichael case had haunted him like few other murders had. Before he'd hung up, Ayden had promised to call as soon as he had more information.

Ayden cringed when he looked at the horrendous shots. No one deserved to die like this.

Rage roiled inside of him. Now more than ever he wanted to get to that bank and find evidence linking this murder to a killer. Whoever had killed Claire Carmichael deserved to rot in jail. He replaced the pictures in the envelope.

He glanced at Nicole. No wonder the woman had been afraid to commit to him. She'd lived with the devil. God only knew what horrors she'd survived. He'd been arrogant and wrong to expect so much from her so soon.

He knew now he'd give her as much time as she needed. If light and easy was all she could give, he'd take it. He wanted her in his life, even if the terms weren't his.

Nicole's hand slid leisurely to his side of the bed and when she realized he wasn't there she rolled on her back and then sat up. The sheet dropped from her breasts and he felt his insides tighten.

For a moment her eyes looked a little wild, confused, as if she didn't know where she was. And then her gaze settled on him. Instantly, the wildness vanished and a lazy smile tugged at the edge of her lips. She lifted the sheet casually over her breasts but the left side dropped low enough for him to see the soft mound just above her nipple.

"How long have I been asleep?" she asked. Her voice sounded husky.

Already, he ached to touch her. He wanted to take her in his arms, make love to her again, and banish all the violence she'd suffered from her memory. "Not long. An hour maybe."

She studied his face and frowned. "You look worried."

He deliberately smiled. "I always look worried. It's part of the job."

She swung her legs over the side of the bed. Dropping the sheet, she rose. She walked toward him naked, her gait relaxed and familiar, as if they'd been together for years. She sat on his lap, draped her arm around his shoulder, and kissed him lightly on the lips.

Ayden wrapped his arm around her narrow waist. He grew harder, if that were possible. "At the rate we're going, I won't be able to walk tomorrow."

Lightly, she kissed his neck and then nibbled his ear with her teeth. "That such a bad thing?"

He chuckled. "I'll find a way to survive."

She cupped his face in her hands. "Good. I like having you around."

They moved to the bed and made love a third time. This time he took his time. The fever that had consumed them before had eased and they were able to explore each other's bodies leisurely. He'd forgotten how exhilarating the discovery process could be.

Ayden loved touching her. He loved her scent. The way her belly convulsed a little when he kissed her. The butterfly tattoo on her hip.

Nicole's heartbeat raced as Ayden touched her body. In no rush, he took his time kissing every inch of her bare skin. Calloused hands cupped her breasts and teased her nipples into hard peaks. Fire shot through her body and she instantly grew moist.

She hissed when his hand slid from her breast down her belly.

"Nicole, you are so beautiful. So lovely."

Here, now, she felt beautiful. The doubts and fears Richard had tried to brand into her had vanished.

She ached for him to touch her and to bring her desire to a climax. "Please."

He glanced up, his gaze skimming over her to meet hers. The devil's glint sparked in his gray eyes. "Not yet. There's no rush, darlin'."

Purposefully, he slid lower. Nicole moaned as he kissed the most sensitive spot between her legs. He cupped her buttocks and lifted her hips as if he couldn't get enough of her. Nicole's head dropped back against the pillow. So wrapped in desire, she was helpless to speak or move.

Nicole slid her fingers through his thick hair. The fire inside of her had reached a peak and she knew if he didn't enter her soon, she'd go mad. "David."

The single word held a wealth of meaning that he clearly understood. He rose up and stripped his pants off. And then he straddled her and in one steady thrust he entered her.

She wrapped her legs around him, taking him in as deeply as possible. He moved inside of her, his thrusts hard and sure. She matched his rhythm, willing to accept what he offered.

When her release came, she called out his name and he drove into her to the hilt. Their bodies clenched in a hard spasm that seemed to last forever and then in a rush the tension fled their bodies.

Ayden collapsed against Nicole. Sweat from both their bodies mingled. Their heartbeats hammered in unison.

He held her for a long time, content to trace his finger up and down her arm and to kiss her hair. He whispered in her ear. "You are beautiful. I love touching you." The endearments made her smile.

Later they opened the boxed lunches that had gone untouched until now. They sat on a towel on the floor, picnic style.

She'd slipped on her sweater and panties, and he'd slipped on his trousers. "I don't want any of this to end. If it wasn't for Beth, I'd never leave this room."

Ayden didn't want to destroy the magic of this afternoon either. He would have gladly locked them both inside for as long as humanly possible. But there was a life out there that neither could deny. And there were problems that had to be addressed.

"I understand," he said. "But we both know there are things we need to talk about."

She dropped her gaze to the half-eaten sandwich in her hand. Some of the light faded from her eyes and he could have kicked himself for dousing it. "You want to talk about Richard."

"It's not something I want. But it needs to be done."

Nicole set down her sandwich. Even as she nodded her agreement her shoulders tensed. "What do you want to know?"

He tightened his jaw. Like it or not, he had to think like a cop now. "Anything you can tell me. I'm trying to figure out what kind of game Braxton is playing."

"Richard was very stylish and sophisticated. Appearances were everything."

"He owned his own business."

"Yes. Though I couldn't tell you what he did. Many times he'd have a dress sent to me along with a note. 'Be ready by six.' I learned to do as he said and not question. I met some of the men he did business with but they rarely spoke in great detail around me." She sighed. "All of the men who worked with Richard were afraid of him. I only remember one questioning him. And he vanished from the party within minutes. His body was found by the Golden Gate. He'd been shot."

Ayden nodded. "San Francisco police suspected Braxton in several unsolved murders."

"I wouldn't be surprised if he committed them all. He didn't like being crossed."

"Tell me again how you met."

"When we met I had a small photography studio in San Francisco. I was living hand to mouth but I didn't care. I was having a ball and some of my work was starting to catch on. Local art galleries were carrying my work. I had a bit of a following."

"I've no doubt."

"Richard ducked in to avoid a rainstorm. He was very charming and asked me out. I agreed. For a time it was like magic. Flowers every day, small gifts, phone calls. When he asked me to marry him, it seemed so natural. I saw us growing old together." She frowned. "But after the wedding things changed almost immediately. When I spent time with my friends or working, he would get angry and annoyed. Said I didn't love him. I don't know why I felt like I had to prove my love to him, but I did. So I gave up my friends. Soon I was so isolated. Then he really started to criticize me. And then he hit me."

Ayden was adept at keeping his expression neutral but it was hard. It angered him that Braxton had treated Nicole so viciously. "I wish I'd been there to protect you."

She shook her head. "I probably wouldn't have listened. I thought if I tried a little harder I could fix his anger."

He touched her cheek with his hand. For a moment neither spoke and then softly he said, "Would Vincent have killed Claire for Braxton?"

"Yes." She sighed. "He would have done anything for Richard. He was intensely loyal. But I don't think he did."

"Why?"

"Because Vincent was very efficient. He did the job he was paid to do and there was no emotion. He didn't waste time inflicting pain. Claire's killer was angry. And she suffered. No matter what Richard said on that video I think now that he killed her."

"What do you think is at the bank?"

"It would only be guesses now. But knowing Richard, probably another clue or even nothing. Jerking me around like this—controlling me—would have given him great pleasure. He knew driving north on the interstate would have terrified me. He knew I'd have no one up here to rely on. He should have been laughing in hell right now." A smile lifted her lips. "What he hadn't expected was you being here with me."

He took pleasure knowing his presence would have driven Braxton insane. "I doubt he envisioned the scenario that's played out."

She smiled. "No. He didn't."

"Do you have regrets?"

"About us?" She sounded surprised by the question. "None. Never. You?"

"None." He chose his words carefully. "This is what I've wanted for a very long time, Nicole."

"I know." She grew silent. "I'm sorry again that I pushed you away in the spring."

"Don't be."

He had promised himself that he'd be patient, but with Nicole it was hard. He feared if he weren't careful she'd slip through his fingers and they'd return to Richmond and all this would be just a sweet memory. "I'd like to see you when we get back to Richmond. And I don't mean as friends."

"I don't want to make promises. I just don't know what I can give over the long term."

Ayden would be lying if that remark didn't disappoint. "I know. Let's just take it one step at a time. We can go at your pace."

She leaned forward and kissed him lightly on the lips. "I think I can do that."

Nicole's lips tasted sweet. He was very aware that she'd made no commitments.

Denny had altered his appearance after he'd left Charlotte's office. He'd changed out of the black wig and glasses and chosen an auburn one. He'd slipped on a turtleneck and tweed jacket over his T-shirt and selected a pair of wire-rimmed glasses from the collection in the trunk of his car. He lost time bandaging his foot, which had a deep puncture wound. It ached like a son of a bitch and he knew he'd definitely double back and pay Charlotte back for the inconvenience.

Now he looked more like an attorney than a biker. The change in appearance meant few would question his presence. And, in case he couldn't get back to Charlotte, he wouldn't be connected to her attack.

It had taken him more than an hour to visit three of the four hotels in a mile radius of the bank. No one at the first three hotels had heard of a Christina Braxton or a guy named Ayden. No one recognized the picture he had of her. He was tired and getting frustrated when he reached the Layfette House just after eight. Irritated, he was ready to be done with this job. The pain in his foot had migrated up his leg.

Denny welcomed the heat of the lobby as he moved gingerly across the carpeted floor to the front desk. A young woman stood behind the counter. She was young, heavyset, and had dark hair and chocolate eyes. He smiled, knowing that most women liked the way he looked when he was dressed like this. Chicks digged the brainy types.

He laid his right hand on the counter but didn't lean too close so that he didn't invade the woman's space. "Good evening."

She smiled. Her teeth were crooked and her mascara a bit too thick for his tastes. He'd liked the way Charlotte had looked. Clean, simple, elegant. He couldn't wait to return to her.

"Good evening, sir."

"I'm looking for someone."

She frowned. "We can't give out the names of our guests."

Everyone said that but the fact was that desk clerks didn't make much money and for a couple hundred bucks they'd toss him all kinds of information.

He laid Christina's picture on the table along with two one hundred-dollar bills. "She's my sister. She lives in New York and came home for the holidays. Long story short, she and Mom had a fight during the big family meal we were having. See, we normally eat on Christmas Day but Mom has cancer and was in the hospital until yesterday. Anyway, figured it was best to eat today seeing as she's so weak. We got the table set and the turkey and trimmings on the table when Mom asks Chris, my sister, if she's going to ever get married. Chris got all mad and stormed out. She's always been dramatic."

The desk clerk seemed to sympathize with his story. "I haven't seen her."

"Are you sure? My job is to find her so we have peace on earth. It's a big family dinner. And frankly this could be Mom's last Christmas." He dropped his voice a notch. "The cancer's spread to her bone."

The woman's eyes softened a little as her gaze dropped to the picture and the money. "I'm so sorry, but I can't really say."

Not an out-and-out *no* like he'd received at the other hotels. "It's Christmas and you could really help me out."

She nibbled her lip.

He pushed the money toward her. "Mom has been crying

for the last couple of hours. Dad is near tears. It's a mess." He nudged Christina's picture toward her. "A little extra change couldn't hurt this time of year."

She glanced from side to side and then laid her hand over the bills. She pulled them toward her.

Denny's first reaction was to slap his hand over hers. He didn't want her to take the money until she told him what he wanted, but he played it relaxed like a novice might. "So you've seen her?"

"She checked in with a man this afternoon. She came down for soda about a half hour ago and then went back to her room."

He leaned forward. "What's the guy's name?"

She glanced at her computer screen and punched a couple of buttons. "David Ayden from Richmond."

David Ayden. That fit. "I didn't realize her boyfriend had come with her." He smiled. "Are they still here?"

"Yes."

"That's excellent."

"I can't tell you the room." She glanced from side to side. "Then people will know we talked."

"No sweat. I'll just take a seat in the bar and wait. They've got to come out sometime."

She lowered her voice. "You're not going to say I told you anything."

He pretended to lock his lips closed and toss away a key. "Just between the two of us."

Charlotte checked her wristwatch. Denny had been gone almost an hour. She'd half expected him to double back and kill her but the lapse of time told her he'd gone after Nicole. She said a prayer for the woman and hoped Ayden could save her.

For as long as she lived, she'd regret that phone call. But regrets had never gotten her anywhere and they wouldn't get her out of this room.

As bad as she felt for Nicole she knew she had a little time to figure out an escape plan. If she got out of here, she could help Nicole. She kicked off her high heels and rose from the bathroom floor.

Every inch of her body ached. The bleeding in her side had slowed and the blood had started to clot and crust on her skin. She'd not bleed to death today, but the pain in her side did not ease her fears.

With a wince, Charlotte unfastened the pearl buttons of her blouse, peeled back the silk, and inspected her wound. The left side of her blouse was crimson and wet. With trembling hands, she slid off the blouse. The first glance at the blood and wound nearly made her stomach reel. She'd never been fond of the sight of blood, especially her own.

Faint heart never won . . . The words had been her mother's mantra for as long as she could remember and it had been hers since the day she'd decided to leave the trailer park behind. She grabbed a wad of toilet paper from the spindle, rose up gently and turned on the tap. She ran the tissue under the water and then squeezed out the excess. She placed it on the blood caked over the wound. Immediately, she yelped. "Damn it!"

The pain took her breath away and for a moment she had to pause and wait for her heart to stop thundering in her chest.

Gingerly, she dabbed the wound until the area around it was clean. A tentative touch to the skin told her that the bullet was in her, lodged deep inside. There was no getting it out now. She'd cleaned it as best she could. Her best bet now was to find a way out of this room.

She'd tried the door several times but the desk Denny had shoved in front of it ensured it wouldn't budge. She pressed her ear to the door.

"Help! Can anyone hear me?" There was no answer but she shouted for another five minutes before pain and fatigue got the better of her.

No one was going to save her. It was up to her to get out of this damn bathroom.

She wondered if Denny had found Nicole and Ayden. The Layfette House was an out of the way, romantic place few knew about. Most tourists went for the chain hotels.

Though the couple had tried to play it cool, the sexual chemistry between them snapped.

"You're getting soft, Wellington," she whispered. Normally, she didn't encourage romance. Fanciful and foolish as far as she was concerned. But it was Christmas after all.

Now she prayed her moment of weakness had saved the couple's lives.

A wave of dizziness washed over her. Her vision blurred. She moistened her lips as she closed and opened her eyes. She focused on the wallpaper, a hunt scene that featured strong greens and reds. She'd chosen it because she'd seen it in a magazine. It had looked expensive and spoke of old money.

The time and effort she'd put into decorating a bathroom now seemed so foolish. "Gracie Jane Wells, Grannie always said your high ambitions would come to no good. And look where it got you. Dying, alone, and during the holidays no less."

Tears welled in her eyes. Not so much from dying, which she didn't want to do, but at the waste. She'd scrimped and saved and worked so damn hard to get out of the trailer park and make herself into a person worth knowing. And now a job that had bothered her from the beginning was biting her in the ass.

"I ain't dying today." Wincing, she straightened herself up and glanced around the bathroom again. The vent on the ceiling was too small for her to fit through even if she could have climbed on the pedestal sink and hoisted herself up there.

There were no windows. The only way out was the door and it was jammed.

She stared at the door, hating the thick walnut that she'd been so proud of when she'd purchased the place. The old wood was as hard as iron and it would take an ax to penetrate. Even if she had an ax she doubted she'd be able to wield it.

She laid her head against the cool wood. "I'm not dying here. I am not dying here."

Raising her head, she ran her manicured hand over the smooth wood. That's when she noticed the hinges on the door. Why the devil hadn't she noticed them before? Brass pegs secured each of the three brass hinges. If she could remove the pegs, the door would fall open. Once it was open she could crawl over the desk and get to her phone.

The middle peg was the easiest to reach, so she started with it. She tried to pull it free of the hinge, but it didn't budge. She tugged harder, her hand slipped, and she snapped the French manicured nail on her index finger. "Shit."

For a moment she was incensed. She'd just had her nails done last night. And then the absurdity of it all made her laugh. Good Lord, she was bleeding, trapped, and most likely would have to face down a killer. And she was worried about a damn nail. She laughed so hard, tears rolled down her cheeks.

Finally, she stayed her nervous laughter. She'd have to find something to jab the hinge free. She didn't want to be here when Denny returned.

Charlotte needed something stronger than her finger to wedge the peg out of the hinge. Glancing around the room, she saw nothing that would work except the sharp heel of her pumps.

Grimacing, Charlotte leaned over and picked up the shoe. The pumps had cost her three hundred dollars a few years ago and she'd lovingly cared for them like children.

She started to work on the peg. In seconds the soft leather ripped. She cringed and then reminded herself dead women didn't wear shoes.

Chapter Seven

Wednesday, December 24, 8:00 A.M.

Nicole couldn't remember the last time she'd felt, well, complete. She loved Beth and couldn't imagine her life without her child, but last night with Ayden had filled a need that went beyond the mind-blowing sex. For the first time, the idea of a life with him didn't scare her.

She stepped out of the shower and toweled off her hair. She dressed in yesterday's clothes and dried her hair quickly with the hotel's blow dryer. When she stepped out of the bathroom, Ayden was standing with his back to her. He'd dressed and stared out the window. His cell phone to his ear. Under his white shirt she saw the outline of his bulletproof vest and frowned. She didn't like the idea of him being in danger.

"The roads have been cleared and salted, so we'll be able to get on the road. It just depends what we find at the bank," he said into the phone.

At the bank. Richard. For the last few hours, she'd felt so much like her old self—a vibrant, twenty-nine-year-old woman. And then the thought of Richard's name made her feel a hundred again, as if the weight of the world rested on her shoulders.

Ayden hung up. He smiled and winked. "It's going to be okay."

In that moment the weight drifted from her shoulders and she felt as if she could do anything. She would get through this. She would survive. And life would be good again. "Let's go."

Charlotte worked on and off through the night on the door-jamb. Her side pinched each time she shoved her hand up and jammed the heel into the peg. Sometimes it was so painful she had to stop and rest. A couple of times she'd sat down and drifted off into a fitful sleep.

Now, however, she was wide awake. She'd removed the middle and bottom hinges and now had only the top one to tackle.

She lifted her gnarled, scuffed shoe over her head and jabbed the heel under the peg. The upward motion made her grimace but she kept working. Slowly the peg started to budge.

"Come on, you son of a bitch. Move!"

Charlotte shoved with all she had and the spindle wriggled free of the latch and fell to the floor with a loud ping. She cast her shoe aside and yanked on the door handle. The lock remained fused but the other side opened several inches. It wasn't enough for her to squeeze through.

Charlotte rested her head against the door and swallowed. "Please just get me out of here." It was the closest she'd ever come to a prayer. Until now she'd never asked God for a favor because, well, she never figured he listened. "Please."

She straightened her shoulders and pulled against the door-knob. This time the door opened more. It was a tight squeeze, but enough for her to get through.

Charlotte pressed through the opening, crying in pain when the hard wood grazed her wound. She tumbled out into her office onto the floor. She curled her fingers into fists. "Take that, you son of a bitch."

She glanced up to her desk to the phone. Half pulling and

half climbing up the side of her desk she laid her hand on the phone receiver and lifted it. The line was dead.

"Damn."

She moved around behind her desk and dug her purse out of the bottom drawer. She burrowed her hand deep in the leather sack until she found her cell phone. She dialed 911 and waited for the operator.

"Nine-one-one. State your emergency."

Charlotte had never been more grateful to hear another human being in her life.

Denny sat in the lobby drinking his eighth cup of coffee. He'd waited in the lobby an hour for Christina and when she'd not appeared he'd decided to put his time to use. He got his laptop from the trunk of his car, found a corner of the lobby and hooked up to the hotel's WiFi service.

He searched the Internet for anything he could find about Christina Braxton, aka Nicole Piper. Her Web site showcased impressive pictures, and newspaper accounts detailed that she'd survived.

Too bad she had to die.

His mind drifted to Charlotte. He wondered how she'd fared last night. No doubt time alone coupled with her injury had subdued her. He smiled. He looked forward to doubling back to the law firm.

Denny turned his attention to Ayden. Ayden, it turned out, was a decorated cop who'd proven he was more than worth his salt. Not good. He'd have to be careful when he snatched Christina because he'd prefer not to tangle with Ayden.

Now as he sat in the lobby watching the guests checking out, he knew it was a matter of time before he saw Christina and finished this damn job that had taken far too long.

* * *

Ayden pulled open their hotel room door. "I'm sorry to say good-bye to the place."

Nicole glanced back into the room at the rumpled sheets on the bed. "Me, too."

"Maybe we should come back sometime."

The offer hung in the air. She knew Ayden wanted so much more. And something inside her whispered again that the time had come to take a chance. "Sounds good."

He grinned and pressed his hand into the small of her back. He guided her to the elevator and pressed the DOWN button.

His touch on her back was light, but the points of pressure sent shivers of delight down her back.

The doors dinged open, he kissed her on the lips, and they stepped inside the car. The doors closed behind them.

Ayden stood straight, not touching her but close so that she felt the energy radiating from his body. She missed touching him, missed the connection they'd shared in the room. She slid her hand into his and he gently squeezed it. He rubbed her palm with a calloused thumb.

"I love you," he said.

Speechless, emotions swirled in her. She'd never heard anything so sweet and so frightening. She wanted to love him, but still feared the vulnerability and pain that came with it. She squeezed his hand and kissed him on the lips.

He stared at her as if trying to peer into her mind. "I don't expect you to say anything back. I just wanted you to know how I feel."

"I want to be fair to you. I don't want to hurt you again."

He squeezed her hand. "I know."

The doors to the elevator opened and they walked into the lobby and moved to registration so Ayden could check out.

The Christmas tree in the lobby winked and sparkled in the corner. As Ayden gave the clerk his information, she headed toward the tree. She loved this time of year and she loved looking at the different trees. She touched one of the teardrop glass balls hanging from a branch, mesmerized by the way the morning light hit it.

"They're beautiful, aren't they?"

Nicole turned toward the unfamiliar male voice and smiled. The guy wore wire-rimmed glasses and had reddish hair. He looked nice enough, but instinct had her tensing and moving away. "Yes."

The guy looked at her. "Do I know you?"

"No." She glanced over at Ayden, who stood at the front desk. She couldn't go running to him every time a man spoke to her. Still, maybe she'd wander over to the large fireplace. "Excuse me."

He moved and blocked her path. "My name is Denny Smith."

"Okay."

"No, but I do know you, from California. You're the photographer, Christina Braxton."

Nicole's stomach dropped. Her heart pounded in her chest. "No. I'm not Christina."

"You sure? I'm a photography collector and I'm certain I bought some of your work in San Francisco."

"My name is Nicole Piper." She didn't feel the least bit flattered. She felt as if the past were sucking her in again.

Ayden's phone rang as he tucked the credit card slip in his wallet and slid it and his card into his pocket. He flipped open the phone. "Detective Ayden."

"This is Charlotte Wellington."

Her voice sounded fragile. It didn't fit the image of the strong, cold woman he'd met yesterday. "What's wrong?"

"There's a man. Dark hair wearing a T-shirt and biker jacket. Calls himself Denny. He's looking for Nicole. He shot me."

His senses went on full alert. "Shit. Where are you?"

"My office. I've called nine-one-one and they're sending help, but you need to protect Nicole. This guy is dangerous

and I think her husband sent him. Go find her. I'll be fine."
She hung up.

Ayden's gaze swung over the lobby. He spotted Nicole
standing by the tree. A man was talking to her. Her back was
to him and he couldn't see her face. He didn't fit Charlotte's
description but Ayden wouldn't take a chance. Without hesitating, he unclipped the strap on his gun holster and started to
move toward them. "Nicole."

Just as he did, the man pulled out a gun and stuck it in
Nicole's side. She flinched and tried to move away. But the
man yanked her against him. He dragged her toward a service
exit.

In that moment, Ayden realized the man was going to kill
Nicole.

Chapter Eight

Wednesday, December 24, 9:02 A.M.

Nicole struggled to free her arm as the stranger dragged her to a metal door. "Let go of me!"

Denny jabbed the barrel of the gun in her side. "Make a sound and I will kill your friend by the reception desk."

A scream died in her throat as the service door slammed behind them. "What do you want?"

"Your husband sent me."

Nicole jerked against his grip. "My husband is dead!"

"He hired me before he died. I'm kinda his insurance plan." He fired at the lock and the bullet mangled the metal before bouncing off. Nicole cringed. Denny didn't flinch as he pushed her down the tunnellike hallway that led toward stairs.

The air in the hallway quickly grew colder and she could smell the scent of garbage. They were headed to a back alley. She twisted free, lost her balance and pitched forward toward the stairs.

Denny grabbed her arm again, saving her from falling. "Careful, you could have broken your neck."

If he'd meant to kill her quickly, he would have let her fall. If Richard had hired him then whatever he planned was going to be painful. This time she did scream.

The sound echoed in the hallway and Denny cursed. "Shut the hell up."

Anger roiled inside her. "Drop dead."

Ayden's voice could be heard issuing orders from the other side. Frustrated, the man dragged her down the stairs at such a rapid pace she had to take the steps two at a time.

Behind them, she heard pounding on the door before it crashed open with such force it slammed against the wall.

Ayden. She screamed, "David!"

Denny glanced back but didn't break stride. "He won't get to us in time. I've got a car parked outside in the alley by the service entrance. Cooperate and that sweet baby of yours will grow up."

Her heart leapt with grief and fear. "How do you know about her?"

"I discovered a whole lot about you and your boyfriend." He shoved her toward a metal door. "Sounds like you're getting your life back on track. Too bad."

Denny reached for the door handle and twisted it. Outside she could hear the scrape of a snowplow and the honking of a horn.

If they got through this door, she'd be lost to her daughter and Ayden forever. Her heart hammering against her ribs, she reached down and grabbed the gun with her free hand. She twisted it away from him as she drove her foot into his shin and down on his foot. Pain drained the color from his face and for an instant he hesitated. "Goddamn, bitch. Let go."

"Go to hell," she hissed.

Denny grabbed her arm. He was stronger, but a fierce energy rolled through her as if she were possessed. She was not going to leave her child an orphan.

He wrestled the gun free from her and shoved her back against the metal door. Her head hit hard and for a second pain blurred everything.

He whirled her around so that she faced the door. "Now get your sweet ass outside." She felt the jab of metal in her ribs.

Nicole righted and drove the back of her head into his nose. He screeched in pain and grabbed a handful of her hair. "I'm gonna enjoy taking you apart inch by inch."

"Let her go." Ayden's command echoed from behind them.

The man jerked Nicole around so that the two of them faced Ayden. He pressed his gun to her temple.

"This is between Christina and me," the man said easily. "Let us go, Detective."

"No."

The blood trickling from Denny's nose made him sniff. "You've got two boys. I'd hate for anything to happen to them."

Nicole's gaze locked on Ayden's. He had the gun pointed right at them and there was steel in his eyes that she'd never seen before. It was a hard, cold look.

Claire. Lindsay. Now David. She'd brought such terror into so many lives.

"You're not taking her," Ayden said.

Denny pointed the tip of the gun barrel to Nicole's head. "You can't stop me."

Even if Ayden fired, Denny could easily put a bullet in her brain. She couldn't expect Ayden to save her alone. She jerked forward, trying to break his hold.

Denny's iron hold didn't budge. "Stop it."

"Let her go," Ayden said.

Denny shook his head. "Can't do that. There's a hell of a bonus waiting for me when I deliver her body to the right people."

Ayden took a step toward them, the gun steady. "You've been seen. Too many people can identify you."

The man laughed. "I can change my appearance in seconds. When I leave here I'll be a different man in less than a minute."

"You aren't leaving here with her."

"She's not worth dying for. She's not worth making those boys of yours orphans."

Nicole screamed and yanked hard against the man's grip. She managed to shift her weight slightly to the left. Ayden fired his gun. The bullet hit Denny in the shoulder and the impact knocked him off balance and into the door behind him. Blood splattered Nicole's face.

Denny fired his gun. The deafening sound cut through her ears. The bullet struck Ayden in the chest. He dropped to his knees before he fell forward.

Nicole screamed as she watched Ayden hit the floor. Tears burning her eyes, she started shrieking and jabbed her elbow into Denny's injured shoulder. He grimaced and the pain doubled him over.

She grabbed his gun and tried to wrench it free of his grasp. Pain had loosened his grip and the metal gun handle started to slip from his fingers. She nearly had it free when Denny grabbed her hair and jerked back her head. The force was so great she stumbled and fell to her backside.

Denny whirled on her and trained the gun tip right at her temple. He was going to fire. Rage and anger had wiped all reason from his eyes. He was going to kill her.

Seconds passed like days. She saw every detail in excruciating clarity. The blood on his shoulder. The beads of sweat on his forehead. The rapid rise and fall of his chest.

The deafening sound of gunshot exploded and echoed in the hallway. For a moment Nicole wasn't sure if she was alive or dead. And then a plume of blood blossomed on Denny's shirt and he fell back against the wall. He slid down the wall, his eyes wide with shock and anger.

Nicole didn't hesitate. She scrambled to her feet and yanked the gun from his hand. Clutching it tightly, she kept the gun trained on Denny as she backed up.

Ayden was standing now, his gun also on Denny. As they moved toward each other, she could see that his face was ashen with pain.

"You're not dead," she said. She nearly wept with joy.

"No." He sounded as if he were in great pain.

"Your vest," she said, remembering.

"Yeah." He knelt beside Denny and checked for a pulse. "He's dead."

Denny lay on the floor. His eyes had glazed over and his shirt was stained crimson.

"Are you all right?" His voice sounded hard and abrupt.

"Yes."

"Are you bleeding?"

"No. Just bruised." There was no tenderness in his gaze. She wanted him to take her in his arms and tell her it was all going to be fine but he didn't. He was all business.

Ayden flipped open his phone and called 911. He reported the facts to the dispatcher. He hung up. "The receptionist upstairs already called it in like I told her."

She nodded as she stared down at Denny. "Richard sent him."

"It was all a trap."

"Yes."

Neither he nor Nicole moved. She was stunned by the violence. Ayden was wired from the adrenaline.

The Alexandria cops opened the service entrance and entered, guns drawn. Half a dozen uniforms moved swiftly into the small area, first confirming that Denny was dead and then turning their attention to Ayden.

Ayden lowered his gun to the ground and raised his hands as he identified himself. Slowly he pulled out his ID.

Cold air from the alley swirled around Nicole. Her teeth chattered and she could barely breathe. Her hands trembled.

She was aware of someone asking if she was okay, aware of the cops questioning Ayden. She answered questions from the local police. Painstakingly, she recounted her story and Richard, her flight and his attempt to kill her.

She glanced toward Ayden as he spoke to the local cops. His head was bowed and his face grim as the other cops spoke to him. Then, as if he sensed her gaze on him, he looked up. His gaze softened and held hers. Seeing the hole in his shirt made by Denny's bullet triggered a replay of the morning's terrifying events. She tried to offer a quivering smile but in the end had to look away.

Richard had reached out from the grave and smashed her life. She wondered how many other traps he'd set for her. How many other killers were out there waiting to finish what Richard couldn't? What would Ayden do the next time something like this happened? Would he have to kill for her again?

God, death had stalked her since she'd met Richard. She would never escape it.

"I'd like to take you to the hospital." The ambulance attendant's voice cut through the haze in her brain.

"What? No. No hospitals. I want to go home."

"You're pretty banged up. The doctors need to check you over."

She shook her head. "I'm fine. I just want to go home. I want to see my daughter."

The guy had kind eyes. "You can't drive."

"I have a ride."

She'd come with Ayden. He would have to drive her home. He was a good man. He'd take care of her. But was it fair to let him? Was it fair to care for him, knowing that Richard may have set other traps for her?

The energy around her shifted, felt more tense, and she looked up. Ayden was standing before her. He had removed the vest but the bullet had left a gaping tear in the shirt underneath.

He knelt in front of her. "How are you?"

Nicole lifted her chin. "I'm good. I'm good."

"We can leave now."

Leave. It was magic to her. "I want to see Beth. I want to hold her."

Ayden kissed her on the forehead. "Let's go."

The safety deposit box had a note in it. It was written in Richard's handwriting and addressed to Christina. It read:

Christina, I love you so very much. No one can love you like I do. We will be together forever. Your loving husband, Richard.

Nicole's hands trembled as she balled the note into a tight wad.

Ayden laid his hand on her shoulder. "It's not true. You are free of him."

She nodded. "God, I want to believe that."

"Believe it."

But as she glanced at the bloodstains on her shirt, she couldn't summon his confidence.

The two-hour drive home was tense and quiet and Ayden was aware that Nicole was still wound tight. She had every reason to be. To think her ex would have sent someone like Denny to kill her eighteen months after his death.

Ayden had tried to discuss what had happened a couple of times but she'd not wanted to talk. She was withdrawing back into herself and it scared the hell out of him.

The woman he'd made love to last night had been alive and vibrant. This woman was scared and sullen. And she was shrinking away from him.

They pulled up in front of Lindsay's house and Nicole was out the door before he could come around to her side of the car. She hurried to the front steps and rang the bell.

Ayden caught up to her. "You don't have to rush. Beth is okay. We've both spoken with Lindsay."

Nicole tapped a nervous hand on her thigh. "I know. But I've got to see her."

He'd learned long ago never to get between a mother and her child. The bond was too powerful and strong.

Lindsay snapped open her door, took one look at Nicole, and immediately wrapped her arms around her. "I'm so sorry."

Nicole offered a wan smile. "I'm okay."

But her tense tone said otherwise and Lindsay picked up on it immediately. "Come in and see your baby."

Nicole moved into the house. "Thank you."

Lindsay and her husband, Zack, had renovated the whole

place. The front room was decorated in a mismatched collection of furniture that Lindsay had collected at flea markets and antique stores. The pieces shouldn't have worked together but they did. The casual relaxed style was very inviting.

Zack came out of the kitchen. His tall body and broad shoulders filled the doorframe. Short black hair accentuated rawboned features. He had the lean body of an athlete. In his big arms Beth looked so small and helpless despite the wide grin on her face. She was gurgling and grabbing at Zack's ear. But the instant the child saw Nicole she pouted and started to whimper.

Nicole went to her immediately. "Oh, baby girl."

Zack looked confused. "I swear she was fine while you were gone. She and Jack were best buds."

Nicole buried her face in the little girl's curls, inhaling the scent of baby soap and milk. Beth calmed immediately when Nicole kissed her on the forehead. "Hey, sweet girl."

"Why don't you two come into the kitchen for a cup of coffee?" Lindsay offered.

Ayden wanted that. He wanted to sit down with Nicole and get her around friends. He wanted to see her nerves calm and he wanted to see the light return to her eyes.

"I'm taking Beth home. Thanks, Lindsay, but I just need some quiet."

Ayden glanced at Lindsay and Zack's worried expressions. "Your car is still at the station."

"I brought it back," Zack said. He went to retrieve the spare key Nicole always left with Lindsay.

Nicole smiled. "Thank you."

"Nicole, don't go home now. You need to be around friends," Lindsay said.

"Honestly, I will be fine." A part of her worried that they were all in danger just by her very presence.

"I'll follow you home." Ayden's voice was hard, unwavering.

"A good idea," Lindsay said.

"I'm fine," Nicole said.

Ayden was aware that Lindsay and Zack watched them closely. Lindsay's gaze sharpened as she stared at the two and it seemed in seconds she'd guessed something more had happened in D.C. So be it. Hell, he wanted them and everyone else to know that Nicole was his.

He loved her. He wanted her in his life forever.

"I'm following you home," Ayden said again.

Nicole glanced at Ayden, realizing if she wanted to go home it would have to be his way. "Okay."

With Beth balanced in her arms, Nicole dug her keys out of her purse. The paramedics had washed the blood from her face and hands but the would-be killer's blood still stained her shirt. He had no doubt her arms would be bruised.

Just the thought of Denny sent anger shuttering through his body. He half wished the guy was still alive so that he could kill him again.

Nicole loaded Beth in her car seat, kissed both Lindsay and Zack, and thanked them before slipping behind the wheel of her car. Ayden got into his car. He followed her home.

Nicole lived on the second floor of a historic building in the city's historic district. Called The Fan by locals, the area was home to young couples and artists. He didn't like her living here. The crime stats were too high for his comfort. A woman alone and her baby . . . it just wasn't safe.

"Let me come up with you. I can stay until you get the baby settled," he said.

Sadness had drained the life from her. "That's okay. Really. I'm fine."

He studied her. "You're doing it again."

"Doing what?"

"Shutting me out. Let me help you. You don't have to do this alone."

She shook her head as she glanced at Beth's smiling face. "I know."

"Do you?"

"Yes."

He shoved his hands in his pockets and leaned toward her, lowering his voice. "Don't shut me out."

"It might be better that way."

"Why the hell would you say that?"

"I thought I was free of Richard, but I'm starting to believe that I will never be free of him. He's managed to taint what we had. What if there is another Denny out there waiting? What if he hurts you or your sons?"

"Don't borrow trouble."

"I don't want to. But I can't ignore it."

He rattled the change in his pocket. Yesterday, they had been so close. He truly had felt that nothing would ever come between them again. And now here they stood, a sheet of glass between them. They might as well have been a thousand miles apart.

"I want us to be together, Nicole. We can move past this."

Tears welled in her eyes. He saw genuine hurt and confusion and it nearly broke him. "You deserve someone who doesn't have so much baggage."

"Hell, I've got enough of my own damn baggage. And whatever is eating you is affecting us both. It's our problem." He softened his voice. "Let me help you."

She stepped back into her apartment. "You can't. I've got to do this."

Ayden wasn't going to beg. Some problems had to be worked out alone. But it was killing him to see her pull away. She smiled sadly and softly closed her door.

He pulled his hand from his pocket and fisted it. It was all falling apart and there wasn't anything he could do about it.

Chapter Nine

Thursday, December 25, 8:00 A.M.

Nicole tossed and turned all night.

Several times nightmares woke her up. *You are mine forever.* Richard's words reached out from the past and there were moments she could almost imagine his hot breath on her face.

At one A.M. she had sat up in bed soaked in sweat and fear. She was certain she heard footsteps several times. She ran to her front door and checked the locks. She also peeked in on the baby, who slept peacefully in her crib.

She and Beth were safe.

And yet the fear clung to her like a wraith.

At dawn, she had swung her legs over the side of the bed and gave up on sleep. Checking Beth again, she padded into the kitchen and made herself a cup of coffee. As the pot dripped and spit she glanced at her hands. They were clean now but the memory of the would-be killer's blood was sharp and clear.

She'd been so excited about this Christmas. This Christmas was to be her new beginning. Her fresh start. And Richard had found a way to ruin it all.

Nicole pushed away from the counter and her untouched coffee and walked into her tiny living room. She stared at her tree, now a reminder of her own foolishness.

Her cell phone rang and automatically Nicole started. She picked it up from the kitchen counter and checked the number. Lindsay.

Nicole cleared her throat hoping her emotions wouldn't reflect in her voice. She flipped open the phone. "Lindsay."

"Merry Christmas."

Nicole made herself smile. She would not let her mood poison Lindsay's Christmas. "Merry Christmas to you."

"Is Beth up?"

"Not yet. I think you wore her out."

"It wasn't me; it was Jacob and Kendall." Jacob was Zack's partner and Kendall his wife. "Jacob tossed the kid around like a sack of potatoes—all of which she loved."

A faint smile tipped the edge of her lips. "I noticed Kendall painted Beth's toenails again."

"Sinful Ruby Red. It's Kendall's new favorite color. She said every girl should be glamorous at Christmas."

Kendall was always dressed to the nines. Nicole glanced at her own plain short nails. "Kendall's going to get my girl hooked on manicures and pedicures."

"She has a stunning outfit to give Beth at the party tonight. So cute."

The thought of the party did not excite her. "Beth is going to be spoiled rotten." Despite her efforts to sound happy, sadness leaked into the words.

Lindsay picked up on it immediately. "How are you doing?"

"I'm good." The lie tripped off her tongue as automatically as it had in the days she'd been married to Richard.

"Bull. You sound like you didn't sleep a wink."

Lindsay's perceptive mind missed little. "I'm fine. Just trying to get my feet back on the ground since yesterday."

"Don't let *him* do this to you. It's what he would have wanted." Her voice cracked.

She straightened. "Lindsay, don't let this get to you. It's not your fault."

"The bastard managed to reach out from the grave and ruin your Christmas. I blame myself for giving you that stupid letter."

"This is not your fault. You had no way of knowing. Richard was a clever man." Tears filled her eyes and she had to tip her head back to keep them from spilling.

Lindsay sniffed and Nicole pictured her friend swiping away a tear. "Ayden filled Zack in on the details. Richard tried to kill you."

"But he didn't." She'd been unable to boost her own spirits, yet here she was trying to cheer Lindsay up.

"When I think of all you've been through . . ."

"And I'm still standing." She couldn't bear the sadness in Lindsay's voice.

"That's right, *you* are still standing." The steel was returning to Lindsay's voice.

"It's all good." She didn't believe that but wanted Lindsay to.

Lindsay changed tactics. "Something happened between you and Ayden."

Nicole didn't speak, not trusting her own voice.

"I *was* right!" There was no missing the triumph in her voice. "Are you going to see him again?"

"I don't know."

"Nicole, I am not going to let you give up on David."

"Lindsay, let it go."

"You weren't like this in college."

She didn't want to ask but did. "Like what?"

"Closed off. You were so open and expressive. Richard taught you to bury your pain and retreat. He taught you how to be afraid."

That made her angry. "I am not afraid for myself. But I am afraid for the people in my life. I can't put them in more danger."

"We can all take care of ourselves."

"That's what Claire said."

"Stop doing this!"

Nicole could picture Lindsay's green eyes blazing. "God, Lindsay, would you just let me deal with this on my own?"

"Nicole, I can't let anything go. Just ask my husband."

The hint of humor in Lindsay's voice cut through some of her dark mood.

"Ayden is a good guy. And I could tell by the way he looked at you last night that he is crazy about you."

Her heart constricted and this time the emotion erupted to the surface. The image of Ayden's face when he dropped her off last night flashed in her mind. His features were stony and hard but she'd sensed the unbearable sadness in him. Guilt ate at her. "Lindsay, please stop."

"No, I will not, Nicole. You have a chance to reclaim your life fully. Not just career-wise and mother-wise but romantically with a great guy."

More images flashed. This time she saw Denny shoot Ayden in the chest. "David could have been killed." A sob caught in her throat. It was hard to say the words out loud because it made her feel like such a coward. "I'm afraid to love him."

"Don't be." She softened her voice. "Love makes life so worth it all."

Nicole didn't speak.

"Stop hiding out in your apartment and rejoin life." Her voice had grown gentle again. "If you don't take a chance and try to love Ayden, Richard will have won."

That last statement infuriated Nicole.

Beth started to fuss in her crib. "Beth is awake. I've got to go."

"Will I see you at the party tonight?"

"I'll think about what you said."

"Don't think. Do." Lindsay hung up.

Beth's wails grew louder and Nicole went to her. The baby was standing in her crib gripping the side rails. When Nicole's gaze met hers, she cried louder and started to jump up and down.

Smiling, Nicole picked up the child and held her close. "It's okay."

Almost immediately Beth stopped crying and grinned. She grabbed a chunk of Nicole's hair with her chubby hand.

The weight of the baby's diaper felt heavy in her hands. "Your diaper is about to explode."

The baby tossed her a sloppy grin that held no hint of apology.

Nicole laughed and took the baby to the changing table. She laid her down and unsnapped her one-piece sleeper. As she pulled the little feet off, her gaze was drawn to the bright red nail polish that Kendall had put on Beth's toes.

The splash of color had her smiling. "Your aunt Kendall is going to turn you into a diva after all."

The baby kicked and laughed. Nicole removed the soggy diaper and cleaned the baby up. Within ten minutes the baby was dressed in a clean outfit and laying in Nicole's arms. Nicole steadied a bottle in the baby's mouth and the child greedily slurped.

With Beth in her arms, the stresses and worries of last night faded. As long as she had Beth, she would always be at peace and she would know the love of her child.

But what of the passion she'd shared with Ayden? He'd revived a part of herself that she'd thought dead. Lost forever. He was offering a full life to her. One filled with her child's love as well as passion.

Lindsay's words replayed in her head. *Don't let Richard win.*

Ayden sat in his house in the family room, staring at the tree he and his boys had decorated. The job was a sloppy mess at best. The lights were uneven, none of them had bothered to put ornaments on the back of the tree, and the tinsel clung to branches in thick clumps. Julie would have been appalled.

Ayden rose and walked to the collection of pictures on his mantel. Julie had seen to it that the boys had had their picture taken on Santa's lap every year. Often he'd been working and been unable to help her with the boys but she'd steadfastly gone each year.

Last year when he'd stood here and stared at the pictures he'd wished so hard for his old life back. He wanted what he'd had so much he could taste it.

Now, as he looked at the pictures, he knew the past was dead and buried. No amount of wishing was going to bring it back. And for the first time, he didn't want to look back but forward. His thoughts turned to Nicole.

She had her whole life ahead of her. She had so much in life that she could embrace. But she was trapped by her past. He knew from personal experience that no amount of talking or begging was going to make her look forward. Lord only knew how much his friends and family had lectured him about letting go. About moving on.

And now he was ready to move forward and the woman he loved couldn't.

As much as he wanted to march over to Nicole's house and push, cajole, and persuade her to embrace life, he knew it would be for naught. She had to *want* it. And the sad truth now was that she didn't.

It was Christmas Day. The boys wouldn't be home until tomorrow. He had no desire to go to the Kiers' open house after his shift.

He sipped his coffee. It had grown cold and bitter.

"Shit."

He reached for his coat, determined to head to the office and bury himself in work. The doorbell rang. Irritated by the intrusion, he set the cup down and moved toward the door. He snapped it open, ready to send whoever it was away.

To his shock, it was Nicole.

Nicole had never been as nervous as she was right now. Embracing life had never been so frightening but she knew if she didn't go for it now, Richard would have won and she'd always regret it.

"Nicole, what are you doing here?" Ayden's face was a stone mask and revealed no hint of emotion.

That didn't help. She'd hoped he'd see her and take her into his arms and tell her that he loved her. Instead, he stood rigid, his hands fisted at his sides as if he were bracing himself.

"I came to see you," she said.

"Where's the baby? Is everything all right?"

"Yes. Yes. She's fine and with Kendall."

Nicole felt like she could jump out of her skin. Good Lord, where was the brave, fearless woman who used to camp alone in the mountains? "Can I come in?"

"Why?" His tone was cool, distant.

Nicole hadn't expected this. She'd expected him to welcome her with open arms. Refusing to retreat, she held up a neatly wrapped box. "I have a Christmas gift for you."

That seemed to darken his mood. "You didn't have to do that."

"I wanted to." She kept her smile bright. "Can I come in?"

He stepped aside. "Sure."

Ayden closed the door softly behind her. Her gaze went to the tree. It was a disaster and yet it was wonderful. "I love the tree."

His look was openly skeptical. "Why?"

Despite all the hits this family had taken, they'd taken the time to put up a tree. "It is a signal of hope and life. And it's a pure reflection of your boys and you."

Silent, he glanced at the tree as if seeing it with fresh eyes.

Fearing that her emotions would turn her into a blithering coward, she handed him the box. "Here."

He took the package but made no move to open it. "Thanks."

"Open it."

"Nicole, what's this all about?"

"Open it." She'd resolved when she'd started this trek that there was no going back.

Annoyance flashed in his eyes. He tore at the paper as if he wanted the accursed gift open so that he could acknowledge it, and then, as quickly as possible, send her away.

As the paper ripped, he found himself staring at a cereal box. He raised a skeptical eyebrow. "I already ate breakfast."

"Oh, don't look at the box." She laughed. "It was the only box I had that the gift fit in. Open the box."

She'd taped the box securely and it took him a few frustrated seconds to peel the layers of tape off so that the lid opened. He reached inside and pulled out a flat square object nested in tissue paper.

Nervous anticipation bubbled inside of her as she watched him toss the cereal box aside and with long, lean fingers rip the tissue paper from her present. It was a framed picture, only he was staring at the back of it.

"Turn it over."

He hesitated, sighed, and complied. It was a picture of Nicole and Ayden taken at Beth's christening. Nicole held Beth and Ayden's boys flanked them.

"Lindsay took the picture with my camera. I would have set the whole shot up differently. And I would have coaxed a fuller smile out of Zane. And the frame and mat were all I had on hand this morning. The colors are all wrong for that picture."

Ayden closed his eyes. "Why are you giving me this?"

She nibbled her lip. "That's the day I told you I couldn't see you anymore."

He stared at her with an intensity that made her skin itch. But he did not say a word.

"I was still reeling with a lot of emotions then and I wasn't whole enough to care for anyone other than Beth at the time. But I'm different now."

Ayden still didn't speak. And a muscle in his jaw started to pulse as if the hold on his patience was slipping.

God, she felt like a fool. "Don't you have anything to say?"

"No."

"Right." He wasn't going to make this easy. It had to come from her. She shoved her hands in the pockets of her worn jeans and then pulled them out. "This year was about healing for me. Getting my feet back on the ground. And I did a good job of that."

He continued to stare but his jaw had relaxed a fraction.

"And then that damn letter arrived and I felt myself sliding backwards. It was as if the last eighteen months had never happened. I felt like a wreck all over again."

"You don't give yourself enough credit."

Just hearing him speak gave her the courage to keep talking. It wasn't so much his words that she heard but the tone of his voice. This tone wasn't exactly ecstatic but the anger had faded.

"After what happened in that hotel hallway . . . well, I just felt even more like I was back at square one. I was just so damn afraid."

"Of me?" Bitterness coated the words.

"No. I was afraid of opening my heart again and then watching Richard destroy another person I cared for."

He set the picture down. "What's your point?"

"I'm trying to fix this and I'm just making a mess of everything."

"You're trying to fix our friendship? Our affair?"

"No. I mean yes. I mean *no*. I'm trying to fix *us*. I'm trying to tell you that I love you. And that even though I may seem like a coward at times I am doing my level best to tell you that I do have a backbone and that I can stand up for what I want. I want you—"

He closed the gap between them in an instant, cupped her face with his hands, and kissed her on the lips. The kiss was hard and searing and so full of emotion she forgot the entire speech she'd practiced on the way over here. She wrapped her arms around his neck and pulled him toward her. He banded his arms around her waist and held her so close she could feel the beat of his heart against her chest.

Finally, the kiss ended but they remained entwined in each other's arms. "I love you, David Ayden."

He traced her jawline with a calloused finger. "I love you too, Nicole. And I will take you on whatever terms you have."

"Actually, I came here to make an honest man of you, if you'll have me."

A grin tipped the edge of his mouth. "An honest man?"

"Well, it seems like the honorable thing to do."

"I wasn't expecting marriage."

Her heart sank a little. "So you don't want to get married?"

"I didn't say that."

"So you do want marriage?"

He kissed her on the lips. "I'm saying I don't want it if you don't. Life isn't quite so black and white when I'm with you."

She nibbled her lip. "That's the thing. I do want it. Despite all the past . . . *stuff* . . . I believe in marriage. I believe in us being married." His eyes filled with so many emotions she couldn't begin to name any of them. "I'm making a mess of this."

"You're doing just fine." He pulled away from her and crossed the room to a desk in the corner. He opened a drawer, pulled out a small box, and returned to her. "I've had this since April. I saw it days before the christening and thought it was perfect for you. I hoped one day to give it to you."

Tears filled her eyes. Good God, he'd bought her an engagement ring days before she'd shot him down. "I'm so sorry."

He brushed her tears away with his thumb. "Don't be sorry. You were being honest. You weren't ready. I wasn't crazy about what you'd said that day but I understood."

He cracked open the box to reveal a stunning ring. It wasn't a traditional solitaire diamond but a gold band embedded with a string of small diamonds. She stared at it amazed. It was perfect.

"I thought about a big single diamond, but I figured that just wasn't you. When I saw this ring, it just seemed to suit who you were."

Tears streamed down her face.

"If you don't like it . . ."

"I love it. You know me better than I know myself."

He pulled the ring out of the box and slipped it on her ring finger. "Will you marry me, Nicole?"

More tears followed. "Yes. Yes. Yes."

They made it to the Kiers' party that night. But they were late.

A Mulberry Park Christmas

Judy Duarte

Chapter One

When the doorbell rang the first time, "Mac" Maguire was stretched out on the floor with his head and shoulders under the kitchen sink, trying to fix a leaky P-trap. He wasn't in the mood for visitors, so he ignored the interruption.

But then it chimed again.

And again.

In his haste to get to his feet, he banged his head on the cupboard overhang and cursed under his breath. By the time he reached the entryway, his forehead was throbbing and aching like a son of a gun. So when he swung open the door, he found it difficult to smile, even when he found seventy-nine-year-old Charlie Iverson standing on the stoop wearing a blinking, battery-operated Santa hat, a white shirt stained with tobacco juice, and a red and green argyle vest.

"I need to report a theft," the elderly widower said.

"Did you call the police?"

"You *are* the police."

Yes, but Mac was also off duty and on vacation. "What was stolen?"

"An angel that's been in my family for years. It was standing in the front yard, right by the nativity scene. Just like it's been every Christmas since Grace and I moved to Sugar Plum Lane."

"Is that the only thing missing?"

Charlie slapped his hands on his hips. "That's plenty, as far as I'm concerned. And it shouldn't be too hard to find the culprit. I know who he is. It's that little hellion who lives next door."

Mac wasn't up for this right now. Not while his forehead hurt and the kitchen sink was torn apart.

"I'm not one to fight with my neighbors," Charlie added, "but that brat has gone too far this time. So I thought you could go next door, demand that he return my angel, then tell him and his mother what happens to naughty little boys whose parents don't control them."

Mac had pretty much raised himself, so he had firsthand knowledge of what happened when parents didn't play an active role in their children's lives. But he wasn't about to get involved in a neighborhood dispute, especially when he planned to list the house he'd recently inherited with a Realtor right after New Year's Day.

"Don't tell me you haven't had a run-in with that kid yet," Charlie said.

"No, not yet." The majority of the homeowners on the street were senior citizens, but Mac had seen several children playing outdoors. "Which kid are you talking about?"

"The one who moved in a week ago." Charlie pointed to the pale green Victorian house on the opposite side of the cul de sac, the one Jillian Grant had lived in when she was growing up.

"What makes you think that boy stole your angel?"

"Who else would do it? He's as ornery as all get out, and this isn't the only thing he's done to spite me. Last week, while I was pruning the roses, he sprayed me with the water hose. And yesterday, he pelted me with pine cones. He also thinks it's funny to ring my doorbell and then run away before I can get to it."

Right now, Mac wished Charlie had rung the bell and then run off.

"How old is the kid?" he asked his temporary neighbor.

"Eight or nine, I suppose. Just the right age for a good spanking. But he doesn't have a father, and his mother coddles him."

Mac raised a hand to his forehead, finally giving in to the compulsion to probe the wound and determine how badly he'd hurt himself.

Great, he thought, estimating the lump to be about the size of a walnut. As he lowered his hand, he checked his fingertips for blood, but didn't find any.

Mr. Iverson cocked his head to the side and studied Mac's injury, squinting to get a better look. "What happened to your noggin?"

"I bumped it." Mac again fingered the tender lump. "It's no big deal."

And neither was Charlie Iverson's problem. The boy was probably just mischievous. Not that Mac was making excuses for his behavior.

The elderly widower scanned the house and yard. "I see you still haven't gotten your Christmas lights up yet."

No, and Mac didn't intend to. He only had a week to get the house in shape, then he'd be back on the job and living in his loft apartment in downtown San Diego again. "I've been too busy."

"I can imagine. Too bad Ray had to go and die before he could fix up the place. Still, he always found time to decorate for Christmas, which is a tradition on Sugar Plum Lane. I'm not sure if you know this, but folks come from miles around to see the light displays on our street."

Yeah. Mac had already been approached by several well-meaning neighbors. And he'd told them all the same thing. He really wasn't into Christmas. Never had been. Not even as a kid.

"By the way," Charlie said, "Ray stored his decorations and lights in the attic, so if you need anyone to help you put them up, just let me know. I'll give you a hand."

"Thanks, Charlie. But I really don't have time to drag it all out, then put it away a week later."

"But yours and that boy's house will be the only ones on the street without lights."

"Yeah, well, that can't be helped."

Charlie clucked his tongue. "That's a shame. Christmas won't be the same this year."

Before Mac had time to consider a response, Charlie added, "'Course, it won't be the same without my Grace either. Everyone in Fairbrook used to call her The Cookie Lady. She'd start baking just after Thanksgiving and freeze what she could. Then she'd fix a platter of goodies for all our friends and neighbors. She'd even remember the mailman, the folks at the bank, and her hairdresser."

From what Mac had heard, Charlie didn't have any family left. And since he'd lost Grace just months before Ray passed away, he had a lot to grieve this year.

As the old man's eyes glistened, Mac decided to change the subject to one they'd both be more comfortable discussing, but Charlie blinked back his grief and beat him to it.

"Anyway, back to that kid." Charlie crossed his arms. "I suppose I'll have to go next door and give his mother a piece of my mind. But I've done that already. And when she got all weepy eyed, I backed down. I never have been able to handle a woman's tears. That's why I think an official visit from a police officer might work better."

"It would have to be an *unofficial* visit. I'm off duty, and Fairbrook isn't even in my jurisdiction."

"So you're suggesting it would be better if I called FPD and made a formal complaint?"

Mac sucked in a deep breath, then slowly blew out, hoping to expel his frustration as well. As much as he'd rather let his temporary neighbors squabble, he didn't like the idea of a kid being dubbed a troublemaker at such an early age. He knew firsthand how easy it was for a boy to start believing the adults who'd called him a bad seed and predicted he'd never amount to anything. But he didn't like the idea of a budding sociopath living in the quiet, tree-lined neighborhood either.

"No, Charlie. There's no need to call FPD yet. I'll talk to the boy and his mother." And if Mac thought the kid was going to graduate to setting fires and hurting small animals, he'd encourage Charlie to file an official complaint.

"Thanks, Mac. It's nice having a cop in the neighborhood again." Charlie adjusted the Santa hat he wore, then turned and started down the steps. "I sure miss Ray Burke."

Mac missed him, too. Ray had been Mac's first partner, and in spite of a thirty-year age difference, the two had become best friends. Of course, thanks to all the overtime Mac pulled, they hadn't gotten to see each other as often as they would have liked after Ray retired. So when Mac received word that Ray had died of a massive coronary in his sleep, he'd been slammed by regret as well as grief.

By all outward appearances, Ray had been in excellent health, so his death had been totally unexpected.

And so had the news that Ray had created a trust and had named Mac as the sole trustee.

Still, Mac didn't plan on staying in Fairbrook more than a week or ten days. Just long enough to fix up the house and put it on the market. He sure couldn't take care of two places, and his apartment in San Diego suited him best.

Besides, Mac wasn't into the Christmas hullabaloo or life in the suburbs. And if by some fluke he decided to go the white-picket-fence route, it wouldn't be on Sugar Plum Lane, the one neighborhood in which he'd been the least welcome as a teenager.

Mac stepped onto the porch, then closed the front door and made his way to the sidewalk, where Charlie waited for him.

"See there?" Charlie pointed to the nativity scene at the far corner of his yard. "The angel used to be looking over the manger, but now it's gone."

Mac hadn't noticed the angel before, but he'd keep an eye out for any stray ones in the neighborhood that matched Charlie's figurines.

His focus shifted to the pale green Victorian where the so-called hellion lived. The house and yard were as devoid of holiday adornment as his was.

As Charlie shuffled up his driveway and headed home, Mac continued to walk toward the house that had once belonged to the Grants. Shortly after Jillian had left for college, her father had packed up and moved. At least, that's what Mac had heard. He wondered who lived in the house now. Someone who'd just moved in, Charlie had said. A single mom who coddled her ornery kid.

Mac strode toward the front door. Each time he'd come to visit Ray, which hadn't been often enough, he'd noticed that particular house and how it had been going steadily downhill. When the Grants had lived here, Jillian's father had spent a lot of time outdoors, creating a garden showcase, but time had certainly changed things. The lawn, once neatly trimmed, was overgrown. And the colorful array of flowers, plants, and bushes that had lined the driveway and porch now grew wild.

But the yard wasn't the only thing that had been neglected. The white gingerbread trim had yellowed with age, and the faded green paint on the exterior walls had chipped and cracked. He hoped the new resident was planning to refurbish the place, which would increase the value of all the homes on the street.

He rang the bell. At least, he thought he had. Dead silence suggested it might not be working, so he lifted the squeaky brass knocker and rapped. As footsteps sounded within, he shoved his hands in the front pockets of his jeans and waited for someone to answer.

His breath caught when an attractive, thirty-something brunette opened the door, and as recognition dawned, his heart slammed against his chest.

There stood Jillian Grant.

Chapter Two

As Jillian welcomed her old boyfriend into the house, her pulse rate soared through the roof, and her heart tripped all over itself trying to regain control.

Yesterday she'd spotted a man in the neighborhood who'd resembled Mac, but she'd shrugged off the similarities, thinking her eyes had been playing tricks on her. But, apparently, they hadn't been.

Now here he was.

"You look great," Mac told her.

She wanted to believe him, but she'd gained weight during her marriage—ten pounds with each child she'd borne and then some. But she thanked him anyway and added, "You look great, too."

And he did. He still wore his sandy-blond hair stylishly mussed, and his blue eyes were just as bright and intense as they'd ever been. His face had matured nicely, and in keeping with the memory she held of him, a light stubble of day-old beard added to the bad-boy aura she'd found so attractive when she was a teenager.

A nasty lump, which appeared fresh, marred his forehead, though. She wondered how it had happened—a fight maybe?—but the question stalled on the tip of her tongue. After the way she'd ended things between them, she didn't have the right to be so curious.

Nor did she have the right to gawk at him, but she couldn't seem to help herself. He still resembled the lanky teenager she'd once known, and she found him just as intriguing now that he'd grown up. Maybe more so.

As they strode through the entry and into the living area, he scanned the room from top to bottom. She imagined he was noting the yellowed water spot on the popcorn ceiling, the curled up edges of the blue floral wallpaper, and each gouge and scratch on the original hardwood floor.

She was taking in a few things, too, like the way he'd bulked up over the years and filled out the white T-shirt he wore.

He was either working out regularly or his job required physical labor. Construction maybe? She could imagine him driving a bulldozer or wielding a jackhammer.

Her gaze returned to his shirt, but this time she actually noticed the red and black lettering that read: JIFFY BAIL BONDS—We'll have you out in a jiffy.

Did Mac work at the place?

Or maybe he'd used their services. Her heart sank a bit as she entertained the possibility.

"I always wondered what the inside of this house looked like," he said, reminding her that this was the first time she'd ever invited him in.

She'd had her reasons for not doing so at the time, but wouldn't stew about that now. "I'm afraid the house was in much better shape when my dad and I lived here."

"I thought your father sold this place when he left town."

"No, he didn't. While I was in my first semester of college, he moved up to the Sacramento area to be closer to me. But instead of selling the house, he rented it out. Now I'm trying to get it back into shape, and it's a lot more work than I expected."

"Tell me about it," Mac said. "I'm refurbishing one of the Victorians, too. The beige and white one that's on the other side of the cul de sac."

So they were practically next-door neighbors; only Mr. Iverson's house separated them.

"In fact . . ." Mac laughed and pointed to the knot on his head. "This is a result of my latest fix-it project."

He seemed to be doing a good job in the chitchat department, but she was almost speechless. All she could seem to do was marvel at how good the years had been to him.

"Are the neighbors giving you a hard time about decorating the house and yard for Christmas, too?" he asked.

"A couple of them have made comments, but I'm pedaling as fast as I can to turn this place into a home, so stringing lights along the eaves and around doors and windows is the last thing on my list."

She didn't mention that when she and the kids moved out of the house they'd once shared with Jared in Roseville, she hadn't thought to bring any decorations or ornaments with her. And even if she had the money to buy new ones and the time to put them up, she just couldn't get into the holiday spirit this year.

Of course, she blamed Jared for that. If she were still living with him, she'd be wrapping the last of the gifts, polishing the silver, and planning elaborate menus for Christmas Day.

"Charlie told me the woman living here was a single mom," Mac said, "but I didn't realize it was you."

"Are you talking about Mr. Iverson, the old man who lives next door?"

Mac nodded.

She wondered what else her crotchety neighbor had said. He'd been on Tommy's case about one thing or another ever since they moved into the house next to his.

In fact, he'd come to the door and voiced another complaint yesterday, but he'd caught her at a bad moment. Jared had just called to say his child support check would be late, which meant, after paying a repairman to get the furnace working again and then purchasing a new hot water heater, she was going to be strapped for cash. So she would be buying groceries instead of the tree she'd promised the kids they would get this weekend.

She'd been on the verge of tears when Mr. Iverson had knocked on her door, and when he started in about Tommy, calling him a hellion and saying that he needed a firm hand, the floodgates had opened.

Fortunately, Mr. Iverson had been so taken aback when she fell apart that he couldn't back off the porch and skedaddle fast enough.

"It's good to see you," Mac said.

"Thanks." She offered him a smile, wishing she hadn't postponed her diet until after the holidays. "I'm glad you stopped by."

She glanced down at the pink cotton blouse she wore, noticing a grape jelly stain on the front. She definitely would have changed her clothes if she'd known she was going to see Mac, and she would have combed her hair and applied a bit of lipstick, too.

Uh-oh. Her thoughts shifted and her movements stilled. If Mac was living in her neighborhood now, she hoped Tommy hadn't had a run-in with *him*.

"So why did you come by?" she asked.

"Charlie wanted me to talk to you."

"Why?"

"He mentioned calling the police, and I thought he was overreacting. So I figured it might be best if I took care of it."

The police? Jillian crossed her arms. "What is it this time?"

"Apparently, he had an angel decoration in his front yard, and now it's missing."

"And he thinks Tommy took it?"

"That's about the size of it."

Jillian let out the breath she'd been holding. "Tommy is angry with his father, and I'll admit that he's been acting out and is difficult at times, but he wouldn't have taken anything that didn't belong to him."

"I'm sure you know the boy better than anyone."

"Just for the record," she added, "Mr. Iverson has been picking on Tommy. And I'm not saying that because, as he told me a couple of days ago, 'every old crow thinks her baby's white as snow.'"

Mac smiled. "Would you mind if I talked to your son?"

"No. Not at all." Maybe it would be good for Tommy to talk to another adult—and a male for a change. She nodded toward the doorway that led to the rest of the house. "Come on. I'll put on a pot of coffee."

As Jillian led Mac through the entryway and into the living room, she spotted a pile of Barbie clothes Megan had left in the center of the area rug. She stooped to pick them up, hoping Mac didn't think she was a lousy housekeeper as well as a negligent mother.

To be honest, though, she had to accept at least a bit of responsibility for the divorce. After all, she'd gotten so caught up with her dad's failing health, with baking cookies for the P.T.A., and driving on field trips that she'd slowly stopped thinking of herself as a wife and lover. But she'd always been a good mother, and when Mr. Iverson had implied otherwise, she'd bristled.

She held the doll clothes close to her chest, like a shield to protect herself from anything Mac might hurl at her. "The divorce has been a big adjustment for all of us." Well, at least it had been for her and the kids. Jared hadn't seemed to lose a wink of sleep over it.

"I'm sorry to hear that," Mac said.

She'd been sorry, too. "The breakup was completely unexpected, although, in retrospect, it shouldn't have been. It was more than a little unsettling at first, but I think, with time, we'll all be better off."

Her ego had taken a beating when Jared had left, and while she knew his affair had been more of a reflection on his lack of morals than on her personally—or the twenty-some pounds she'd gained since they got married—that didn't keep seeds of doubt from sprouting every now and then.

"I imagine your father is happy that you moved back into his house," Mac said.

"Actually, my dad passed away a little more than a year ago, so it's just the two kids and me living here now."

Mac raked a hand through his hair. "I'm sorry about your dad. And divorces are tough. It sounds like you've got your hands full."

The way he'd said *divorce* made her suspect that he'd experienced one, too. So she yielded to temptation and asked, "Have you . . . ?"

"No, I've never been married. But with my job, it's just as well."

Now *there* was another topic they could discuss and stay on neutral ground. She shuffled the tiny clothes in her arms. "What line of work are you in?"

"Law enforcement. I'm a homicide detective with the San Diego Police Department."

"Oh, really? That's a . . ."

"Surprise?"

"Yes, I guess it is. Dad would have been . . ." She paused, realizing she'd veered right back to a touchy subject. "Well, to be honest, he always figured you'd be riding in the backseat of a patrol car, not in the front."

Mac tossed her a wry smile. "I guess there weren't too many people in Fairbrook who expected me to make something out of my life."

"*I* knew you would."

"Did you?" His gaze locked on hers, demanding complete honesty.

She *had* believed in him. But she had to admit that even though she'd tried to sing his praises to her father, there had been a niggling fear that Mac would always have an edge about him, that he'd never kick his rebellious streak. That if she'd married him, she'd end up . . .

. . . in the same boat she was in now.

She chuffed inwardly at the irony.

Still, she suspected it had been Mac's bad-boy reputation and the slim prospects for a law-abiding future that had been part of his appeal back then.

Before she could conjure a response, Megan skipped into the living room, her blond ponytail swinging from side to side. "Mommy, have you seen my . . ." The six-year-old froze in mid-step when she spotted Mac. "Oops."

"Megan," Jillian said, "this is Mac. He's an old friend of mine. We went to high school together."

Mac reached out his hand to her daughter. "It's nice to meet you."

The child seemed a bit perplexed by the adult greeting, but she nibbled on her bottom lip and smiled at the same time, then took the big hand he offered.

"You look a lot like your mommy," Mac said, straightening. "She used to wear her hair long like yours, too."

Megan shot a glance at Jillian and smiled, her shyness abating some.

Jillian took the opportunity to hand over the doll clothes. "Now that you're here, young lady, I have a job for you to do. You forgot to put these away when you were finished playing with them."

"Sorry." Megan reached for the clothing, but an evening gown, a tiny wedding veil, and a bathing suit dropped to the floor.

"It might be easier to make two trips," Jillian told her. "And by the way, lunch is almost ready. Where's your brother?"

"He's in the backyard making a fort. As soon as I put this away, I'll tell him to come in."

After Megan left the room, Jillian turned to face the man whose visit had momentarily shaken her world. "Have you eaten yet? I'm afraid the pickings are slim since I need to go grocery shopping. But I can offer you all the peanut butter and jelly sandwiches you can eat."

He chuckled, the rich timbre of his voice tilting her world

further yet. "I might take you up on that. I worked through breakfast and my cupboards rival Mother Hubbard's."

She led him into the kitchen. While he sat at the table, she sliced several apples and poured two glasses of milk. Then she took a pitcher of tea from the fridge and a tub of ice from the freezer. Before preparing a drink for herself and for Mac, she turned and leaned her denim-clad hip against the counter. "Let's get back to Mr. Iverson and his angel. I really can't believe Tommy took it."

"It might have been a childish prank. When I was a kid, I was involved in more than my share of those."

"I suppose it's possible. Tommy seems to have been hit harder by the divorce than Megan. That's probably because the woman his father got involved with has a son who used to sit across from him in school. And right now, that boy, his mother, and my ex are . . ." She glanced at the clock on the microwave. "Well, they're probably sunning themselves on the deck of their cruise ship as we speak."

"Does Tommy know that?"

"I wish he didn't. Before we moved back to Fairbrook, the boy was telling everyone in class how his mother's new boyfriend was taking them on a Disney cruise out of Orlando." Jillian tucked a strand of hair behind her ear. "And, just for the record, Jared was the classic workaholic who never had time for school programs, dance recitals, or family vacations."

"No wonder your son is hurt."

"Before the divorce, Tommy was a happy, loving child." She straightened and stepped away from the cabinet. "So, needless to say, I'm in uncharted water when it comes to dealing with hurt and angry little boys."

She couldn't read Mac's expression, although she searched carefully, looking for skepticism or disbelief and finding neither. She suspected that holding his thoughts and reactions close to the vest had been part of the skills he'd garnered at the police academy and later on the job.

Still, she couldn't help but add, "In spite of what Mr. Iverson may have told you, I'm a good mother."

Mac got to his feet and closed the gap between them. He placed a hand on her shoulder, sending her reckless pulse rate soaring again. "No one could convince me otherwise, Jilly."

"Thanks."

His touch lingered long after he removed his hand, and his musky, mountain-fresh scent taunted her even as he returned to his seat. She struggled not to take in another heady whiff, but before she could regroup, the back door swung open.

"What's for lunch?" Tommy asked.

"Peanut butter and jelly sandwiches," she answered, before introducing Mac to her son.

Again, Mac addressed the child respectfully, taking the small, dirt-stained hand in his.

Since Megan had yet to come into the kitchen, Jillian decided to lay the latest problem on the table. "Mr. Iverson had an angel in the nativity scene in his front yard, but now it's missing. Do you know where it might be?"

"I saw it when we moved in," Tommy admitted. "And it was there a couple of days ago, I think."

"Mr. Iverson seems to believe that you might have taken it," Jillian said. "I hope you aren't playing a trick on him to annoy him."

"I didn't take it. Why would I want a dumb ol' angel?" Tommy crossed his arms and frowned. "And I don't try to annoy him. It just happens. But he tries to mess with me all the time. And he does it on purpose."

"Oh, yeah?" Mac asked. "How does he mess with you?"

Tommy furrowed his brow, scrunched his face, then shrugged. "Like the other day. I was playing with my little parachute guy and throwing him up in the air, but he accidentally flew over the fence and landed in Mr. Iverson's yard. Any nice, regular person would have thrown it right back over the fence. But not Mr. Iverson. He kept it instead. And he still has it."

Jillian eased closer to her son. "Did you tell him the parachute guy was yours and ask him to give it back?"

"I tried. I knocked a bunch of times, but he didn't answer. Then I rang the bell. But he never came to the door. I knew he was home, though. I could hear the TV on some news show. So I looked in the window and accidentally bumped into one of the big plants on his porch. It fell over, and the pot broke. I knew he would be super mad, so I ran away. But then he came over and yelled at my mom instead."

"He didn't *yell* at me," Jillian said in the old man's defense. But he certainly hadn't been happy about it.

Again, Tommy shrugged. Then he used a dirty index finger to push his glasses back up the bridge of his freckled nose.

"Why didn't you tell me about your little parachute man?" Jillian asked. "I would have gone next door and asked Mr. Iverson to please return it. And rather than run away when you broke the pot, you should have told me about it."

"But what if it cost a whole lot of money? I heard you talking to Dad on the phone, and you said that you didn't even have enough money to buy a tree and presents this year. So how could I tell you about the pot?"

Jillian took in a sharp breath. She hadn't meant for Tommy to overhear the financial discussion she'd had with his father. Nor had she wanted Mac to be privy to that same piece of news now, but it was too late.

"My dad is a jerk," Tommy told Mac.

For once, Jillian didn't correct him.

Megan entered the kitchen, and Jillian sent the children to the bathroom to wash their hands.

She probably ought to have said something to Mac, like, "I'm sorry you had to hear that." Or maybe even, "See what I've been up against?" But she bit her tongue instead, hoping the frustration wouldn't well in her eyes.

But, hey, if it did? Maybe Mac would disappear as quickly as Mr. Iverson had.

"You know," Mac said, "I've got an idea."

He did?

Jillian had run through every idea she'd had when it came to dealing with Jared's selfishness and Tommy's anger. And she hadn't had much luck. So she was game for almost anything.

"After lunch, why don't I take you guys for an ice cream cone at The Creamery?"

Jillian hadn't stepped foot in that place since the day before she and Mac broke up.

Why would he suggest they go there?

And why did she later go to get her purse and grab jackets for the kids?

Chapter Three

It was mid-December, but the air was still a bit crisp and chilly for a southern California beach community.

Mac probably should have suggested taking the kids to Happy Donuts, which was only a few shops down from The Creamery. But the ice cream cone invitation had just rolled off his tongue, and the kids and their mother had been okay with it.

So here they were, parked in his black Ford Expedition on the shady, tree-lined street, where The Creamery was flanked by Specks Appeal, an eyeglass store, and Café Del Sol, a trendy eatery that offered both indoor and sidewalk dining.

While Mac slid out of the driver's seat, Jillian and the kids climbed from the SUV.

Most children had a natural sweet tooth, so he figured he'd get on Tommy's good side by buying him a treat. And maybe, if he was able to connect with the boy on some level, he could help Jillian put an end to the cold war that seemed to be brewing between her son and Charlie.

As they entered the shop, a bell—probably the same one that had announced new customers years ago—tinkled, alerting an older man who was reading behind the counter.

The sixty-something man, who wore a red-and-white-striped shirt, stood and made his way to the freezer display case.

A black plastic badge said his name was Ralph. "Can I help you folks?"

"We'd like some cones," Mac said.

The gray-haired man grinned. "You betcha."

Megan and Tommy approached the freezer display case and peered at twenty or more flavor options, while Ralph awaited their decision.

"This place certainly hasn't changed much," Jillian said, perusing the interior.

Mac had to agree, noting the black and white checkerboard flooring, the chrome-trimmed, white Formica tables, and the red vinyl chairs. Several matching booths still lined the back wall, including the one in the far corner, where he and Jillian used to sit whenever they'd found it empty.

"Oh, cool," Tommy said. "Look, Meggie. Bubble gum ice cream. It has chunks of gumballs in it, and when you're all done eating it, you end up with a mouth full of chewing gum."

"Ooh, yuck," Megan said, scrunching her face. "I want strawberry."

Mac nudged Jillian's arm as though not a day had passed since they'd met here regularly. "How about you?"

"Thanks, but I'll pass."

"You didn't eat anything except apples at lunch," he said. "Aren't you hungry?"

"A little. But I just started a diet." She offered him a smile, then glanced at the small bulletin board behind the cash register, where a snowflake-trimmed flyer had been posted.

He'd noticed that she'd put on a bit of weight over the years, which was probably why she was dieting, but it didn't matter to him. There'd always been something special about her that had caught his eye and gripped his heart.

Her dark brown hair, which had once hung to her waist, curled at the shoulders now. The style suited her, he supposed.

"Mac?" The way she said his name, her voice as soft and lyrical as he'd remembered, stirred up all the good memories he'd ever had. She pointed to the announcement.

"Did you see that? They're having another Christmas Under the Stars. It's this weekend. Apparently, it's become a community tradition."

As the children gave their ice cream orders, and Ralph prepared their cones, Mac's thoughts drifted back fifteen years to the day Fairbrook readied for the very first outdoor holiday event.

That particular December afternoon, the sun had been sinking low in the western sky, and Mac had been hanging out in Mulberry Park with a couple of friends. They'd been discussing what they were going to do that night for fun, while several men on ladders ran extension cords and connected a sound system. A few women had set up tables and were covering them with red and green plastic cloths.

Mac had been looking forward to joining his friends for another aimless night on the city streets, when he noticed Jillian's car pull up. And suddenly, his interest shifted.

He'd never been shy around girls before, but Jillian had been different. She'd been a college-bound senior, and he was a year younger and a grade behind, wondering if a high school diploma was all it was cracked up to be. So their paths had rarely crossed, but on those few occasions when they'd spotted each other in the cafeteria or down the hall, Mac had sensed that the attraction had been mutual.

Jillian had parked along the curb that afternoon, and as she was trying to get a platter of brownies out of her car, Mac had gotten a burst of testosterone-laced courage.

So, after telling his friends he'd catch up with them later, he'd made his way toward the girl who was clearly out of his league, figuring he'd bite the bullet and introduce himself.

Jillian, who was still studying the flyer behind the register in The Creamery, interrupted his thoughts. "Do you remember the first Christmas Under the Stars?"

"Yeah." Being with her again had brought it all rushing back to him.

"I'll never forget that night," she said, her tone soft and wistful.

Neither would Mac, but he didn't want her to know he'd been waxing nostalgic, so he made light of it. "I believe that was the first and only time I'd ever heard you say a bad word."

She batted his arm the way she'd done when they were teens on the verge of adulthood and he'd teased her about something. "The word I said wasn't so bad. And it just slipped out. I'd baked four dozen brownies earlier that day, and I was supposed to drop them off with the refreshment coordinator. And then you called my name."

And when she looked up, she'd dropped both plates, frosting side down, in the dirt.

He grinned, remembering it all clearly. "Hey, I helped you pick them up."

In the process, their hands had touched, their gazes had locked, and Mac had fallen in love for the first and only time in his life.

Three months later, she'd dumped him.

But hey, he should have known better than to imagine anything could have really developed between them. Jillian had grown up as an only child in a loving home on Sugar Plum Lane. And Mac had spent his early years in a rundown apartment on the east side of town with an alcoholic mother and a father who'd been an on-again, off-again druggie. So the cards had been stacked against them since day one.

Suddenly, a little tiptoe down Memory Lane had turned into a full-on run. Mac tried to backpedal, but something in Jillian's pretty green eyes zeroed in on him, just the way it always had, and he felt like an awestruck adolescent all over again.

"That'll be four dollars and twenty-eight cents," Ralph said. "That is, unless you two want a cone or something."

Mac turned to Jillian and smiled. "It's your last chance to cheat on that diet. For what it's worth, you look just fine to me. And this has got to be the worst time of the year to be watching what you eat."

"Thanks, but I'm going to pass. You go ahead. How about one of those triple-scoop Rocky Road cones you used to like?"

"Not today." He wouldn't feel right eating in front of her. "I think I'll just have a cup of coffee."

Jillian ordered hot tea, and as the clerk prepared their drinks, Megan and Tommy tasted their ice cream cones, then wandered to the back of the shop and slid into a booth. Mac had almost suggested they move to the one in the back corner, but he didn't. Instead, he took a twenty from his wallet and waited for Ralph to tally the tab.

"I heard you talking about Christmas Under the Stars," Ralph said, handing an insulated cup of hot water to Jillian, as well as a teabag. "It's an annual event, and the kids will love it. I hope you'll consider taking them. We sing carols by candlelight and drink hot cocoa. There's also a live nativity display."

"You know, I think I will take them." Jillian dropped the teabag into her cup. "It'll provide them with a bit of the holiday spirit since we won't be celebrating in the usual way at home this year."

Ralph handed Mac a large coffee and nodded to a table to the left of the counter. "You'll find sugar and cream over there."

"Thanks." Mac would drink his black, but he wasn't sure about Jillian's preferences.

He watched her stop by the table and pick up a packet of sugar-free sweetener. Then she looked at him, her eyes just as bright and expressive as ever. "How about you? Will you be going?"

"No, I've never made a big deal out of holidays." There'd never been a reason to. The last time he'd tried was when he'd dated Stacy Pernicano, a hairstylist by trade and his longest lasting relationship. A few years back, she'd taken him home to meet her family and to spend Christmas evening with them.

Her parents had gone all out with the outdoor lights and a *Nutcracker* scene that moved around the lawn. And inside, a ten-foot tree, its branches fully lit and loaded with ornaments, took center stage in the living room, surrounded by a mound of colorfully wrapped gifts. Stacy's mom had gone all out on a gourmet feast, too.

But Mac had been uneasy all evening.

It was more than just the over-the-top holiday scene that had made him skittish. It was because Stacy had gotten a little clingy, and he preferred not to let women get too close. He was more of a loner than most, and he liked it that way. So he'd broken things off after New Year's.

"I can't imagine not celebrating Christmas at all," she said. "It makes me sad to think of you being alone."

"Don't worry about me. I keep busy." He usually volunteered to work extra shifts so the other officers could spend the holidays with their families.

As he and Jillian approached the table where Tommy and Megan were sitting, she slid in first and made room for him.

He tried to focus on the kids and their ice cream cones, rather than on Jillian, whose arm touched his. Whose light, floral scent reminded him just how little had changed.

Fifteen years ago, she'd always insisted that they meet somewhere, which was probably because Mac had been a budding delinquent her father hadn't approved of.

Of course, that was the old Mac, a guy who no longer existed. Still, as he sat at a table with Jillian and her kids, those same adolescent insecurities began to surface again, reminding him of how star-crossed his crush on Jillian had been. And being together again at The Creamery, where the walls seemed to be closing in on him and forcing his memories to the surface, was making it worse.

He suddenly wanted to be anywhere but here.

"Look, Mom." Tommy pointed at the window that looked out at the park. "There's a playground over there. And it's got a teeter-totter, a slide, and all the stuff Meggie likes."

"Where?" His sister scrambled to get to her knees, ditching all signs of her shyness. "I want to see it."

Mac glanced across the street, noting that the playground

hadn't been anywhere near as grand fifteen years ago and wondering when it had been remodeled.

"It looks fun," Jillian said. "Before school starts in January, I'll have to take you there."

Sensing an escape route, Mac slid out of the booth and got to his feet. "What's wrong with going there now?"

Chapter Four

Jillian and Mac, each with an insulated cup in hand, steam rising and twisting in the cool, wintry air, walked the children across the street to Mulberry Park.

Today had been surreal, Jillian thought, first with Mac showing up at the door and then with him suggesting they take the kids to The Creamery. And now they were headed to the playground.

She'd always wanted Jared to take part in outings like this, and while they did occasionally go to dinner or to school programs together, he usually had a reason for not joining her and the kids.

"Sorry, babe," he would say, sometimes placing a kiss on her cheek and sometimes not giving her so much as a glance. "I've got another meeting I have to attend. And you know that business comes first."

She just hadn't realized he'd meant monkey business.

Of course, now Jared was probably strolling the deck of a cruise ship with his new family in tow, which wasn't fair to the two children he'd left behind.

But she shook off the thought. The divorce was behind her, and it was best if she focused on the future. Whatever that might bring.

She stole a peek at Mac, who was looking ahead and scanning the park. He'd always been keenly aware of his surroundings, a tendency that, whether innate or learned as a child, probably came in handy with his job as a detective.

"Come on," Tommy said as he and Megan reached the end of the crosswalk and stepped onto the curb. "Let's go ride the teeter-totter first."

"Okay, I'll race you." Megan took off across the grass, running toward the playground, her blond ponytail swishing across her back. Yet even though her brother reached the sand several strides ahead of her, she didn't seem the least bit disappointed to come in second place.

"I'm glad I made the kids put on a jacket before we left," Jillian said, noting that Mac only had on a white T-shirt. "Aren't you cold?"

"Not really." He took a sip of coffee.

She again noticed the red and black lettering on his shirt, and curiosity got the better of her. "What's with Jiffy Bail Bonds? That seems like an odd shirt for a police officer to wear. I thought it was your job to lock up the bad guys and make sure they stayed there."

He glanced at the block lettering across his chest, then tossed her a crooked grin, his eyes crinkling at the edges, and chuckled. "One of my buddies had these made up for a department softball game. It was our way of razzing our opponents. The captain of the other team was a public defender."

"Cute. I'll bet your opponents loved that."

"Yeah, but don't worry. The shirts they wore were blue and said The Donut Stop, the Safest Place in Town."

"That must have been some softball game."

"It was a lot of fun. Especially the heckling." He nodded toward a green fiberglass picnic table. "Why don't we sit over there and watch the kids play? Unless, of course, you'd rather join them on the playground?"

Like they'd done on the night they'd met?

Her thoughts drifted to the first Christmas Under the Stars event, when she and Mac had wandered away from the couples and families holding candles and singing carols, away from the twinkling lights that adorned the trees.

They'd teeter-tottered for a while, their only light coming from the ornamental electric lampposts located near the cinder block building that housed the restrooms. Then they'd moved on to the swing set.

For two teenagers with very little in common, except a mutual attraction that had caught them both off guard, they'd hit it off that night. And when no one was looking, they'd slipped behind the restrooms and shared a kiss that began sweet and hesitant, then grew hungry and urgent.

Had Mac been remembering it all, too?

As they each took a seat on the bench, their backs to the table, they faced the playground where Tommy and Megan had joined several other children. She stole another look at her teenage crush, but couldn't tell what he was thinking. His gaze was on her son, who, fortunately, seemed to have left his troubles at home today.

"Tommy's always been a happy child," she said. "It's just since the divorce that he's been a little . . . down and snappy."

"Have you taken him to see a counselor?"

"Not yet." She would have done it by now, but the new insurance plan Jared had recently acquired didn't cover anything other than basic medical and only some dental. And with the expense of the move and a delay in the child support check . . . "I've enrolled the kids at the new school, and their first day is on the fifth of January. So I thought I'd see if the district psychologist might talk to him at that time. And then we'll see what he or she recommends."

"I'm sure that'll help."

"I hope something will. I've been at a loss. It's tough to see your kids hurting and not know what to do about it." She'd always been a mother-knows-best sort of woman, but in this case, she was treading water and hoping for the best. "I've prayed about it," she added, not sure at all how Mac would feel about that. Her father had taken her to church regularly as a child, while Mac, according to what he'd once told her, had never stepped foot inside one.

Had that changed?

She slid another glance his way, but couldn't read his expression. For some reason, she felt compelled to explain. "A couple of days ago, Tommy blew up over a lost toy. Not the parachute guy, but another one. And he started crying, saying that everything he loves gets stolen or lost or broken. I knew he was talking about more than just the toy."

"What did you say to him?"

"I brought up his father, planning to explain—again—that the divorce had nothing to do with him at all, but he just stomped out of the room and slammed the front door. I probably should have gone after him, but I was feeling so helpless when it came to knowing what to say and how to deal with his pain and anger, that I fell apart and started crying. All I could do was pray. I heard the front door open again, and some footsteps in the hall. They paused for a moment or two, then continued on to his bedroom. I suspect he might have heard the desperation in my sobs, but if so, he never mentioned it."

"If he's like most males I know, he probably didn't know what to say to a woman in tears so he chose to keep quiet."

"You're probably right."

"Does his father see him and his sister very often?"

"No." And now, since she'd moved to Fairbrook, Jared would see them even less. But she'd needed the distance, even if the kids didn't. She'd gotten tired of running into friends they'd had as a couple, people who were uncomfortable with the situation and didn't know what to say to her anymore.

Sometimes, she'd spot one of them at the market, and they'd either hem and haw, opt to study something on the shelves to keep from addressing her, or make a quick U-turn and take their cart down another aisle.

Bottom line, though? She'd also come home to lick her wounds. But Mac didn't need to know any of that.

Silence stretched between them like a frayed rubber band, ready to snap in two.

Then he turned ever so slightly, his knee grazing her leg, his gaze locking in on hers. "Your husband was a fool to ever let you go."

The sincerity in his eyes and the kindness of his words were a balm to her bruised ego, and she clung to them as long as she dared.

If more time had passed, if she were even ten pounds lighter . . . If they were teenagers again and could start all over . . .

But there were way too many ifs, too many memories and emotions balling together in her chest that made her want to get this conversation headed in another direction.

Yet it wasn't memories of Jared that caused her uneasiness. It was the memories of Mac, of what they'd once had. Of what she'd given up.

She needed to change the subject, to break eye contact, but his penetrating gaze wasn't letting up.

Fortunately, her daughter came to the rescue, her little arm extended with a pink, gooey, strawberry mess. "Mommy, can you please hold my ice cream for me?"

As Jillian's fingers stuck to the soggy paper cover, which already bore traces of sand, she scrunched her face, then opened her mouth to object. But Megan was already heading back to the playground.

"That doesn't look too appetizing," Mac said.

"You're right. I'll hold this for a little while, then I'll encourage her to throw it away."

"Look on the bright side." The laughter in his voice was calming, soothing. "At least you won't be tempted to eat it."

"That's for sure. I've been known to finish off a few treats, but this won't be one of them."

He leaned his back against the edge of the table and stretched out his legs, crossing them at the ankles. "I'd never be able to steer myself away from sweets for more than a day or two, so I admire your willpower."

She wondered what he would think if he learned that her self-improvement program had only begun the minute she'd laid eyes on him again.

At the beginning of the year, though, when she'd first learned that Jared was having an affair, she'd started a diet and exercise plan, hoping she could entice her husband to end things and come back home. But then she'd connected the dots and realized the man she'd thought was a workaholic had actually been a womanizer. And she'd decided not to stress about carbs or calories until after the divorce was final and she'd gotten the kids resettled in Fairbrook.

But settling in was more difficult than she'd imagined it would be, and her last plan had been to start watching her weight as a New Year's resolution.

She glanced at Mac, saw him studying her, and forced herself to look away. Shrugging off the possibility of mutual interest, she stood and called Megan. When the child acknowledged her, she began walking to the trash can that was located near the drinking fountain. "I'm going to throw this away, Meggie. It's melting."

"Oh, okay."

After dumping the cone, she used the fountain, its water brisk and cold, to rinse her hands. She wiped them dry on her denim jeans, then shoved them into her pockets for warmth.

Upon her return to the picnic table, she decided to take control of the conversation, shifting it from her and her children to him.

"I'm curious, Mac. How did you decide to pursue a career in law enforcement?"

He looked beyond the playground, then seemed to study his feet. About the time she thought he wasn't going to answer at all, he said, "Your dad was right about me. I'd had a lousy home and very little parental direction. I'd already started down the wrong path, but when you and I were seeing each other, I was determined to change. To be the kind of guy you thought I could be."

She felt the need to argue, to defend the boy he used to be, but she kept quiet.

"And to be honest?" Mac's gaze reached deep inside of her, where there was no need for arguments, excuses, and false sentiment. "I wasn't sure I could be that man. But, for what it's worth, your grades might have slipped, but mine had begun to climb."

Her father had believed that Mac would drag her down, and he'd done his best to discourage her from seeing him.

"After we broke up and you went to college, I figured to heck with it and fell in with a bad crowd, a group of bad-ass delinquents who were in trouble more times than not." He lifted his hand and pinched his index finger and thumb. "I was this close to crossing the line and facing some jail time."

"What happened to change that?" she asked.

Again he looked into the distance, and when his gaze returned to her, a crooked grin formed, crinkling the edges of his eyes with wry humor. "I'm probably the only guy you know whose life was turned around by a homeless man."

"You mean you saw a guy living on the streets and realized you might end up like that?"

"Nope."

She turned in her seat, her knee brushing against the warmth of his leg. She considered pulling away, but she missed what little connection they still had. "Then how did he . . . ?"

"One day I was cutting through this very park to meet up with some of my friends, and I ran into this homeless guy. At least, I assumed he was homeless. He wore a dark jacket with a torn sleeve, a faded black shirt, and brown frayed pants. His long, stringy hair hung to his shoulders, and he had a bushy, silver-streaked beard."

"Who was he?"

"He said his name was Jesse—just Jesse. And he had the bluest eyes I'd ever seen. He seemed to know a lot about me, and he talked the way I always imagined a father might speak to his son." Mac shrugged a single shoulder. "You know, in a Ward Cleaver or Pa Ingalls sort of way."

"What did he say?"

"Among other things, he told me that I couldn't change the past. But I could change the way I perceived it. And that I could choose a better future for myself. One that would put me on the right side of the law and lead me to the family I deserved."

"And you took his advice to heart?" she asked.

"Yeah. I guess I did." Mac looked off into the horizon, and for a moment, she thought he wouldn't share any more about the epiphany the homeless man had provided him. But he turned, caught her gaze, and reconnected. "Jesse gave me an interesting lecture about doing the right thing, even though it took a lot more effort than doing the wrong thing. 'Sometimes it's easier to concoct a lie than to brave the truth,' he said. 'And a weak person will find it easier to take what someone else has earned rather than risk working hard and achieving something on his own.'"

"I hadn't thought of it that way," she said.

"Neither had I. He went on to say that doing the right thing, even when it seems like the hardest thing in the world to do, is a reward in and of itself. And that the biggest reward was reaping the kind of life I deserved." Mac uncrossed his ankles and stretched his legs out in front of him. "So, on a whim, I decided to give it a try. Instead of going out with my friends that night, I just went home. I learned later that it was a good thing I did. My friends had been arrested for vandalism, breaking and entering, and burglary."

"You lucked out."

"Yep. But it felt like the kind of reward he'd been telling me about."

"Whatever happened to him?"

"I don't know. I never saw him again, but I always figured he had some kind of psychic ability. Then again, maybe I'd just decided to make sure his prophecy came true. Either way, I hit the books and ended up with a college degree in criminal justice. And six months after that, I became a police officer. The guys in my department are my family now."

"Mommy!" Megan's voice shattered the conversation Jillian had been having with Mac. She turned to the child, who was stooped over a filthy, shaggy mutt. When she looked up, she grinned from ear to ear. "Look, Mommy! It's a dog."

"Don't touch him, Meggie. You don't know where he's been."

"That's because he's lost and doesn't have an owner," the girl said.

"You don't know that." Jillian glanced up at the sky, which had grown darker while they'd been at the park. The air had become colder, too.

Megan ran her hands along the dog's ribcage. "I can feel his bones. He's starving. We have to give him something to eat."

Tommy joined his sister. "Hey, boy. What's your name, huh?"

Jillian again looked overhead, noting a storm moving in from the northwest. Then she turned to Mac. "We really ought to be going home. I think it's going to rain."

Mac stood and made his way toward her.

"But we can't leave the dog here," Tommy said, looking up and pushing his glasses back on the bridge of his nose. "He'll get sick."

He was probably already sick. And flea-bitten. The closer Jillian got to the animal, the more neglected it appeared. Its fur was matted and filthy. Brown, soulful eyes peered at her through shaggy bangs, as if pleading for sympathy and help.

"Can we keep him?" Tommy asked. "*Please?*"

Jillian certainly didn't need to take in a stray dog, and she opened her mouth to tell the boy no. But the word wouldn't form.

Maybe the kids needed a new focus. Maybe they needed that poor little stray more than it needed a home. And maybe a new pet would make up for the Christmas presents she wanted to buy them and couldn't afford.

She approached Mac. "Do you mind if that dog rides in your car? If so, I can come back for it in mine."

Mac studied the mangy critter, then crossed his arms. "Sure. Why not? I owe a lot to a homeless man. Maybe finding this mutt a new home is a way to pay it forward."

Chapter Five

The rain began as a light sprinkle, dotting the pavement and plumping the dust in the air with moisture.

As Mac, Jillian, and the kids entered the crosswalk on their way back to where the Ford Expedition was parked, the kids used words of encouragement, kissing sounds, and pats on their thighs to coax the stray dog to follow. Apparently, the shaggy little mutt realized it was in his best interest to keep up with the children, because even though it favored its left hind foot, it managed to hobble across the street at a pretty good lick.

"What are we going to name him?" Megan asked her brother.

Mac's first thought was "Lucky," but he didn't offer any suggestions. He'd already gotten more involved with the little family than he ought to.

"He looks like a Wookiee," Tommy said. "So how about Chewbacca? We can call him Chewie."

"I don't want to call him that. Besides, he's not going to look like a Wookiee forever. After he gets a bath, I'm going to use one of my barrettes to keep the hair out of his eyes. I don't think he can see very good."

"He's not going to wear girl stuff. We'll just give him a haircut." Tommy opened the passenger door, then bent to pick up the dog.

"I'll do it," Mac said, reaching for the animal and getting

more involved by the minute. "You get in first and buckle your seat belt. Then I'll pick him up and give him to you."

If Mac had any qualms about getting sucked in deeper, they disappeared the moment Jillian placed her hand on his forearm, her fingertips pressing gently into his flesh and throwing his pulse out of whack.

Her pretty green gaze reached deep inside of him. "Mac, I really appreciate you being a good sport about this."

Yeah, it definitely wasn't his usual MO, but he decided not to think about why that might be. He picked up the filthy mutt and grimaced. "Oh, man. This dog smells like it's been Dumpster diving."

The boy opened his arms, ready to take the four-legged Wookiee on his lap.

"Be careful, Mac. He has a sore foot." Jillian stood at Mac's side, watching the transfer of the dog to the boy. "I hope it's nothing serious. If it is, we'll have to take him to the pound. I can't afford a vet bill right now."

"I'm sure it's no big deal," Tommy said. "He'll be fine. Besides, we don't mind if he's crippled. Everyone needs love and a family."

Maybe so, but they didn't always have one.

Mac certainly hadn't.

He'd always wanted a dog, too, but his old man had never let him have one. There'd been a Labrador mix that had hung out at the apartment complex for a while, and Mac used to feed him and talk to him every chance he got. He'd even pretended the dog was his—until it was hit by a car. When Mac had spotted that big black dog lying on the side of the road, he'd cried for a week.

Weird how that dumb mutt had become so important in a matter of days.

After closing Tommy's door, Mac told Jillian, "I'll pay for any treatment the dog might need."

"I can't ask you to do that."

"You didn't. And you don't have to." He shrugged, then

reached for the handle of the passenger door. "Having a dog will probably help the kids through the holiday."

"You read my mind." She offered him a wry grin. "And that's the only reason I agreed to let that stray come home with us."

Mac opened the door for her, and as she climbed into the vehicle, he glanced first at his grungy hands, then at a dirty smudge on the front of his rain-splattered shirt. The dog wasn't the only one in need of a bath. Great. He closed Jillian's door, circled the vehicle, and climbed into the driver's seat.

"It reeks in here," Jillian said. "We'd better roll down the windows."

"Good idea." Mac started the ignition, then turned on the windshield wipers, letting them make a few swipes to clear his vision.

Jillian glanced over her shoulder and into the backseat. "The first thing we're going to do when we get home is to give that dog a bath."

"But Mommy," Megan objected, "can't we feed him before that? He's awful hungry."

"Okay. But just a snack. We've got to get him in the tub before we can turn him loose in the house."

"He sure is cold and shaky," Tommy said. "We'd better get him home in a hurry."

"Yeah," his sister chimed in. "We don't want him to get sick."

She was probably thinking about the dog catching a cold, but Mac sure hoped it didn't get carsick. Then he'd have to call a mobile auto detailing company, which he might have to do anyway to get the doggy stench out of the upholstery.

"I'm going to owe you for this," Jillian told him. "But the best I can offer is dinner. We're having tacos tonight, and you're more than welcome to join us."

The peanut butter and jelly sandwich had worn off an hour ago, and Mac would have to fill up on something soon. He usually just drove through a burger place or called out for pizza, so there were plenty of options. But in spite of having several reasons why he ought to thank Jillian and decline, none of them seemed to matter. "Tacos sound good."

Mac backed out of the parking space, then pulled into the street. Other than the slow swishing of the windshield wipers and a few groans and complaints about Chewie's smell, they returned to Sugar Plum Lane in silence.

As Mac parked in front of Jillian's house and climbed out of the vehicle, the rain was still a light drizzle. But he suspected it would start coming down harder before too long.

He began to circle the car while Jillian slid out of the passenger seat.

"I'll carry the dog in the house," he told her. "There's no need for all of us to be stinky and dirty."

"Thanks. I appreciate that." She tucked a strand of hair behind her ear. "Let's give him a chance to go potty first. I have a feeling he isn't housebroken."

"You're probably right." Mac opened Tommy's door and took the dog from him. Then he carried it to the grass in front of Jillian's house.

He expected the little dog to sniff around and gain its bearings or maybe lift its leg to mark its territory, but instead, it trotted over to Charlie's yard, its left hind leg bobbing behind it.

Uh-oh. *Don't pee over there,* Mac thought. Before he could chase after the mutt, Charlie's front door swung open, and the old man stepped out on the porch, that silly Santa hat still on his head, a cane in his hand, and a frown on his craggy face.

Great. Talk about radar. Charlie must have been sitting by the window when they drove up.

"Hey!" the elderly man hollered from his stoop. "Where did that mutt come from?"

Tommy stood tall and lifted his chin. "He's our new dog. And his name is Chewie."

"Well, get him off my property. I don't want you or your pets here."

"See what I mean?" Jillian whispered to Mac. "For a man who went all out with his Christmas decorations this year, he sure is an old Scrooge. He doesn't make it easy for the kids and me to get along with him."

Who knew what Charlie was thinking? Either way, Mac supposed he'd have to mediate. Maybe, if the aging widower knew what the kids had been through this past year, what they'd lost, he'd be a little more understanding.

As Megan and Tommy tried their best to shepherd the collarless dog back to their own yard, Mac called out, "Hey, Charlie. Did you get a chance to see that San Diego/Denver game on TV? I'm afraid I missed it."

"Yep. Sure did." Charlie leaned against his cane. "The Chargers lost in overtime. That new rookie, Grady Chathers, got a chance to show his stuff today. But they should have left him on injured reserve."

"If you don't mind a visitor," Mac said, "I'll come over to your house in a minute or two and have you give me a run-down on what happened."

"Be glad to. They're still showing some highlights on ESPN."

The dog, which seemed intent upon staying in Charlie's yard and adding to the drama in an otherwise quiet neighborhood, finally pulled away from the kids and dashed back to no kid's land. It barked several times, then hobbled up the steps and jumped up on Charlie, apparently forgetting about the sore leg it had been favoring.

Charlie brushed the mutt aside. "Get off me."

The dog didn't seem the least bit fazed by the scolding, and jumped up on the old man again.

Charlie grimaced. "That fool critter stinks to high heaven." He glanced down at his dirt-stained slacks and clucked his tongue. "Its feet are all muddy. Just look what it did to my good trousers!" He shot Tommy a frown and shook his head. "Now I gotta take them to the dry cleaners, and that isn't cheap."

Mac strode to Charlie's stoop. "I've got a few things that have to go to the cleaners, Charlie. So I'll take your pants for you. And it'll be my treat."

"I've got some spot remover I can try first," the old man said.

"All right. Just let me know if that doesn't work." Mac picked up the dog and carried it back where it belonged. With a possible vet bill and the charge for cleaning Charlie's pants, Mac suspected being Jillian's neighbor might get expensive.

But hey. It seemed like the right thing to do.

Jillian met him halfway and, reaching out her arms, took her new pet from him. "Thanks, Mac." A breezy smile didn't last long, and she scrunched her nose at the mangy little mutt. "I'm going to take him inside and bathe him."

"Good idea."

She glanced down at the squirmy critter, who seemed determined to wiggle out of her arms and dash back to Charlie's yard. "I sure hope I didn't make a big mistake in bringing this dog home with us."

Mac feared he'd made a few mistakes today, too. In San Diego, he usually kept to himself and didn't get involved with the people who lived in his building. But for some reason, he was letting himself get in deeper and deeper with his Sugar Plum Lane neighbors.

"Dinner will be ready at six," she told him.

He nodded, hoping dinner with Jillian and the kids wasn't the biggest mistake of all.

Chapter Six

After his visit with Charlie, Mac took a shower, then finished working on the drain under the kitchen sink. As he'd planned to do earlier, he also replaced the garbage disposal and changed out the hot water valve.

Now, at a few minutes before six, he stood at Jillian's door, wearing faded Levis, a black jacket, and a white button-down shirt. The wind had really kicked up during the past half hour, and the light rain that had continued to drizzle had dampened his hair and clothes. He probably should have looked for an umbrella so he didn't get drenched on his return home, but it was too late now.

He knocked at the door, and moments later, Jillian answered wearing a crisply pressed lime-green blouse, a pair of black slacks, and a smile. She'd also curled her hair and applied some lipstick, which suggested that she might have wanted to look nice for him. But he wouldn't take that assumption to heart. The dinner invitation had been a neighborly response, and so had his acceptance.

Still, he couldn't downplay his interest in the way her outfit complemented each womanly curve, the way her glossy hair curled at the shoulder, the way her eyes lit up when their gazes met.

"Hi, Mac." She stepped aside so he could enter. "Come on in."

Megan and Tommy, who sat on an area rug in the living room playing with the dog, glanced up at him and smiled.

"Look at Princess Leia," Tommy said.

The stray, while still thin and scraggly, had completely morphed into a poodle/terrier mix. Its fur, which had appeared dark when they'd found her, had lightened considerably with soap and water.

"Can you believe how cute she turned out to be?" the boy asked. "She's practically a brand new dog."

"So now that she no longer looks like a Wookiee," Mac said, "I guess the name Chewie is out."

Jillian laughed. "Actually, we made a critical discovery at bath time. And as long as we stuck with a Star Wars character, Tommy agreed to a more appropriate name."

Mac shook his head and chuckled. "She certainly doesn't look like that same pitiful creature we found in the park."

Jillian crossed her arms and blessed everyone in the room with a dimpled grin. "Isn't it amazing what a haircut, three shampoos, and some conditioner will do?"

"Yeah." Tommy laughed. "For a while, Mom smelled like a dog. Now our dog smells like our mom."

"Very funny," Jillian said.

"Princess Leia isn't limping anymore," Megan added. "At least, not very much. We found a thorn in her foot, and Mommy pulled it out with tweezers."

"We put medicine on it," Tommy explained. "But not the kind that stings."

"That's great." Mac crossed his arms and studied the former stray that had gotten a new lease on life. He hoped having a pet helped the kids adjust to all the changes they'd gone through.

Jillian pointed to the beige, overstuffed sofa. "Why don't you have a seat? Dinner will be ready as soon as I fry the tortillas."

"Want some help?" he asked.

"I've got everything under control, but I'd love to have some company."

"All right. You lead the way."

Mac followed Jillian into the kitchen, where a pan simmering on the stove provided the warm aroma of beef, tomatoes, and spices. He scanned the bright, cheery room, noticing lemon-yellow walls and white café-style curtains that trimmed the window over the sink.

The appliances appeared to be fairly new.

A couple of rooster pictures adorned the walls, and a few ceramic hens dotted the white tile countertops.

"I see you like chickens," he said, taking a seat at the polished oak table and watching as she reached for a black, cast-iron skillet from the cupboard nearest the stove.

"Well, I used to. I brought them from the old house, but I'll be replacing them when I can."

"Trying to reinvent yourself?" he asked.

She reached inside the pantry and pulled out a bottle of vegetable oil that was almost full. "Yes, I suppose you could say that, but I'm afraid it'll be a long time before I'm able to do everything I'd like to do to this house."

He opted not to comment about that, realizing her ex-husband's cruise had taken precedence over the child support check he was supposed to send her. Mac knew he wouldn't have liked the guy anyway, but his selfishness was hard to stomach.

Instead, he steered his thoughts and the conversation back to the only thing he and Jillian had in common—the renovations they were both tackling. "This house must hold a lot of memories for you."

She leaned her hip against the counter. "It does. Both good and bad."

So much for intending to talk about fix-it projects. After that comment, he couldn't help wondering about the bad memories she'd admitted to having. It was hard to imagine that hers could compete with some of his. "I always thought that you had the perfect childhood."

"The early years were wonderful, but I lost my mother when I was twelve, and things were never the same again."

"I'm sorry."

"Me, too." She cast him a wistful smile, then shrugged.

They'd never really gotten into the past before. Instead, as teenagers were prone to do, they'd clung to the here and now. He'd known she'd lost her mother, though, but he hadn't been aware of the details. "How did your mom die?"

"In a car accident. She was driving home from the grocery store one night and the roads were wet." Jillian glanced at the rain-splattered kitchen window. "It was a December night like this one: rainy, cold, and miserable."

Mac really hadn't meant to stir up any uncomfortable memories and, with the weather being what it was, he was sorry he'd asked.

"I think that's why this time of the year is so . . . sad." She tucked a strand of hair behind her ear and scanned the interior of the kitchen with eyes that glimmered with nostalgic yearning. "It wasn't always, though. My mom loved antiques and old Victorian houses. In fact, when we first moved to Fairbrook, Dad wanted to buy a place in one of the new developments off Applewood, but Mom insisted they find something on Sugar Plum Lane. He gave in to her, as he always did. And she went to great lengths to make this house a home for us. She was always picking up old knickknacks and furniture to add to the charm."

Mac wondered why Jillian had really moved back home. Was it for financial reasons? To escape the memories of a marriage gone bad? Or had she come to the one place she'd been able to call home?

Either way, he suspected the move had been bittersweet.

"My mom would begin decorating for Christmas the day after Thanksgiving, and it would take weeks for her to finish. She'd start from the inside out. It was really something. You should have seen it." Jillian let out a wistful sigh. "But after the accident, it was hard to get excited about anything anymore. Dad felt that way, too, which was another reason he didn't want to remain in Fairbrook without me."

Mac knew Jillian and her dad had been close, but he hadn't realized they'd had to cling to each other following their loss.

"Christmas was her favorite holiday," Jillian added, "but after she was gone, it no longer held the same appeal. In fact, even after I got married and tried to re-create my own traditions, I just never could seem to get into the Christmas spirit. Without my mom, it . . ." She paused for a moment or two, then shrugged. "Well, enough of that."

Mac didn't want to drop the subject. He wanted to find out everything he could about Jillian, about her hurts and disappointments, about her life after she'd moved up north. But he didn't suppose he could press her about it. Not if thinking about it hurt.

That's the way it had always been with them, though. There was a side of her she'd refused to share with him. A side he'd known better than to ask about.

The rain began a steady tap-tap-tap at the window, and they both looked out to see that the raindrops had turned to ice.

"Hail," Jillian said.

Before Mac could comment, Tommy ran into the kitchen. "Mom, look outside. It's snowing! I hoped and prayed that it would."

"I'm afraid it never snows around here," Jillian said. "That's hail, honey."

"But it's turning the ground white," the boy argued. "So Megan and I are going to make a snowman."

"I'm afraid you can't make anything out of ice," Mac said. "And you'd better not put too much hope into having a white Christmas. The last snowfall recorded in Fairbrook was back in 1976." At least, that's what Ray had told him. It was easy to remember the date because it was Mac's birth year.

"Well, this is practically the same thing," Tommy added before dashing back into the living room.

"He's a lot like his father," Jillian said.

Mac wanted to know in which ways the boy and his dad were alike—in looks? In temperament?

He wouldn't ask, though, even if he couldn't help being just a little bit envious of the man who'd married Jillian, then let her get away. A guy Jillian hadn't been ashamed to bring home. A man her father had undoubtedly approved of.

When Mac and Jillian had been teenagers, it hadn't taken him long to realize she was making up excuses to meet him away from her house—at the library, at the park, at the beach, at The Creamery. And when he'd finally realized she was ashamed to have him meet her father, his pride had taken a direct hit.

The rebel in him had refused to accept the slight, and he'd actually planned to end things. But a part of him had needed Jillian. A lonely, hurting part that had needed her innocence and her healing touch.

As Jillian placed the skillet on the stove, then poured a bit of oil into the pan and turned the flame on high, Mac watched her work.

A few years after she'd moved away, he'd quit thinking about her on a daily basis and had figured he was over her for good. But right this minute he wasn't so sure.

"That little dog sure seems to have settled right into the family," he said, changing his focus to something they'd both feel more comfortable talking about.

"It certainly looks that way." Jillian reached for a pair of tongs from the cupboard drawer. "We'll have to keep her in the house, though. I have a feeling she's going to run over to Mr. Iverson's yard every chance she gets. With my luck, she'll probably dig up his petunias or something. And all I need is one more thing for him to complain about."

"Charlie's getting older," Mac said by way of an explanation. "And he's facing his first Christmas without his wife of fifty-some years. They never had any kids, so I suspect this one will be especially hard."

"I'm sure it probably will be."

Mac watched her expression drift. He knew this particular Christmas was going to be especially tough on her and the kids, too.

"Did you mention Tommy when you went over to Mr. Iverson's house this afternoon?" she asked. "Or did you just talk about the Charger game?"

"A little of both." Mac leaned back in his chair, the old wood creaking in complaint. "I told Charlie that the more I got to know you and the kids, the more I think you'll make great neighbors. I suggested he give you a chance."

"What did he say to that?"

Truthfully? He'd grumbled about it, and Mac had gotten the idea it might be easier to get through to Tommy. But he wasn't sure that was going to help build a neighborly relationship where none existed. "I'm sure, with time, things will work out."

"I hope you're right." Jillian placed the first fried tortilla shell on a paper towel, then dropped another into the skillet. She jerked her hand back as the hot oil hissed and spattered.

"Charlie and I watched the game highlights," Mac added. "Then we chatted for a while. I've noticed that he's been especially talkative lately, and I suspect that's because he's lonely."

"I'm sorry to hear that." Jillian removed another fried tortilla shell from the pan and replaced it with a new one. "It's too bad he couldn't have been a little more understanding of Tommy. If he had been, I would have been a lot friendlier to him."

She had a point, but Mac still couldn't help feeling sorry for the old man. "I met Charlie about ten years ago, and he wasn't nearly as crotchety back then. Before he retired, he was an insurance agent for the most part. But during football season he was an NFL referee. You can't believe the stories he had to tell. I really used to enjoy talking to him."

Actually, Mac still did, but he hadn't had much time for the elderly man since he'd been staying in the neighborhood. With only ten days of vacation time available to him, he'd had a lot to do in order to get Ray's house back into shape, and only a short time in which to do it.

"I didn't realize you'd known Mr. Iverson that long," Jillian said.

"Ray Burke, my first partner, invited me to a barbecue about ten years ago. He'd also included a couple of his neighbors, and that's when I first met the Iversons."

"So you knew Charlie's wife, too?"

"Her name was Grace, and she was a great lady." Mac smiled, as he was prone to do whenever he thought about the short, matronly woman who'd mothered the entire neighborhood. "Grace used to make killer brownies that were loaded with nuts and covered with a fudge frosting. Ray was allergic to chocolate, but when she found out how much I liked them, she'd make him bring a plate to me each time she made a batch."

"What happened to Ray?" Jillian asked.

"He died of a heart attack about six months ago." It was a loss Mac was still grieving.

Years ago, the homeless man Mac had met in the park had predicted that Mac would find his place in the world and that he'd get the family he'd always wanted. Ray had been his first real human connection, his first real sense of belonging.

But Jesse had neglected to mention how much it hurt to lose someone who'd come to mean so much.

"Ray owned the house you're fixing up?" Jillian asked.

"Yes. It's mine now."

It had been a shock when Sam Dawson, Ray's attorney, had called Mac the day before the funeral and told him Ray had created a trust, making Mac the sole trustee. Sure, Mac had known that Ray had really liked him, but he hadn't realized that Ray had considered Mac the only family he had.

So that's how Mac had ended up with the old Victorian and everything else that Ray had owned.

Of course, he'd give it all up in a heartbeat to have his old buddy back.

A child's scream tore through the house, and a shot of adrenaline rushed through Mac's veins.

"Nooooo!" Megan yelled.

Jillian ran to the living room, with Mac on her heels.

The front door was open, and both children stood on the porch, frozen droplets of hail bouncing on the steps and the sidewalk.

"Tommy opened the door, and Princess Leia ran outside," the girl explained. "We gotta get her back."

"I think she went over to Mr. Iverson's house," Tommy said.

Jillian slid a glance at Mac. "Hopefully, she'll realize that she's better off inside and come back home."

"I'll go and get her." Tommy started for the steps, and Mac stopped him.

"Hold off a minute or two," he told the boy. "Maybe she went outside to relieve herself."

"What does that mean?" Megan asked.

Mac shot a glance at Jillian, who explained, "Princess Leia probably had to go potty and didn't want to make a mess on our floor."

"That's a good thing," Tommy said. "Right? And so she'll come right back."

Before either Jillian or Mac could respond, the fire detector screeched out an ear-piercing alarm.

"Oh, my gosh." Jillian dashed back toward the kitchen, taking time to look over her shoulder. "I forgot to take the skillet off the flame!"

Chapter Seven

Mac jogged after Jillian, hoping she hadn't caught the house on fire and kicking himself for not being more alert when they'd dashed into the living room to see what all the fuss was about.

When he reached the smoke-filled kitchen, Jillian had already removed the burning pan from the flame. He opened the window, and she grabbed a dishtowel and began fanning the smoke out of the house. Still, the alarm continued to screech like a banshee.

"Where's the smoke detector?" he asked. "I'll remove the batteries."

She nodded toward the doorway, her towel flapping in the air. "It's at the top of the stairway."

He turned to leave the kitchen, and she reached for his arm, stopping him. Again, her touch reached something deep inside of him.

"I'm really sorry about this." A blush on her cheeks revealed sincerity, as well as embarrassment.

He lifted his free hand and skimmed his knuckles along her cheek. "Don't be sorry."

Her lips parted, and her breath caught. Yet she didn't step back, didn't turn away.

If he had any doubt about the strength of the attraction he still felt for her, he didn't anymore. But he figured a relationship with her now would be just as doomed as it had been fifteen years ago. So he decided it was best to laugh it off. "I could be eating take-out all by myself, and this beats watching television."

A slow grin stretched across her lips, and she released his arm. "It's not always this hectic around here."

He wasn't sure he believed that, but he returned her smile before heading toward the stairway to turn off the annoying alarm. Thirty minutes later, the house was quiet, the batteries had been put back into the smoke detector, and the smell of burned oil and corn tortilla was just a whisper in the air.

To appease the kids, Mac had braved the hail-turned-rain with an umbrella Jillian provided and had gone out to look for Princess Leia. He'd found her on Charlie's front porch. Fortunately, the old man's television had been blaring too loudly for him to hear her yappy barks. So Mac had scooped her up and carried her home.

"This is your house now," he'd muttered to the little dog. "And if you want to stay on everyone's good side, you'll figure that out before you head outside again."

Now, while Princess Leia lay snoozing near the fire in the hearth, the adults and children sat in the dining room, where an oval, dark-wood table was laden with bowls of taco fixings: spicy beef, golden-brown tortilla shells, shredded lettuce and cheese, chopped tomatoes, salsa and sour cream. Two casserole dishes, one filled with Spanish rice and the other with refried beans, rounded out the meal.

This, Mac decided, had to be an example of family style eating at its best.

As he reached for the rice and scooped out a second helping, he glanced at the table, the varnish darkened by age. It matched the hutch against the wall.

"I like this antique furniture," he said. "It really suits the house."

"Thank you." Jillian placed her hand on the dark, polished

oak, her agreement and appreciation apparent. "It used to be my mother's. My dad sold a lot of her favorite pieces, but I kept this set in storage while we lived in Roseville. Jared liked a more modern style, and this didn't fit."

Mac wondered if having her mother's things and being in this house made Jillian feel closer to her mom, or whether it made her feel worse. A little of both, he suspected. Just as being in Ray's house, surrounded by Ray's things, made him feel good, yet sad.

Jillian, who'd skipped the tortilla shells and had made a taco salad for herself—light on the meat and cheese—asked, "How long will you be staying in the neighborhood?"

"About a week. I need to go back to work before Christmas."

"Where's home?" she asked.

"Downtown San Diego." He took a sip of the iced tea she'd poured for him. "I'm afraid a loft apartment in the Gaslamp District suits me and my lifestyle a lot better than an old Victorian in the suburbs."

"It's too bad that you'll be leaving." Jillian lifted her napkin and blotted her lips. "I liked the idea of knowing a police officer lived close by."

Tommy, who'd been drinking milk, set the glass back on the table with a thunk and a wobble. He used both hands to prevent a mishap, then brightened. "You're a cop?"

"Yes. Actually, I'm a detective now."

"Cool," Tommy said. "Do you arrest guys and put them in jail?"

"If they're guilty, I do."

"And do you shoot guys, too?"

Mac glanced at Jillian. He wasn't sure how honest she wanted him to be. "I don't like drawing my gun, but if I have to protect myself, my partner, a victim, or an innocent bystander, I do what I have to do."

"Wow." The boy's eyes lit up. "Did you ever catch any bank robbers?"

"I'm in homicide, so I don't usually get called out on those kinds of cases. But yes, I've caught my share of thieves and burglars, too."

"How many bad guys have you locked up?" Tommy asked, clearly enjoying the grittier aspects of Mac's job.

As much as he hated to admit it, Mac kind of liked being the subject of hero worship, especially in the eyes of Jillian's son. "I've arrested plenty of them."

Tommy turned to his sister and gave her a nudge. "Did you hear that? We have a real live policeman living on our street."

Megan didn't appear anywhere near as impressed as her brother was.

The phone, which sat on a small table in the hall, rang, and Jillian excused herself to pick it up. "Hello?"

Mac didn't pay much attention, but when he glanced through the open doorway and saw her stiffen, his curiosity was piqued and he found himself listening to one side of a conversation.

"They're fine." Jillian looked at the kids. Tommy was chomping on a taco, and Megan was studying her plate with an intensity that had erased the smile she'd been wearing earlier.

When Jillian and Mac made eye contact, she shrugged and tried to hide a grimace.

"Just a minute," she said, covering the mouthpiece with her fingers. "Tommy, your father's on the phone."

The boy scooted his chair away from the table, then entered the hall and took the receiver from his mom. "Hey, Dad. Are you home yet?"

His expression fell. "Oh."

Apparently, the man was calling from the cruise ship.

"Yeah. Me and Meggie are doing okay. We're eating dinner."

Mac lifted his glass and took a swig of tea, but it didn't taste nearly as cool and refreshing as the last sip had.

"We're having tacos tonight. And guess what? Mac's here. He's Mom's really good friend. He's a policeman, and he's been telling me all about the bad guys he caught."

Mac slid another glance at Jillian, noted her rosy cheeks.

Did she care if her ex-husband knew she was entertaining a man? Not that this was remotely datelike. But the boy's explanation made it sound that way, and if Mac had been her ex-husband, he would have at least been uneasy about it.

"Meggie," Tommy said, "Dad wants to talk to you."

The little girl slid out of her chair and hurried to the phone. When she grabbed the receiver, her voice cracked and her tone turned weepy and whiny. "I miss you, Daddy. Come and get us and take us home."

Mac stole a glance at Jillian, saw her standing ramrod straight, saw a slight roll of her eyes. He didn't think the kids had noticed, but he had.

Was she sorry that Mac was privy to all of this?

"Why *not*?" Megan pleaded. "Why *can't* you?"

Mac suddenly wished he was anywhere but here. The poor kid. Tommy, who'd apparently been the one harboring anger and resentment, seemed to take it in stride right now. Talk about kids being resilient. But Megan, who'd seemed fine earlier, was certainly showing her grief.

"A week is way too long," Megan countered. "I don't want to wait to see you. *Please,* Daddy!"

The man must have started sweet-talking the kid because her small shoulders hunched. "Okay, but hurry. I don't like it here."

Jillian stepped closer to her daughter. "Megan, don't hang up. I need to talk to your father, but I'm going to pick up the phone in the other room."

When Jillian had walked away and Megan returned to the table, Tommy continued quizzing Mac about the bad guys he'd caught, and Mac did his best to answer the onslaught of questions. Yet the little girl seemed to completely shy away from the conversation.

She hadn't seemed all that bashful or sad in the car or at the park. But what did Mac know about little girls?

Not much. Yet that didn't make him feel any more comfortable about being here, about observing the child's disappointment and Jillian's discomfort. Maybe he ought to call it a night and head home.

Jillian didn't return right away, so he focused his attention on Tommy. And on completing the task he'd originally set out to do this morning.

"Do you like sports?" he asked the boy.

"Yeah, especially baseball and football."

"Football, huh?" Mac sat back in his seat. "After dinner, maybe your mom will let me take you to my friend's house. He was an NFL ref, and he has all kinds of photographs and autographed balls. I think you'd really enjoy it."

"Cool." The boy sat up straight. "Does your friend live very far away?"

"Actually, he lives right next door."

Tommy furrowed his brow. "Which house?"

Mac nodded in the direction of Charlie's.

"You mean Mr. Iverson?"

"Yep."

"No way. He hates me."

"Mr. Iverson—Charlie—isn't so bad when you get to know him. When he finds out you like football, I'll bet he warms right up to you. He loves talking sports with guys like us."

Tommy nibbled on his bottom lip and furrowed his brow. "I don't know . . ."

"What could happen?"

"He could turn the sprinkler on me or something. He did that once before. Or he could shoot me full of buckshot, like he said property owners used to do to trespassers when he was a kid."

Mac blew out a sigh. What was he going to do with Charlie? Apparently Tommy had been right. Charlie had been "messing" with him.

"I think you need to know something about Mr. Iverson so you can understand him better. His wife died earlier this year, and his good friend and neighbor died shortly after that. He's crippled up with arthritis, and the cold, wet weather has been making it worse, so he hurts all over. I think what he really needs, even if it doesn't seem like he deserves it, is kindness and friendship. What do you say?"

Tommy thought about it for a moment. "Do you have your gun?"

Not with him. "Why?"

"In case he flips out or something."

"If he does, just leave it to me."

"Okay."

When Jillian returned, Mac told her what he wanted to do. "I came over here this morning to try and help the problem you've been having with Charlie. And I think taking Tommy to visit him this evening might do the trick."

"Are you sure?"

No, he wasn't. But he had a hunch it would help. "It can't hurt."

"All right. I'm willing to give it a try."

Minutes later, Mac and Tommy stood on Charlie's porch, the wet umbrella collapsed at their side. The television still blared inside, so Mac opted to ring the bell rather than knock.

As they waited for Charlie to answer, Tommy scanned the lighted yard. His gaze seemed to skip the animated snowmen and zero in on the lit nativity scene. Was he checking out the missing angel?

Charlie swung open the door, wearing a green plaid robe and a pair of brown slippers. He'd finally removed the Santa hat, but he still held his cane. He offered Mac a ready grin, but when his gaze drifted down to Tommy, he stiffened. "What's this all about?"

"I'm not sure if anyone formally introduced you to our new neighbor, but this is Tommy, and he's a big sports fan." Mac put his hand on the boy's shoulder, felt the small muscles tense. "I told him about your collection of football memorabilia and wondered if you'd let him look at the photographs and the autographed balls you have displayed on your living room wall."

Charlie seemed to give it some thought, shot Mac an are-you-sure-about-this? grimace, then stepped aside and let them into his house.

Mac wiped his feet on the mat, glad to see that Tommy was following his lead.

Charlie turned off the television, then led them to the built-in, cherrywood bookshelf near the fireplace that displayed the finest and most impressive pieces in Charlie's collection. As the old man proudly pointed out pictures of himself standing next to such football greats as Johnny Unitas, Bart Starr, and Joe Namath, the boy stood transfixed.

Before long, it appeared that a temporary truce had been reached, just as Mac had hoped.

"Wow," Tommy said for the umpteenth time in just a matter of minutes. "It's super cool that you know those guys, Mr. Iverson. And I'm lucky to live next door to you."

Charlie, who'd finally begun to let down his guard around the kid, puffed up like a peacock.

As they turned away from the shelves, Mac said, "While we're here, Charlie, we want to ask you about that missing angel. Tommy and I'd like to help you find it. So can you describe it for us?"

The old man stretched his hand about three feet from the floor. "It was about this high, and it had long gold hair, a white flowing robe, and wings. It was hand painted, although a few places on the face had cracked. After Christmas, I planned to take all the figurines to an antique shop and see if they could refurbish them for me."

"I'm sorry about your angel," Tommy said. "But at least you still have that cool snowman that moves his head. No one else on the street has one of those."

Charlie snorted. "Those snowmen are a dime a dozen, but that angel is priceless. My wife's parents gave us that set the first Christmas after we were married, and every year we'd put it up. The angel was her favorite piece."

Charlie shuffled toward the mantel over the fireplace, where several photographs were on display. He picked up a gold frame and gazed at the picture fondly, his eyes welling with tears as he passed it to Tommy. "This is Grace. If she would have been alive, she would have baked her famous, seven-layer coconut cake and taken it to your house the first day you and your mother moved in."

Tommy, who was studying the photograph, brightened. "Hey, that's a cool dog she's holding."

Mac took a peek over the boy's shoulder, noting a long-haired, cream-colored poodle/terrier mix that sat on Grace's lap. It wore a pink collar adorned with faux jewels.

"That's Bobbie Sue," Charlie said.

Tommy handed the photograph back. "She looks a lot like our new dog."

"Just in size." Charlie was obviously thinking about the mangy creature that had leaped up and put its dirty, rain-soaked paws on his pants.

A dog that seemed compelled to run to Charlie's house every chance it got.

Mac's gut knotted. "I didn't know you and Grace had a pet."

"Yep. I bought that dog and gave it to her the Christmas before last. It was her pride and joy." Charlie's thoughts seemed to drift. "We had a lot of people in and out that last week before Grace passed on, and little Bobbie Sue was acting skittish. I don't know if she sensed what was happening or not, but she spent a lot of time either on Grace's bed or underneath it."

"What happened to the dog?" Mac asked.

"Someone left the front door open, and from what I can piece together, she must have dashed outside. While the fellow from the mortuary was loading Grace into the hearse, Bobbie Sue jumped in back. Either way, when he got back to Crandall's Funeral Home, he opened the door and found her. When he tried to pick her up, she got away and ran off. I checked the pound each day for a month, but no one turned her in. And since she was an indoor dog, she didn't have any street smarts. I suspect she may have been hit by a car. Who knows?"

The knot in Mac's gut swelled, then twisted with a vengeance. He couldn't be sure, but it was certainly possible that Princess Leia was Bobbie Sue. And if so?

It was only right to return her to Charlie, yet how could he ask those kids to give up the dog they'd just adopted?

Mac didn't have a clue how to handle the latest development.

Not if he wanted to keep the neighborhood peace.

Chapter Eight

Jillian sat in an overstuffed easy chair in the living room, listening to the rain splatter the window and waiting for Mac and Tommy to return from Mr. Iverson's house. She sure hoped Mac knew what he was doing, but she'd never had any trouble with her neighbors before and didn't want any now.

With Tommy gone and Megan in her bedroom playing with Princess Leia, the house was quiet—other than the steady tick-tock of the antique clock on the mantel and the occasional crackle from the fire in the hearth.

Dinner had been pleasant this evening—until Jared had called. Yet it wasn't just the call that had surprised her. She'd also sensed something in his tone. Something . . . off.

He seemed a bit down, but she wouldn't try to analyze why. She was just glad that he'd thought about the kids and had wanted to talk to them before bedtime.

Megan's desperate outburst had clearly caught him off guard, though, and Jillian understood why it had. Early on, the six-year-old had been brokenhearted about the split, but up until this evening, she seemed to have been taking it much better than Tommy.

Jillian combed her fingers through her hair. Would her life ever get back to normal? Not that she hadn't accepted the divorce and adjusted to being a single mother, even if it wasn't what she'd signed on for. She'd come to grips with that reality months ago. It's just that she was sorry about what the kids had been forced to endure—all because of the choices their father had made.

Of course, Jared had always had a selfish side, even though she hadn't realized it at first. When they'd met during her last year of college, she'd been charmed by his good looks and his outgoing manner. But what she'd considered self-assurance had been egotism in the classic sense of the word.

In retrospect, she wasn't totally convinced that she'd been in love with Jared back then, but at the time, her father had been fighting a losing battle with cancer, and she'd known that he was worried about dying and leaving her on her own. So marrying Jared had seemed like the right thing to do.

Tommy had been born ten months after her wedding, and Megan had come along three years later. Jillian adored her children and had been happy with her life. Her only complaints had been that her husband traveled a lot on business, and that she spent too many nights alone.

Last Thanksgiving, after her dad died, she'd found herself lonelier than ever. She began to realize that she'd been so tied up caring for her children and her ailing father that she and Jared had drifted apart. Yet she'd soon learned that Jared's job hadn't been the only thing drawing him away from home.

Jillian stood and made her way to the window, where she peered out into the rainy night, her breath fogging the glass. There was no sign of Tommy and Mac yet. Hopefully, that meant Mac's plan was working.

It had been a godsend when he'd shown up on her front porch earlier today, and she couldn't help thinking that her prayers for some kind of relief had been answered.

She suspected that Tommy thought so, too. His excitement had been obvious when he'd talked to his father on the telephone earlier—so much so that Jared had quizzed Jillian about Mac when they'd talked privately afterward.

"Who is that guy?" Jared had asked.

"Just someone I went to high school with," she'd replied.

When her ex had pushed for more information, she'd downplayed the relationship she'd once had with Mac. After all, their time together today and their dinner tonight hadn't been anything more than old friends reminiscing—even if she found herself increasingly attracted to the man he'd become.

There'd always been something about Mac that had drawn her to him, something dark, edgy, and sexual. Something wounded and gentle, too.

Thinking back, they really hadn't had anything in common when they'd been younger, although she suspected that might not be the case any longer.

Of course, if her father were still alive, he'd probably argue that point. He never had liked Mac, even though he'd refused to even give him a chance.

One day, suspecting Jillian hadn't been honest about where she was going and who she was meeting, her father had followed her to The Creamery, where he'd found her and Mac cuddling in the corner booth. Mac had stood up and extended a hand, but her father had refused to take it. He hadn't made a scene, but he'd insisted that Jillian leave with him. She'd decided it was in everyone's best interest if she quietly got into his car.

Once they were alone, he'd blown up.

Jillian had never rebelled a day in her life, but she'd been determined to stand up to her dad, to tell him that he couldn't choose her friends. But then he'd dropped the bomb and told her he'd been diagnosed with cancer.

Her whole world had fallen apart at the seams. Afraid to put any more stress on her dad than necessary, Jillian had told Mac she couldn't see him anymore.

As footsteps sounded on the porch, drawing her from her musing, she turned toward the door, eager to know what had happened at Mr. Iverson's house. And, if truth be told, she was eager to lay eyes on Mac again, too.

When he'd gazed at her and skimmed his hand along her

cheek earlier this evening, he'd sent her senses reeling. Still, she was afraid to read too much into that. She doubted a good-looking bachelor would find an overweight single mom attractive. Yet every now and then, she'd caught him looking at her, and her fantasies would take flight.

As the door swung open, Mac reminded Tommy to wipe his feet. Then he closed the wet umbrella and left it on the porch. A hank of sandy-blond hair fell over his forehead, and Jillian had the strangest urge to brush it aside.

She stood to greet him, yet she forced her arms to remain at her sides as she waited for Mac and her son to give her a report.

"You ought to see all the cool stuff Mr. Iverson has," Tommy said, his eyes bright, a blush on his cheeks. "He's not as mean as I thought he was."

"I'm happy to hear that." Jillian glanced at Mac. His grin set her heart on end. Then she returned her focus to her son. "Why don't you take your shoes off and leave them on the rug by the door? Then tell your sister it's time to get ready for bed."

"Okay." The boy did as he was instructed before dashing off.

"Tommy and Charlie seemed to have gained a new respect for each other," Mac said.

"Good. That's a step in the right direction."

Mac scanned the living room, then lowered his voice to a near whisper. "How's Megan doing?"

"She's been pretty quiet." Jillian nodded toward the stairway. "She took Princess Leia to her room."

An awkward silence filled the air, and Jillian wasn't sure what to do about it. She supposed she could thank Mac and walk him to the door, indicating their time together was over. But she couldn't quite bring herself to do that. There was still so much she wanted to know, so much she wanted to say.

The girl she'd once been pressed her to ask if he was seeing anyone special right now. She suspected that he wasn't, but the woman she'd become wouldn't allow her questions to get that personal.

"Do you want a cup of coffee?" she asked, letting him make the decision to stay or to go.

Something told Mac he ought to decline and head home. He'd hoped to solve a neighborly dispute earlier today, and it appeared that he'd succeeded. Sure, now he had the Bobbie Sue/Princess Leia dilemma to contend with, but he wasn't ready to tackle that one yet and had already decided to sleep on it.

Yet, while he passed on the coffee, he wasn't ready to say good night. "I know it's none of my business, but what did her father have to say about her sadness?" It would have turned Mac inside out if he'd had a daughter and heard her cry like that, begging him to come home.

"He didn't say much. How could he?" Jillian began to close the gap between them. "But I think it really bothered him."

"Good." If Mac would have had a wife like Jillian and kids . . . Well, the guy ought to feel like crap for leaving them.

He kept his thoughts to himself as he watched Jillian draw near. Seeing her again had awakened the attraction that had lain dormant for years, and he didn't have a clue what to do about it. Could he trust his feelings after only spending a few hours with her?

She tucked a strand of hair behind her ear, and he fought the growing need to touch her. To slide his arms around her and draw her to him, just as he used to do when they'd been young.

"I think it also bothered him to know that you were here for dinner," she said. "I told him that we were old friends, but he seemed to think there was more to it than that."

Was there?

"Jared doesn't realize that I'm not in a hurry to jump into a relationship," she added. "I made one big mistake already, and I don't plan to make another."

He wanted to ask just what that mistake was. Her marriage? The divorce? Did she blame herself for not seeing it coming?

When she and Mac had dated, their split had left him heartbroken, but he'd been too proud to admit it. After all, back then, he hadn't had a thing to offer a girl like her.

In fact, he still didn't.

"Hey, Mom!" Tommy yelled from upstairs. "Come quick! The toilet is all stopped up!"

Mac couldn't decide if he was glad to have the conversation interrupted or not.

"I'm coming!" Jillian, her cheeks a pretty shade of pink, managed a wistful smile. "Every time I turn around, something goes on the blink around here."

"Let me take a look at it. I've developed a real knack for unclogging sinks and pipes in the past week."

She scrunched her face in that cute way of hers. "Gosh, I can't ask you to do that."

"Why not?"

Her lips parted as though she had a good reason, then she stepped aside. "I'm probably going to be sorry for this, but to tell you the truth, I haven't honed too many fix-it skills yet."

"Why would you be sorry about me taking a look at your toilet?"

"Because you've seen me—and the kids—at our worst today. And something tells me that you're not used to all the domestic drama."

He wasn't. Yet he lifted his hand and trailed his fingers along her cheek, relishing the silky softness of her skin, as well as the arousing effects of touching her. It was a ballsy thing to do, he supposed. But he couldn't help it. And the fact she didn't pull away or flinch suggested that she hadn't found his move out of line.

"Don't worry about it," he said. "That's what friends are for."

But as he turned to head for the stairway, he found himself wondering if this was just the kind of drama he'd been missing all of his life.

Chapter Nine

Talk about domestic drama.

Jillian stood in the bathroom doorway and watched Mac kneel beside the toilet, roll up his sleeve, reach deep within the now-empty ceramic bowl, and pull out a small toy motorcycle. Then he got to his feet and dropped it into the sink.

As he washed his hands with hot, soapy water, he glanced over his shoulder and flashed Jillian a boyish grin. "I've had plenty of experience with plumbing these past few days, but I've yet to run into this same problem at my place."

She was sure he hadn't. Finding toys that had been flushed down the toilet was the kind of thing only parents and grand-parents had to deal with. She turned to her son, who sat on the edge of the fiberglass tub, the pale green bathmat bunched up at his bare feet.

"How did your motorcycle get in there?" she asked.

He shrugged. "I don't know. I didn't do it."

Jillian knew better than to believe everything her children told her, but since Megan had disappeared the moment Mac had entered the bathroom, Tommy wasn't the only suspect. Jillian would have to question Megan about it, but she didn't have the heart to scold her right now. Not after the child's tearful chat with her father tonight. So she would wait until bedtime to bring it up.

Mac held the three-inch-long motorcycle under the running faucet. "What do you suggest we do with this? It definitely needs to be sanitized."

"Don't bother doing that," Tommy said. "It's gross now. Just throw it away. I don't even want it anymore."

When Jillian nodded her agreement, Mac dropped the toy into the trash can beside the sink.

After he'd filled the toilet to the proper water level and made sure it was in working order, Jillian began to back out of the bathroom, clearing a path to the hallway.

"Okay," she said to her son, "now that the crisis is over, it's time for you and Megan to go to bed. I'll be in shortly to tuck you in and listen to your prayers."

As the boy headed to his bedroom down the hall, Jillian led Mac downstairs. "Thanks so much for solving another dilemma for me. I'm sorry to be such a nuisance."

"Don't worry about it."

They continued to the living room, their weight creating an occasional creak on the wooden steps. Once at the bottom landing, she wasn't quite sure which way to turn or what to say.

Mac had already declined coffee, and she feared, with her luck, something else would go on the blink before the night was over. So she walked him to the door, still not quite ready to let him go, but unable to conjure an excuse for him to stay when it was probably in his best interest to leave.

"Well," he said, "I guess I'd better head home."

"Thanks again for all you've done today."

"No problem. Thanks for the best tacos I've had in a long time."

"You're welcome."

In the lingering silence, their gazes met and locked. Something powerful swirled between them, something heart-spinning and warm.

Memories began to rush Jillian's mind: their first kiss; the taste of the peppermint-scented toothpaste he used; that musky, mountain-fresh scent that had belonged only to him.

Her heart rate kicked up a notch, and anticipation swept through her. She may have gotten rusty at this sort of thing over the years, but she sensed he was going to kiss her. And if he did, she feared she'd let him.

There were a hundred reasons why she shouldn't, but each one slipped her mind as quickly as it popped up.

Standing only a heartbeat away from Mac, the past and present blurring together, Jillian was afraid to speak, afraid to move, afraid to break the spell.

Was he just as caught up in it as she was?

Mac had dated his share of women since his breakup with Jillian, and he'd had plenty of hot, lusty kisses to ease his heartbreak. But none of those kisses had ever compared to the sweet innocence of the first one he'd shared with Jillian. Or with the hungry, youthful intensity of those that had followed. And now an opportunity to kiss her again was presenting itself.

The kid he used to be would have been reluctant to step out on a limb like that, but Mac was no longer that same gangly teenager on hormone overdrive who'd had a hopeless crush on the high school valedictorian, the good girl who'd turned the bad boy's life on end. So he took a chance, lowered his head, and brushed his lips across hers, relishing the breathy intimacy.

He knew he was probably out of line, so he expected her to tense, to balk, to pull away. Instead, she leaned into him, wrapping her arms around his neck, and kissed him back as though she'd been missing him for as long as he'd been missing her.

When her lips parted, his tongue swept into her mouth. The feel of her in his arms, her taste and scent, were better than he'd remembered, and his head swam in a sea of possibility.

But Mac was a realist, not a dreamer. He'd witnessed Megan's response to her father's phone call tonight. And he'd been aware of Jillian's need to speak to her ex in private. Things weren't the same as they'd once been; he and Jillian were no longer teenagers with their futures lying before them. There were complications now, as well as old baggage.

Mac had always made it a point to avoid dating single mothers for that very reason. There were too many extra hurdles, too many variables to make a man's life more difficult than it had to be.

Besides, when it came to dealing with kids, Mac was way out of his league. There was no way he was daddy material, so he slowly drew back, breaking their kiss and loosening his hold.

As he did, Jillian reached for his shoulder to steady herself. The kiss, he realized, had knocked her off balance, which shouldn't be the least bit surprising. It had unbalanced him, too.

Her cheeks, which had flushed several times throughout their day together, were a rosier shade than ever now. And a red splotch along her neck and throat suggested that she'd been just as swept away by their chemistry as he'd been.

His ego wanted to rise up and pound its chest, yet common sense tamped it down. He and Jillian still couldn't be any more star-crossed.

So now what?

Mac raked a hand through his hair. "I . . . uh . . . don't know what to say. I hadn't planned to do that."

"Neither had I." Her voice was soft, yet husky.

A rash of excuses lay on his tongue, yet he couldn't think of one that was entirely accurate, so he let them all remain unsaid. "I'd better call it a night."

She managed a smile tinged with shyness. Or maybe it was embarrassment; he couldn't be sure how she was feeling.

"Do you want to borrow the umbrella?" she asked.

Then he'd have to return it, and he wasn't sure if it was wise to make even that much of a commitment. "Thanks, but I won't need it." He glanced at the windowpane, saw no evidence of the heavy rain they'd had earlier. "It's only drizzling now."

He turned away and opened the door, letting himself out.

As he walked down the front steps, he knew she stood in the

doorway, watching him go. It took all he had not to turn around, but he pressed on. He was nearly to the driveway when he finally heard the click of the door shutting behind him. It was only then that he seemed to falter, but just for a moment.

The winter air was cold and damp, yet he relished the chill and the subsequent shiver that chased his dreams away with a dose of reality.

Now what? he asked himself.

The answer never came.

As he continued along the wet sidewalk in front of Charlie's house, the colorful outdoor lighting in the old man's yard seemed to proclaim hope and goodwill, as did that of nearly every house on Sugar Plum Lane tonight—every house but his and Jillian's.

At least hers had lights on inside. His, which he was now approaching, looked like a big black hole ready to suck the life out of the neighborhood.

His feet sloshed along the wet concrete, and as he neared the streetlight, he glanced at his wristwatch. For the most part, the day was over. He'd had a lot of things he'd wanted to get done and not much to show for his time, thanks to the decision to get involved in a neighborly dispute. Everything else just got more complicated by the minute.

What was he going to do about his attraction to Jillian?

As he continued in a fog of indecision, he sensed that he wasn't alone, and a feeling of being watched shivered through him. He glanced behind him, then looked to his right and left.

Down the street, near the fire hydrant, he spotted a shadowed figure with long hair and wearing what appeared to be a dark trench coat.

Jesse?

His steps slowed, but the shadow, as well as the feeling, disappeared as quickly as he'd imagined them.

Weird, he thought, shaking it off.

Still, he wondered what the homeless man would have had

to say about all of this. About the kiss he and his old high school sweetheart had shared tonight.

Do the right thing, Jesse had once told him, and you'll get the family you've always wanted.

Before Jillian moved back to Fairbrook, Mac had considered the department his family. But had Jesse's comments been a prophecy? Was there a real family in Mac's future?

Or was Mac's hope of finally hooking up with Jillian merely an attempt to spit into the wind, like he'd done fifteen years ago?

Chapter Ten

The rain stopped around five o'clock that morning, and by the time Mac finally rolled out of bed and peered out the window, there were only a few clouds left in the sky. The day promised to be clear and bright, yet Mac's thoughts were anything but.

Ever since that kiss last night, he'd been unable to focus on anything other than Jillian and what he felt for her.

Okay, so that wasn't entirely true. He also thought about her kids and the lousy Christmas they were going to have. Not that he was any expert on what they were missing out on. He'd learned not to put much stock in any holiday—especially *that* one—but he knew most kids were counting down the days by now.

Around nine-thirty, as he poured his second cup of coffee, he had what could only be considered a lightbulb moment.

What would it hurt for him to purchase Jillian's kids a Christmas tree?

There was a lot at the north end of Applewood Drive, so it wouldn't take long to pick one up. He wasn't sure what she had in the way of decorations, so before heading out to his Expedition, he climbed the stairs to the attic, where he turned on a dusty forty-watt bulb that dangled from the ceiling of the small room.

He scanned a hodgepodge of junk Ray had been storing—a wrought iron birdcage that was big enough for a parrot or two, an old oak rocker with a slat missing in the back, a guitar with a macramé strap, and a beat-up canvas golf bag with several wood-shaft clubs.

Those golf clubs had to be really old—antiques, maybe. He wondered where Ray had gotten them, why he'd been saving them, and if they were worth anything.

Against the east wall, near the only window, several boxes had been stacked from floor to ceiling. Ray had marked the outside with black capital letters indicating the contents: 2005 TAX AUDIT, DAD'S ARMY PAPERS, and XMAS STUFF. Mac pulled the Christmas boxes away from the rest and found colored lights and ornaments in them.

Behind the boxes, life-size, painted plywood cutouts of a red-nosed reindeer and a drummer boy leaned against the wall. A couple of Victorian-style carolers had been placed next to them.

Two wicker laundry baskets held strands of outdoor lights that had been rolled up neatly around shortened pieces of PVC pipe.

Maybe Mac ought to take some of this stuff to Jillian's and use it to decorate her house and yard. The kids would probably be happy about that. So he stacked a couple of boxes on top of each other, picked them up, and carried them downstairs. It took several trips, but soon he had it all placed by the front door.

All he had to do was share his intentions with Jillian and hope she agreed with his plans.

But why wouldn't she? This way she and the kids could have a Christmas they would remember, even if it wasn't at all like the holidays they'd had in the past.

He stepped outside and, after locking his door, strode toward Jillian's house. The sun was out, and a temperate coastal breeze had chased away the crisp wintry chill that had settled over Fairbrook yesterday.

Across the way, a middle-age man who lived a few doors down from Jillian was tinkering under the hood of a red '56 Thunderbird. Charlie had mentioned that one of the neighbors had refurbished the car and rebuilt the engine himself. If the guy would have glanced up from his work, Mac would have given him a nod or maybe even strode closer to take a look at the classic car. As it was, he continued on his way.

In front of Charlie's house, his steps slowed and he studied the display of Christmas decorations that, in the daylight, merely littered the yard.

Mac had told the old man that he would try to solve the missing angel caper. So, on impulse, he crossed the wet, soggy lawn and approached the nativity scene, where the Madonna gazed lovingly on the infant in the manger and Joseph looked at the two in awe. A shepherd was flanked by two lambs, a cow, and a donkey. Mac wasn't sure where the missing angel had stood, but as he surveyed the grass surrounding the other figures, he didn't see anything amiss. As he turned to go, he noticed a small piece of gold ceramic floating on a puddle of muddy water. He stooped and picked it up, turned it over, and studied the broken edges.

A second, closer scan of the surrounding area revealed another small piece just steps away from the first. And then another.

It didn't take a forensic expert to come to the conclusion that the angel had been broken or to follow the trail from Charlie's lawn to Jillian's. The pieces didn't lead to her front door, but there were at least two smaller chunks on the side of her yard.

Had Tommy been lying when he'd insisted he hadn't taken the angel?

As a homicide detective, Mac had honed a skill at reading facial expressions and discerning when a suspect was lying.

Most liars tended to skate around the question, to blink, and to fidget in one way or another. But the boy had looked Mac right in the eye when asked about it. Of course, his answer might have been different if Mac had asked if he'd broken the angel and hidden the evidence that led to his house.

Mac blew out a heavy sigh and raked his hand through his hair. He wasn't exactly sure how to handle this, but he didn't want to accuse Jillian's kids until he had something solid. He supposed he ought to play it by ear. So he made his way to Jillian's front porch and rang the bell, then, remembering that it was on the blink, grabbed the brass knocker and banged it several times.

When Jillian answered wearing a pair of cream-colored slacks and a pink cotton blouse, her breezy smile nearly knocked him to his knees. The kiss they'd shared last night hovered over him, and he'd be darned if he knew what to do about it. Ignore it, he supposed.

"Can you come outside for a minute?" he asked. "I want to talk to you in private."

Her smile fell, and she stepped onto the porch, closing the door behind her. "Sure, what's up?"

"I'd like to pick up a Christmas tree for you and the kids."

"That's nice of you, but . . ."

"The kids need a tree, Jillian. It'll be my treat."

Her expression seemed to lighten, so he reached into his pocket, withdrew his wallet, peeled out two hundred-dollar bills, and handed them to her. "I want you to take this and pick up a few gifts for them—from you. And then buy anything else you need for Christmas dinner—ham, turkey, whatever."

"I can't accept this, Mac." She tried to hand the money back, but he wouldn't take it.

"It's my Christmas gift to you. And if you have a major problem with that, then consider it a loan until your ex-husband comes through with the child support."

"I don't know what to say."

"A simple thank-you works for me."

She folded the bills together, clutching them in her hand, and her gaze sought his. He was usually pretty good at reading between the lines, but in this case, he was afraid to. She looked too appreciative, too touched, too . . .

He cleared his throat. "I'll tell you what. If you want to go shopping now, I can keep an eye on the kids while you're gone. Or you can go later. It's your call."

She didn't respond right away, and about the time he wondered if she would, she relented. "You're right. The kids deserve to have a nice Christmas. And I'll consider this money a loan."

He'd kind of hoped she'd take it as a gift, but he supposed it didn't matter. "While I was in Ray's attic, I found a box of decorations I won't need, so I'll bring them over for you to use—if you want them."

She started to lift her arms, and for a moment, he thought she was going to hug him. But she brushed her hands along the fabric of her slacks and crossed her arms instead. "I don't know how to thank you, Mac."

"There isn't any need to." He hooked his thumbs in the front pockets of his jeans, then nodded at the door. "Come on. Let's go tell the kids you have a few errands to run and that I'm going to watch them while you do it."

Ten minutes later, Jillian had done just as he'd suggested and had driven off. Mac hoped he hadn't made a mistake in volunteering to babysit. He didn't know much about kids, although he figured the most important thing was keeping them safe while she was gone.

Tommy appeared to be pleased about the setup, but Megan, with her blond hair pulled back in pigtails, pursed her lips together, then took the dog out into the backyard. Mac couldn't be sure, but he had a feeling she somehow blamed him for her parents' breakup.

"Hey!" Tommy, who'd dragged a soccer ball from his bedroom, tossed Mac a grin. "Do you want to come outside and play?"

Now that Mac was an adult, playing soccer with a kid was definitely a first, but he returned the boy's smile and said, "Sure. Why not?"

Tommy led the way through the kitchen and out to the yard, where Megan stood in the shade of an elm tree with Princess Leia.

Or was the little dog actually Bobbie Sue?

Mac wasn't sure, but it was certainly possible. He again realized that telling Charlie about the similarities was the right thing to do, but he wasn't in any big hurry to do that. Nor was he ready to have a chat with the kids about something that was sure to upset them.

He supposed, if the dog turned out to be Bobbie Sue, he could always beg Charlie to let the kids keep her, but who knew what the old man would say to that?

As Tommy dribbled the ball with his feet, Mac said, "I've been thinking about something."

"What's that?"

"I don't think anyone stole Mr. Iverson's angel."

Tommy stopped the ball with his foot. "You don't?"

"Nope. I think what really happened is that someone broke it and hid the pieces."

"No kidding?" Tommy kicked the ball to Mac. "How come you think that?"

"I found some small chunks of gold ceramic in Charlie's yard."

"Who do you think broke it?" Tommy asked.

"I don't know for sure." Using the side of his foot, Mac kicked the ball back to the boy. "Did you break it?"

"*Me?*" The boy slapped his hands on his hips, letting the ball slip right past him. "Heck, no. I didn't even touch it."

"Are you sure? Not even accidentally?"

"*No.* Don't you believe me?"

Mac studied the boy's expression, his eyes blazing with indignation and his chin lifted in defiance.

Truthfully? He didn't appear to be lying.

"Do you know anyone who might want it to look like you broke that angel?" Mac asked.

"No, I don't think so. There's a kid who lives down the street, and his name is Danny. He said hi to me once, but he doesn't know me good enough to like me or hate me. Oh, and there was a homeless guy who was hanging out by the fire hydrant once, but he was pretty cool."

A homeless guy? Mac's thoughts drifted to Jesse, to the image he'd imagined seeing last night. But he shook it off as coincidence, even though Sugar Plum Lane was a long way from where any of the homeless tended to gather.

They kicked the ball around in silence for a while, and Mac decided to drop the subject. He really wanted to connect with Jillian's son, but he had a feeling any further questioning was going to backfire if he wasn't careful.

His gaze drifted to Megan, who was still playing with the dog, her back to Mac and Tommy. Did she know anything about the broken angel?

He supposed she might, but he wasn't sure if he should quiz her. She'd withdrawn since yesterday afternoon, and he was afraid she thought he was trying to take the place of her father. For that reason, he figured it was best to let Jillian talk to her.

As Megan wandered to the very back of the yard, near the rose garden that had been pruned for the winter, the dog trotted behind her. Mac focused on the soccer ball and on making friends with Tommy.

Several minutes later, he heard a thump, a shriek, and a howl.

He looked up to see Megan sprawled over a rose bush.

Oh, no. Mac dashed toward her, hoping she hadn't been hurt too badly. So much for thinking he would make a competent babysitter. Jillian would probably never leave the kids with him again, which was wise on her part. And maybe he ought to be grateful for that.

He lifted the screaming child from the sharply cut, thorny branches, trying to avoid hurting her any more than she already was, and placed her feet on the ground. "Are you okay, honey?"

"Nooo!" She screamed, leaning into him.

He checked her carefully, noting a nasty scratch across her

cheek and down one arm. She raised her blouse and showed him a red, raw scrape on her tummy.

"Come on, Megan." He picked her up and held her close. "Let's get you inside and cleaned up."

"I want my mommy," she cried, tears streaming down her cheeks.

"I know you do. She'll be back soon." At least, he hoped so. He might have had first aid training, but he was way out of his league when it came to dishing out TLC.

As they crossed the lawn, he asked, "What happened?"

"I was running and tripped on a rock and fell in the thorns and pokers. And it hurts really, really bad!"

Mac carried her into the house and to the bathroom, where he sat her on the counter. Next he turned on the water and searched the drawers for a washcloth.

"I'll get the medicine and the Band-Aids," Tommy said from the doorway. "They're in my mom's bathroom."

"Thanks." Mac's heart was pounding a mile a minute as he tried his best to doctor the little girl.

She really wasn't hurt too badly. The fall, he suspected, had frightened her more than anything. Still, the scratch on her face announced that she'd been wounded on Mac's watch.

Great.

After cleaning the wounds with an antibacterial soap and water, Mac dabbed them dry and applied a salve. "Is that a little better?"

She nodded.

"I guess I'm not a very good babysitter," he said.

"Sure you are," Tommy argued. "Who could be a better babysitter than a policeman? Besides, you knew just what to do when Meggie got hurt."

Oh, yeah? Mac was a novice at this sort of thing, but he didn't see any point in setting the boy straight.

Of course, he'd done a better job of it than his old man had done. Whenever Mac had been injured as a child, he'd known better than to complain. "Just rub a little dirt on it," Jim Maguire used to say. "That'll toughen you up."

Mac was lucky he never followed those instructions. He might have gotten blood poisoning or something.

He let out a sigh, glad the girl had finally stopped crying.

"Why don't we go watch some TV?" he suggested. An indoor activity would ensure that no one else got hurt before Jillian returned.

When the kids seemed to accept the new game plan, Mac scooped Megan into his arms and carried her downstairs.

Hey, if she wanted to milk it, he was okay with that.

"Thank you for fixing me," she said.

"No problem." He tossed her a grin. "That's what friends are for."

She seemed to think about that for a bit, then smiled. "Are we really friends?"

"Sure we are."

As he set her on the sofa, she looked up at him with eyes that were every bit as expressive as her mother's. "Can I ask you a question, Mac?"

"Of course."

"Do you always put people in jail?" she asked. "Even kids?"

Was she afraid of him? "I only arrest adults who've broken the law. There are special courts that deal with children who get into serious trouble. Why do you ask?"

"You don't put kids in jail?"

"Nope." He couldn't see any need to explain the intricacies of juvenile incarceration.

She nibbled on her bottom lip, then glanced up at him, those eyes so much like her mom's threatening to make a tough guy soft. "What happens when kids do bad things?"

"Usually their parents take care of the situation. The police don't get called in unless the kids do something *really* bad."

"Like breaking something on accident?" she asked.

Uh-oh. Was Mac about to hear a confession?

"When kids break things, their moms and dads handle

that." He pulled lightly on her pigtail and offered her a gentle smile. "But I think, when it's an accident, most parents would understand and go easy on the child."

Her green eyes, expressive like her mommy's, glistened with emotion. "Even when it's something that belongs to someone else? Something they weren't supposed to touch?"

"Accidents happen, Megan. Did you break something?"

The tears that had been welling in her eyes overflowed onto her cheeks. "It was an accident, Mac. Don't put me in jail. *Please!*"

"No one is going to put you in jail, honey. I won't let them."

She wrapped her arms around his neck, nearly squeezing the heart right out of him. "I didn't mean to do it, Mac. I touched Mr. Iverson's angel, and it fell over all by itself. And the arm broke off. And the halo, too. I was so scared he was going to get mad at me and hit me with his cane, like he said he was going to do to Tommy. So I picked up all the pieces and hid them so no one could find them."

"Where'd you hide the angel?" he asked. "I'd like to see it. I might be able to fix it and put it back where it belongs."

"Really?" She loosened her hold to search his face for sincerity.

He tapped his finger on the tip of her lightly freckled nose. "I haven't seen it yet, but even if it's as badly broken as Humpty Dumpty, I'll figure out a way to fix this whole mess for you. Okay?"

Her smile lit up her face, and she wrapped her arms around his neck again. "When I heard you were a policeman and you were Mr. Iverson's friend, I thought you would take me to jail."

"Nothing doing, sweetheart." Mac held her close.

"You're the best police in the whole, wide world."

Mac didn't know about that. But he sure liked having this little girl think so.

Chapter Eleven

The next day, Jillian stood beside the kitchen table and studied the broken ceramic figurine she and Mac had painstakingly repaired. Rather than return the angel broken, they'd decided to take it back to Mr. Iverson in one piece, although at one point, she hadn't been sure that would be possible.

Yesterday, they'd had trouble getting the pieces to attach properly, but the new glue Mac had purchased earlier today had worked much better than they'd expected. A little putty had filled in the gaps and holes, so if their luck held, they would be able to return the angel to Mr. Iverson before heading to Mulberry Park for Christmas Under the Stars.

"I think it looks pretty good," Mac said as he surveyed their handiwork.

The paint was chipped and cracked in numerous places, but they'd left those spots alone. Instead, they'd only tried to match the white, gold, and flesh color to cover the putty and the places where they'd glued the arm and halo back together.

Tommy tiptoed and craned his neck to assess the angel. "You can't even see the broken lines anymore. That glue and paint you bought worked really good."

Jillian had no idea what Mr. Iverson would say when they returned his angel, but they'd done their best to repair the damage. She'd also made a batch of sugar cookies this morning—stars, bells, and Christmas trees—that she and the kids had frosted and decorated with candy sprinkles. She hoped their elderly neighbor would accept the platter of cookies as a peace offering, along with their apologies.

Megan, who was kneeling on the seat of her chair and resting her elbows on the kitchen table, had closely watched their attempts to glue the angel back together. "Do I have to go with you when you take it back to Mr. Iverson? I'm scared. I don't want him to get mad at me."

Mac placed a hand on the child's shoulder. "Sometimes it's hard to do the right thing, Megan. But if it makes you feel better, your mom, your brother, and I will be right there with you."

"Yeah," Tommy said, "and Mac won't let Mr. Iverson yell at you or anything."

"That's right." Mac glanced at Jillian and winked.

What had she done to deserve a man like him? Not that she *had* him by any means. It's just that they'd somehow become a team in the past couple of days.

Of course, they hadn't even broached the subject of how or even *if* he was going to fit into their lives. He'd just seemed to slide right in, as though he'd always belonged. And for the first time in ages, she was actually looking forward to Christmas.

Thanks to Mac's efforts, a fully decorated noble fir sat in the living room, surrounded by ten or twelve wrapped gifts. Lights adorned their front yard now, even though their decorations weren't anywhere near as elaborate as those of most of the other neighbors.

In spite of the comments he'd made about his inexperience with kids, Mac had proven to be wonderful with hers. He might not have had a paternal role model growing up, but he was a natural. In fact, he was everything she'd ever wanted in a father for her children.

He was everything she'd ever wanted in a husband, too.

The kiss they'd shared the night before last had turned her knees to Jell-O, just as all of his kisses had once done to her. But interestingly enough, they seemed to be pretending it hadn't happened, and neither of them had dared to mention it again.

Too bad, she thought, as she stole an appreciative glance at Mac. She'd love to throw her arms around his neck and kiss him again, although she wasn't sure how to orchestrate something like that without being obvious.

"There's something else we probably ought to discuss," Mac said, sobering and stepping away from the table.

Tommy perked up, as he was prone to do each time Mac spoke. "What's that?"

"Do you remember that picture Mr. Iverson showed you of his wife?"

The boy nodded. "Yeah, she was holding a dog that looked a lot like Princess Leia."

"Do you remember what he said happened to his dog?" Mac asked.

"It ran away after Mrs. Iverson died."

Mac appeared to study the statue, and Jillian studied Mac.

"Remember the day we brought the dog home from the park?" he asked both kids.

"She was all dirty," Megan said. "And we had to give her a bath."

"Yep. And that very first day, when we set her down in your front yard, she dashed off to Mr. Iverson's house. She did the same thing when she got out later that day."

"Yeah," Tommy said. "So what?"

"Don't you think that's kind of weird?" Mac asked.

Jillian tensed. Uh-oh. Did Mac suspect the kids' dog had once belonged to Mr. Iverson?

If that was true, their peacemaking efforts could blow sky high.

"You mean like the two dogs and the kitty in *Homeward Bound: The Incredible Journey*?" Megan asked.

Mac glanced at Jillian, a question in his eyes.

"That's the story of three lost pets that make their way home."

"Yes," Mac said. "That's what I'm thinking."

"But Princess Leia is *our* dog." Megan sat up straight, although she still knelt in the seat of the chair. "Mommy said we could keep her."

Jillian couldn't voice the words. Mac was right, of course. If the dog belonged to Mr. Iverson, they'd have to return it to him.

Mac shifted his weight to one foot. "The only reason your mom told you that it was okay to keep that dog was because she thought it was a stray. She didn't realize it might have an owner."

"But Mr. Iverson was mean to her," Tommy said. "Remember? He pushed her away and called her a mangy mutt."

"You'll find that things always work out for the best when you do the right thing," Mac said, "even when doing the right thing hurts."

"Maybe our dog only *looks* like his dog," Megan said.

"You might be right." But when Mac glanced at Jillian, she suspected that he had his doubts.

"We can talk to Mr. Iverson about the dog later," Mac said, as he picked up the figurine. "Let's return the angel first."

Moments later, as they stood on Mr. Iverson's porch, Mac held the angel in one arm and rang their neighbor's bell with the other.

Charlie Iverson answered the door wearing a green flannel shirt, red suspenders, and a pair of black trousers. His gray hair stuck up in back, as Tommy's sometimes did.

"What's all this?" He glanced at the plate of cookies Jillian held. When he spotted the angel, he brightened. "Where'd you find that?"

Megan slid behind Mac and wrapped an arm around his leg.

A heartfelt confession might be the right thing to do, but Meggie was only six and afraid, so Jillian made the plea. "My daughter was admiring your angel the other day, and it accidentally fell over and broke. She was so afraid that she'd get in trouble, she hid the pieces. And when Mac and I found out what had happened, we glued it back together."

Charlie peered at Megan and frowned.

The child tightened her grip on Mac's leg, but managed to say in a soft voice, "I'm sorry, Mr. Iverson. I didn't mean to break it. I just wanted to see how the wings fit on her back. My grandpa is in Heaven, and before he died, he told me not to be sad 'cause he was going to have fun flying around the clouds."

Charlie merely chuffed, then took the angel from Mac and looked it over carefully.

"It's as good as new," Mac told him. "No harm done."

The old man didn't answer, and Mac nudged his arm. "Come on, Charlie. Tell Megan that you accept her apology. She's afraid of you and thinks you're a mean old man. Let her know that's not true."

Charlie's brow furrowed, and one side of his lip quirked up in an attempt to grin.

"I suspect Grace has a pair of wings right now, too," Mac added. "And knowing how much she loved children, she's probably fluttering up a storm overhead, frustrated with you for not welcoming the new neighbors like she would have done."

Little Megan glanced up, as though wondering if there really was an angel looking down on them, and Jillian held her breath, hoping for the best.

Charlie ran a hand over his head, just now figuring out that his hair was mussed. Then he inhaled deeply, slowly blew it out, and looked at Megan. "I'm not such a bad sort. It's just that I've lost a lot this year, and I'm trying to hang on to whatever I can."

"We've lost a loved one, too," Jillian said. "My dad passed away last year, so, like you, we're facing a lonely Christmas."

"It's tough," Charlie admitted. "I'll sure be glad when it's all over."

Jillian offered the old man a warm smile. "I know just what you mean. Maybe it would help if we had Christmas dinner together this year. I'm fixing turkey and all the trimmings, and we'd love to have you join us."

Charlie's eyes glistened, and he offered Jillian a weak smile. "Thanks, but I hate to put you out. I'll just stay home and eat a TV dinner."

"Oh, you won't be putting me out," Jillian said. "It's a huge turkey. Besides, I'm inviting Mac, too, and it would be nice if he had another man to talk to."

Charlie shot a glance at Mac, then shrugged. "Okay. I guess I can always save that TV dinner for another day."

"Good." Jillian lifted the platter of cookies. "By the way, the kids and I made these for you."

As Charlie looked at the yellow stars and green trees, a tear slid down his craggy cheek. "I didn't expect to have any homemade goodies this year."

"You know," Jillian said, "that's the nice thing about Christmas. We can usually expect a surprise or two."

As another tear slid down Charlie's face, he swiped at it with a gnarled hand, then glanced at Mac. "Looks like there's a new cookie lady on our street."

Jillian wasn't sure what he meant by that, but Mac slid an arm around the old man's shoulders and gave him a squeeze.

After leaving the angel and the platter with Mr. Iverson, they all headed back to Jillian's house. As soon as they got home, she was going to tell the kids to grab their jackets and to help her pack some lawn chairs and blankets in the car. It might be nice to arrive at Mulberry Park early. That way, the kids could play before the event started.

As they stepped onto the sidewalk, Jillian noticed a familiar figure standing on her front porch, and her heart turned inside out. She slid a glance at Mac, as though he could somehow fix this awkward situation, too.

"Daddy!" Megan clapped her hands, then dashed off to meet the guy who was supposed to be on a cruise with his new family.

Chapter Twelve

Mac hadn't needed a crystal ball to figure out who'd shown up at Jillian's house, and Megan's enthusiastic response to seeing her daddy had only validated his assumption.

"Jared?" Jillian asked, her voice indicating she was every bit as surprised to see her ex-husband as Mac was. "What are you doing here?"

The tall, dark-haired man in his late thirties stooped to pick up his daughter. "I came to see you and the kids."

"I realize that," she said, "but you're supposed to be on a cruise."

"I flew back early." Jared's gaze drifted from Jillian to Mac. "Who are you?"

Tommy, whose steps had slowed, didn't appear to be as happy to see his father as his sister was. "This is Mac, our friend, the cop."

Mac knew he ought to reach out and shake the man's hand, but he'd rather send him packing instead. Yet while he didn't feel like making the first move, he did so anyway. "Mac Maguire."

"Jared Ridgeway."

An uncomfortable moment stretched between them, as they assessed each other like two adversaries with their hearts set on the same prize.

Jared broke eye contact first and returned his attention to

Jillian. "I . . . uh . . . got to thinking that I should come and see what was going on here. Megan was pretty upset when I talked to her on the phone the other night."

Can you blame her? Mac wanted to ask, but he clamped his mouth shut and crossed his arms instead.

"We need to talk," Jared told Jillian.

Mac could understand that. Like it or not, they had children together. And over the next few years, they'd have a lot of reasons to talk. Of course, even when the kids grew up and went on to college, Jared and Jillian would still have to see each other at social events, such as graduations, weddings, christenings. So if Mac was going to be a part of her and the kids' lives, he'd have to get used to times like this.

"Can we talk later?" she asked. "The kids and I were planning a trip to the park."

"You can come, too," Megan told her daddy. "It's got a really fun playground, and we get to stay there even when it gets dark. We're going to sit on blankets and drink hot cocoa and eat cookies and other good stuff."

Now things had really taken an awkward shift, and Mac realized he'd better give the man the privacy he undoubtedly wanted.

"Listen, Jillian." Mac uncrossed his arms and nodded toward his house across the cul de sac. "I've got some things I need to do, so I'll see you later."

Her lips parted as though she wanted to object, but she didn't. How could she?

On the other hand, Jared seemed relieved that Mac was leaving, yet Mac didn't feel so good about it. Still, it wasn't his place to stick around.

And he had to face the fact that it might never be.

He watched as Jared placed a hand on Jillian's shoulder and gave it an affectionate squeeze. The effect was so distressing that he had to look away. In fact, he couldn't stay here any longer.

As he turned to go, Mac overheard the other man say, "I

started thinking about a lot of things after my call the other
night. And I began to realize I'd made a mistake."

He'd made a mistake, all right. A *big* one. And while re-
morse was usually a good thing, the guy shouldn't have left his
wife and kids in the first place. Not when that wife was Jillian.

Still, as she seemed to ponder the words her ex had said,
and as Mac read between the lines of silence, he continued on
his way, waiting for fate to slam into him once again. To take
every last bit of hope he'd ever harbored and to dash it against
a wall of reality.

And reality sucked.

No matter what he'd told himself over the past fifteen
years, he'd never really gotten over Jillian. And he probably
never would.

He wanted to slam his fist into something rock hard and
solid. Maybe the pain of tearing flesh and cracking bones
could take his mind off a breaking heart.

Yet he trudged on.

"Let's go in the house," Ridgeway told his family.

Mac supposed they did deserve some privacy, but he
wasn't about to stick around and listen to their discussion,
even if he'd had the heart to.

He was losing Jillian all over again, and he couldn't help
but kick himself for allowing it to happen.

Why hadn't he told Charlie he didn't want to get involved
in a neighborly dispute? Or why hadn't he just broached the
subject with Jillian, then gone about his own business?

Instead, like a fool, he'd followed his heart. And now he
was heading back to his house, determined to hold his chin
up. But he wasn't going to stay on Sugar Plum Lane another
day. It might only be a fifteen minute drive to downtown San
Diego, but it was a world away from Fairbrook.

Out of the corner of his eye, he saw the neighbor who'd
been working on the '56 T-bird was outside again. This time
he was buffing a layer of Turtle Wax on the hood.

When the older man glanced up from his work and noticed

Mac, he shot him a friendly smile. "Hello, there. How's it going?"

Under different circumstances, Mac might have used the excuse to check out the man's handiwork, to shoot the breeze about rebuilt engines and classic cars. But other than a brief nod and uttering, "Great," Mac didn't want to be bothered.

Right now, he couldn't care less about cars or neighbors or even being polite. All he could think of doing was to get out of Dodge with his pride still intact.

It was time to pack up his stuff and head back to the loft apartment in the Gaslamp District. Maybe he'd just go ahead and list Ray's house with the Realtor as a fixer-upper and sell it as is. That way, he wouldn't have to stick around any longer.

Yet even the thought of escape didn't seem like an easy way out. Walking away from Jillian was going to be tough for a man who'd fought for everything else he'd needed in life. But why make it any harder on himself than it had to be?

"You'll find that things always work out for the best when you do the right thing," Mac had told the kids earlier today, "even when doing the right thing hurts."

And that's just what he was going to do. He just hadn't realized how much truth there was to that statement.

Letting go of Jillian and the kids hurt like hell.

Chapter Thirteen

When the doorbell rang, Mac was shoving his shaving gear into the top of the black carry-on bag that sat on the bed. He'd packed up his stuff and was ready to take it to the car.

The Realtor he'd called earlier had wanted to come by and see the house later this evening, but Mac told her he'd meet with her tomorrow. He wasn't in the mood for visitors right now, which was why he ignored the bell—until it chimed again.

And again.

After zipping the canvas bag shut, he made his way to the door. He'd just have to tell whoever was there that he was leaving and didn't have time to chat or to get involved in another neighborhood dispute.

But he hadn't expected that someone at the door to be Jillian.

"Are you still up for Christmas Under the Stars?" she asked.

Since he figured her ex-husband's arrival had altered everyone's plans, the question caught him off guard. Yet even if it hadn't, Mac was planning to make an excuse and bow out.

Surely, she didn't expect him to go with all of them to the park. No way would he be a part of that circus.

"What about Jared?" he asked.

"He's looking for a hotel. I told him he could spend time with the kids tomorrow and maybe take them somewhere, but he can't be with them tonight. I already have plans with them."

Mac didn't know what to say. He might have made a commitment to Tommy and Megan to take them to the park, but he wasn't about to tiptoe around Jillian anymore, pretending that he was just an old friend, when he wanted to be so much more. Maybe he would tell her that there'd been a new lead on a case that had gone cold and that he'd been called in to work this evening.

Hey, what would one little lie hurt if it shielded his pride?

But there were still a few questions tumbling around in his mind, and he decided to ask the biggest one. "What's Jared planning to do in Fairbrook?"

"I guess that Disney cruise was more family oriented than he'd anticipated, and he started feeling guilty about being with someone else's kids, when the children he'd fathered were spending Christmas without him."

As far as Mac was concerned, the guy should have realized that before he even considered booking a trip during the holidays. But apparently, Jared Ridgeway was self-centered and jumped into all kinds of situations without giving his wife and kids much thought or consideration.

"So when the guilt finally kicked in," Mac said, "he decided to fly to San Diego to play the part of a loving daddy?"

"That's about the size of it. And he gave me that child support check he'd forgotten to mail, too."

"Great." But that still hadn't provided the answer Mac most needed to hear. "How do you feel about all of this, Jilly? You left Roseville to put some distance between the two of you and to start a new life. Now here he is, standing on your front doorstep and wanting to right a multitude of wrongs."

She combed her fingers through her hair and shifted her weight to one hip. If she thought anything about why he was keeping her on the porch, rather than inviting her inside, she didn't let on. "I'll admit that I got a certain amount of satisfaction out of his apology. My pride took a low blow when he left me for someone else, so it was nice to hear him say he was sorry, that he'd made a mistake in leaving."

And . . . ?

Did Mac need to pry it out of her? Was she going to give her ex-husband the second chance he was asking for or not?

He hated to come right out and ask, though. His own pride was at stake, and he didn't want her to suspect how vulnerable he felt right now. So he skated around what he was really feeling. "If you two are going to give your marriage a chance, there's no point in me complicating matters by going with you and the kids to the park tonight."

"Jared was hoping I'd welcome him back home," she said, "but I can't do that. I told him that I would fully support his efforts to have a better relationship with the kids, but that whatever we had as a couple is over."

A sense of relief swept through Mac, yet that wasn't enough. He wanted the chance to re-create a relationship with Jillian, and he wasn't talking about them being "old high school friends." Did he dare admit that to her? No matter what her response would be?

He hadn't been able to do that fifteen years ago.

"The woman Jared hooked up with this time wasn't the first one he'd gotten involved with while we were married," Jillian added. "And I want a man I can trust. A man who knows how to make a lifetime commitment and who won't bail out on me on a whim or when the going gets tough."

Mac knew without a doubt that, given the chance, he could be that man for her. And, more than anything else in the world, he wanted to be. But wishes hadn't gotten him anywhere before. He was going to have to admit how he felt—no matter what the risk.

He lifted his hand and skimmed his knuckles along her cheek. "Life is full of uncertainties, Jillian, and this is one of those times. Fifteen years ago, I fell in love with you. I know I never said it, but I was afraid to put my heart on the line. And when you broke up with me, I told myself it was a good thing I hadn't leveled with you."

"So that's why, when I told you I couldn't see you anymore,

you just shrugged it off as though I was one of your teachers, and I'd just announced a pop quiz."

He let his hand drop, missing the warmth of their contact immediately. "In truth? I wanted to beg you to give me one more chance, but my pride wouldn't let me. So I acted as though it was no big deal. Then I watched you walk away, taking the only good thing that had ever happened to me with you."

"I loved you, too," she said, her voice coming out whisper soft.

"I wish you would have told me." It would have made it easier for Mac to admit his feelings back then if she'd gone first.

Her eyes welled with unshed emotion, but he'd be darned if he knew what it was—regret? Disappointment?

Holding back their feelings in the past hadn't gotten them anywhere. Now it appeared as though Mac had been given the second chance he'd wanted. But this time he was going to have to do something about it.

He cleared his throat and stepped out on what felt like a shaky limb that might crack under his weight. "Seeing you again has not only made me realize just how much I once loved you, but how much I still do."

Tears slid down Jillian's cheeks, and her bottom lip quivered. "I know just what you mean, Mac. I love you, too. And in the past couple of days, I've come to the conclusion that I always have."

A warmth swelled in his chest, and he slid his arms around her waist, drawing her close. "You have no idea how badly I've wanted to hear you say that."

She wrapped her arms around his neck. "Well, you'd better get used to hearing it."

As she lifted her lips, he kissed her with all the love in his heart, love he'd been bottling up for as long as he could remember.

Her fingers slid into his hair, and she leaned into him, opening her mouth and allowing the kiss to deepen. She tasted of sugar and spice, of magic and dreams, and he lost himself in her embrace, relishing every heated touch, every ragged breath.

When they finally came up for air, Mac cupped Jilly's face in his hands. "Now that I've said the words, I'm not sure if I'll ever be able to hold them back. I love you, honey. And I promise to do everything I can to make the rest of your life happy."

Her eyes glistened with joy and an intensity he'd never seen in them before. "There's bound to be some rough spots along the way, but overcoming them together is what life and love are all about."

"Hey!" Tommy's voice sounded behind them, and they both turned to greet him.

Mac had no idea how the kids were going to react to him being a permanent part of their lives, but he was willing to do whatever it took to help them see that they were all better off this way, even if domestic drama was an everyday occurrence.

"What's taking you guys so long?" the boy asked. "Meggie and I are ready to go to the park."

"Then what are we waiting for?" Mac asked. "I'll grab my jacket and the keys."

An hour later, Mac and Jillian strolled hand in hand through the grounds of Mulberry Park, appreciating the work volunteers from Parkside Community Church had put into decorating for Christmas Under the Stars. Tiny blinking lights twinkled in the trees, and a mouthwatering spread of home-made goodies filled tables covered with red cloths. Off to the side, industrial size thermoses filled with coffee, decaf, hot cocoa, and hot water provided drinks to warm the crowd.

Christmas music, as well as the sound of laughter and happy voices, filled the air. Talk about Christmas cheer. Mac had never understood it all before, but he did now.

Jillian's fingers threaded through his as though she'd never let him go. With her free hand, she motioned for Tommy and Megan, who'd been playing with several other children on the swings and slides.

Mac watched as the kids approached, and he marveled at

their smiling faces and at how right it was for them to be together, here and now and always. They'd be his kids, too, he realized, and the thought pleased him.

There was still a lot up in the air, but for the time being, he would let his apartment go and stay in Ray's house, getting it ready to sell. The commute to work would be a breeze, and even if it wasn't, it wouldn't matter. He'd be coming home to Jillian, one way or another.

"Is it time for everything to start?" Tommy asked.

"I hope so." Megan's excitement lit her face. "I want to hear them read the Christmas story."

"Look." Jillian pointed to a man handing out candles for people to hold. "I'm sure they'll be starting soon, so let's sit on the blanket we brought."

Mac gave Jillian's hand a gentle squeeze. "That's probably a good idea."

As they gathered together on an old patchwork quilt, Mac couldn't help noting the intricate design. Someone had carefully taken scraps of cloth and stitched them all together into something useful, something beautiful. And he couldn't help thinking that's how families were supposed to work. Individuals bound together by love and a creator.

His first family might not have been what every kid deserved, but look at him now.

What a gift he'd been given.

His thoughts drifted to the day he'd met Jesse, the day Mac had listened to some fatherly advice and opted to make a change in his life.

If he closed his eyes, he could still hear the homeless man's prophetic words.

Doing the right thing, Jesse had said, *is a reward in and of itself.*

Maybe you're right, Mac had responded. *But it's not that easy.*

I know. Sometimes it's the hardest route to take. But I'll tell you this, Mac. If you choose to do right over wrong, every chance you get, you'll get that family you always wanted and reap the kind of life you deserve.

Jesse had been right. Mac had finally found everything he'd ever wanted in Jillian. And his future had never looked brighter.

They would, however, still have to deal with the Bobbie Sue/Princess Leia dilemma when they got home, but he suspected that was just one of those rough spots Jillian had talked about.

One way or another, he knew they'd work it out.

After all, Mac had promised Megan that he would "fix things" with Charlie and the broken angel, and with Jillian's help, he'd managed to do just that. So if Princess Leia proved to be the dog Charlie had lost, then Mac would fix that, too— somehow. Perhaps he'd talk Charlie into giving up the dog. Or into entering some kind of shared canine custody agreement.

The microphone roared an annoying squawk, and the senior pastor of Parkside Community Church welcomed those who'd gathered on the lawn to the fifteenth annual Christmas Under the Stars. Then he introduced a teenage girl who would read a passage from the second chapter of Luke.

Mac had never considered himself a religious man and didn't even own a Bible, but he listened intently to the story of a child born in a manger and wrapped in swaddling cloth.

As the young girl continued to read, he surveyed the others who sat in the park, strangers now, but people in a community that would soon be his. He couldn't imagine where his life might have led if a stranger hadn't taken him under his wing when he'd been an unhappy, aimless teenager with a broken heart and shattered dreams.

"An angel of the Lord appeared to them," the girl read, "and the glory of the Lord shone around them . . ."

A light caught the corner of Mac's eye, and he turned to see a figure in the distance, a man with a silver-threaded beard and a glowing face.

Jesse?

"Excuse me a minute," Mac whispered to Jillian.

She questioned him with her eyes, and he nodded toward the man dressed in a trench coat who stood at the fringe of the park. Then he got to his feet and made his way toward the guy.

As Mac drew nearer, the man turned to walk away.

"Hey, wait!" Mac called.

The man stopped long enough to smile and raise his hand in a little wave. Then he continued on his way, disappearing into the night.

Mac decided not to chase after him, but he still fought a wave of disappointment as he made his way back to the blanket where he'd left Jillian and the kids. He hadn't gone far when he heard a pathetic little whimper.

Several feet to the right, a small, dark-haired puppy, its hair matted, looked up at him with the saddest eyes he'd ever seen.

"Where'd you come from, little guy?" Mac scanned the immediate area, but didn't see anyone with the scrawny little thing.

So he stooped and picked it up. "Come on, little guy. You look like you need a family. And I've got just the one for you."

Then he carried his find back to Jillian and the kids.

Together, they were going to make this world a better place—doing the right thing, one day at a time.